MW01225690

Here's a poignant story of the old west that I relished. I found the book captivating, with each new chapter introducing characters that you fall in love with. I found myself hesitating to get to the final chapter as I did not want the story to end. I longed to read more about their lives and how the families evolved. PH Garrett is a gifted writer evoking the texture and feeling of life in the 1850's.
—Claire Passanisi

Trail of Hearts
Copyright © 2019 PH Garrett

All right reserved. This book is a work of fiction. References to historical events, real people, or real places are used fictitiously. Other places, names, characters, and events are wholly products of the author's imagination. Any resemblance to actual places, events, or persons living or dead is entirely coincidental.

Except for brief passages quoted in newsprint, magazine, radio or television reviews, no part of this book may be reproduced in any form, electronic, mechanical, or online, including photocopying, audio recording, or by information storage and retrieval system, without the express permission of the publisher.

The sale of this book without its cover is unauthorized. If you purchased this book without a cover, be aware it was reported to the publisher as unsold and destroyed. Neither the author nor publisher has received payment for this "stripped book."

ISBN: 978-1-7335089-0-2

Author's website and contact information:
www.wordwranglingwoman.com
wordwrangling.press@gmail.com

Published by:
wordwrangling press
Cotati, CA 94931 USA

Interior book formatting: fonts, pages, graphic art and much needed assistance through the maze of the self-publishing business: Berkana Publications, Skye Blaine

Cover layout: Vicki Dougan, promotional marketing, publications, and graphic arts services including logo design. Dougan is a member of the Promotional Marketing Association of Northern CA

Original Cover art: Western Artist Don Weller. Find his work at Don Weller.com A visit to his website is a delight.

Photographic images: Alamy and Getty Images

Printed in the United States of America

I have fallen in love with American names,
The sharp names that never get fat,
The snakeskin-titles of mining-claims,
The plumed war-bonnet of Medicine Hat,
Tucson and Deadwood and Lost Mule Flat.
—Stephen Vincent Benét, *American Names*

Looking behind, I am filled with gratitude.
Looking forward, I am filled with vision.
Looking upwards, I am filled with strength.
Looking within, I discover peace.
—Unknown Native American

How 'Kah'-kah-loo' The Ravens Became People

Amongst the Northern Miwok of what is now Central California, the story of Raven begins with a world covered in water except for a single mountain top where people gathered during the flooding. As the waters receded The People tried to come down from the mountain, but the land was so soft with mud that those that tried would sink into the ground. Wherever a person sank, a raven would come to stand on that spot. One raven at each hole. Once the ground hardened, the raven turned into a person.
—Miwok Legend

This book is dedicated with love
to my daughters
Paula Cristi and Olivia Dawn

Trail of Hearts

by
PH Garrett

For Ken
Happy trails
to you

PH Garrett

Summer
1850

Southern Arizona
Chapter One

Lost

Clothes streaked with dust, mouth dry as dirt, a young man staggered along rough crusts of desert sand. A blaze of midday sun seared his face. He stumbled, fighting to stay upright. Black pooled at the edges of his vision, threatening, closing in. His shoulders tensed against the inky tide. Then, losing the battle, he pitched forward onto the gritty track, his battered hat landing close by.

Near dusk, consciousness returned. Shivers snaked his arms, warning of the cold night to come. He rubbed a stiff hand across his face and winced as it connected with the bruised flesh of his jaw. His body ached. Feels like I must a' took a towellin', he thought.

The stocky-built man shook his head, tried to clear his vision. His pupils rattled side-to-side of their own accord. He saw two of everything; rock and cactus jumped. Jagged outcrops swam in the twilight. Dazed, he lay back down.

When his eyes opened again, ribbons of brilliant red and orange licked underbellies of clouds that scudded above the horizon. He recognized long-armed ocotillo and giant, spiny saquaro silhouetted in the setting sun. He blinked. They stood still. Relieved, he pushed away from the ground and struggled to sit up.

His gaze darted into growing shadows as he waited for the painful pounding in his head to subside. Bugaboo sounds invaded his senses. Scurrying critters, the near silent brush of body against sand, provoked visions of hairy tarantulas coming from their holes, snakes on the prowl. Where am I? he wondered.

Under a shock of brown hair, he touched a tender lump just above his temple. His hand came away sticky. He stared at the dark wet on his fingers. "Blood."

The man puzzled over his situation. As eventide became full on night, questions whirled. He grappled with his vanished memory. *Was there a fight? Did my horse throw me?* He broke into a cold sweat. *Holy Jesus, who am I?*

Panic brought him scrambling to his feet. *Is someone after me?* If only he could remember. No answers came.

Grateful for a risen moon in the star-dappled sky, its brightness pouring silvery light across the cooling desert floor, he glanced around. He had no weapon. No horse. No shelter . He needed to find a hidey-hole in which to survive moonset's cold and its pitch darkness. He brushed desert debris from his homespun shirt. He examined the crushed felt headgear that lay beside him. Exploration of his pant pocket contributed naught but a small collection of coins.

His shirt's tuck-in yielded a neatly folded, lace trimmed, white square. He fingered the soft fabric, willing it to give up its secrets. Pressing it to his nose he breathed in the fragrance of lavender. Surely a lady's thingamabob. But the elegant hankie brought no memories. Its lingering scent carried no image of its owner.

Weary as an old hound dog, the cowboy shoved the pretty cloth back into its poke and turned his attention to the task of finding a safe place to sleep. Desert track stretched endless before him. He ignored persistent dizziness and looked for something familiar, a place to rest. Determined, he forced one canvas-covered leg in front of the other.

The toe of his boot scraped a circle gleaming in the sand, he jabbed at it and uncovered a small, silver piece. Curious, he scooped it up. Cradling the round in his calloused palm, he flipped it over. An inscription shone in the moonlight. He ran fingertips across the roughened script, unable to decipher the words. The last bit was smooth except for a dent, the engraving nearly worn away. A watch? He searched for a connection. Nothing.

When the metal fell from his unsteady grasp, he followed it with his eyes, but did not reclaim it. Instead, he resumed his labored walk, until, giving in to exhaustion, he stepped three feet to the left of the old roadbed and lay down. His back pressed into a small mound of desert sand. He wondered if he was destined to die alone, without a name. Then, with no defense against dropping night temperatures, he slept.

Chapter Two

The Traveler

A half-day's ride east of where the cowboy lay, morning sun rose red as an cardinal's wing in a clear blue sky. Its brightness awakened a young Miwuk Indian woman, far from home. Reluctant to abandon her vivid dream, she rubbed at her eyes, grateful that *Kiwil*, Wind Man, who lives in the breezes, had allowed a heart-visit with her parents. It had been good.

She clung to the vision of Father's brown face smiling in welcome as Mother brought her to the home fire. *Oloki Kalanah*, Raven Dancer, her Spirit name, had spilled from her parent's lips, not the nickname Father favored. This showed their respect. She felt pride to be recognized as a healer. As was the custom, her name had been bestowed when she reached her third year of life. She remembered the formal ceremony and the words Grandmother Owl Woman, clan shaman spoke—telling the name marked her grandchild's bright eyes, black as midnight, and honored her ability to see things others did not, even then.

Now, full awake, wrapped in a sleeping blanket, she felt her isolation. The burden of travel over vast lands and unknown dangers lay ahead. It was to be a long quest from this dry place to the home of her father and mother at the edge of the big water. The place white men called California. She was eager to see family again, to touch their shoulders in true greeting.

More than nine round moon-times had passed since she had begged her father, Standing Bear, for permission to visit a sister-cousin, married to an Apache and living in the wild and sacred mountains of the *Chiricahua*. He had given his consent reluctantly and only after much discussion about the dangers she might find along the way.

Headman of their *Olumpali* village, Father had entrusted her—his precious, only daughter—to his friend Many-Buffalo-Skins for the long trip. Father had been solemn, his words stern: she was to respect and follow the loyal warrior.

Many-Buffalo-Skins chose an arduous trail that forced much dismounting and walking. The pace he set wearied her. When at last they reached the Apache village, she offered a grateful prayer. Her sister-cousin welcomed her warmly, gripping her shoulders. "You come," Little-Fox-Who-Walks said, and led the way to a spacious teepee built by her new husband.

She'd enjoyed her time in the *Chiricahua* camp. It was good to be a guest. But, after several months of visiting, she yearned to return to her own clan before the mountains grew white. Although a woman traveling for many moons without a protector was not a passage her father would bless, Many-Buffalo-Skins had joined a group of Apache warriors to make a hunt. The time of their return was uncertain. She had been unwilling to wait.

Her decision made, she sat with Little-Fox. "From you, I have learned much about courage and making my own way far from salt waters. I am daughter of a chief. I will make my journey home," she said, and placed her hands on her knees. "I have spoken."

Concerned, her sister-cousin asked a tribal elder to give counsel on the matter. He spoke of the route she must take and questioned her plan and preparations. Only after his guidance, and a dance ceremony held to ask for her protection and success, did she bid her sister-cousin and new friends farewell.

This morning, resting alone on hard ground, she wondered what Father might arrange upon her return. Would he have one more group of men who were not yet husbands, prepared to seek her hand in marriage? While she was of marriageable age, men of Father's choosing did not please her. She scowled. It is my decision to make. Perhaps I will never take a husband, she thought. She fingered the eagle feather Mother had given her as special protection. It hung around her neck on a narrow rope of deer sinew.

Feeling unsettled, she sat up, stretched, and climbed from her sleeping blanket. She smoothed the fawn-colored leather shift that covered leggings sewn from soft, chewed hides. To warm her toes, she stomped feet sheathed in blue and white-beaded moccasins whose tops rose to wrap her calves and knees. She had much to do before moving on. The young woman knelt and gathered the dusty blanket that had been her bed. Close by, a chestnut and white pony nickered softly, eager to be off. She looked his way. "Patience, Washee," she murmured, and swept her long, dark hair, thick as a mare's tail, over supple shoulders.

After a breakfast of cactus fruit and pinion bread, she stowed her cook tools, rolling them into the blanket's folds. Leather straps she had fashioned for the trip tied her belongings securely. Standing, she slid a thick deer hide thong over her left shoulder and between her breasts. The bedroll rested secure against her back.

The young woman turned her attention to the tiny clearing which had given her shelter this past night. Red rock soared on three sides, creating walls of grotesque and wild shapes. A thick mix of stunted trees and cactus anchored in desert sand stretched to the West. Sky spirits had made a round moon that allowed Washee to find his way into this protected place. In return she gave thanks as she collected a handful of twigs and carefully brushed away all traces of their visit.

Stepping lightly, she approached her pony and grabbed his mane. With her fingers wrapped in its thickness, she swung herself up and settled on his warm back. Urging him forward with her heels and soft chucking sounds, she steered the pinto toward the desert wash that would carry them into the mountains. They had been traveling for many days. Ahead, on the next leg of their journey, the hills that touched the sky must be crossed.

Chapter Three

The Apparition

Morning sun threw early heat on the sleeping man's face, waking him. Its rays burned like a branding iron. He squinted against its glare and turned onto his side. Even that slight movement gave misery. Groaning, he sat up and ran his tongue over parched lips. "I'd trade a good horse for a drink a' water," he muttered.

The cowboy closed his eyes and tried again to remember what had happened. It was hazy—he recalled a wagon wheel. Maybe a fight? A rifle lifted and used as a club? Fright flickered, quickened his breathing. Then nothing.

He still could not give himself a name.

His head throbbed. Hunger, thirst, and the increasing swelter of the desert morning left him weak. Shading his eyes against the brightness, he searched the horizon and an uneven track that appeared to be a road. He saw no landmark, no sign of human habitation. Defeated, he sank back onto his bed of sand.

The day wore on as sunshine blistered a cloudless sky. Merciless, hot as a wild fire, it scorched the edge of his reason. Separating reality from the conjurings of his mind became an effort. Snarling creatures, teeth sharp as razors, seemed to creep toward him from among the cactus and ocotillo, only to disappear as he flung his arms outward in defense.

"No," he groaned, sprawled face down, his head heavy against desert grit. Hellish dreams, loud with screaming, tormented him. As he struggled to escape the nightmare, he heard the beating of his heart. Faint, but growing stronger, it thudded in his ears. Suddenly, the thumping stilled. His breath froze. Blinding terror surged through him.

Was this death?

He waited to fall into nothingness.

Seconds passed. His eyes fluttered open, and he strained to lift his head. The shape of a pony wavered before him in the seething heat. Unshod hooves pawed the ground. A woman's face floated in his vision. Her moccasin-covered feet shimmered, dancing on the sand. Breathing in shallow gasps, barely able to whisper, the cowboy moaned "water," and with his last conscious gesture, reached out to touch the apparition.

The woman stood unmoving, silent, wary of the cowboy lying facedown in hot sand. The circling birds that spoke of carrion had been visible from a distance. They gave warning: rein in Washee, approach with caution.

The stranger was helpless. Although he was *waliki*, a white man, she knew he must have strong medicine because he still lived. Few men could cheat death in a place of endless sand without water or pony.

This situation was unexpected. She had much to consider. Her hand went to a small pouch that hung around her neck. Hidden at her breast alongside her eagle feather rested a parting gift from her cousin's husband—the gleaming dust white men so revered. "Keep it safe. The little sack will make good feasting for your village," he had said. She pressed it against her chest, marveling that bits of soft yellow were valuable. It was her secret. She planned to travel with care, to stay away from settler houses and soldier camps between this sand and her home.

Instinct told her this man was neither outlaw, nor blue-coat. In truth, she most feared the horse soldiers who would shoot her, or worse, because they thought her an Apache. She had seen the injuries and heard tales of soldier cruelty from her mountain cousins. Even babies were not safe. Greedy whites would kill an Indian girl for a cache of the golden metal. *If I heal him, perhaps he will give me safe escort home,* she mused.

Taking her water basket from her shoulder, she knelt, turned the cowboy over, and supported his head. Surprised by short sharp face hairs that scraped her arm, she gave him drops of the precious liquid, first to moisten his parched lips, and then many small swallows to ease his thirst.

Although she wanted to touch him, explore the little hairs that sprouted around his mouth, so unlike the smooth faces of men in her tribe, she did not put her fingers against him. After a time he stirred. She watched as his eyes slowly opened and could not help but smile. His burning demons had retreated, leaving him weak and groggy, but conscious.

The color of his eyes amazed her. They were grey as mountain rock, then, as if a shape-shifter spirit lived within, they turned to blue stone and back again. He seemed puzzled, maybe to find an unknown young woman hovering over him. She did not imagine that he found her beautiful, with her long, dark hair and eyes like polished obsidian. Nor did she know the cold fear that spread tendrils in his belly.

"We need ride, find good shelter from hot," she said in broken English, certain he would not know her people's way of speaking.

She peered at the pale-skinned stranger, and wondered if she could get him onto her horse. If she'd be strong enough. In his face, she saw confusion, and something else … something unreadable.

"I help you *hac-i-cy,* to be standing. Mount pony." She gestured at Washee. The man seemed to understand that she would take him from the killing heat. He struggled to his feet, allowing her to assist him. "Good place no sun, not far." She surveyed their surroundings and pointed west. "We go big rocks. You rest, drink water. Be strong for journey."

Chapter Four

A Puzzle

Seventeen-year-old Sara Durann Colton spurred her mustang, Cherry, deeper into the Arizona canyon that had been home to her family for more than a century. "If only Matthew had heeded my advice!" Her words sliced, sharp as rifle shots, through the dry August air.

She'd never been so worried in her entire life. Of course, she'd had never had a beau before. She couldn't shake her fears. He had been missing for nearly two weeks. Her last conversation with him had been wretched. She pulled at the damp bandana already sticking to her neck. In truth, he was not qualified to ride shotgun for Wells Fargo. It was best left to hired guns or the law. He courted disaster and she'd told him so! Stubborn, as usual, he refused to consider the perils. Indeed, he'd been argumentative, his eyes pinched and intent. Downright ornery, he'd saddled his big grey stallion, Thunder, bid her a cool goodbye, and headed for the livery stable.

The stagecoach, bound for Tucson, had never arrived. Matthew, passengers, and payroll had vanished. There'd been no news from the stationmaster, only frightening silence. The entire town was alarmed over the disappearance but no one had been able to provide a single clue.

One of her father's ranch hands found the big grey wandering, thirstin' something awful, and brought him home nearly a week ago. She bit back tears. Surely Matt would have sent word to her or Pa if he were able.

Brows knit, Sara pulled to a halt in the blazing sun. Her hopes for the future were slipping away. She scowled. She'd expected to be choosing a wedding dress, not fearing for his life. Their marriage, her hope of setting out upon her own destiny was in jeopardy. Her leather-gloved fingers tensed on the reins, and Cherry shifted in response.

Driven to discover what had befallen him, Sara threaded her way to the top of a small rise that offered a wider view. She gazed at the forest of Joshua trees and cactus that peppered the sandy canyon floor. This would have been a fine day to enjoy Durann Canyon's glories if it weren't for misgivings that scrabbled in her head. She gnawed her lower lip; the puzzle of Matthew's whereabouts left her baffled.

Skeersomes—Pa's favorite word for horrible, frightening ideas—bit at her like tiny "no see-ums." She knew her beloved desert could be dreadful fierce. Tranquil at first glance, it was a keeper of secrets. Intolerant of mistakes, it meted out punishment, swift and final.

"I am going to have a conniption fit," she hissed, fighting a wave of flusteration that threatened to explode. Patience was not her strength. Although she didn't care to admit it, Pa was right when he looked to the heavens, shut his eyes and shouted, "The Good Lord has not seen fit to bless you with forbearance, daughter." But something was terribly wrong. The feeling bit at her like a wasp sting. *Matthew must be found.*

Sara forced herself to recall happier times. Thoughts of Matthew's strapping good looks, his broad shoulders, unruly brown hair, and sweet, open smile allowed the tension in her arms and legs to fall away for a few moments. Then seeking relief from the unrelenting sun, she guided Cherry down into the thin shadows of Wild Horse Mesa. The spirited, stocky-built, wild mustangs that called the canyon home were gone today. No pounding hooves, no snorting, no whinnies. Silence. Still as a grave. She swallowed hard. This is big country. A man could get lost in it and never find his way home.

Inhaling air laden with the fragrance of desert sage, Sara scanned the creviced walls of Durann Canyon. Centuries-old Indian dwellings, guardians of ancient bones, mysterious carvings, and hidden relics were concealed in the imposing pink and brown rock face. Alert for any sound that bespoke the irregular, she endured the afternoon swelter. What route had the stage taken? Could they have reached the mouth of the ravine and been unable to continue? Her eyes widened. Not ten feet away lay the bleached skull and bones of a longhorn. *Was it an omen*? She shuddered.

In need of comforting, she leaned forward and laid her head against Cherry's thick mane, almost as flaxen as her own tresses. Her fingers entangled gently in its length. "I do wish I hadn't quarreled with him before he left," she whispered. Her hand slid beneath to stroke the mustang's silky dark-red coat. Muscle rippled under her fingertips. The mare turned her head and nibbled the brim of Sara's John B. "Quit it," Sara yawped, as the hat threatened to slip off. Heaving a sigh, she tightened her belly muscles, pulled erect in the saddle, and readjusted her favorite shade-maker atop tousled ringlets.

"Matthew! Where *are* you?" The echo of her words gave the only reply. Sliding feet from the stirrups, she wiggled toes curled and cramped in high-top boots. Ominous thoughts like scavenging crows, continued to wheel and dive. Cherry jigged, golden tail switching. The saddle creaked, a settling of leather on leather beneath her, and Sara, discouraged, decided to head home.

"We'll take the lower track," she informed her horse. "Perhaps the swash of water will calm my nerves." Lifting the reins, and leaning into the pommel, she put heels against Cherry's sides. The mare moved forward, picking her way along a narrow trace that led down the Canyon to the river's edge.

Chapter Five

Waylaid

Sara called it the wet trail. It was her favorite stretch of the ride home. Miles to the north, the sparkling Arroyo River tumbled into Durann Canyon. Its occasional deep pools, clear and cold, were refreshing in the blister of summer. She thought of many afternoons when she'd tether Cherry in a cluster of leafy green cottonwood trees at the Arroyo's edge, then, bold as you please, step out of her split skirt, shirtwaist, riding boots and stockings. Clad only in lacy white bodice and pantaloons, she'd splash into a quiet sink. Savoring the sweet smell of water and sunshine, she'd float, watch dragonflies dart overhead, and hardly move except to waggle her feet.

Today, shoving tickling wisps of hair behind her ears, she bent an ear to the far off gush of the torrent. "It's the life source of this canyon," Pa had told her. She did love how water swept along crevices carved in the canyon floor, disappeared mysteriously into the earth, and bubbled up again to rush over boulders. But, at the moment, she had only a passing fancy for the rippling wet that flowed several feet away. Instead, uneasy thoughts continued to burst in her head.

Suddenly, the breeze picked up, fast turning to hot canyon gusts. She brought a hand to the brim of her hat, settling it with a tug. Afternoon blows were stingers, full of fine bits of sand—an onerous circumstance to be sure. Peevish, she pulled her bandana up to cover her mouth and nose as she rode. Thus protected, she continued on.

In the distance, unexpected puffs of dust dotted the horizon. The clop of hooves striking the track was clear. One rider. Who on earth can that be? she wondered, watching a dappled grey come into view. She squinted. It looks to be Matt's stallion, Thunder. By Christopher, surely it is!

She pulled to a halt, huffing short, sharp breaths. Her pulse raced with hope. She stared into the distance. *Dash it!* The man astride the big grey was not Matthew at all. As he loped toward her, she couldn't help but notice the cowboy sat taller in the saddle, seemed longer legged and leaner, too. What is he doing on Thunder's back? His countenance was not familiar to her. A ripple of unease rode along her spine.

Horse and rider broke to a dusty walk and stopped, blocking her way forward. Brash green eyes explored her person. Sara pushed her bandana down and returned his impudent stare with the haughtiest glare she could muster. The unwelcome burn of an embarrassed blush flamed her cheeks. She drew back a step. Quick thoughts raced in her head. Who is this bold-faced cowboy? Has he no breeding? Might he be a roadman? A rapscallion? Hiding her alarm, she held herself aloof, lips pressed into a straight line. She'd not cower. Her fingers inched toward her rifle stock.

"Miss Coulton?" he said, breaking the taut silence between them.

"Who might be wanting to know?" she said, surprised he'd addressed her by name.

"Handle's Gage Evans." He never dropped his impertinent gaze. "In your father's employ as ranch foreman." He tipped his hat. "I've seen you around the ranch, Miss." His handsome brow lifted and eyes the color of young pine tree shoots drilled her.

The man was certainly nervy, she decided, fear gone. "Hmmph. I don't believe we've been properly introduced, nor have I seen you on the property, Mister Evans. My father *has* mentioned your name. I do recall him stating you were on the trail to Utah, delivering a string or two of our working horse stock."

"Yep. Pulled in home day before yesterday. I'd say it was a good trip. Big doings up north. Lots of excitation just now, seeing as Utah's tossin' in with Arizona to become part a' the Territory." Amusement leapt in his eyes. "The place was wild with celebratin'." He flashed her a roguish smile, showing even, white teeth, daring her interest.

He is insufferable! "I have no care in the sort of carryings-on you've been involved in," she retorted, infuriated as her cheeks pinked again. "By the bye, that will be my fiancé's horse you ride." She hoped her words stung.

Unperturbed, the foreman rubbed Thunder's neck with copper browned fingers. A devilish smirk appeared on his lips. "He's quite a fine ride. His spirit suits me." Then like quicksilver, the man turned grave as a mustard pot. His tone biting, he reproached her. "Needs exercising. You ought know that, ma'am."

Sara, thunderstruck with his proddy reply, found herself rendered mute. His audacity galled her.

"Miz Lena asked me to find you, Miss Coulton, and fetch you home."

"I have no need of your fetching," she declared. "I am perfectly capable of getting myself there." Her eyes narrowed. "Your message has passed to me, Mister Evans. I thank you," she snipped. "I shall require no escort."

"As you wish, Miss." He tipped his hat again, nodded her a cheeky sort of farewell, whipped his mount around and took off at a gallop. Sara stared after him, thoroughly provoked. *He surely thinks himself fine as cream gravy.*

Flustered, she looked at Thunder's disappearing rump and frowned. What on earth did Lena want? "Best find out," she muttered, and pushed Cherry into a trot.

As they jogged steadily down the track, Sara went to reminiscing. Durann Canyon, the ranch, and her father's newspaper would be hers someday, hers and her husband's. At least that was what Pa expected, she thought, feeling a stab of guilt.

The first time her father had taken her into town to his newspaper office she couldn't have been more than five years old. "Someday this will be yours," he'd said. Then he placed an editing pencil in her small, eager fingers and deposited her in the big leather chair behind his desk.

Although she was much too young to grasp the full meaning of his words, Sara understood the seriousness in her father's voice. And he'd been sowing the seeds ever since, encouraging her to learn the business and the land. "Well, teaching me to fill his shoes kept me under his thumb, but hasn't dampened my free spirit," she muttered.

Then, two years ago, Pa sent her off east to Miss Evelyn's Girl's School aiming to "tame her wild streak." Instead, she became more determined than ever to experience life. Truth be known, though writing excited her, she was not at all persuaded she wished to run a newspaper. It was adventure she sought. She'd yet to tell him. Hers was a significant decision. She concluded it best to bide her time, especially now, with Matthew's whereabouts unknown.

Sara's thoughts drifted to Matthew and his talk of their future as man and wife. Only a few weeks past, he had shared his dreams over one of Lena's fine dinners. He was determined to do business in the California gold towns. Even in this little corner of Arizona, word came regularly of thousands of men flocking west, swarming the rivers in a frenzied search for the prized yellow metal. It was simply laying around for the picking, according to some.

"I believe a bonanza to be a scarce thing," he'd said. "But cattle and horses and even eggs are worth their weight in gold."

It must be true, she'd thought. Mining camps were in need of all things: food, blankets, tools, wagons. She relished the idea of being right in the midst of the fever-pitch pursuit of real treasure. It was an exciting time.

"I could write some wonderful stories," she'd suggested sipping her after-dinner coffee, her tone bright with the contemplation of such opportunity. Matthew had smiled at her enthusiasm. Her father's eyes turned cool. Father clearly wasn't interested in losing his only child to the commotion in California. Nor to marriage for that matter.

When she had first spoken of her desire to wed he'd set his jaw and growled, "Matthew is betwixt hay and grass, Sara. Not a boy, not yet a man." He'd pounded his desktop and shouted, "Why, you scant know one another."

He refused to further discuss the subject for weeks, regardless of what she said or how much she wept. Thank goodness that ordeal was over. He'd finally agreed to give the issue thought, but had yet to show any sign of giving his blessing. It was aggravating, to be sure. He simply could not accept that she had attained her majority, seventeen years of age, now a grown woman ready to make her own life. She shook her head. Between Lena's watchful eyes and Pa's, she always felt corralled.

Cherry trotted steadily on. In the distance, the family rancho came into view. The Durann-Coulton spread—a rich gleam of adobe, whitewash, and spots of green set against the silhouette of jagged, volcanic peaks—always gave her pleasure. She sighed and wondered again what Lena wished of her?

She never expected to find visitors anxiously awaiting her arrival.

Chapter Six

Odd Companions

For several days, both travelers straddled Washee, although the Indian woman often climbed from the saddle, and led her pony.

"We move forward like snail people," she grumbled, as they made their way up above the foothills of the Sierra Colorado Mountains. Green, high-country trees filtered harsh sunlight. Afternoon shadows brought chill breezes that whispered of an even colder night. The cowboy said little—once mumbling that he was grateful for the cool of a shaded track. She felt him relax. Perhaps his mind drifted in and out of blank spaces.

Among the trees fresh water came strong to her nose. She halted. Here they would make camp alongside a deep stream that flowed between big boulders, high above the desert valley. She slid off the pinto, stepped into a clearing to the side of the streambed, and peered down at the endless sand below them. Satisfied that she would see any who came this way long before they could find her, she chose a sheltered, level spot.

So weary he had been unable to dismount without her help, the injured man rested beneath a tree. She knew he fought the overwhelming urge to sleep, yet his curious gaze tracked her as she made camp. Under his scrutiny, she prepared a place for sleep and cooking, then turned toward him. "Healing plants make ... hmm ... medicine," she said, showing with finger movements and soft words that she would attend to his head gash, sun-ravaged face and swollen hands. "This safe place. You sleep."

He nodded, but she felt his eyes follow her as she disappeared, soundless as a snake, into the nearby trees in search of the necessary ingredients.

In the shallow hollow of a nearby boulder, she used scant drops of water and a rounded stone to grind her gathered leaves and moss into paste. Then she approached the white man. "You come fire circle," she instructed, and helped him settle against the slope of the rock. Her fingers scooped the mash and gently pressed it to his head wound, smoothed it on his wrists and hands. "Good you. Make well," she said.

Inspecting his sun-reddened face, she asked bold questions. "How you in hot desert place? What name call you?"

He shook his head and could make no answers. The man took a small bite of the acorn cake she'd baked on a flat rock set in the cooking fire. "Good," he mumbled, and devoured it along with a deer jerky strip she soaked in stream water. Although they did not speak, his company at the evening meal brought comfort.

She glanced across the remains of their small fire. Embers flared, mimicking the orange ribbons that flamed bright against the darkening Arizona sky. Gold and red streaks gave way to purple dusk as nightfall drew its cloak ever tighter. Firelight cast its glow on the man's face, throwing just enough light to show the smudge of a bruise still visible on his temple.

He must have taken a hard blow, she thought, perhaps from a long gun or club. She saw him stir, push his back into the granite, and lift his head until he gazed across the coals. His eyes, fixed on hers, were filled with questions.

There was effort in his slowly spoken words. They broke the long silence as drops of water disturb the surface of a quiet pond. "How do you come to speak the white man's tongue?"

"Father teach me. He learn many ways talk," she replied, proudly. "He taught as young man by *ilesja*, Mission priest. He Standing Bear, son of great chief. Leader *Olumpali*, my home. Many come, visit our village."

"How are you called? What is your name?" he asked.

She considered his question. "Hard to make right words. Father call *Olu* … Mmm … I think better you make sounds you know," she said. "How *you* want call me?"

He stared at her for a long moment. "I sure would call you Dark Eyes. Will it do?"

She smiled mischievously. "You choose name very fine. I like."

"Where … where is your village, Dark Eyes?" the man asked, surprising her with his wish to know more.

"My home over mountains." She pointed, waving a long, slender finger in the general direction. "Americanos call 'California'," she said, pronouncing the word carefully. "Is very beautiful, much good food, have warm lodges. Many big waters give fish. Tall trees. You like my village. You come? Meet Eagle Feather Woman, my mother, and Old Grandmother. She name Owl Woman, gathers plants. Makes healing for many sorrows."

Dark Eyes moved closer to the fire, needing its warmth in the chill of the high country night. Her mind sought to understand how it was with the white man she found near death in the desert. He rests and gets stronger, yet after many new suns his thinking is not whole. Perhaps Coyote, The

Trickster, keeps his memories. He cannot say how he came to be prisoner of bad dreaming, lying in the hot sand. Though she tried to speak of this with him, he cannot identify his people.

She wondered about the small square of white with pretty tangles around its edges that hid in his pocket. Twice he had pulled it out and lingered over it. It was woman gift. Of that she was certain. How does he come to carry it? What power did it hold over him?

His name had been taken from him, probably from the blow made to his head. She saw this once before when a young boy, a visitor to *Olumpali*, stood dangerously close to his pony's flying feet. For many winters the boy was called "No See Old Days." Then, during a sweat lodge ceremony the Great Spirit returned the boy's past times to him. Will this man be given such a gift? It may be so.

Bowing her head, Dark Eyes quietly made a prayer to thank her Grandmother, Owl Woman, for teaching her the ways of plant healings. She wished she had learned more of Grandmother's art. She had much to understand before her power to fool Coyote could grow stronger—maybe force him to loose his hold on the white man. It was something she could not offer now.

Her eyes again sought the cowboy sitting on the other side of the coals, lost in thought. I am drawn to this pale-skinned man with the long hairs pushing out like fur on his face, she realized with a shock. She drew a long breath. Was this some sort of witchery? No. I like he listens with care to my words. It is good to make talk with him. Her breathing slowed.

"I want give you brave name, want show spirit guide," she said, studying him. "You look into me with hungry eyes grey as coat of wolf, and sometime soft, like mist near water."

He made no response.

Dark Eyes pulled her sleeping blanket tight around her shoulders to protect against the cold and the unfamiliar feelings that licked at her.

As the last spangles of orange faded, the evening sky went black, unveiling tiny lights that spilled across the high place of Spirits. Dark Eyes sat beneath the glittering stars. Her mind, like a creeping vine, stretched along burgeoning branches. She considered the unexpected thoughts that slipped around her. Does he have a woman? she wondered. Someone that makes the ways of loving with him? She imagined resting her lips against his mouth as she had seen white women do with their men.

I will make best sound for his spirit, she decided, and drew further within herself. Lids lowered, she sank into her place of quiet, to make careful thoughts and good choice. Naming was powerful medicine. After some time Dark Eyes lifted her head. "I choose name you," she stated. "Your eyes and face hair tell me how call. You Greywolf."

Still braced against a good-sized boulder, he returned her gaze. She was like a cat, he thought—soft, but strong and mysterious. The way she saw the world was strange to him. "*Greywolf.*" He pulled the sound around in his mind, as he unrolled his shirt-sleeves against the chilly evening. "It'll do as good as any," he responded.

Bits and pieces of the past few days spun in his head. Remembering the easy warmth of the woman's memories as she spoke of family and her home, he fell silent. He thought himself a cowboy. His efforts to recall kinfolk, shared meals, or even a place he once might have lived seemed useless.

Everything but the time he had spent with the dark-eyed woman came up a troubling blank. Lost to him.

This woman, an Indian, a stranger, had cleaned and placed healing herbs on his wounds, cooked for him, and nursed him toward health. She had offered kindness, yet he felt the sharp edge of uneasiness. *Why?*

Greywolf watched Dark Eyes stand and lean toward the fire. Her long legs, booted in deerskin, provoked his interest in a most basic way. He wanted to touch her long, dark, shiny hair, to know what went on behind her guarded black eyes. She is beautiful, he mused. The attraction was undeniable. But so much is wrong. I cannot even provide a name for myself.

Sadness and sense of desolation washed over him. "My head hurts," he mumbled, and pressed his palm to his temple. He hoped she would favor him with her soothing touch.

"You rest," Dark Eyes said, her tone cautious.

It was almost as though she was aware of his jumbled thoughts, his longings. He wondered if she felt stirrings of her own.

She pushed at the last of the glowing coals with the toe of her moccasined foot. Her black eyes held their secrets.

"In new day we speak more," she promised.

Chapter Seven

Unexpected Visitors

Sam Brenner, sheriff of Arroyo County, settled himself in the shade of the veranda, his calloused hands wrapped around a thick rose-colored pottery mug. Even in the afternoon heat, Lena's steaming cafe con leché, dark and rich with cream, was just what he needed. His booted feet rested on large terracotta tiles that he and his friend Will Coulton had laid out more than twenty years ago. That was when Will and his young Spanish bride, Antonia de Anza Durann, first built the one-room house that had become the heart of today's sprawling Durann-Coulton ranch.

Adobe walls, high as a man's shoulder in places, shared space with large pots hosting cactus and pink desert flowers, marking the edge of the patio. He figured the graceful trees tangled in a canopy overhead had been there a hundred years—before white men even found this valley. Sam leaned his head against the well-worn, brown leather chair-back and gazed into the green jumble of branches and leaves above him, remembering better days than this particular one.

The sheriff watched his deputy, Bob Raley, tall and stick thin, peer over the whitewashed adobe wall, sighting straight down the ranch track and well beyond the corral where their horses dozed. Raley, usually given to biding his time, had been up and down looking at the road for nearly an hour. How much longer they'd be waiting for Miss Sara was a stumper. Being Tubac's elected lawman, Brenner reviewed his full plate of problems. All needed tending back in town.

"Here she comes, boss, riding that purty sorrel a' hers," Bob rasped.

His deputy's voice jolted him back to the situation that brought them to the ranch today. He reluctantly set his coffee mug down on a small table and rose from his seat. Running a rough hand through his mane of almost white hair, he prepared to share his news.

Sara guided Cherry past the rancho's outbuildings and several fenced pastures. Horse and rider moved at a walk toward the large corral her father had put up to the left of the main hacienda.

She took in two geldings standing quietly at the far end of the corral, and the unease that had gripped her all day grew with a thudding leap. "It looks like we have guests," she said aloud, fretting over what would bring visitors in the middle of a too hot afternoon.

She rested her reining hand on Cherry's neck and reached down to lift the rope that held the corral gate closed. Rider and horse eased the wood planking open. Voice low, she turned the mare and urged her forward. Together they pushed the rectangle shut and she looped the rope to hold it firm. Her eyes swept the enclosure. Those horses are familiar. That buckskin is Sheriff Brenner's. And he's brought his deputy with him. Cold prickled her spine. Sara dismounted quickly. Swinging her leg easy over the saddle, she jumped down into dusty sand. Her mind swept through the litany of troubled thoughts she'd entertained all afternoon. She moved close to stroke Cherry's velvet nose and tried to ignore the foreboding that hung thick in the air.

The mare, get of a wild stallion and one of her father's fine broodmares, responded with affection, nuzzling Sara along her neck just below her ear. Usually a comfort, today the gesture made her frown. She stepped away from the insistent lipping.

"Jose." She motioned to a bearded ranch hand, who was busy repairing a worn halter. "Por favor, unsaddle my horse and see that she has water." Out of habit, she checked the level of the drinking trough. Then with a worried glance at the house, Sara handed the reins to Jose, gave the mare a gentle push, murmured "Go Cherry," and strode toward the corral gate.

Her feet traveled swiftly along the pathway leading to the big adobe ranchera. She fair ran up the few steps onto the wide, stone ramada that stretched along the front of the house.

Blooms of yellow Chiricahua roses curled thick around rough-hewn posts that framed the porch edges, but she barely noticed the fragrance of her favorite flowers as she moved into the shade of the Spanish-tiled overhang.

Sara grabbed at a black iron handle and tugged hard. The heavy door, crafted in Spain some one hundred years before, its intricate carvings smoothed by decades of relentless polishing, gave way. She slipped into the cool recesses of her beloved home.

"Lena," she called, using the affectionate nickname she'd first pronounced when she'd learned to talk. "Where are you, Elena?"

"*Mi niña*," came the quick reply as Elena, long skirts rustling, hurried across the large parlor toward Sara.

Elena Rosaria had come to the Coulton's seventeen years ago, on the occasion of Sara's birth. She was to help Señora

Antonia with the birthing, care for the baby, and keep up of the house. The young Señora had gone to God just days later, and Señor Coulton had asked Elena to stay on. She had happily agreed, serving as wet nurse, mother, friend and teacher to the golden-haired little girl, daughter of Antonia.

"*Sarita,* Senor Brenner is here. He waits for you on the patio."

Sara looked into the older woman's dark-as-coffee eyes. Lena's round brown face, often wreathed in smiles, now mirrored Sara's anxiety. Apprehension wrapped them like fence wire.

"Our Lord will protect you, *niña,* and those you care for, little one," the housekeeper whispered.

Sara threw herself into Lena's ample arms. "I'm frightened!" she said, the words catching in her throat. "What news might they bring?"

Sara, clinging like a child, could hear Lena murmuring.

"When you were young, always I could give comfort. *Cristo* has blessed us with many *años,* easy years. Now we must pray for guidance."

Silently, each woman offered up a petition. Then Lena patted Sara on the back with a gentle hand. "*Sarita, mi niña, por favor,* your guests await."

This woman who had been a mother to her always gave her courage. Today was no exception. She allowed Lena to untangle her from the safety of their protective embrace, then stepped back, slowly brushed a hand across damp eyes, and smoothed her dusty riding skirt with shaky fingers. As if to gain energy from the very air around her, Sara pulled several deep breaths, lifted her chin and walked purposefully toward the patio, hat bouncing against her shoulder blades.

Chapter Eight

Disturbing News

Sara watched Sheriff Brenner stride across the patio toward her, his boots scuffing against the hard terracotta tiles. Fear curled in her heart at the determined brush of his steps.

"Hello, Miss Coulton." He fixed her with a level, grey-eyed stare.

"Sheriff Brenner, Deputy Raley," she said, looking from one to the other. "It's Matt isn't it? I knew it. Something's happened. What's wrong?" She stood dead still, her legs gone heavy, unwilling to tread forward.

Sam Brenner moved to her side. He grasped her arm and gently led her to a chair. "The payroll never made it to Tucson, Sara," he said. His eyes were sober. "A rancher found our driver and the passengers wandering a ways north a' here. The stage was ambushed and robbed. Folks described 'em as highwaymen. Faces covered. Rough trade, armed to the teeth," he said. His voice coarse with emotion spoke volumes. Sara sank into the chair he offered and waited, hands fisted at her sides.

A frown carved his leathery face. "There's more to it." He couldn't bring himself to tell her they had been half dead from thirst. And that wasn't the worst of it.

"Matthew … Matt, was one of them?" she asked, staring up at the two lawmen. Dread churned in her belly.

"T'weren't no sign of your young man," Brenner said, keeping his tone even.

Bob Raley shook his head. "We was tol' he took a beatin'."

The words screamed in her ears. Slowly, Sara brought her gaze to the floor. She studied her boots, noticing deep scratches in the leather along the toes. She fought to keep her breath steady, as panic came alive and slammed around like a *bolo* inside her ribcage.

Brenner and Raley exchanged a worried look.

"I will *not* accept losing him," she sputtered, fingers wiping tears that came unbidden and spilled onto her lap.

The Sheriff yanked a square of red from his back pocket, and squatted down next to her. "Here," he offered and placed the bandana in her damp hands.

Sara managed a choked "Thank you." After a moment she raised her head. "My father," she said. "I must tell him right away! My pa will know what to do."

Brenner stood and pulled a chair over to where Sara sat, motioning his deputy to do the same. The lawman covered Sara's clenched fingers with one of his large hands. His paws, lots of town folk called them. They were strong, toughened and scarred by a lifetime of riding in the searing sun, roping cattle, and working at a hundred other frontier tasks.

"He knows, honey. He was writin' the story for the *Star Dispatch* when I rode out of town. The news came in late mornin'. Tain't no need for you to fret. We'll handle it."

Sara slowly pulled away from the sheriff's protective grip. She carefully folded the red square and handed it back. "I *have* to get to my father's office." A mixture of misery and fear in her voice, she turned to Sam Brenner. "Someone," she said, looking at him intently, "has to find Matt, immediately. I'm riding to town now," she announced, her words husky with tears.

Struggling to control her emotions, she could feel the two men come to the pinch. *They are teaming-up against me.* She saw it in the set of their faces. They deemed her tearful resolve irksome. They'd prefer she draw aside, bide her time. "I'll not argue. I've made up my mind."

To confirm her intentions, Sara stood and bent her look upon both men, shooting them a piercing glower. "I'll not sit and wait." Then she turned and walked toward the interior of the house.

Sheriff Brenner dispatched Raley to saddle her horse. As the deputy slipped over an adobe wall and set off at a run, the sheriff followed Sara through the screened patio door.

Two pairs of spurred boots clattered across the dark wood planking of the parlor floor, spurs making a counterpoint metallic jingling, that took Lena's attention from her task in the kitchen. Hurriedly, she wiped her masa-dusted fingers on her white apron and made the sign of the cross.

Out of the corner of her eye, Sara saw Lena wringing her hands, her face shaded in the wide arched adobe doorway that led from the kitchen into the big comfortable parlor.

"*Niñita, adonde va?* Where do you go?"

"Matthew is missing. I'm riding to Father for help," Sara answered, as she barreled across the room and ran toward the oaken door. There was no time for further explanation, although Sara knew the older woman would return to her tortilla making, heart heavy with concern.

The sheriff's long-legged stride kept him right behind the distraught girl. He paused only to retrieve his battered white Stetson from the iron hat rack that stood just inside the entryway. *"Adios, Senora."* He flung his goodbye over his shoulder.

The intricately carved door opened and quickly swung closed behind them, but not before Sara heard Lena's whispered *"Via con Dios, Niña,"* rush toward her like it had wings.

Midafternoon sun assailed young Sara and the lawman as she continued to run, without a backward glance, down the hacienda steps, along the walkway, and across to the corral. Her boots kicked dust and bits of rock. She could feel a still damp streak along the small of her back where her blouse stuck to her spine. On any other day she would have stopped and changed her clothes, but not today. In moments she halted at the corral's edge, breathing hard. Looking across the evenly spaced fencing, she saw Cherry and the sheriff's buckskin saddled and ready to ride.

Sara reached for the rope that held the gate in place. She shoved it wide as Bob Raley swung onto his horse. The deputy spun neatly around, grabbed Cherry's reins and those of the buckskin in one fist. He led both horses through the break at a fast walk. In seconds Sara looped the gate. She and Sheriff Brenner mounted immediately.

Sara turned in the saddle, face tense, her hand resting for a moment on the mare's broad croup. "Are you moving on?" she inquired, her focus hard as rock.

Sheriff Brenner pushed his hat back on his head. His big horse danced restlessly under him, eager to be off. "Well, I kinda thought we'd ride along back t' town with ya," he said, returning her gaze. "If ya'd have us."

In answer, Sara turned and urged Cherry into a trot, then a lope.

Chapter Nine

The Stallion

Dark Eyes arose to welcome a clear morning. As she did at each new dawn, she made her prayer to greet the day and spoke of her grateful heart to the four spirits who bring warmth, wind, rain, and all life.

Under a sun-filled sky, she rummaged through her small baskets. "We eat, Greywolf. Come now you," she called softly, offering a piece of her dried meat. She watched him tear at buffalo jerky, the traveling food given by her cousin. "You like?"

Greywolf scratched his chin and worked his still sore jaw. He grinned. "I have a big hunger," he said, thwacking his belly. She could not help but look to each place his fingers touched. His gestures pleased her. After their sparse meal, he rolled himself into the blanket and slept.

Dark Eyes made her way to the edge of the clearing. She chose a vantage point and eased her body into a crevice in the rocks. Perhaps the spirits will allow him a visit with his people in the dream world, she mused, wondering if *waliki* knew such journeys. She would ask him.

Hidden from sight, she scanned the valley below. Her eyes focused first on small puffs of sand. Dust devils the whites called them. She waited. Before long, two riders, men, were visible moving along the dry track far beneath her camp spot. Twice they climbed off their horses and walked in small circles, their heads bent toward the ground. They look for something, Dark Eyes realized.

Light flared for an instant as the sun struck the bigger man's chest. "Ahh," she murmured, and pictured the piece of metal he must be wearing. He was probably what the white man called "the law." She had seen such men before, when they came to *Olumpali* to speak with her father. They had been looking for a particular horse and rider. It was not a happy visit. They wished to jail their quarry. Father sent them away with no answers.

Do these two seek the man who lost his name, she wondered. What might Greywolf have done to cause them to hunt him. If they find him, they will take the small pouch of yellow metal I carry as a gift to my family. Maybe they want take me prisoner as well. Fright shook her, but she did not flinch.

She waited until sun shadows grew long and the trackers turned to ride north, toward the place of the big soldier fort called Tucson. Her movements were swift and sure as she returned to the campsite. Though her *sikenah,* her patient, needed rest, she knew they had to move quickly. "It is wise to leave danger behind." More than once she had heard her father, Standing Bear, say those words.

Finding the man still asleep, Dark Eyes knelt on the ground and gently shook his shoulder several times. His sleep was deep. "Greywolf," she hissed, regretting she must pull him from the powerful dream world. She knew his spirit journey would be unfinished, but he had to awaken. His dreaming must fall away, maybe taking with it questions unvoiced and unanswered. At last he stirred and came from his vision place.

"What is it?" he groaned.

"We leave now," she said. "Bad men come. Maybe seek you. We not know. Bring much danger me, Miwuk woman." She pulled at the blanket that covered him, her voice urgent. "I must return my family. Many long times not see them. You want make journey me?"

Coming fully awake, the cowboy stared at her. "I don't reckon I have much choice, do I?" he said, and sat up. "But we can't get over the mountains to California. We only have one horse, Dark Eyes, and that'd go hard with him. We're in a scrape."

"I find more horse. You stronger now, need own pony," she responded, pleased by the way his voice sang her name. "We leave camp" she repeated. "Go from this place."

Riding double, Greywolf and the Indian woman made their way along the upper reaches of a dry creek bed. They traveled deep into the mountains during the long afternoon. Toward evening, Dark Eyes, though reluctant to feel his arms drop from the warm circle they made around her waist, put concern for her pony first. "Washee need rest now. We stop here," she said.

They dismounted in the fading light, and she ran ahead to scan the surrounding area. She slowed, stood motionless, and listened intently. All of a sudden she whirled, and stepped to his side, two fingers set across her mouth. His eyes found hers, questioning what she had in mind.

"No speak. Follow," she mouthed, tugging the pony's rope halter, leading Washee into a clutch of junipers.

Greywolf, weary, stepped after her into the trees. He was exhausted, as much from the ride, as from the odd pictures that burst into his mind from time to time all afternoon, images shadowed by sharp head pains.

"What are we doing here, Dark Eyes?"

Still as death, her attention focused straight ahead. She motioned toward a gap in the trees. He peered through the brush, and understood. All but hidden from view, three horses grazed in a small corral, built where the land dipped into a shallow depression. It was made in the old way, of twigs and branches entwined and stacked to the height of a small woman. Farther up the mountain he saw the outline of a cabin.

"This is a bad idea. You can't just take a fella's horse." Fear flickered in his belly. He wondered briefly if he had been a horse thief in the time he couldn't recall. *They hang horse thieves.* The thought startled him. Sweat spiked along his spine. "What if they catch you? I see a cabin right up there." He pointed. "It's likely they won't be askin' questions. Just shoot us both."

"Great Spirit bring here. Have many mounts, no miss one." Dark Eyes turned to him, triumph in her eyes. "I get horse soon," she whispered, her voice a song. "We need for be safe, go quick over high places. I choose best animal."

"I don't like it."

"This chance for fine ride. Strong. Great Spirit show good way. I follow." She thumped a clenched fist against her breast, ending the discussion.

He sighed. *Well, if that don't take the rag off the bush!* She seemed to think it a plum acceptable act. Although his unease did not slide away entirely, it was useless to argue with the woman. Frustrated, he said no more on the subject.

Partnered in an uneasy truce, the two hunkered down side-by-side, speaking little. When blackness began its relentless seep into the sky, Dark Eyes rummaged again in her food baskets bringing out corn cakes to be shared.

The edge off his hunger, the cowboy, grateful for an escape into sleep, nodded off.

His shoulder pressed into hers as she sat unmoving, listening to the night sounds. Critters scampered, dusting up dry vegetation. Somewhere close by an owl hooted. Coyotes sang their yipping songs on hillsides while he slept.

In the deep shadows that follow moonset, he awakened refreshed and found himself leaning into the girl. He stretched his arms and legs, aware of the contact. Liking it, he wondered if the closeness pleased his companion.

She fixed her eyes on his. "You rest plenty longtimes. Now you sit Washee," Dark Eyes whispered, and pushed him away from her, all business.

Reluctance in his posture, brow creased in a worried frown, Greywolf mounted the pony. His eyes bored into her back, watching her steal toward the corral. He felt menace in the air.

Scouting the makeshift circle of fencing, Dark Eyes found an opening. She slipped inside and waited, motionless. Silent as a secret, she stood at the corral's edge and allowed the animals to take her measure. After many minutes she broke the hush and murmured softly to the ponies.

Evaluating the strength of each, her eyes returned again and again to the large black stallion standing, ears erect, at the farthest turn of the pen. Alert, he watched her every move. She felt the great and proud heart of this horse. The choice was made.

Her hide-covered feet stepped lightly as she moved toward him, holding his eyes with her own. Blowing soft breaths, the stallion allowed the Indian woman to approach.

In low tones Dark Eyes spoke to him of her need for his swift feet and fearless heart. Her hands moved against his long neck, calming him when he tossed his head. In one fluid move she slipped a rope from around her waist and laid it over the stallion's withers.

With a long, unhurried motion, her left hand slid beneath the big neck and grasped the end of the braided hemp, gently pulling it across itself and toward her. She fit the end piece through a loop she'd twisted to receive it. Her fingers worked without hesitation, creating a sturdy halter for the horse.

Dark Eyes stood quietly next to the stallion, her senses attuned to heed anything unusual. No sound but the distant hoot of an owl came to her ears. She knew the bird to be harmless, the spirit of someone who had died. Only the voices or footsteps of living men were of concern now.

Whispering to the black horse of her pleasure in his company, she tugged on the rope. Together they moved across the enclosure and out through the makeshift gate. In silence she led him away from the corral, the specter of the cabin, still dark on the slope above them.

She slipped along the rim of the juniper thicket with her prize, searching for sight of her waiting pony, when the sudden clatter of the stallion's hooves against loose stone whipped loud into the night. Startled, she tightened her grip on his rope. Rough voices shouted in response, jarring her and alarming the great beast. She looked up to see dim light glowing in a square that must be a window.

Shots peppered the darkness. Making the sound of a hawk's cry, Dark Eyes signaled her pinto. She soothed the stallion and hung on to him, as Washee, soundless as smoke, appeared out of the trees, Greywolf astride him. She could smell the man's panic. Hear it in his breathing.

The black horse danced, nostrils flared. He snorted and pawed great dust clouds from the ground. Speaking of fleeing in low, urgent tones, Dark Eyes grabbed the stallion's mane and leapt onto his back. She prayed to her spirit protector for the cooperation of the big animal.

Holding her prancing ride in check, she twisted her body around just enough to grab her pony's halter rope and wrap it in her outstretched fingers. "Hehey," she called sharply, digging her heels into the stallion's sides. It reared, pushed off its powerful haunches, and leapt forward.

Dark Eyes, forced to loosen her grip on Washee, flung the lead rope toward Greywolf. She prayed terror did not cripple her fellow traveler, that he'd caught the pony's rope and would spur the pinto forward. Only when she heard Washee's unshod hooves at her back did she lean into a gallop. They would outrun the snarling voices that carried to her ears in the cool night air and escape the angry men with rifles.

"Hell to damnation. Injuns, Jedidiah! They took m'best horse."

"Mebbe it's Apache raiders took 'm," offered his companion. "Near t' pitch black out there. Cain't hardly see."

"Twern't no Apaches, boys! I sawn what I sawn. Looked a female sittin' my Blackie. See here, you two old buzzards, I ain't losing no stallion to a danged horse thievin' woman, an' a injun to boot," he shouted.

"If that don't beat all," another voice protested, as Dark Eyes and Greywolf disappeared into the trees, kicking up sand and bits of rock and twig.

"Well then, come on now, Jonas. Quit yer yakking. My feet 'er iced cause I ain't got but stockin's on and it ain't sun-up yet. Too damn dark to get a good shot at them horse rasslers 'n I ain't traveling these hills t'night. Chester n' me aim t' track 'em first light."

"I ain't pulling in m' horns jest yet." Jonas hefted his rifle, sighted down the barrel and took one more shot.

Chapter Ten

Tubac

Sara leaned forward in her saddle and urged Cherry on as she and the two lawmen moved steadily along the sandy track toward town. The Arizona sun settled into its late afternoon rhythm, painting canyon cliffs and crevices with deep shadows. Durann Canyon soon gave way to flat, Saguaro studded desert. Craggy black peaks beckoned in the distance.

Her eyes swept the darkening vista. It seemed so like the setting of a ghastly story that tore, unbidden, at the edges of her mind. Long before they met, Matthew had survived terrible danger. When he was but a boy of fourteen, his life had forever changed. It had happened not far from here, he'd told her. "That is how I came to live in Tubac," he'd said.

Her breath came fast, and her fingers white knuckled on the reins. She winced, remembering the day Matthew had described his parent's coldblooded murder and the disappearance of his sisters. It had been horrible to hear, but she had listened.

Goosey bumps prickled her arms as she again saw the frightening scene through the eyes of the innocent boy he had been. He'd spoken of screaming women and children. The desperate shouts of their men when Apaches had swept down from a mountain ridge. Fierce and savage as a desert brush fire, the raiders laid waste to the small wagon party of panicked farmers and their families.

The war party had overwhelmed the unsuspecting immigrants at nightfall with lances, hatchets and rifles, killing all but a handful. Matthew's eyes had glazed in horror as he relived the unspeakable tragedy. Sara shook her head attempting to dislodge the ugly images.

Doc Crow, an Indian guide, had pulled Matt to safety beneath a wagon bed, and held him there. Huddled against its heavy wheels, Matt had watched his parents' desperate attempt to shield his sisters from two fearsomely painted attackers, galloping toward them at breakneck speed. His mother and father were felled in an instant.

Same as she had when Matt first recounted seeing the braves ride down upon them; tonight Sara could just about taste the terror of the two young girls. She knew his grief as his sisters, one a moppet of only six years, and one nearly a young woman, almost twelve, were pulled shrieking into the painted arms of the murderers. And then they were gone.

"I can still see their faces ... the piercing eyes of the men, their yellow and black war paint reflected in the light of the burning wagons. I'll never forget the blood chilling whoops of the war party. It all happened so fast," Matt had said, looking rather puzzled.

Just thinking of his dreadful night caused a flutter of fear in her belly. The renegades were never caught. Although the desert air was not yet beginning to turn icy, Sara shivered in her thin shirtwaist. Beset by a storm of worry, she considered the possibilities of lurking dangers: Apache warriors, hatchets raised. Waiting.

Fearing the black of coming nightfall, her heels closed hard on Cherry's flanks. The mare bolted ahead. Startled, Sara pulled up on the reins. "Easy girl," she commanded, slowing the beast to a measured lope as she tried to steady her own breathing and feverish imagination. She wondered if Matt, wherever he be, feared the setting sun.

Wary, she scanned distant flat-topped mesas and the backdrop of ridges. Behind her she could hear the comforting drum of the buckskin's hooves and Deputy Raley's horse. Ahead, against a murky sky, the town of Tubac seemed perched on the edge of the world. It drew her on; a jumble of odd shapes sitting between two sharp, black peaks.

The small group rode three abreast down Tubac's main street. Cowboys, gamblers, and family men had deserted the grimy dust of Main Street for soap and hot water, an early evening meal, and preparations for other pleasures of the night. In the silence Sara rode with ghosts. Perhaps Matthew and others on the stagecoach perished, never to be seen again. Veiled in twilight, she shuddered at her foolishness and hoped that Matt was warm and safe this eventide.

Falling behind, Brenner's leggy golden horse and the deputy's gelding settled into a walk. Sara heard the Sheriff dispatch Bob Raley, sending him to check on the town's tiny jail and the drunk it currently hosted. "The feller'll be needing supper," he instructed.

She rode on down the street, never breaking a trot.

Next to Murphy's Mercantile—stacked barrels sitting outside its doors like so many wobbly columns—the familiar newspaper office façade came into view. Its white plank sign with black letters barely readable in the fading light proclaimed, *Tubac Star Dispatch*. Two large, dusty windows, both aglow with flickering oil lamplight, guarded its solid entryway set smack between them.

Relief replaced some of her distress as Sara abruptly turned Cherry toward the tie rail. "*Madre Dios,*" she sighed, and slid off the mare's back. Tossing the reins over a hitch post, she fairly flew up the wooden steps that separated raised walkway from parched, rutted street. Rushing past a window, Sara saw her father look up from his desk. She knew in a heartbeat he'd heard the thud of her booted feet and sensed the urgency apparent in her manner. "Panic," she admitted to herself.

Flinging the door open with trembling hands, she ran into the newspaper office. Sheriff Brenner shouldered through just behind her. "Pa! Pa, Matthew is in trouble!" The words tumbled out as she hurried across the planked floor. "We've got to help him."

Their eyes locked as her father stepped around the long counter that kept customers separated from the working area of the paper. A tall man of considerable years, streaks of silver shot through his once dark hair, Will Coulton carried an air of vigor and authority. He was her rock. He'd make a plan. He crossed the lobby toward her hurtling body and Sara fell into his arms, burying her head against his white shirt. "Oh Pa, we've got to find him. Now!"

Coulton, arms occupied with the task of calming his frightened daughter, signaled Sam Brenner with a lift of one dark eyebrow and a nod toward his inner sanctum. "Sara," he said, "Look at me."

She heaved a wordless sob and released clutching fingers that gripped him. As she stepped back, he lifted her chin until she was staring directly into his elegant aristocratic face. Her eyes were hot with raw terror. "Let's sit down and talk this over," he said keeping his voice level.

Will Coulton knew his daughter well. She was bright, stubborn, and emotional—traits that made raising her both a challenge and a delight. More than four generations of Arizona settlers ran in her blood. In times of childhood crisis, he had often seen her display that strength of spirit. He knew that somehow she'd handle whatever was to come. Together Sam and Will guided Sara toward the editorial office doorway.

Chapter Eleven

Decisions

Sara stepped into her father's private workspace and moved to the only window. She grasped the shade and lowered it against curious passersby afoot in the night. Behind her, chair legs scraped the floor. She turned to look at her father.

"Come on over here," he said, offering her his editing chair.

Was he hoping the large old frame and familiar worn seat-pad would give her some measure of comfort? That would be just like him. With a nod of thanks and a sigh, she settled into what had been one of her favorite childhood roosts. She glanced at the desktop. It held the usual jumble of papers, lead type, and pieces of printer's machinery in need of tinkering. The familiar smell of ink and machine oil, both earthy and acrid, hung in the air. Nothing showed evidence of the catastrophe that had befallen them. Everything looks so ordinary, she thought with a frown.

Will Coulton gestured to an oversized leather-cushioned chair. "Have a seat, Sam," he said. In the dim light of a kerosene lamp that hung from the ceiling, he proceeded to the far corner of the small, sparsely furnished office, dragged a second chair across the room and settled himself next to Sheriff Brenner.

Sara turned her attention to the two men. Leaning forward, elbows propped on knees, they spoke in measured tones, rehashing the story, trying to place the probable location of the hold-up. She hung on every word, eager to glean any new particulars of Matt's whereabouts.

The sheriff pushed the fingertips of one calloused hand against the other. "Anyone besides that ranch hand give information, Will? I want to know bout' what time that stage was hit."

"Seems the driver and passengers weren't all that sure." Coulton scowled. "They were pretty shaken up. You'll need a couple of men to search the wagon road."

Brenner agreed. "I know three men took the blasted strong box and pocketed every valuable the travelers were carryin'.."

Debate warring in his eyes, Will looked at his daughter. Sara, saw discomfort on her father's face. He sat back, shifted his gaze to the sharp creases of his woolen trousers, smoothing them with long elegant fingers. Obviously he didn't relish sharing all the facts with her. What secrets did he keep?

Finally, he cleared his throat and looked straight at her. "One fellow, the three ladies, and the drover are still resting up at the Barr Three Ranch just north a' Tucson. There was hard scuffle with a fair amount of gunplay when Matthew refused to hand over the payroll. I'm sorry," he said.

Her heart skipped a beat and panic settled in her throat. The time for listening was over. Unable to sit still she pushed against the thick oaken chair arms and stood up. A nameless new fear tingled deep inside her. Terror for Matt propelled her in a circle around the room, her boots clicking sharply against pine floorboards. "I'm going directly out to the Barr Three and speak with the ranch hand that found the passengers." She stared at the two men. "He may know where Matthew is ... if he is hurt. They must have told him something! I don't have to wait for a posse."

Alarm flared in the sheriff's hooded eyes. "Sara, yore not goin' anywhere," he said, and turned a black stare on Will.

Coulton's lips met in a curve of disapproval under his thick salt and pepper mustache. He squinted, brows drawn together, voice harsh. "That's out of the question. It's too dangerous, Sara."

She stared defiantly at her father, her imagination conjuring rattlesnakes, hungry coyotes, and worst of all, marauding Apaches—each waiting to prey on Matthew as he lay unconscious and defenseless.

"Pa," she whispered, her gaze cast downward, "if he's without water or shade it could be a death sentence."

Sara saw the two men exchange studied glances, surely rife with information she didn't have. Defeated for the moment, she sank into her chair desperately hoping Matt would be found alive.

He was too young to die. Her tumble of gold curls barely hid the tears that slid down her cheeks. Silent, berating herself for weeping, Sara raised her head as Will Coulton rose and moved to her side, plainly concerned about the misery sitting raw on her face. She allowed him to take her hand and wrap it with his own, as he turned his attention to the sheriff who slouched, one booted leg crossed over the other.

"I agree that deputizing a couple of men is a good idea," Brenner said. "But," he continued, shaking his head, "it ain't reality. So many's gone on with them California wagon trains, I'll be lucky to get me one good tracker. I'll find 'im tonight, and plan to ride with 'im. That'll make two. Raley can handle the town's riff-raff."

Still holding Sara's hand firmly enfolded in his own, Coulton nodded. "That makes plenty of sense, old friend. You'll leave at daybreak?"

"Yep. We'll follow the stagecoach road, and circle 'round to check with the ranch hand, and them that's got rescued. I ain't yet certain all the passengers is accounted for. Best you stay here in case someone comes ta' town with new factuaries."

"Sounds like the right plan," Coulton agreed, considering the few facts they did have.

"Pa," Sara pleaded, "Two men searching is not near tolerable. You know they will never cover enough ground! It's been more than a week since the stage was hit. How much longer can Matthew survive if he's bad hurt?"

"Honey, we have one problem on our plate. Finding him!" Her father tightened his grip on her hand. "If I let you go, I'm creating a second situation, and I'll not have you putting yourself in that kind of danger. I have plenty of writing and numbers work for you at the paper. It'll help keep your mind off all this mess."

Tears of frustration burned. "Please, Pa," she said, determined to continue the debate until he gave in.

"I suggest you forget this foolish notion," came the quick reply.

Fury rose hot in her face. "This is tiresome talk. I simply won't listen to it." She flicked her eyes from one man to the other. Withdrawing numbed fingers from her father's grasp, she rubbed her reclaimed hand and stood up. "Please excuse me." She lifted her chin, and nodded curtly at Sheriff Brenner. Turning toward her father, she offered him a calculating glare.

"I won't be long, now," he said. "Why don't you sit in the front room for a spell?"

She knew his reassuring smile was meant to comfort, but angry tears welled, spilling over. Sara walked toward the door. It had been a bare six hours since she learned Matt was officially missing, but it felt like forever.

In the lobby, she stood with her forehead pressed against one of the windows. She peered at the shadowy movements of the few men who strolled along the uneven plank sidewalks. Amber light spilled from saloon doorways and hotel rooms, poking holes in the darkness that cloaked the street. Half a dozen horses stood tethered at the rails while owners went about their evening pursuits. For a few heart-stopping seconds, she was almost certain she saw Matt.

Irritated, she glanced toward the office. She wanted to talk with her father. Privately. He had to know she had no intention of sitting around like a barrel cactus waiting to bloom while Matt needed her. She paced back and forth. Deciding not to wait any longer, she lifted her feet and stomped purposefully toward the counter, spurs jingling. Moments later, she heard the scrape of chairs, a signal that the meeting was over.

Sara sat astride Cherry, wearing one of Pa's old dusters as protection against the cold night air. She waited with unconcealed impatience as her father bolted the *Star Dispatch* doors, hefted his rifle into its leather boot, and climbed into his saddle. "Finally," she sighed, and reined in next to him, sullen.

She was in an ill temper, more angry than frightened now, and dogged in her determination to help Matt. Under a waning moon, the two rode in tense silence as the horses picked their way toward Durann Canyon. Although her pleas to stay the night in town, sleep in the newspaper offices, and at least ride out with the Sheriff in the morning met with repeated thin-lipped refusals, Sara knew her father did not expect her to simply let the matter rest.

"Pa, no one knows Matthew better than I do!" Sara began again, spilling words into the quiet night. "You must understand, I can help. I will simply die if something terrible happens to Matt." Her voice caught. "I know Matthew is capable. You think he's tough, but this is different."

"Sara Durann Coulton, this is naught but carrying on," he replied, as though he hadn't heard a word she said. Hard weariness edged his voice as he reminded her of his expectations, and the strengths that were part of her heritage.

He's always telling me that, she brooded, feeling decidedly rebellious. Besides, if the Durann's—her mother's people, Lena's family, and others had survived sickness, Indian revolts, droughts, floods, bandits, and invasions for more than 200 years, surely she could find Matt. "Oh, Pa," she said, her exasperation clear as the canyon cliffs shining in moonrise. As they traversed the last stretch of the ravine, howling coyotes were the only voices. She knew the set of her shoulders told him more than the strained silence that hovered between them.

Will Coulton swung the corral gate open, allowing Sara and Cherry to ride in before him. Sara worked in silence as cinches were loosed, saddles and blankets hauled off, bridles and reins put away. She refused to meet her father's eyes.

"I'll hay the horses, you check the water troughs. They'll want to drink," he said.

She barely nodded in response, and was instantly ashamed of her stubbornness. She knew her father loved her. Guilt battled with anxious thoughts of Matt.

Their animals bedded, the two made their way to the house. In the dimly lit parlor they stood and eyed one another. Distraught, Sara tried to control the turmoil churning in her head.

Her father folded his arms across his chest "Sheriff Brenner and the posse are our best bet to find Matthew, girl. Why don't you get some rest?"

"Pa," she entreated, "you are simply being pigheaded."

"Sara! Hobble your lip. I'm done up with fool talking." He stepped toward her. "I'll get into town early come morning to see if there's some news. You plan on giving Lena a hand around here," he ordered.

Feeling offish, she scarcely returned his brief hug. Without another word he turned down the kerosene lamp and headed to bed as though everything was settled. Sara soon made for her own room, although aggravation rankled, and she didn't expect sleep to come easy this night.

Chapter Twelve

Sara's Plan

A nearly full moon threw shafts of silver across the old four-poster, giving the comfortable, thick, down bedcover an eerie glow. Sara sat wrapped in its soft folds, gazing at the moonlit landscape outside her bedroom window. Even at this late hour, sleep was the furthest thing from her mind.

Picking absently at a goose feather that had poked its way to the surface, she anxiously wondered if Matthew was on foot. She remembered the many times they had argued, then laughed about his unwillingness to walk anywhere that he could ride. She still marveled at how inseparable he and that big muddy grey stallion of his were. Matt often told her that until they were married, Thunder was his only family. Now, Sara thought with a lump in her throat, he was alone, without even the muddy grey for comfort.

Her fingers pushed a tangle of curls from her face. She sighed. It had been nearly two weeks since she'd felt the touch of his hand warm against her back, guiding her across Tubac's dusty main street.

Matthew was my true graduation present, Sara mused, recalling her return from Miss Evelyn's College for Young

Women little more than two months ago. From the moment she stepped off the dusty stage and found him waiting to convey her home, his smiling brown eyes had beguiled her.

He'd approached shyly. "Miss, are you Sara Durann Coulton?"

In answer, she'd turned up the corners of her lips and fixed him with a bold gaze, her blue eyes wide, and full of mischief. "I'm Miss Coulton," she'd confessed.

"I'm Matthew Davies," he'd said, stretching out his sturdy hand to help her into the buggy. "Your Pa sent me to fetch ya."

She'd found his voice delicious. There were very few opportunities to meet young men at Miss Evelyn's, certainly no chances to speak with a fellow, and never to flirt. The old biddies were like hawks, always watching them. She had practically forgotten the timbre of a man's voice!

She'd noticed his browned arms right away, and how easily he'd lifted her heavy trunk full of dresses and Miss Evelyn's schoolbooks. His rough grace pleased her. Aware that he was unable to keep himself from sneaking looks at her, Sara had blushed under the brim of her traveling-bonnet, secretly thrilled that he appeared taken with her saucy demeanor and halo of curls.

When it was time to climb down, she liked the way his strong fingers had closed around her waist and set her lightly on the ground, as though she were made of glass. He'll be my first beau, she'd decided as she ran up the path toward the hacienda and jumped into her father's welcoming embrace.

Over the past months Matthew shared his dreams of a life in California, and when she'd spoken of her adventurous ambitions for the future his eyes had widened with pleasure, delighting her. He, at least, didn't consider her notions foolish.

He is simply devotion itself, she thought, feeling tears starting. "I know Matt would contact me if he could," she said to herself for the hundredth time, flinging her body backwards, onto goose feather bed pillows resplendent with Lena's colorful hand embroidery.

Too agitated to sleep, trying to ignore defiant thoughts that roiled insistently in her head, Sara extricated herself from her comforter. I cannot lie here and wonder about Matt's safety, she fumed. I know in my heart he's alive. I can ... I must ... find him without delay. Swinging her legs over the side of the bedstead, her mind made up, she tried hard not to think about her father's ultimatum.

Sara padded barefoot across the cool, moon-silvered floor and opened her armoire doors. Standing on tiptoe, she probed the top shelf. To the right, her fingertips identified a stack of lesson books she'd stored away, then the round contours of her leather travel case. Sighing with exasperation and effort, she pressed her lips together in a hard straight line, and rocked back on her heels. "Blessed Virgin," she hissed through clenched teeth, "I know I put it up there."

Determined, she pushed up on her toes again and stretched her fingers to the left, willing them to lengthen. When her hand slid over the silky smooth surface of fine cowhide, Sara knew she'd found what she was looking for. The saddlebags had been a Christmas gift from her father.

"Perfect," she breathed, scrabbling at the leather, working the hand-stitched bags to the shelf's edge. Grasping a corner, she pulled them toward her, only daring to inhale when they fell safely into her arms. "Please, *Madre Dios*," Sara implored silently, throwing a meaningful look toward her *retablo*—a depiction of the Holy Mother, that hung above her headboard.

"Do not let my preparations wake the household. Allow them to slumber in peace."

She carried her treasure to the bed, swift steps whispering across the floor, her white flannel nightgown billowing around chilled legs. Gingerly, Sara crept into the pile of blankets and pillows and listened intently. No sounds of stirring sleepers came to her ears. "*Gracias a Dios,*" she murmured, crossing herself, gratefully acknowledging the Holy Mother's collaboration in her scheme.

Then, turning her attention to the cowhide bags, she slid their bulk under the comforter and settled down to think out a plan. Saddling horses and packing food at this hour was out of the question. It takes very little to rouse the entire ranch, so tomorrow would be the big day. She stifled a yawn and hoped she was drowsy enough to sleep at last.

Starting from the scrap of slumber she'd managed to catch during the uneasy night, Sara bolted upright, awake, apprehensive, her heart pounding. No soft edge of dreams cushioned her return to consciousness or her fears for Matt. Her eyes surveyed the blackened sky. The moon had set hours ago, blending the rims of canyon cliffs into darkness. Though the Arizona sun did not yet show its earliest morning gleam, stars had begun to fade into the vast pre-dawn sky. It was time. Sunrise would come soon enough.

"Ooh, frosty," came an involuntary gasp, as she shoved back the goose-down mound that enveloped her. Don't be such a weak-kneed sissy, she told herself, imagining how Matt might be chilled to the marrow right now. The setting sun left the desert to the icy fingers of darkness, even in late summer. Hunching her back against shivers, due only in part to the frigid night air, she pushed herself out of bed.

She needed to be careful. Staring across the room in the direction of the small dresser that had been her mother's, she willed its edges to become visible. "I wish to heaven I could simply light my lamp," she complained as she stepped into the shadows and crept forward until the dresser's squat outline took shape in front of her. Feeling for the iron pulls, she opened one drawer after another, and yanked bloomers, camisoles, and stockings from their tidy bins, clutching them against her chest.

Turning to the armoire, she felt for the doors. "Hmm," she smiled as her free hand connected with cloth and buttons. Her fingers recognized the ruffled neck of a favorite shirtwaist. Pulling it from its dark cave, she tossed it across her shoulder. She added another frock, warm flannel smocks, a sweater, and a jacket to the pile. Finally, her hand closed on a leather riding skirt.

Garments in tow, Sara glanced toward the window. "Blessed Lord," she groaned, sure she could see the thinnest line of shimmer rimming the cliffs. "I'd best make haste." She moved swiftly to the bed where she slipped out of her white cotton nightdress and into her frilly underpinnings, flannel smock, stockings, riding skirt and jacket. Quickly, she rolled and stuffed everything else into the saddlebags.

Draping the bulging cowhide over one shoulder, she scooped her riding boots from their resting place and carried them to the window, where quiet as a cat, she slid her feet into the comfortable scuff of brown leather.

Through the bubbled glass of a hand-blown window, Sara traced the shapes of barely visible cactus and mesquite. The cliffs, like silent sentinels, were revealing their majesty. *You must do this in a hush,* she admonished herself, nervously recalling childhood uproars, when the clatter of her unscheduled exits had resulted in extra chores, scoldings, and once, the loss of a favorite pony. Lena's son Marco, her very best friend, had often shared the blame back then and, she admitted to herself, will share it now.

With fingers hooked under the wood of the window frame, she took a deep breath and pulled slowly upward. Making nary a sound, the window opened. Sara sighed in relief and lowered the saddlebags, then herself, onto the desert floor, three feet below. Her lips formed a silent litany of prayerful requests for Marco's cooperation, Matthew's well being, her father's unsuspecting slumber, and protection from Lena's sharp eyes.

She stepped away from the house and crept across dry scrub, threading her way between mesquite and prickly pears, toward the bunkhouse Marco shared with Matt. It was the smallest of three mud and straw bale structures that housed Durann Canyon ranch hands. "I'm glad it's set apart from the other two. The last thing I need is to awaken that new ranch foreman," she mouthed. The men say he has eyes in the back of his head. Striding up to the porch, she whistled softly.

As she peeked toward the still dark rancheria, the bunkhouse door opened, and Marco appeared, grinning sleepily above a rumpled shirt and canvas trousers not fully buttoned.

"Take these, I don't want anyone to see them," she whispered, thrusting the brown cowhide bags through the open door and letting them drop.

Startled, Marco eyed the leather pile at his feet, curiosity quickly replacing drowsiness.

"Ahh, *Sarita*, wait a moment, and I will welcome you properly," he said.

"Marco, be quick. This is important. Don't fiddle about."

He nodded, pulled his head back and closed the door, leaving Sara to sit on the bench that rested against the white-washed building.

If he's not out here soon, I'll go in and fetch him, she vowed, tapping her heels impatiently against the hard-pack floor. She cast a glance upward to the porch roof, drawn by the faint pink threads of dawn visible through the strips of dried ocotillo cactus that lay across the beams.

Anxiety spiraled up the center of her chest and into her throat. Every moment we are not riding is a moment wasted, she thought. Leaning back against the white washed wall, she attempted to swallow her fear, to rehearse the things she planned to say. He wouldn't be happy. He'd look at her like she was loco as a coyote with the "water fear" upon it. Gritting her teeth, she said softly, "You are my best friend. You simply have to help me!"

"Help you what?' Marco slid, quiet as a shadow, onto the bench beside her.

"Oh, thank goodness." She lowered her voice to a whisper. "It's Matthew. He was hurt when the stage was held up, now he's out there somewhere, alone and—"

"I am sorry, *Sarita*. What can I do for you?"

Sara's words flooded out as she recounted the story of the evening's meeting and her frustration with her father's decision. In the early morning light she saw alarm flash across Marco's face. Her eyes locked on his, daring him to refuse her.

"*Madre Dios, ¡Estás chalado! Loco*. Have you lost your reason?" he demanded, leaping up.

"I'm going to find him, Marco. I know exactly what I need to do."

"You will break your father's heart with this," he said, staring at her, his words sharp with anger.

75

"Hush. You'll awaken the whole ranch! I'll go alone if you won't help me. I mean to find Matt. Now."

"*Sarita*, you know I would do anything for you, but—"

"By the saints, Marco. I will do this thing," she spit out. Then instantly ashamed, she pleaded in gentler tones, "We must get started." Sara grabbed his hand. Tears shimmered in her blue eyes. "Please help me."

Marco slumped against the wall. "Your father might kill me for helping you with your wild plan, but he'll certainly kill me if I let you go on this journey alone. Why is it, I cannot say no to you?" He fixed uneasy brown eyes on his childhood friend. "*Tu diablo*," you devil, he said, resigned. "We will go."

Blonde and dark heads bent together in hurried conversation until the faint scrape of boots on gravel caused them both to turn toward the house. Together, they watched Sara's unsuspecting father saddle his horse and start down the canyon toward his newspaper offices. She shrank back against the bunkhouse wall, wishing herself invisible, Marco sat motionless. Face grim, he followed Will Coulton's progress with hooded eyes.

In the dim light, sudden movement caught Sara's attention. "Oh perfect," she snapped, as she recognized Gage Evans, her father's new foreman. He was heading up to the mess hall for coffee and tortillas, his long legs eating up the pathway. Every time I see that man I feel uneasy, she thought with annoyance. Her heart skipped uncomfortably, certain he must have noticed them.

"We must leave right away," she hissed. "I may lose Matt forever if we don't. Hurry," She inched from under the *ramada*. "I'll get food and meet you at the stables."

Marco watched Sara's retreating form for a long moment, before he turned to the business of saddling the horses, and gathering supplies.

Sara stepped into the familiar warmth of Lena's kitchen, her nose accosted by delicious aromas of cooking onions, tortillas, and *Anazazi* beans. Remorse at involving Lena in her plot, and fear of being found out vied with her determination to succeed in the deception. She ignored the tiny voice that whispered of disgraceful behavior and hellfire its price. Then casting all concerns but those of finding Matthew from her mind, Sara settled her face into a sham of innocence, and crossed the adobe-tiled floor to stand next to Lena at the cooking stove.

"Morning," she said casually, as she reached over copper pots and painted earthenware bowls to pluck a cast iron ladle from its wall hook. She gave the stewing beans a half-hearted stir.

"Buenas dias niña. Queres café?" Lena responded without looking up from her sausage making.

"No. No thank you, Lena. No *café* this morning, but *por favor*, make a picnic basket. Marco and I are going to the river to swim," she said, struggling to keep her tone light.

Lena nodded as her rapidly moving hands slapped masa dough into thin, flat rounds. *"Bueno, Sarita*, it will be ready shortly."

Grateful that she hadn't been forced to meet Lena's eyes, she hurried from the room.

In her bedroom, Sara leaned against her dresser. Painted with doves and tiny, blue flowers, and topped by a copper-framed mirror, it was where she laid out her special belongings. She fingered the tortoise shell hair combs and a small carved box that held favorite doodads. Both had been her mother's. "This is as wicked as I have ever been," she said, making a face and staring at her reflection in the glass. Pulling a breath, she dragged her silver hairbrush through stubborn curls, tied them back with a short blue ribbon, and jammed the brush into her boot. At her desk she penned a note, splashing dots of ink in her haste. Then, closing the bedroom door behind her, she tiptoed down the hallway and placed the folded sheet of paper on her father's big oak chest of drawers.

Returning to the kitchen, Sara gave Lena a brief hug. "See you later," she mumbled, and picked up the food-laden basket. Grabbing her Stetson from the hat rack, she let herself out through the ornamental front doors. Head down, lost in thought, she rushed past the corral, toward the stables, imagining her father would wish to wring her neck when he found the note.

"Well, well, if it isn't Miss Coulton," came an amused voice directly in front of her.

Lord. The ranch foreman. She pulled up short. He was certainly the last person she wanted to see. Sara lifted her head, furious that their paths had crossed. She wondered if he'd done it on purpose? What if he had heard something of what she'd said to Marco?

"This is becoming a habit," she snapped, as he barred her way.

"Having a picnic? Looks like fun." His glance was anything but innocent.

A flutter of guilt shot through her, headed straight for her face. "I, uh … we …" she began, flustered and irate at her tongue-tied response.

Gage Evans tossed her a lopsided grin, put a hand to his hat, bobbed his head and strolled toward the hay barn without another word.

Lord love a duck, the man is obnoxious! Fuming, she gazed after him, and hurried along through the stable doors. "Let's go!" she demanded.

"Mount up. I'll take the basket." Marco said, his voice tight.

She grabbed Cherry's reins and heaved herself into the saddle, glad to see a rifle included in her gear. Marco emptied the food into his saddlebags and tossed the basket into the corner of an empty stall. He placed his long gun in the boot behind his cantle, produced two pistols, pushing one into his waistband and stowing the other, then draped a coiled rope around his saddle horn and mounted his favorite ride, a bay gelding called Valiente.

Unnoticed, the two rode out through the new ranch gates as the rising sun pushed Durann Canyon into full morning.

"*Dios*," Marco huffed, and crossed himself as he passed beneath the smithy's heavy, wrough-iron signage, "Durann-Coulton Ranch."

Chapter Thirteen

Slipping Away

Reveling in their undetected escape, Sara kicked Cherry up to a lazy lope and passed Marco. Disgruntled, he poked along on Valiente. She led the way steadily southwest until the canyon was behind them, slowing to a walk only to let the mare safely cross the Arroyo along a shallow bend. She knew without question she'd have been locked in her room for a week had her father caught them. Now she was free to search for Matt. Her heart pounded with the boldness of her actions.

Closing her eyes, she pictured Matt's face. Every fiber of her being yearned to see him alive and well. Marco's low whistle sliced into her thoughts. He called her name as he rode toward her through the knee-high current. Reluctantly, she allowed the image of her sweetheart to slip away, her reveries replaced by the accusing tone of her friend.

"Your pack is in need of strapping down," Marco scolded, churlish. He pointed to the leather piece and buckle that hung loose behind her. "We must stop now to care for it." His eyes, dark and unreadable, fixed on her.

"I can tend it later." Her voice climbed a notch. "What we need is to move on," she replied. Stubborn as a jack-eared mule.

"Sara, take a look!" he retorted.

Twisting in her saddle to check the pack she saw the reason for his concern. Her blasted bags were tilting, threatening to spill clothes and gear the first time Cherry startled. They had to stop. Resigned, she shaded her eyes. Ahead, glowing in the mid-morning sun she could see the bell tower of the old Tumacacori Mission, a place she had known all her growing-up years. It was a landmark visible for miles, standing graceful and pink against the black silhouettes of the mountains that ringed the flat Santa Cruz Valley.

"*Venga*, Marco. Come. We'll make a quick stop at the Mission," she agreed, trying to control her frustration at the delay. "It's certain to be the safest place. No one's likely to be there. And I can ask for a blessing."

Marco, nodded, his relief obvious. She hoped it wouldn't take long to tighten cinches and redistribute the equipment and supplies they had so hastily thrown together. They picked their way through scrub grass and saguaro cactus in silence, each lost in thought.

Sidestepping prairie-dog holes, the two riders moved single file through the old adobe-walled mission entrance. Climbing down, they tethered their horses in a clump of smoke grey, mesquite trees, across from the imposing old church. Valiente stood quietly, tail switching unseen insects, head low, back leg cocked. He looked as though he was already dozing in the growing heat.

"I'm going into the Nave," Sara said.

Marco slipped his hand under Cherry's cinch. He offered an unfriendly grunt in response.

"Call to me when you are ready," she said and turned to walk across the hard clay of the courtyard.

Tears threatened as she stepped through the arched doorway onto once shining red tiles, now cracked and dusty beneath her feet. Her arms prickled as if with sudden chill. The long walk down the empty central space was eerie. No benches remained. Even the richly colored carvings of the apostles were no more. It seemed only ghosts lingered. Outside, she heard the familiar chirrup and twitter of cactus wrens, as they rode the breezes down, to land atop the sharp spikes of the Yucca.

Standing under the sanctuary's soaring dome, Sara gazed at once lovely Pima paint work, the intricate designs chipped and fading. Against the wall where Fray Emanuel had given her first communion, a handful of fresh flowers lay, someone's recent gift, the only bright spot in the dim recesses of the old church.

She breathed deeply, searching for remembered scents of frankincense and myrrh, but only the fragrance of abandonment lingered. Nothing but the music of the wrens was as it had been. How lonely, she thought. Even the lifelike statues of the Virgin and the saints had been moved to Il de Bac, a larger church, farther away.

Sinking to her knees in the thick dust, she made the sign of the cross. "Holy Father," she whispered, bowing her head. "Please let Matthew be well. And please don't let Pa and Lena worry too much. And help me keep a civil tongue with Marco, and—"

"Sara, I am ready." The sound of Marco's voice, echoed in the stillness of the deserted church. "*Andalé*," he demanded. "Let's go!"

"The façade looks as though it's melting," Sara said, as they rode past the mission's decaying colonnades, where cracking terracotta plaster revealed the mud of adobe beneath.

She'd always dreamed she would marry in this *iglesia* like her mother and grandmothers before her, but Tumacacori had been abandoned nearly a year ago, and, sadly, the last of the Spanish Friars chased out by the Mexican government. As the mare carried her away from the crumbling walls, Sara realized she and Matthew would never take their vows here.

It seemed impossible. Durann women had given their marriage vows, made their confessions and bid their loved ones a final goodbye at the mission for a hundred and fifty years. Her great grandparents had pledged their troth in the original adobe building—no more than a hut really—barely ten miles from her Durann Canyon home. Over time, this church had prospered, welcoming Pima and other Indian tribes to the worship of Christ. The modest hut had been replaced by the grand *Iglesia* of her growing-up days.

Sara sighed. Tumacacori and the occasions of her childhood were threads woven surely and tightly into a colorful blanket of memories. Even now she could taste the excitement of Sunday masses gone by.

"*Amigo*," she called, and rode up close enough to pull on Marco's sleeve. "Remember the pretty Spanish ladies in their Sunday finery, being helped from their gleaming surreys by handsome *caballeros*?"

"I remember *Mexicano* families arriving on dusty mules, and a fine feast of good breads baked by the Fathers," he said.

Visions of Indio mothers, babies bound tight against their sides, walking behind their men into the Mission courtyard sprang into her head. How she loved to be amidst all that commotion. How comforting it was to kneel in the cool shade of the nave with her father and listen to the deep musical voices of the friars.

Feeling the weight of her losses, Sara shook her head and urged Cherry forward. So much had vanished. Little more than two years ago, after the Apache attack at Tubac, several of her friends were laid to rest in the mission cemetery. And now the mission itself was dying. Even my future with Matt may have slipped away, she thought sadly.

Morning passed into afternoon as the riders followed the wagon track southwest.

They stopped at intervals and circled, their attention fixed on the ground, searching for any sign of Matthew. When he wasn't looking for tracks, Marco stared at her, sullen.

"I think we look in the wrong place," he said. "We should have ridden north."

Sara, baked dry in the heat of the noonday sun, brushed a fine coat of dust from her face. His challenge sat between them as she considered his words. She felt from the start they were moving in the right direction.

"Marco, you simply have a poor attitude," she piped sharply, and legged Cherry around until she could see the pout sitting on his lips and the resentment in his eyes. She'd begged and bullied Marco into making this trip and taking this road, and she mulishly decided to keep to her plan. Besides, Sara knew she was correct. She'd not go against her canny female sensibilities—as her father called her "feelings" about things. Her best instincts told her to ride south. And anyway, the sheriff was planning to be off to the north. "No," she said with some bravado. "This is the right way; I know it in my heart."

Turning from him, she pushed negative thoughts from her mind and absently reached over to stroke Cherry's neck. Her eyes traveled idly across the sand beneath her. There, in the dull yellow of an ancient lakebed, metal glinted, bright in the unrelenting sunlight.

"*Aguarda un minuto.* Hold up, I've found something." Sara swung off her horse, her attention on the surface directly before her. She knelt and gently lifted a thin silver circle, brushed away the dust, and turned it over in her hand.

"Look, it's a pocket watch. By God, it's Matthew's," she said, voice unsteady, fingers shaky. "I recognize the inscription and the tiny dent near the 'W.' See?" She held it out to her friend. Then Sara pressed the circle tenderly against her cheek, feeling the heat of the metal. "I wonder how long it's been lying here," she whispered. "He would not have just left it. It was so special to him."

Memories of the first time Matt had shown it to her rushed in. He'd pulled her toward the bunkhouse door. "Come in Sara," he'd said, as they stole into the room he shared with Marco.

Feeling decidedly wicked, she'd wandered around the edges of the room where he slept, sensing the maleness of it. When she came to a wall hung with two whitewashed shelves, Matthew pointed out a beautiful old pocket watch sitting next to an ancient Bible.

"This was my grandpa's," he'd said, the sadness of his grandfather's death after the terrible wagon-train massacre, raw on his face. "See the dent? An arrow nicked it."

Sighing, Sara tucked Matthew's treasured old timepiece into her pocket. Thoughts of him dying alone of thirst and starvation returned unbidden. She looked around at an army of misshapen saguaro cactus, arm-like limbs reaching heights of twenty feet. The forest extended all the way to the horizon, where the shapes of black volcanic giants halted their march.

A terrifying image of Matthew's hand, darkened and swollen with the venom of an Arizona rattler, flashed in her head. Her breath came in quick, shallow intakes as fright rode roughshod over her renewed hope of finding him. The shudder of her breathing amplified in the desert's silence.

Marco urged his horse forward, his eyes focused on the ground again. "*Sarita, mira.* Look!" His voice intruded on her emotional turmoil. His face was closed. Did he keep secrets from her, his closest friend?

She saw nothing of his wish to have her hold tender thoughts for him. Her eyes followed his outstretched hand. "Boot prints," she breathed. "Oh, we are going in the right direction."

Climbing into her saddle, Sara followed Marco eagerly along the rough track. Hope again lifted her heart, rendering even the midafternoon heat insignificant until the footprints abruptly ended.

"Merciful heaven," she sputtered as she watched Marco, several yards ahead, circle his horse and peer intently at the surrounding desert floor. "How can they simply cease?"

He didn't answer for a minute or two, then, "Hoof prints," he shouted. "They go deep. One horse, yes? Perhaps two riders."

She spurred Cherry forward and looked down, mightily thankful for Marco's keen eyes, and, she admitted, his loyalty. Sometimes it seems as though we are two pieces that make one whole, she thought—like twins, one of us always seems to know the next step. She vowed to keep her temper no matter how trying he became.

Side by side, the riders tracked the deep prints until they disappeared into the gravel of a dry creek bed.

Chapter Fourteen

The Note

Will Coulton stepped into the house, trying to shake the unease that had shadowed him all day. He closed the heavy door, shutting out fiery orange streaks that blazed across the darkening sky. A commanding sunset often drew his admiration. This evening his mind was busy with other things. The lack of new information from the sheriff troubled him. He dreaded the questions Sara was sure to fling at him.

He put a hand to his brow. "All I can say is Sheriff Brenner and his posse have not yet returned. It's true enough. There's been no word." He imagined her reaction and did not look forward to it.

His well-worn riding boots clattered against tile flooring, alerting Lena to his presence. Flour flew like dust in all directions as she pushed herself from the kitchen worktable and hurried to meet him.

"Señor Will!" Lena rushed across the dining room, clearly distraught.

"What happened?" he demanded. He tossed his battered hat toward the couch and pinned Lena with intense blue eyes.

Agitation replaced her usual calm demeanor. Flour-covered hands worried one another as her words spilled out.

"*Los niñitos*," she said, using the affectionate term for children in her native Spanish. "I am troubled. Marco and Sara have not come from their afternoon ride. I prepared a fine picnic lunch for them *temprano*, quite early, more than seven hours ago. Then they rode off and have not returned."

She pulled a handkerchief from among her skirts and pressed it to her lips. "I sent the *caballeros* out to look along the river. They have not found them injured. *Madre Dios*, they have not found them at all," she sputtered. Fright washed her face pale and shivered in her eyes.

Will felt tension build along his neck and jaw. *Tarnation. Those kids know better than to get Lena riled up. They've got her jumpy as a brood mare.* He paced the length of the big room. Her eyes tracked him; he could feel it.

"*Malo*," she whispered at his retreating back. "*Este es muy malo*. Very bad."

He refused to allow outrageous possibilities that nibbled at the edges of his mind to gain purchase. Instead, he turned and placed a reassuring hand on her plump shoulder. "I'll change for dinner, Lena. Don't worry," he said. "They'll show up to eat. They better," he grumbled.

Will strode through the silent hacienda, headed toward the long hallway that led to the bedrooms, and considered what he would say to the two of them. His annoyance grew with every step. Those kids are about grown and too old for such disrespectful behavior; of that he was certain. He pushed open his bedroom door and walked across the room, boot heels scuffing over the dull gleam of old, polished floorboards, tracing steps worn by a century of ancestors.

He sank down on the over-sized bedstead with its ornately carved, wood frame, and hoped the headache that threatened would retreat. His fingers worked the buttons of his white cotton shirt. He wished he had just a little time to stretch out. He could use a catnap before dinner and dealing with Sara and Marco. Instead, he sighed, and separated another button from its furrow.

In the silence of late afternoon, Will glanced around the room, marking its orderly state with satisfaction. A comfortable oak armchair, a pine chest of drawers, and a carved armoire, complimented by big, decorative, wrought iron pieces mounted on the walls were the only other furnishings. He looked up at the long beams, browned with age that ran sturdy against the whitewashed ceiling. The simplicity pleased him.

I'm downright grateful for one peaceful spot: my refuge, he reflected, as his eyes came to rest on a square of white paper, propped neat against the dresser mirror. "Now what the devil is that?" His fingers dropped from their task of unbuttoning and reached instead for the folded sheet of paper.

Written in Sara's generous scrawl, the note had Will Coulton's complete attention. His sandy brows drew together like a band of storm clouds as he read the few lines…

Dearest Father,

My concern for Matthew, his wellbeing, and perhaps his life, has forced my decision to act. I must ask your forgiveness. Be assured I am carefully prepared, and have determined seeking him to the south is the proper plan. Marco and I are well provisioned, and you know, fair skilled in the saddle. Please do not worry. I shall contact you when time and circumstances allow.

I remain as always,
Your Loving Daughter,
Sara Durann-Coulton

Astonishment, outrage, and fear for her safety slammed through him as though he'd been kicked by a damn horse.

As he neared her kitchen, the strident sound of Will's boots hitting the floor in hard fast bursts startled Lena. This does not sound like a man who has no worries, she thought, turning toward the clatter. A chill crawled along her spine, as he stepped in close and caught her arms in his hands, his fingers pressing deep into her flesh.

"You were right to worry, Lena!"

She stared up at him, her dark eyes filled with alarm. She could feel the blood drain from her limbs. The *Señor* was more angry than she ever remembered seeing him. His face was red hot with it.

"*Ahora*, now, tell me every doggone thing that happened this morning," Will ordered, giving her a small shake. "I mean every detail."

"Ah," she sighed, trying to breathe evenly. "*Señor*, let us sit now and speak." She allowed him to lead her to a settee.

He did not sit. "See this," he said, pulling a piece of paper from his shirt pocket and tossing it toward her. "The two of them are off on some crazy mission to save Matthew. I forbade Sara to do this! And to have Marco assist her is an outrage." His look bespoke accusation. "How did this come to pass?"

His voice shook with fury as he paced up and down. "God knows where they are, and how long they might be gone. Anything can happen," he flung at her. "This is Apache country … and Lena, not just that. You know how close they are. Marco worships her. They are both near at their majority. I … I have to find them."

Lena's eyes glistened with barely contained tears, all her terror for Sara and Marco's safety now spoken aloud, alive in the room. She reached for him. "Perhaps we should have told them, ¿*Verdad*? True? We have been silent for a lifetime … now we pay the price, *mi amigo*."

Will's pacing slowed. He looked down at the woman sitting before him. "Ahh, Lena, what a mess," he said and settled himself beside her. "You were right. A mother's wisdom rings true. I should have listened to you. What you warned of those many years ago has come to bite us."

"I can tell you again what I remember of today," Lena mopped at her face with a corner of her apron. She retold her story, knowing he committed every detail to memory.

Then he lifted ink-stained fingers, rough with callouses, and gently brushed at her still wet cheeks. "I'll find them, Lena." He stood up and proffered his hand. "Come," he said, and strode to the old silver encrusted *retablo* that adorned the dining room wall. "A prayer might help."

She rose to follow him searching his face, craving the comfort of hope. "You must go," she said, at last. "You must ride after them at first light. I will help you to prepare."

Chapter Fifteen

Following the Creek

Marco stood in the sand ten feet from Sara. He stared straight ahead, Valiente's reins clenched in his hand. The sharp grit of the desert lay on his tongue. A bandana dark with sweat circled his neck. Before them lay the foothills, a place unfamiliar to him. He had no illusions. Moving forward meant crossing an invisible line. A line Sara's father would plainly see. Apprehension rode on his shoulders, uncomfortable as an ill-fitting shirt. "It is best we camp here, before sunset. What of the horses? They must rest," he said.

Pulling miserly sips from her water bag to ease her parched throat, Sara refused. "Certainly we cannot fall to exhaustion." The flint in her voice was unmistakable. "We will continue." She pointed toward a gently rising track alongside the bone-dry creek bed.

"These mountains. We don't know them," Marco insisted. They may be *muy peligroso*." Someone must be concerned with the dangers. We should make camp."

"Blessed Virgin! You know I cannot stop. We have daylight still and cannot waste a single second of it." She gave Cherry a gentle poke with her heels, and the horse moved slowly forward, her tail swishing lazily in the relentless heat. "Let's follow this slope up into the hills."

Stalking behind horse and rider Marco led Valiente, deliberately refusing to mount. *Dios, she is determined.* He wiped beads of moisture from his upper lip and tugged his hat down over his brow. Glancing at the unrelenting descent of the afternoon sun, he attempted to reason with her once more.

"Hear me, Sara. It is likely *Señor* Coulton has found your note by now. He knows of this foolishness we are doing. If we move ahead, we will never be able to explain this excursion away. *Nunca!*"

Giving voice to the words filled him with dread. He could practically feel the old man's penetrating blue eyes, slamming into him, the edge to his voice hard as iron, demanding explanations. Though Marco had endured those uncomfortable experiences in the past, the fury this terrible mistake would bring, could not compare. "I wish I'd never come," he spat.

Sara rejected his warning and pointed at an outcropping of ruby-colored quartz where the trail widened. "Stop moping. Let's go up through that ridge."

He shuffled forward, inches at a time, hoping she'd give in.

She turned and glared at him, surly as any cowboy could be. "Quit wool-gathering!"

"Aah ...*no tengo ninguna opcion,*" Marco murmured darkly. "I have no choice, do I?"

He shoved a booted foot into the wood of his stirrup and swung into the saddle, resigned to disaster one way or another. Sometimes she was so high-handed he wanted to throttle her.

Grim, he rode at the walk, his horse now close behind hers, eyes alert for the sudden movements of rattlers, javelinas, or God forbid, he thought, Apaches. Sara seemed unconcerned. She let Cherry pick her way along the rocky trail upward—through thick clumps of mesquite and sharp spikes of pencil-thin ocotillos, and finally a smattering of grey pines. As though she hadn't a care in the world, she hummed some unfamiliar tune.

Where the trail curved and broadened, an unexpected, broken wall of basalt rose on their right—huge, uneven blocks of volcanic rock stacked toward the sky just across a narrow divide. The horses snorted, pricked their ears forward and kept them at attention. Cherry danced on her bit and Valiente pulled, wild-eyed, away from the steep rock formation. Sara fell silent.

"Someone or something is scaring the horses. Hold up!" Marco urged his bay backward to calm him. He ran his eyes along the black palisade and found trouble. There, against towering pillars and jutting outthrusts, a large mountain lion claimed a shallow ledge. The creature stood motionless, but for its tail. Yellow eyes, bright with menace inspected them. Muscles rippling under tawny fur hinted at its coiled strength. Toothy snarls rode the breeze.

"That damn cat wants our horses," Marco said. Sara paled beneath the flush of her heated face. Her hand crept toward her weapon. "Stay still," he ordered, and slowly dismounted. The cat crouched.

"Marco!" Sara blurted, hysteria threading her voice. She pulled her rifle from its scabbard.

"Don't move," he whispered. To fire a shot which might bring hostile Indians, bandits, or even *Señor* Coulton down on them was ill-advised. Instead, he held his frightened horse steady, reins tight in hand and knelt to gather rocks and heave them at the creature. The huge animal, ears flattened against its head, sank more deeply into its crouch, belly skimming the ground, eyes fixed intently on its tormentor.

"Oh God! It's going to attack!" Sara screamed. She lifted her rifle and fired at the ledge. Startled, the beast moved backward a step, and launched from its hazardous perch. Her second shot ricocheted off the rocks. The thwack and whine of the bullet frightened the big cat mid-jump.

Marco flinched. His breathing froze as the powerful golden body twisted in the air and landed on a lower ledge. The cat turned, its heavy tail switching with annoyance. Displaying long canine teeth in a fearsome hiss, it slipped away through a crevice in the basalt wall.

"That was not so smart, *mi amiga*. Your shots could be heard for a long way, my friend," he said softly, catching a breath he hadn't realized he needed.

"I thought he'd kill you for sure. You should be thanking me," she snapped, indignant.

"Rocks would have sent him away. You never think. I worry always for both of us."

Glaring at him, she turned to the task of calming her mare.

Maybe that cat should have had me for dinner, he thought, smarting from Sara's words and the unpleasant set of her face. Shrugging his shoulders, he climbed into his saddle and pushed his heels into Valiente's belly. As he swept past her, he swung his arm forward. "We have to move—and move quickly. *Vamos!*" he bit out through gritted teeth.

Chapter Sixteen

Search Party

Gage Evans worked a pick around the hooves of the big grey that belonged to Matthew, dislodging sand and tiny stones. He'd already brushed the dappled coat as he made ready to tack up. Now, he tossed a saddle blanket onto Thunder's wide back, checked for creases, and added a second layer atop it for solid padding. He swung the saddle up, yanked the blanket edges up off the critter's withers, and pulled the cinch tight against Thunder's belly. Next to him at the hitch rail, Will Coulton tied a slip-knot to hold his favorite ride, a thick-maned, Spanish mustang.

"Mister Coulton, I saw the two of them, Sara and Marco, chatting on the bunkhouse porch real early yesterday mornin'. I wish I'd a known what they were up to."

Will, grim-faced, eased a bit between his horse's teeth and tossed the reins across the mustang's brawny back. "I'll get the saddle bags. You finish tackin' up my ride, pronto," he said and started toward the house.

"Yessir, boss."

Young, good-looking, and tough, Gage Evans, the oldest of three sons, had seen a lot of life and death growing up on the frontier, and he had the scars to prove it. At age sixteen, when his pa died of the influenza, he became protector and provider to his mother and two younger brothers.

Showing maturity far beyond his years, he saw to it that his brothers kept up with their schooling and their chores. Times were hard, but the boy proved to be made of even harder stuff, perfecting his riding and roping skills until they were the equal of any man's.

His reputation for accuracy with a rifle and deft handling of his father's six-shooter grew during hunting trips and occasional shooting contests. As his long legs took him into manhood, his levelheaded sense of right and wrong, and inherent fearlessness made him a fellow to be reckoned with. The sixteen-year-old was hungry for book learning. He devoured every piece of printed material he came across.

"Ma, I want to be able look any man in the face and not feel the fool," he told his mother, Lottie Evans. He knew she quietly offered up a daily prayer that book learning would be his way in the world, rather than handling a gun.

Their small ranch and his mother's vegetable garden barely kept them fed, forcing Gage to hire on at neighboring ranches from time-to-time to keep boots on the Evans boys' growing feet for the next three years. Nevertheless, his mother set her mouth in a hard line when she heard that town elders were whispering about making a lawman out of him. "Even a steady salary doesn't justify compromising your safety," she warned her son.

Dressed in her Sunday best, leaving biscuits cooling on the table, his usually soft spoken ma promptly hitched up the family buckboard and made a special trip into town to give the gentlemen a piece of her mind. Gage knew she'd rather die than have him earn his keep at the business end of a pistol, and as he watched her retreating back, he hoped he never would. But he was growing restless, anxious to see the world.

By the grace of God, they made it through the hardest times. No angry injuns caused them hurt. No one tried to run them off their land, and the small ranch began to prosper. When the younger boys were old enough to run things, Gage figured it was his time to go adventuring. Certain he'd had enough of domestic responsibilities to last him a lifetime and then some, he packed up, hugged his weeping ma, told his brothers the ranch was theirs, and rode off to go cowboying around the West. He moved on, into a different life. One that would have made his ma burst with grief had she known of it.

Some ten months ago, on his twenty-third birthday, he recalled, he rode into Tubac and came upon the Durann Canyon Ranch. Will Coulton and the horse ranch offered him an opportunity to change direction, a chance he'd been hankering for, for some time. "I'm right fine with handlin' horses," he'd said first off.

Coulton, in need of a dependable foreman asked a lot of questions. Questions Gage answered truthfully. The man's eyes narrowed when Evans recounted his acquired knack for playing cards at whiskey-soaked frontier saloons—and how, in those same places, he learned to defend himself with his fists, and when necessary, with the cold metal of his pistol.

"Mr. Coulton, my ma wanted me to make something of myself. I've been doing it poorly. I know now with certainty that the life of a hired gun, carousing with bawdy women, and hard drinking is not what I want," he said. "My ma was right."

He looked steady into Coulton's piercing squint. "I am done with it. My last encounter with the working end of a revolver nearly took my life, sir, and worse, that of a youngster cowering nearby. I am a fair cowboy, Mister Coulton, and an honest man. I sure would appreciate the opportunity." Gage shut his mouth, then shifted his attention to the ground and awaited the older man's decision.

"Name's Will," the man said after several seconds, and offered his hand in welcome.

He'd been ranch foreman comin' a year now. It was going well. Durann Canyon was a satisfying home and he enjoyed his responsibilities. But, he'd not missed the fire and beauty of the boss's daughter over the past few days. She was fine bred he allowed; all the same, it seemed she needed a strong hand. "That girl's just plain spoiled rotten," he informed his horse on numerous occasions while working the longhorns and horses. "She has her dad wound 'round her little finger. Young Matthew is hard put to keep pace with 'er. And that young *vaquero*, Marco, why he acts like a blasted love sick calf most every time his eyes light on her."

He'd watched her fly around the ranch, tossing her curls and turning gleaming eyes on one cowhand or another. "Well it won't work on me." He pulled his weathered Stetson off, and ran a hand through his thick dark blond hair. "Damned, I hate dealin' with foolishness," he muttered, shoving his hat back on his head.

Pushing the thoughts from his mind, Gage hefted his boss' tooled leather saddle, grabbed a saddle blanket, and set about following his employer's instructions.

Lena and Will stood together on the shaded ramada, looking out at the corral where Gage was saddling the mustang.

"Lena, I'm going to find them," Will said softly. *"Por favor,* don't worry. We'll handle this."

She turned toward him, focusing on the saddlebag that lay across his shoulder. Her fingers moved, checking the closures she had secured only moments before. Her brown eyes, full of apprehension, met his. She was exhausted. "I will make my petition to the Virgin Mother," she said, dropping her hands to the folds of her skirts.

Silently, she bent to lift his heavy cowhide jacket from the bench where it lay. This was the covering he wore when he was away on cattle drives and other working journeys that kept him far from Durann Canyon. It protected him from sudden desert rains and the deep chill of long nights. Only her eyes spoke when she handed him his weathered *chaqueta,* a jacket as full of cracks and scars as the land they called home.

"I promise you, Lena," he said, and took the garment from her trembling fingers.

His words seemed to come from far away, as though they were slipping on the wind to reach her ears.

"It will be okay, I promise you," Will repeated, his voice heavy with emotion.

"My prayers travel with you, *Vaya con Dios,*" she whispered, gathering her self-control and turning her eyes toward the corral.

"It's time, *Cara,* my dear one." He stepped off the veranda, kicking up dust as he strode toward his waiting horse.

She wondered what he would find. And how soon.

Chapter Seventeen

On the Trail

Hawks circled and chattering redbirds swooped, following Marco and Sara as they made their way up and across the sun-seared ridge. There, they again picked up the hoof prints of a single, heavily weighted horse moving toward the hills that lay beyond. The blazing late afternoon sun was brutal, forcing Sara to agree to take a break in the shade of a rock overhang.

Marco rode on, skirting the shadowed platform to scout the immediate area for signs of habitation. Sara watched him disappear. Now she hoped her shots that frightened the mountain lion hadn't also alerted other, more cunning, two-legged hunters to their presence.

Grateful for a reprieve from the punishing summer heat, Sara dismounted and stretched her saddle-sore body. She ached from thigh to shoulder. Cherry's reins hung loosely in her right hand. She leaned back against the slant of moist granite wall. It was cold to the touch. Relief swam through her. She pressed into the slab, and shivered with pleasure at the cooling of her skin under the cotton shirtwaist that lay sweat-damp along her back. She caught the welcome scent of fresh water on the breeze and turned her head in search of the wetness.

There, nearly within arm's reach, a spring gurgled through jagged cracks in the rock face, creating clear, puddles deep enough to water the horses. She straightened and led Cherry to the nearest sink, where the flaxen-maned sorrel nosed at the shallow pool and began to drink.

Sara pressed her hands into the cold flow and wished the little basins were deep enough to bathe in. Opting for the next best thing, she yanked off boots and stockings, and stepped barefoot into one of the ankle-deep hollows. "Holy Mother, thank you. It feels so good," she sighed in pleasure. Her grimy fingers untied the kerchief wound around her neck and held it in the spilling water. "Lord, it's hot and I'm dirty," she said to no one in particular. It was a glory to at least wet her dusty bandana and mop the trail grit from her face and hands. Wanting more, she pulled off her hat, let a stream collect in it, and sloshed its contents on her curls.

Wiggling her toes in the wet, she recalled sitting alongside the Arroyo River with Matthew. She smiled. She'd loved the feel of her hand entwined in his as rivulets of cool water slipped across their feet. Her reverie was short-lived. Without warning tiny pebbles cascaded down from the overhang and skitter-scattered against her ankles—she glanced up and saw Marco's legs dangling above her.

"Have you refilled your water bag?" His voice brought her back to the present. She looked up again and saw his brown eyes and a shock of dark hair peering over the rock face.

"Not yet, but I will. Come down, aren't you hungry? Was there any sign of the horse we've been tracking?"

"No, *mi amiga.*" His voice was flat.

Neither of them spoke as they laid out portions of Lena's biscuits and cornhusk-wrapped packets of meat and beans. Sara chose to ignore Marco's mood. All day, his unhappiness with the way things were going showed plain in the set of his jaw, the down-bowing of his mouth. He was given to sulking on occasion. Feeling a rumble of temper beneath his pout, she knew fear of her father's wrath weighed heavily on him. Perhaps Lena's feast would raise his spirits. It would be a treat. Soon enough they'd have to forage and hunt for their meals.

Gazing across the small canyon at strangely shaped cliffs—colorful rock formations that spiraled down like melted candle-wax, each fusing into the next—she dug into her share of the vittles with abandon. A day's riding had made her ravenous. Was Matthew hidden somewhere in those cliffs? she wondered, wiping a drip of chocolaty *mole* sauce from her chin. No. He's got to be ahead of us.

"Marco, I'd rather not make camp. Let's go on after we eat," she proposed between bites of Lena's delicious pork *tamales*. Only the chitter of birds and the rustle of trees promising cool evening breezes broke the stillness as Sara waited, impatient for his response.

"The horses are exhausted," he said at last. "We'll stay put and sleep for a bit, then move on when the moon rises. That is best. We have good shelter here."

"I will not waste time sleeping." Sara straightened her spine, drawing up her shoulders for emphasis. She braced herself to get her way—to weep, if necessary.

"I am not going on until we have rested the horses and ourselves," Marco said, his mouth set in a stubborn line. "And I don't care if you cry," he added, his eyes hard. She heard an unmistakable edge in his voice, a tone she didn't often hear from her oldest friend.

"Fiddle-faddle. You are simply on the prod," she accused with less vehemence. She bit into a biscuit. In truth, she was dragged out, and with Marco digging in his heels, well …

maybe it is prudent we take our ease, she thought. I don't wish a fight. Lifting her chin she studied him for a long moment. "All right," she agreed, allowing her voice to waver a bit. "But only if you ride up a ways and check the trail one last time … Matthew may be just ahead."

"Fine. I'll take a look," came his terse reply. He tossed his bedroll toward her. "You make camp."

She found a small grassy area at the edge of the overhang that would do for the animals and gathered enough fallen wood, pinecones, and twigs to create a modest fire. Sara unpacked their bedrolls and laid them out nearby, side by side. Her saddle made a good headrest, as would his.

Marco rode in as she finished preparing the hobbles that would keep both horses close during the night. "*Nada.* Nothing," he said, shaking his head. "No sign." He pulled his saddle down.

In a short while, the horses were grazing peacefully on bits of wild grass and brush. Under shelter of the overhang, embers of their campfire gave some small warmth in the cooling mountain air. Sara settled into her blankets as dusk threw down its cloak, creating deepening shadows. She watched Marco hunker down in his bedroll.

"*Madre Dios,*" he grumbled, cursing the moment of weakness that had brought him on this wild chase.

She chewed at her lower lip. He was being impossible. But then, she wasn't as patient as she promised herself she'd be.

"You were right," she whispered, from under the folds of her blanket. "I am tired. I worry so for Matthew. I'll wake you …" Sara's drowsy chatter slowed, and her eyelids fluttered.

Sleep overtook the small encampment even before the sun dropped fully behind the cliffs, leaving the world in darkness, save for starlight. Their dreams did not tell them that less than fifteen miles away as the crow flies, Matthew rested, while his companion, a beautiful Indian woman, tended a dinner fire.

Chapter Eighteen

The Cabin

Fingers of light barely grazed the sky when Sara's eyes flew open. The predawn chill prompted her to yank the blanket up around her ears. As she lay there on the cold ground, head resting on the slick leather of her saddle, the veil of sleep dropped away. Blinking to clear grit from her eyes she peered into the morning gloom. We never did wake at moonrise, she realized—all the more reason to move quickly now.

Just a few feet away Marco stirred. Sara heard his boot scrape dry ground. Slowly a leg appeared from under his bedroll.

She struggled to standing. Shivering, she pulled the coarse saddle blanket tightly around her and shuffled her cold feet. Even my boots are frozen, she thought, as she wriggled her toes and worked her way up to a stomp in an effort to warm them. "Marco," she whispered, then, getting no response, raised her voice a notch. "*Amigo*," she hissed.

Marco came full awake, his attention focused on Sara's voice in the near darkness. "*Sarita*," he mumbled, "come sit beside me. Let us talk of what we will do." Wrapped against the cold, the two sat side by side.

"I'm sorry for being so bossy," Sara said softly, her eyes aimed at the ground. "We've rested as you wished, but I still believe Matt is alive, and we've lost a lot of time." She offered him a fetching smile. "I'm glad that you're here with me. I know we'll find him. Please forgive me," she said, hoping her apologies, sweet as ripe fruits, would be hard for Marco to reject.

He turned toward Sara and lightly brushed her cheek with his lips. Startled she scooted away, putting several inches between them. He's never done that before. Was he offering an apology of his own for being so trying? Perhaps ... still it seemed too intimate a gesture.

Sara stood, allowing her blanket to fall from her shoulders. "Brisk up *amigo*. I'm anxious to be off." She unpacked what remained of Lena's generous larder, and shared cold tortillas and beans with Marco. They washed their breakfast feast down with sips of clear water that sprang from the cliff face.

Saddlebags were repacked and horses saddled in the growing warmth of what promised to be another cook-pot hot day. Marco led the way as they rode single file, veering in from the cliff edge to follow a deer trail where the imprints of fresh horse tracks were apparent.

"What is going to happen when your father finds us? Or worse yet, Apaches? We should go home," Marco called back to her, as they wound their way uphill, through a sprinkling of black oak trees and boulders.

His words drifted to her ears between the clop clop of horses' hooves and the scatter of loose pebbles. Sara knew he was right. Trouble would probably catch them. Tearing up, she thought about Matthew. Alone. Injured. Desperately needing her. Her back stiffened. "We must move ahead," she all but shouted.

Her legs pressed hard against Cherry's barrel and the big mare carried Sara forward, close behind Marco. "Don't think about what may catch us. Think about Matthew. You promised," she said sternly, wanting her single concern well understood. There would be no more bedeviling talk of turning back. In response, Marco urged Valiente on, and both riders began to pick up speed.

The sun blazed, unrelenting in a cloudless, late afternoon sky. Without warning the trail opened onto a small meadow. Sara stared at a crudely made corral, standing empty, tucked into a natural depression in the land.

"What on earth is this doing out here?" she asked, and dismounted. Happy to stretch her legs, she led Cherry onto the flat open space. The mare nibbled at sparse green growth and tore hungrily at the tallest grasses, while Sara watched Marco, who was down on his knees peering at the ground surrounding the corral.

"This is a well-used place. There are marks of more than one horse," he said, pushing to his feet. "Some of the tracks are fairly fresh. I wonder where the people are?"

He turned toward Sara and the question died on his lips. She stumbled as she backed away, almost falling into Cherry. The look on her face gave him warning too late. He whirled as he heard the bolt catch and found himself staring into the barrel of an old shotgun topped by two rheumy eyes.

"I reckon I'd jest move on back," the old man said.

"*Bueno*," Marco agreed. He edged away, until he was standing alongside Sara, his mouth dry as a cotton ball.

The man was a tough old bird, and scary, Sara decided, from the look of his rough-made clothing, his matted facial hair, brown-stained teeth, and the map of lines that enfolded the skin around his ancient, but still sharp eyes.

"What's yer business up here?" the old man asked, never moving his shotgun.

"*Señor, buenas tardes*, good afternoon," Marco began, addressing the stranger in the most respectful tone he could muster. "My friend, *mi amiga*," he continued, gesturing at Sara, who was attempting to regain her footing and her dignity, "is searching for her betrothed. We think perhaps he has come this way. We did not intend harm to your family or your home. Forgive our intrusion. *Por favor*. Please."

The old man pulled his eyes toward Sara.

"Yes. It's true enough, sir." Sara pushed down fear and fixed her blue eyes on his. "My fiancé is met with some injury or worse. We simply must find him," she quavered, unable to keep the tremor from her voice. Her eyes widened as the man stepped forward and ran experienced eyes over Cherry and Valiente, taking note of the rifles stowed in their gear.

"Nice horse flesh you got there," said the old timer flatly, giving Marco and Sara an appraising stare.

"Yessir," Marco nodded, nervously glancing toward Sara.

"I'm Jonas," rasped the old man. "Jest you follow me up yonder to the house. We come to some troubles here of late. An' I reckon to be talkin' 'bout it." He gestured with the rifle barrel toward a small cabin tucked into the mountainside. "Best bring yer mounts."

"We don't have much choice," Marco whispered, as he waved Sara, near to tears, ahead of him. Leading their horses, the two reluctantly made their way up the narrow track to the cabin. The old man followed, cradling his long gun in an arm dry as an old cracked log.

Sara, first to reach their destination, peered around. How easily the old man had spotted them; the corral was plainly visible. She pinched Marco's sleeve and pointed. Turning, he glanced back down the trail and shook his head. Following the codger's gruff instructions, Sara and Marco tethered Cherry and the bay to a downed tree limb. They wouldn't go far.

Jonas gestured toward the sturdy cabin, well built of pole timber. "You folks come in and we'll jest settle the hash," he said, grabbing a leather strip nailed into a wood plank door and pulling it open. His weathered hand held the long gun barrel downwards as he ushered them inside.

"His is the way of an old watchdog," Marco whispered, as he climbed through the door first and turned to help Sara negotiate the one, roughhewn step. She clutched his hand with a strength born of terror and moved into the cabin. Unwilling to separate from him, she leaned hard against Marco, sure he heard the pounding of her heart.

Sara surveyed the single room. As her eyes adjusted to the dim light, she saw a simple household. A coarse-built stone fireplace and a cookstove with a battered coffee pot steaming atop its only burner filled one wall. A jumble of small ammunition boxes, a large metal fry pan, sacks that looked to hold beans and flour, a tin coffee container and eating utensils shared space in two dog-eared, wooden crates that sat near the hearth. Cups hung from nails pounded into a log wall next to the stove: three dented tin mugs, and one chipped and cracked porcelain teacup still bright with painted flowers.

A stack of split wood, and two sleeping bunks filled with hay and overlaid with rough burlap filled a second wall. Her eyes took in a hotch-potch of shovels and pick axes resting in a corner. A saddle topped with a dusty blanket stood pommel-end down next to the shovels. Its stirrups poked out, splayed flat on the dirt cabin floor like two feet whose ankles had collapsed.

At the far end of the narrow room, a plank table, well worn and scrubbed, sat surrounded by hand-hewn benches. A solitary lantern squatted on the table, next to an empty, gold pan. Nearby, one small window welcomed a slip of summer's early evening sunshine. Sara knew without question that it, too, offered a clear view of the little valley below. The old man had been spying on them. She shut her eyes against the sudden tightness in her belly.

Surreptitiously Marco watched Jonas prop up his rifle next to the stove.

"Whyn't you two make yerselfs comfortable. I'll be brewin' some coffee," their captor said, picking up the old pot with callused fingers. "Might as well join me."

Sara brought her eyes around to Marco's wary face. Maybe this will be okay, she signaled as their eyes met. "Let's do what he says," she said in a breathy whisper. The two moved slowly backwards toward the benches, and sat together, her hand gripped in his.

She kept an eye on their host. He deftly opened a tin, measured out coffee grounds, and poured them into the heated pot of water.

"Mister Jonas, I'm Sara Durann Coulton," she finally ventured, as he pulled three cups off their nails. Ignoring Marco's glaring frown, Sara continued. "My pa owns a ranch in Tubac. He publishes the local newspaper. Perhaps you've heard of him? Marco, here, is my good friend."

"Don't speak again of your father," Marco warned, his lips against her ear.

The old man gave no sign he had heard her. She shuddered. *What kind of creature was he?*

Moments later he wrapped one hand in an old rag, picked up the pot and headed across the room, cups dangling from his leathery paw. At the table Jonas poured the steaming brew and sat one before each of them, then settling heavily on the bench facing his visitors, he filled the third cup for himself.

"Okay missy," he said looking first at Sara, then at Marco, "What'er you two doin' up here?" His eyes narrowed. "Me an my partners has a claim and don't aim to share it. We don't much like strangers on the place, 'specially after being rustled by durn horse thieves a couple nights ago. Mebee it was yer friends took my stallion," he challenged, his voice a gravelly snarl.

Sara and Marco exchanged a tense glance.

"We are seeking my fiancé. Matthew and I are to be married," Sara responded with haste. She looked indignantly into the old man's watery eyes. "We are not horse thieves, sir."

"Señor," began Marco, "We have no interest in your, er, claim. Sara tells the truth. We track a friend. Her fiancé. He may have passed this way. Perhaps he is injured, or a prisoner. *No sabe.* We don't know."

As the sky turned to pink, then a silvery dusk, Sara and Marco spoke with the miner of the stagecoach robbery and Matthew's disappearance, avoiding any further mention of Will Coulton. Uneasy under Jonas' still suspicious gaze, Sara shared her concerns for Matthew.

"We found Matt's watch and Sara thinks we may have trailed him to your corral," Marco finished.

They listened as Jonas described the fracas on the night he lost his "Blackie" and how he hoped to find the culprits in short order. "My partners grabbed 'em rifles and is went after them doggone thieves. Don't know if it be injuns 'er whut," he said, in raspy tones.

Sara stared at Marco. "Don't you see? It's likely the ones who took Matthew! He must be hurt. But thanks be, he's alive. Someone is certainly holding him prisoner. He would never take a horse." She pushed away from the table and looked at the two men, wild determination flashing in her eyes.

"Mister," Marco said, "She could be right. I saw tracks that showed one horse with a heavy load. Perhaps the ringleader needed a second horse for Matthew."

"Makes em' both horse thieves, don't it?" said Jonas peering at Marco. He slapped a gnarled hand on the table.

"*No. No.* Matthew would never do such a thing," Sara sputtered, her fingers clutched into fists. "You've got to believe me!"

She whirled on Marco. "We'll leave now and we may catch up with them. If Matthew is hurt, they can't be traveling all that fast."

Jonas stood. "Now jesta minute, missy. Fancy yer tale be true, but it's dang late and this be Apache country. You and yer friend best wait fer my partners. They'll be back quick enough. And mebee have sorted the whole mess out."

"He's right, Sara." Marco gestured toward the small window.

She looked out at the settling dark. The old miner spoke well. Stamping a foot in frustration, she picked up the lantern and ferried it to the hearth, where Marco worked the wick until it flamed, casting shadows on the chinked log walls. At least she felt more like a guest. The old man seemed to believe them.

Jonas rummaged among his food stocks and started the evening meal. Pulling out a burlap bag of beans and a dried up onion, he slammed a large iron pot onto the stove top. Whistling through missing teeth, he slid a wicked looking knife from his belt and chopped up the onion, stabbing his pig-sticker into a cracked soup tureen he produced a piece of salt pork.

Soon enough the aroma of cooking black beans triggered thoughts of Lena's kitchen with its wonderful spicy smells.

Lord, we are truly gone far from the ranch, Sara realized with a start. It was almost as if she had stepped through Jonas' leather-hinged cabin door into another world.

Outside, the horses whinnied softly, and Jonas suggested they bed the animals down in the corral. "There be a small water hole runs 'longside the back end," he said, "and some green grasses about it."

Sara and Marco, grateful for a few minutes alone, hurried through the cabin door toward Cherry and Valiente. The horses had been grazing steadily, pulling the downed limb some distance along the ground while they nibbled. The two friends were silent, each considering their predicament. Sara sighed. Sliding her fingers beneath the latigo, she began to remove saddles, blankets and gear, piling them in an untidy heap.

They untied the pair and led them to the corral. In the ever-darkening evening, Marco spoke in hushed tones, keeping his back toward the cabin window.

"Do not let your guard down, *Sarita*. We don't know this man or his partners. He seemed real interested in our mounts. Tomorrow we'll be on our way. Early. And I don't wish him to know that your father may soon be at his door."

Sara trembled, and not with the cold. The horses were their lifeblood. "You are right." She slid the bridle forward over Cherry's ears and patiently waited for the mare to spit out the bit. "Very well," she agreed, as the metal piece dropped into her cupped hand. "I'll say no more of him. I certainly hope Father isn't on his way here. Just don't you tell that old codger where we intend to go," she said. "If his partners return tonight, listen to whatever they have to say, but keep your own counsel." Marco nodded. Wordless, he started up the hill, leaving Sara to scramble after him. She wondered if the miner watched them now. Could he hear everything they said?

The old man was waiting for them. "You put them rifles in that corner," he ordered, moving his chin in the general direction, as they lugged saddles and gear into the cabin. He watched Marco follow his instructions, and satisfied, went back to his dinner preparations.

"May I lend a hand?" Sara asked, shoving her tangled curls behind her ears. As she set about helping Jonas with the meal, she felt Marco's brooding eyes on her. His singular gaze seemed to sit at her back and stay there like a hot coal. Uncomfortable with his uninvited attention, she focused on the cornmeal she mixed, pushing the wooden spoon in hard circles around the bowl.

The unfamiliar behaviors of her childhood cohort troubled her. He has been as a brother since we were babies, a friend, always, she mused. It disturbed her to have others think differently. Why, Jonas looked at us several times, as if speculating on what sort of relationship we enjoyed. Did Marco perhaps hold some other hope for their friendship? If that is so, he may be glad Matthew is missing. "Oh bother," she muttered. "Why does everything have to be so trying?"

Sara shooed the unsettling thoughts from her mind. Instead, she chattered brightly with Jonas as he spiced the iron kettle's steaming mound of beans with salt and sage. She asked him simple questions about life in the mountains—careful not to pry into his secretive activities.

The three gathered around the light of what seemed to be their host's single lantern. And hungry despite the circumstances, Sara and Marco dug into the fixins' of a surprisingly satisfying meal: hot beans, spoon bread and strong coffee.

Dinner done, drowsiness overcame her. She was grateful when Jonas, his thick hands scooping up tin cups and chipped plates, nodded toward the bunk furthest from the rifles.

"I s'jest you folks turn on in over t' there. I'll be doin' the same 'fore ya know it."

Bone-tired, forgetting troublesome concerns, Sara allowed Marco to grab her warm fingers, guide her to the plank and rope-slung bunk, and cover her with one of their saddle blankets.

She was deep asleep, her blanket tucked snugly around her, when Marco stretched out on the dirt floor next to the bunk. Cold and not a little uncomfortable on the hard pack, Marco tossed and turned for a long while. He allowed what he knew to be unseemly visions of Sara to populate the little cabin. Shamed at his unsuitable conjuring, he sat up and made the sign of the cross. "*El Senor. Perdonamè,* please forgive me," his whispered words quiet as goose feathers floating to ground. Sara was an innocent, he reminded himself. His thoughts ought to be about protecting her. He stifled a groan. His fancies seemed to have a mind of their own lately.

Marco watched Jonas tamp down the cookstove fire and set the kitchen to rights. The old man knew what he'd been thinking. He was sure of it. As penance, Marco sat, awake, guarding Sara's sleeping form until Jonas dropped into the empty bunk and began to snore. He could barely wait for dawn and escape from this place. Then he, too, slept.

Chapter Nineteen

Capture

Dark Eyes slipped off the black stallion. Murmuring her thanks against his soft muzzle, she led him to the edge of the small circular clearing and looped his rope reins on a low hanging branch. Her eyes surveyed the ring of trees and dense vegetation. She glanced at Greywolf. He was like a ghost person. Face empty he sat unmoving on Washee's back.

"We stop here. Camp," she said, her tone strident and meant to set him astir. Quick as a breeze she bent to gathering dry pine fodder. "I make soft sleep place."

"Umm," he grunted, and Dark Eyes knew he'd come forth from his shadow place.

In moments, she unrolled her sleeping blanket and laid it over the expanse of pine needles she'd cradled in a shallow gully. "Time rest." She motioned toward Greywolf and sank down, bone weary from traveling through the bitter cold of night and all day in burning heat. "You come."

He stared at her, eyes hollow.

"You take drink. Make good you," she said, holding up a buffalo-skin bladder. "This gift, from cousin's family. Have much water."

He licked his lips. "Thirsty as a desert," he croaked. "Was a danged hot ride." Still weak from his ordeal, Greywolf slid from the pinto and staggered toward his companion.

She could see his exhaustion, and feel her own. Comfort and rest were more compelling than the need for food this moon time.

He covered the distance between them with few steps although he fought to remain upright. Propped on an elbow, she followed his progress, and when he lowered his body to the ground, very near her hip, she thrust the bladder into his hands. "Here, for you."

As she watched him pour the liquid into his mouth, a rush of warmth flooded her face. Embarrassed by her response, she turned away and laid her back to him. "We sleep now."

"Ahhh, I'm plumb played out," he mumbled, and stretched his lean form against hers. Fitting close.

Her heart raced, but Dark Eyes lay unmoving, enjoying the new, but pleasing sensations he brought to her sleeping blanket. His spirit contained fire, she decided. It spread into her at every place their bodies touched. She kept watch as night swiftly fell and enveloped their camp in cool darkness. Smiling up at the glitter of stars, she listened in the stillness for the unwelcome sounds of pursuers, until sleep overcame her, too.

Moonrise had passed into moonset when the faint thud of hooves rose up through the earth and into the senses of the sleeping woman, awakening her. Concerned about the safety of their hiding place, Dark Eyes quietly slipped off the blanket. She turned and lifted the material onto Greywolf who still slept as though dead. Then she moved stealthily away, her body low to the ground.

She crept in widening circles toward Washee, fingers outstretched to meet his rope. Whispering wordless sounds to calm the stallion, she loosed her pony and settled on his back like a soft breath. Turning him, she stretched her torso flat along his withers and brown-and-white neck. As one they moved slowly forward, continuing her outward circles. Dry pine needles crackled under his hooves. She searched with care for a good place to observe those horses whose feet had spoken to her.

Seeing no sign of horses or riders, Dark Eyes turned Washee back toward camp, moving like a secret. She wished to warm herself again beside the man she called Greywolf and close her eyes in sleep, though the stars told her dawn was fast approaching.

The noisy bellow of white men's voices suddenly split the stillness. While she searched for them, the evildoers had come close to her hidden sleeping space. The hard edge of their words told of anger and danger. *The corral people!* She remembered their sounds. "Whoa," she whispered and pressed her hips into Washee to strengthen her command. Not daring to breathe, Dark Eyes slid down the pony's flank and left him tethered to a sturdy pine branch.

In the near-inky blackness she crawled forward and knelt behind a boulder, silently asking the Great Spirit to conceal her from the intruders. Pebbles pushed sharp and gritty through her breeches, biting into her knees. She clenched her jaw, body rigid, her breaths controlled and soundless as she tried to will herself invisible, hoping the intruders would not sense her presence.

The men stopped speaking. In the tilt of their heads she saw that they listened to the quiet.

Her eyes settled on Greywolf. Only yards away, he lay flat in the gully, still wrapped in blankets and motionless in sleep. The trees cast a shadowed tangle cloaking him from easy view. Sudden muffled coughing pierced the silence. Dark Eyes smothered a gasp with her fingertips. Both men turned toward his hiding place. In that small utterance he had made himself known.

Her attention focused on the shorter of the two. Stocky and hairy-faced, he wore a grimy jacket made of poorly tanned animal skins. His unpleasant stench hung strong in the air. He bent an ear toward a nearby pine.

"Grab 'im, Chester. Lookee here, I got the stallion," he snarled, and led the big black horse into the clearing.

The second man, taller than the first, had long matted hair and many weapons hanging from his greasy belt. He pulled Greywolf to his feet and stared hard-eyed at his groggy captive. In no nonsense tones he stated his business. "We knows ye stole ar' stallion. That's a hangin' crime in these parts."

Greywolf remained mute, confused with sleep.

"Ye ain't got t'acknowledge the corn, mister. I catched ye dead to rights." His captor spit a dark tobacco stream for emphasis. "Dang sure I seen some injun gal, Jedidiah," he reminded his partner.

"We got full-on moonset, no more light 'til sun-up," said the smaller man. His voice made her skin crawl. "Ain't no way we'll find 'er."

"Aye," agreed Chester. "I reckon we take this horse thief in ta' the sheriff down Yuma way, and mebbee head fer th' cabin 'fore the sun gits straight up tomorree."

Dark Eyes glared from her hideaway as the two strangers bound Greywolf's arms with thick loops of rawhide and wrestled him onto the stallion's back. Her fingers curled into fists. Unshed tears burned her eyes.

"Ye ain't makin' no more camps son," said the taller man with a harsh laugh as he kicked the toe of his boot into the abandoned sleeping blanket.

She watched the men disappear through the trees, into the murky darkness, taking Greywolf with them. For many minutes she heard the horses' unshod feet, picking their way down the mountain trail toward town.

Mute and still as the boulder that hid her, Dark Eyes waited until no sound but that of the wind rippling through the forest came to her ears. Then she moved quickly. Standing and stretching her long legs, she brushed tiny sharp rocks from her knees. Her fear-laced heart beat like many drums. Her fingers trembled, giving silent voice to terror, as she gathered up the scattered remnants of their campsite. She could hear father's voice within her, speaking his teachings. *Fear is the destroyer, my daughter.*

Dark Eyes stepped to her pony's side. Eyes closed, she gently slid her arm over Washee's neck. Feeling his life strength, she quieted her breathing to match the pony's soft, steady blowing.

Within herself she sought the help of Coyote. "Release my fear to the cool night sky. Allow brother wind to take it beyond the far mountains," Dark Eyes whispered in her native tongue. "Hear me." Her palm felt the powerful heat of the spirit-guide feather that rested between her breasts. Her arm warmed with the good energy of Washee, who stood in silence—his exhaled breaths, like mists of white smoke, disappeared into the darkness.

"Ahhhyea," she sighed, as she opened her eyes and watched a streak of light arc across the horizon. It was a sign. Coyote had given her courage. Her fingers no longer shook. Instead, anger rushed over her like the roar of river waters falling from a high place. It filled her with hot strength. Fierceness was Coyote's gift. "I will go to the white mans' village. I can bring Greywolf's freedom. I wish to keep this man the spirits have given me." No brave who courted her had awakened such feelings.

She readied her pony for the journey ahead, wondering what dangers the new day might bring. She could not await first light to track the three horses. For safety, she'd ride among the trees and not along the white man's wide trail. How soon would the town the taller man spoke of draw near? It will be a place to approach with great care, of that she was certain. She pressed her lips together in a straight line and made ready to move on before sunrise.

Washee carried Dark Eyes alongside the wide track. They moved like shadows, in the early dawn, hidden from view in the trees. When the sun burst upward, tossing a golden rim above the edge of the world, she got off her pony and crept toward the trail to check for the now familiar signs of three riders. Always the signs were there in the dust and pebbles of this road. The track traveled downward, its ruts ugly gouges in the earth. Near her village, she had seen much of this made by the white man's wagons. There would be many big wheels in the town she sought.

Trees thinned as forested slopes gave way to the dense brush of high desert. Growths of shrub oak and jojoba fell away as horse and rider picked their way forward. Her nose and the breeze that tickled her face spoke of increasing dryness in the air. The desert floor was close now. Soon the town would show itself. She felt it like a wall of stones against her heart. The sun climbed steadily, a circle of fire set on a backdrop of cloudless blue. Early morning heat, still gentle, brushed her shoulders. The new day's warmth was always a welcome gift. Dark Eyes chewed thoughtfully on a meal of deer jerky as she rode. She was grateful that her cousin's husband had shared many strips of meat for her journey.

Just below, a forest of Saguaro, prickly limbs, proud and tall, stood like many warriors.

She shaded her eyes with both hands and looked ahead. In the distance ancient dark peaks were visible. At their base, the army of cactus soldiers collided with a mass of jagged black rocks.

She brought her gaze in and scanned the ground, sifting through the odd shapes. There she saw it. A long, straight, wagon track divided the strange army. The rutted road stretched west, inviting her eyes to follow. Dust puffs like pipe smoke in the still air, was a sign of moving horses, three perhaps. Dark Eyes squinted. Beyond, she saw the town. Its hazy jumble of small square shapes was not even a day's ride away.

Protection is the gift of these spiked cactus warriors, she reasoned. They will hide my journey forward. Her path decided, she pressed her heels into Washee's sides and spoke soft chucking sounds only the pony could hear, urging him onward at a lope. Soon she would come to the town where Greywolf was sure to be a prisoner.

Chapter Twenty

Leaving Jonas

The smell of fresh brewed coffee wafted on the air and filled the small cabin with its spicy aroma. Sara, tangled in her covering, did her best to ignore the enticing fragrance. She snuggled deeper beneath the coarse weave of her blanket, eyes still gritty with sleep. The unfamiliar shuffle of heavy boots and the crass guttural splutter of hawking and spitting assaulted her ears. It didn't sound a bit like home.

Unwilling to open her eyes until she felt fully awake, she held herself still, gathering her memories of the events that led to the scratchy bedstead she lay in. It all came back in a rush.

"Marco," she whispered. Getting no response she poked her head over the bunk's edge. Her eyes widened in alarm. The cabin was nearly dark; its one small window provided no morning sun, but she could see well enough to know he was not in the room. Panic pitched her into the morning— icy fingers spreading like cold tea in the pit of her stomach. *Where are you?* Where were the saddles and the rest of their gear? Had he actually abandoned her? Turned tail and run home?

Jonas clumped over to the bunk, battered tin cup in one hand, coffee pot in the other. "Yer friend be gone to tend the horses, missy," Jonas offered in answer to Sara's unvoiced questions. "Wanta cuppa brew?"

She eyed Jonas warily in the dim light. Her heartbeat slowed and her breathing quieted. Sitting up she pulled the saddle blanket tight around her shoulders, gripping its red-fringed edges in one hand. With the other, she accepted the steaming cup he proffered, nodding her thanks. Coffee beans were likely quite dear in this godforsaken corner of the mountains. The old codger was being kind.

She sighed and took a sip, glad to have a warm beverage delivered into her hands even before her feet hit the floor. Jonas grunted and shuffled back toward the stove. It seemed their host was at ease with her this morning, his misgivings put to rest. Kindly or not, he couldn't keep her here. She'd not stay in this dusty miner's abode for one moment longer than necessary. It was time to go. She finished her coffee and brought the cup to the bucket that served as a sink, still holding the blanket slung cozy over her shoulders.

"Thank you for your hospitality—" she began. Getting only a harrumph from the old man, she turned away and moved toward the cabin's only exit and entrance. "I'll be helping Marco now." Sara pushed the door wide open.

Relieved to be standing only inches from the thin warmth of early morning sunshine, Sara negotiated the cabin's one big step and made her way to the privy. At the end of a weedy track, she found the lopsided, wooden shed squatting amidst a gathering of pine and black oak. She shuddered to think of what she might find inside.

Pulling her saddle blanket from her shoulders, she set it atop a sturdy juniper bush, and eyed the flimsy shack. Wrinkling her nose in disgust, Sara tugged at the door. Her eyes checked the dirt floor and the corners for critters. Snakes and spiders would simply be the last straw. Seeing neither, she held her breath and stepped in.

Her morning necessary completed with haste, she threw open the door and gratefully took a gulp of fresh air. The privy's stench lingered. She grabbed a handful of pine greenery and pressed her nose into its sharp fragrance. Rubbing it between her fingers she applied its sap to her shirtwaist. Well rid of the rank odor, she took her blanket from its resting place. It was past time to see what Marco was up to.

Intent upon her mission, Sara trudged down the steep path toward the corral. She lifted a hand to her head and tugged at her curls as she walked. Why, I can't even get a finger through this tangle, she complained to herself. Marco must have my hairbrush. He'd better have!

She found him squatting just outside the corral. Head down, he seemed absorbed in some task. As she drew closer, she saw that he'd spread the entire contents of their saddlebags on the ground and was busily repacking each item. Their rifles rested under the shade of a nearby Manzanita tree.

Pleased that they seemed to have the same goal in mind, she sang out, "Time to go!" He rewarded her with a glance and a small smile, before he returned to his undertaking.

She reached the rough made railing, tossed her blanket over, slipped into the corral, and waited for Cherry to look her way. The red horse lifted her muzzle.

"Hey girl," she murmured, slapping a hand lightly against her leg.

Cherry nickered a welcome and wandered in her direction, head down, eyes soft. Sara leaned into her mare, stroking her muscled neck. She closed her eyes and enjoyed the warmth of her sorrel's sturdy body and slick, soft coat. In a mutual greeting ritual she pressed her face against the velvet of Cherry's nostrils and breathed in and out, glorying in the scent of sweet grass on her horse's breath. There was comfort in the silence and peace of the shared moment—a stillness her father always spoke of as an ancient bonding between horse and rider.

The gentle pressure of a hand against her shoulder was a sudden, unwelcome intrusion.

Sara turned away from Cherry, the spell broken, to find Marco standing behind her. He was close. Too close. Surprised, Sara peered into his face and stumbled backwards a step. His eyes were unreadable. What on earth was going on with him?

"*Sarita*," he said softly.

His tone made her uneasy. Just as uncomfortable as did his eyes boring into her back last night. "Ahem, good morning," she offered, tone curt. He was making her nervous and she didn't much care for the odd strain she felt between them. It certainly didn't help matters. They had to work together or she'd never find Matt. Seeking an ordinary topic to break the tension, she shook her curls. "Look at this mess," she said, yanking at her tresses. "My hair surely needs tending. I need my hairbrush. Have you already packed it?"

"Hmmph." Marco spun on his heel in answer and returned moments later, holding several items. His eyes resentful, he thrust her hairbrush, a horse brush, and a hoof pick at her. "You groom the horses, as well," he suggested, his voice impersonal. No smile now.

"Thanks," she said, tossing him what she hoped was a friendly grin. "I'll saddle them too, and we can be on our way. Jonas' partners might not be back for days. We can't wait."

His nod of agreement was hasty and without enthusiasm, Sara noted, as she watched him stomp back to the bedrolls.

Shrugging, she bent to brushing Cherry and picking her feet. When the reins were loosely wrapped around the saddle horn, she patted the mare's neck. "Good girl," she whispered, and turned her attention to Marco's mount.

"Hold still," she ordered several minutes later, after repeatedly shooing Valiente's nose away from her pockets. "I have no treats!" His indignant snort in response made her chuckle. "We are almost done," Sara assured the restless animal. He really was a young horse and sometimes quite unruly. She pulled his latigo tighter one last time and slipped two fingers between the cinch and his girth area. "You're just fine," she said, scratching his neck. The horse flicked one ear back to catch the sound of her voice. Grabbing her chance, she slipped the bit in his mouth, tightened his cheek strap, and led him out of the corral over to the Manzanita tree, where Marco was checking their rifles.

Marco straightened, brushed his palms against his pants legs, and snatched Valiente's reins from her outstretched hand. "I'll tie down the bedrolls. You bring the saddlebags. Then, before we take our leave, we will bid the old man good-bye. I want to part on the best of terms. You never know; someday we may again require his help."

"Okay, just give me a moment to tame my curls," she pleaded, vigorously applying her hairbrush to the snarls. "I don't want to look like a horse thief and risk getting his dander up again."

He refused to meet her eyes. "*Sarita*, to me, you are always very pretty," he growled.

Sara flinched at his tone. *Was that anger in his voice? Or ardor?* She brushed even harder, in an attempt to banish the very idea.

Leading their horses, the two retraced the steep track to the cabin's door. As they approached, Jonas appeared from around the side of the building, hefting a shovel and rocker sieve, a battered hat jammed down on his unkempt grey hair.

"Reckon you folks aim to be movin' on," he rasped, his rheumy eyes hard beneath the brim of his hat. "Mebbe you'll find m' partners 'longside the trail. Best not be yer young feller took m' horse, missy." He pounded the shovel blade into the dirt for emphasis.

"No sir," Marco agreed, and turned to look at Sara.

Her fingers tightened anxiously on Cherry's reins. "Thank you," she managed to blurt before she spun away and started back down the track, leaving Marco to complete the proper farewell conversation.

"Please, can you name the town just ahead?" she heard Marco ask as she made her way toward the corral.

Jonas spat into the dust. "That be Yuma. Use t' be a fort. 'Bout a hard two day's ride, or three mebbe. Ye find a fair wide track jest offen them trees." He gestured, waving a weather-scarred hand in the general direction.

Marco nodded. "*Muchas gracias, Señor*, for your assistance."

At the foot of the small incline, Sara, already mounted, waited impatiently. What if Jonas' partners had already found Matthew? Her toes clenched in her boots.

Chapter Twenty-One

Finding Greywolf

Dark Eyes leapt from her brown-and-white pony onto the wide, rutted street that ran through the center of town. Her long black hair flew about her shoulders. "Wait, Washee!" she commanded and wrapped his halter rope firmly around the stripped log that served as a tie rail. It lay across two posts and offered space for several horses. The animals stood quietly in the heat. She leaned into her pony and watched cowboys maneuver their mounts along the crowded thoroughfare, riding two and three abreast. Many white-man wagons clogged the roadway just as she predicted.

She swept her eyes left and right, noting several saloons. Inside those places, white men drank the foul tasting water that made them behave like fools. Dangerous fools. Certain she, too, could easily become a prisoner, Dark Eyes drew deep breaths. She must be swift and cautious if she was to free Greywolf. A cloud of fine grit rose around her moccasins as she turned to survey the buildings at the far side of the street.

Her attention settled on an adobe structure toward the end of the wide track. A small, barred window sat high in its cracked and peeling wall. Fear rattled in her breast. Her breath quickened. Deliberately slowing her breathing, she studied the squalid building. Its once bright, whitewashed clay had settled into a yellowing, like the color of dried corn. In places the clay had crumbled entirely, and red-brown mud of adobe brick mixed with bits of straw was visible. This was a jail, the place they held Greywolf. An angry flush crept up her neck. Her heart beat like a drum.

Seeking comfort, her fingertips slid along her breast and connected with the power of the Spirit feather hidden in the deep cleave of her damp skin. To show rage to enemies would waste the strength Coyote had given her. There were many people about. She must stay calm and move without upset. She had much to do.

Warm breezes rippled hair against her cheek. She brushed at the tickling strands and peered at the eating-houses and trade stores that filled the spaces between saloons. In front of one shop she saw wooden boxes stacked with long-handled shovels used to dig for yellow metal in the rivers. Barrels held straw brooms crowded together like many trees. These she knew were used to clear the white man's floors.

Suddenly memories swirled like falling leaves. She hugged herself, recalling life at General Vallejo's Mission rancheria. Father was a powerful headman; he spoke often to the big *Mexicano* chief. Her family had not been forced to move from *Olumpali*, the village of her birth. Going each day to the nearby white man's school had been hard enough. Washee moved, restless, and drew her back to the present. Here, she was alone. Her father could not speak for her. This place held real threat.

Attending to her pony, Dark Eyes rubbed his flank and gave him soft words of reassurance, speaking of her swift return, then walked briskly across the road. She mounted two steps onto the wooden planks of the white man's walking place. Her soft leather moccasins left dusty footprints on the boards as she hurried along, watching for loose or missing planks. She paid little attention to the swells and the stiff-backed, pale-skinned women they squired: white women who threw disapproving looks' her way.

Men filled the boardwalk. Cowboys, prospectors, soldiers, and gamblers loitered in shop doorways and gathered in groups that blocked the easy flow of foot traffic. They were a different story. Long without women to gentle them, their talk was loud and laughter raucous. Young and old, their frank glances were filled with appreciation and no small measure of curiosity as they watched the slender, young woman move with fluid grace through the crowd.

She had seen the ways of these men in the white settlement so near the Mission school. Many times they were rough, even cruel to The People, especially women they found alone and defenseless. Dark Eyes' skin prickled at the thought of such terrible things, and she hastened her pace.

Soon huddles thinned, and at the entrance to an sunless alley, she drew to a halt. The adobe building sat squat and ugly in the heat. Vigilant, she scanned the street and ducked into the tight passageway. She pressed her shoulder against a scarred wall and crouched just beneath a nearly hidden opening. A slit so thin it didn't require bars. Conversation within the building came to her ears.

"As Sheriff, I tell ya, we got that Injun-lover dead to rights," the lawman sneered.

She gritted her teeth. So it was, here Greywolf sat in a cage, awaiting the whim of the man who wore the shiny star. The man's words told the story. He laughed, his voice a nasty croak, as he recounted their arrival. When Greywolf's foul-smelling captors brought him to this place they set upon him with fists and clubs. The sheriff had rolled a smoking stick and looked the other way. Later, he added his own blows.

Chairs scraped and voices rose nearer the window. "He'll hang for horse stealin'," she heard the lawman say. "Yer stallion is official evidence, and you two fellers will need ta be givin' testimony at the trial."

"Hey, sheriff, mebbe he's the one that murdered that old prospector a few months back," declared a new talker.

"You jest look into that, deputy," the sheriff responded, his tone scornful. "I tole ya. We got 'im dead to rights on horse thievin'. Don't need any more make-work."

"Well," the one called Chester drawled, "We ain't know nothin' of murders, but since thar's need fer speakin' up, I guess we'll be leavin' our ole 'Capt'n Black with you law boys for a couple a' days. Take a care with th' horse. We 'spect to be takin' him home follerin' the necktie party."

"Time we be enjoyin' some refreshment. Whar' about parched," added his partner, Jedediah. "Let's git to it."

She'd not forget the sound of their voices.

Fury rose in Dark Eye's heart. "You will never get a chance to put him on your rope," she vowed, startled by her own boldness and the unfamiliar passion that drove her.

As boisterous goodbyes signaled the end of the bad talking, Dark Eyes backed away from the building. She melded into the shadows, observing the two old miners stomp out of the sheriff's office and wander up the walkway to join the stream of men in search of drink.

Studying the row of structures—some sturdy, many part built or leaning, dilapidated—she considered possible plans. As was her way, she asked for guidance. Unable to find answers in the spirits of sand or sky, she understood the choice was hers to make, and settled on the simplest plan.

At the very end of the street, a building constructed of heavy wood planking sat twice higher than its neighbors. The saloon of "two-floors" is the place I will go, she determined. Her gaze fell upon a sign painted above the swinging doors. She shaded her eyes. "Brady's" she muttered, using her Mission-taught reading skills to understand what word the letters made.

Dark Eyes retraced her steps. Willing herself small and unseen, she rode Washee out of town. Far from prying eyes, she removed the small pouch and eagle feather from their warm hidden place and tucked them into her sleeping blanket. Then she circled wide, turning Washee back until she found a spot close to the rear of the white mans' prison house. Here, she tethered her pony in a large clump of ocotillo.

Her water bladder, bow, and few arrows followed the blanket roll into a hidey-hole beneath a thatch of ironwood and pungent creosote, where she carefully covered them with hastily culled desert debris. The leather of her moccasins hid her small knife.

Fighting fear that made her feet wish to run, Dark Eyes gathered her courage and crept to the heavy unmarked door at the back of the saloon. Like a ghost, she slipped inside and found herself standing in front of a shadowy doorway. She stepped into the room. An oil lamp cast gloomy light, revealing a hefty man sitting behind a fortress of a desk.

Chapter Twenty-Two

Doc Brady's

Doc Brady looked up. His cold blue eyes glinted as they moved over her body, assessing, appraising. "What can I do for you, girl?" he said.

She knew that under the deerskin dress with the beaded fringes, it was easy to see her soft, womanly curves. "I wish serve at your saloon," Dark Eyes replied. Her face allowed no trace of apprehension and no sign of the contempt she felt for this sweating man with a face like cold, corn mush. "I give fire-water to cowboys," she said, keeping her voice low and steady.

The saloon owner laughed. "Honey, you're an injun, and I don't hire injuns." But his eyes spoke of something different.

He is like so much clay, she realized, as she stood before the fleshy man. Convincing him would not take long, if she could be bold as a warrior. "Please," she said, and watched the man from under the long dark lashes of her deliberately averted eyes.

She sank into a nearby chair, aimed her gaze at the floor, and stretched out a leather-covered leg. Soft, tan deerskin wrapped her shapely calves to the knees. Her fingers came to rest at her thighs and caused the buckskin fringe of her dress to fall away, revealing dusky bare skin. He made no words, but in the silence his breath quickened. "Please?" she whispered, and stood-up. Pressing her hands against the slender round of her hips, she looked straight at him.

The man sat motionless. Now, only his eyes, leering hot above his pudgy cheeks and thick white mustache gave him away. They followed her every move. "Okay," he growled, placing his meaty hands on the desktop. "You're hired. Get upstairs and have one of the girls find ya' something to wear. Name's Doc Brady," he tossed at her. "Some calls me Boss."

Dark Eyes did not immediately stir for she must appear to be grateful. She forced a pleased smile to her lips. "I am thank you," she said, as she lowered her hands to her sides.

"Yes, you will thank me," Brady wheezed. "I'll be seeing you after closing time." His greedy eyes roamed her body. There was no missing his intent.

She felt him tracking her like a *wakalai*, a snake, as she walked toward the doorway, stepped out of the office, and shut the door behind her. Huffing a sigh of relief, Dark Eyes lifted her chin. She padded across the shadowy hallway that led to the barroom and, closer by, the stairway. She looked up.

Her eyes fixed on the ornate brass lamp at the top of the stairwell. Above it a flickering circle of yellow light wavered toward the ceiling; below, it spilled onto the carpet. She put her hand on the stair rail, curling her fingers around its smoothness, the wood slick with oil and moisture from the touch of a hundred men. Her deerskin-booted feet whispered as she headed toward the second floor. Even as she climbed the scuffed wooden steps Dark Eyes heard the chirp of a female voice.

At the top of the stairs she stepped onto threadbare red carpet, and came face to face with a plump, young woman, who emerged from one of the doors to her right. Dark Eyes stared, fascinated by the sight. The woman's reddish-brown hair was tossed on top of her head in a careless tangle of ringlets. Grimy white petticoats peeked from beneath her soiled pink satin frock. Stale whiskey smells, cigar smoke, and body odor spewed from her clothing—mightily unpleasant to the nose.

"Well, well honey, how do." the woman said. She cocked her head and eyed the tall, leather clad girl standing silently before her. "It looks like Doc's got hisself another canary. Come on, the name's Lily," she said with a smile. "Yah need some proper clothes. I'll getcha fixed up."

Without a word, Dark Eyes followed Lily down the hall. They stopped in front of a curtained doorway and the redhead turned. "In here." she motioned, as she pushed the dusty, faded material aside. "Don't know if I got rags ta fit the likes a' you," the woman said. "Yer a tall one. Say, what do they call yah by?"

Unsure of the proper response Dark Eyes remained mute.

"Don't worry none girl, I'll think yah a fine name." Lily paused. "How 'bout Willa, fer yer long legs? Yah know, kinda like the tree."

Closing her eyes, Dark Eyes sighed.

Her new friend shook her curls. "It's settled then. Good."

Moving to a pile of satin and lace, Lily lobbed dresses at her. Only two of the tawdry garments—shiny and threadbare even in the dim cubicle—fit Dark Eyes' narrow frame, and met with Lily's approval: the first a lacy, red garment with many tiny hooks up the front and skirting that draped to her ankles; the other a sour-smelling green satin dress with wide skirts and petticoats that reached mid-calf. The green, Lily decreed, was the better of the two.

Dark Eyes forced herself to accept Lily's efforts to adjust the none-too-clean dress and its underpinnings on her person. She stood motionless, shifting only when the white woman instructed her to pull in her breath or turn one way or the other.

The layers of material with the corset pulled tight beneath, felt harsh and confining against her skin, so used was she to the softness of the chewed and beaten leather coverings of her people. Reluctantly, she folded her moccasins and the thin metal blade they hid, into her buckskin dress. Crushing Greywolf's lacy gift into a ball, she concealed it in the frock's one pocket.

"Help yourself, dearie," Lily said. Rummaging in a corner, she pointed out two wooden boxes heaped with high-heeled, satin ankle boots.

While Lily explained what Doc Brady would expect of her, Dark Eyes struggled and finally managed to pull the strange footwear onto her slender feet. She tightened the laces as directed. Then the two women made their way back along the carpeted hallway, Dark Eyes unsteady in the un-wieldy shoes.

"This will be your room," Lily said, pointing to a scarred wooden door just to the left of the stairs.

Dark Eyes pushed the battered panel ajar and peered in. She nodded at the redhead and stepped over the threshold, shoving the door shut behind her. Panic kept her company as she gingerly sat on the lumpy bedstead and tried to understand the way of behaving needed in this alien place. Her nose wrinkled. In this small sleeping room the air felt murky and uneasy.

Lily's voice came to her through the thin barrier. "Say, open up! We ain't done yet."

Dark Eyes placed her belongings under the bedstead. Miserable in her new, confining garments, she slowly opened the door.

"Comere," Lily said, and pulled at her arm. "Yah watch me. I'm ta show you how to walk in them shoes." The redhead flipped her skirts with her fingers and stepped forward, swinging her hips.

She looks like a waddling goose, Dark Eyes thought, as she studied her teacher's movements.

"Yah foller' me," Lily instructed, turning around and pointing down the long hallway.

Dark Eyes set out with purpose. "Now I must learn walk on sticks," she muttered, flinging her body from side-to-side in a poor imitation of her mentor. Tottering like a bear that had enjoyed too many overripe berries, she struggled to keep her feet from twisting and tripping in her unaccustomed footwear. Determination quickly turned to disgust, and then to laughter as the two women practiced the harlot's walk, and Dark Eyes learned the ways to lure customers upstairs.

Satisfied at last, Lily maneuvered her pupil into the sleeping place, where she pressed her into the only chair. "Yah gonna do great, honey," she announced, and proceeded to comb out Dark Eyes' long hair and rouge her cheeks in preparation for the evening's festivities. "I'll come getcha in a bit, Willa."

Chapter Twenty-Three

The Saloon

The green satin dress Dark Eyes wore gleamed dully in the greasy light of the saloon's kerosene lamps. Its deep-cut bodice revealed the swell of her modest breasts. Hidden beneath showy frills, she was imprisoned in the whalebone stays of a too tight corset.

Cigar smoke and the ugly smell of bodies that had not sought the sweat lodge or river waters tangled with tinny notes of a piano in the hot, early evening air. No snatch of sunlight gilded any corner. In Brady's Saloon & Entertainment Establishment, she was certain it always looked as if the sun had gone to its home behind the mountains.

Dark Eyes lounged against the worn and polished bar as Lily had instructed. Her black hair pulled up, away from her face, fell in a thick mane almost to her waist. A heavy cascade of petticoats danced beneath her calf-length skirt whenever she shifted her weight. Uncomfortable, she held herself still as a cat. Only her eyes moved, scanning the noisy room.

With studied indifference, she noted four men seated at a nearby table. The empty firewater bottles that sat at their feet told her they had been drinking whiskey and playing poker all afternoon. She heard the slip-slap of cards shuffled and dealt as they geared up for yet another round. Voices rose and fell, the game punctuated by raucous laughter and rough curses. At the long bar, its ornate carvings dented and scarred, two cattle ranchers stood, deep in conversation. Their spurred and booted feet carried the dust of the rutted street. She smelled the faintest odor of manure. The trill of Lily's carousing drifted from a darkened corner, but the general hubbub swallowed her words.

Suddenly, the saloon doors swung wide. A lone man stepped into the large room. His boots scratched against sand-littered floor planks. Dark Eyes noted a gleaming metal star above the pocket of his shirt as he made his way to the far end of the oaken bar.

The bartender, Big Jack, set down a glass and a bottle of vile firewater in front of the lawman. "Sheriff," he called him. Dark Eyes watched the man down two glasses of whiskey in close succession. His free hand rested heavily on the gun belt that encircled his hips. He bent forward, leaning across the massive countertop, and dropped a coin on its scarred surface exchanging a string of words with Big Jack that she couldn't hear.

Glass in hand, the sheriff shoved his hat back on his head and turned to survey the room, one scuffed boot hooked over the beat-up, brass kick-rail. "Finally," Dark Eyes muttered. *It was time.*

She pushed herself away from the bar and turned toward him. This man had beaten Greywolf. She saw cruelty cut deep in his features. The skin along her neck prickled. The tall, star man could hurt her. He would enjoy it.

Dark Eyes swallowed hard, her mouth fear-dry. Breathing in courage, she drew herself up and gathered her resolve. She gripped the white-lace handkerchief Greywolf had given her.

It held big magic. Her fingertips pressed so hard one against another they paled with the tension. She walked toward him with measured steps, her hips swinging slowly from side to side just as Lily had taught her. The skirts whispered against her legs like uneasy spirits. She placed one satin-shod foot across his line of vision and deliberately, dropped the small square of white lace at his feet.

The sheriff looked down at the delicate piece of material resting close to his dusty boots. His eyes took in the tall, dark-haired woman who had dropped it. He inspected the length of her, lingering over the promise of well-shaped legs, bronze under thin cotton stockings. He rubbed his hands against his thighs when his scrutiny found her slender waist and above it the soft swell of her breasts. His survey reached her face, her generous mouth, now curved in an inviting smile, and her glittering black eyes that tracked his every move.

"Well, well," he whispered, and bent to scoop the handkerchief from its resting place on the saloon floor. His lips curled in an insolent grin as he lifted the lacy square and offered it to her. Dark Eyes stepped closer and claimed the gauzy scrap of cloth. Her satin skirts rustled as she backed away. Obviously delighted at this unexpected turn of events, the sheriff followed her as she beckoned him up the wide customer staircase. "Come my sleeping place," she murmured.

Dark Eyes sat on the edge of the meager bedstead and looked at the man slouched in the doorway of the tiny upstairs room. He appraised her with mean, small eyes. She swallowed her anxiety, for Lilly had shared the ways of pleasing these men—and of stopping them. Dark Eyes had been an excellent student. She'd listened carefully.

Fingertips slowly caressing her legs, watching her prey from under lowered lashes, she lifted layers of skirting to show the flesh above her knees. His eyes were hot, hard as stones. She forced a smile and slipped her thumb under one garter.

For a moment the lawman was motionless, a nasty smirk distorting his thin lips. Then he straightened, stepped full into the small cubicle and slammed the door shut with a vicious kick. His grimy hands yanked at the leather of his gun belt and lowered it to the floor. She heard metal and cowhide scrape against wood when he toed it toward the foot of the bed. The taint of evil floated around him like poison.

Dark Eyes lay back, her arms stretched above her head. Waiting. Her body stilled, she welcomed the spirit that lives in the mountain cat and hunting eagle into her heart. She was alert, but without fear.

Hunger plain on his face, he reached her in two short strides. The mattress sank when he sat on its edge and twisted at the fastenings of his shirt. He was so close she could feel his body heat. She pushed down her disgust. Her hand crept unnoticed beneath the soiled, satiny pillow.

"This is fer ya protection dearie," Lily had said when she put her gift into Dark Eyes' hand earlier that evening.

Glad he did not know the pounding in her chest, Dark Eyes grasped the hidden pistol in just the way Lily had shown her. The sheriff turned. He leaned into her, pulling at her skirts. "It is best not to wait," Coyote growled in her ear. She steeled herself, lifted the gun, and holding her breath, swung it hard, striking the startled man on the side of his face. Disbelief flamed in his eyes before he slumped and slipped to the floor like an uncoiling snake.

Sitting up, she inched from the iron bedstead and stepped over the barely conscious lawman. In a fury, she grabbed a pitcher from the tabletop. Water flew everywhere as she leapt forward and brought it down on his head.

Quick fingers searched his pockets. Her nose twitched as the unpleasant odor of his long-unwashed body floated upward. She tucked his two brass keys and revolver into the top of her lace corset. Yanking the red dress from the depths of the closet, she tore at its seams. His limp arms and legs offered no resistance as she bound and gagged him tightly with her makeshift red rope.

Now she must hide him from view, and leave this place. She struggled to move his insensible form. Defiance fed her efforts to push the dead weight of him beneath the bedstead's straw ticking. Sinking to the floor, she drew up her knees and pressed with all her might. The air held prisoner behind her lips escaped with a whoosh, as she shoved his body from view. Catching her breath, she stood.

With the sheriff's pistol nested warm in her bodice, Dark Eyes snatched her soft leather bundle from under the bed. She held the comfort of her moccasin boots and dress under one arm, grateful to regain what was hers. Below stairs the sounds of the piano were louder. Bawdy shouts and howls of laughter were louder still. The stomp of feet and the crack of gunshots were followed by splintering glass and raucous cheers.

She reached for Lily's small pearl-handled weapon and pushed it into the high top of her satin shoe. Turning, she moved noiselessly out of the wretched room and down the back stairs. Doc Brady's office door was closed. The rise and fall of muted voices came from within. Dark Eyes slipped out the rear exit and melted into the evening shadows. It was not safe here, and there wasn't much time. She had to be quick like a fox if she was to save Greywolf.

Chapter Twenty-Four

Escape

Greywolf sat on the floor of his jail cell, staring at dirty, scraped walls, a chronicle of anger and despair. This small adobe cage was about the ugliest thing he'd ever seen. His jailers provided little food—just hard tack and coffee. His belly was riled up, half empty, and feeling like he'd swallowed buckshot. He might starve to death before they had a chance to hang him, he thought with dark humor.

More than once he closed his eyes and tried to figure himself out. Stuck in this cell he'd been racking his brain, but try as he might he could not recall his past. Nothing seemed familiar. Pictures he couldn't quite grasp sometimes flashed like lightning bolts in his mind. The images gave him headaches. His sleep was not peaceful.

He'd tried to speak of his predicament and innocence. The sheriff met every attempt with unconcealed hostility. Maybe it was for the best. The no-good barrel boarders that ran the local law were just a bunch a' low sots. They were on the prod, looking for a fight, and whiskey slewed from sun up ta' moonrise. If he kept his mouth shut, he might live to explain himself to a judge. It's likely my only chance. he thought.

Besides, he didn't want to jeopardize Dark Eyes' safety by talkin' too much. She'd probably disappeared into the mountains by now. He hoped they'd never find her.

He considered the events of the past weeks—the only things he did remember. An Indian woman had saved him from certain death when she found him delirious in the desert. That he was sure of. She had nursed his wounds. And it seemed she most surely signed his death warrant when she stole that black beauty of a horse.

Queer enough, he missed her company. The songlike tones of her speech were pleasing to his ears, although some place deep inside niggled with unease when they were together. He sighed. Another mystery.

The sharp rap rap of knuckles against wood interrupted his reflections, and Greywolf watched with interest as the heavyset deputy stood up, hoisted his trousers over his considerable belly, and lumbered toward the door. He yanked it open, then suddenly backed up. A woman's voice broke the silence.

"Mmm, please, deputy, I like see prisoner." Something metal glittered in her hand, menacing in the dim light.

"Dark Eyes!" Greywolf hissed in surprise. He scrambled to his feet. *I'd know her voice anywhere.* He understood immediately what had to be done, although leaping up still caused him momentary dizziness. He leaned against the wall and cleared his head with a shake. If he could help her, it might work out. Moving fast, he flattened himself against the cold iron bars of the cell and waited.

Dark Eyes seemed fearless as she waved the small pistol at the deputy, encouraging the astounded lawman to back up, step by step. She was oddly dressed. What the heck had she been doing? Her long legs were visible in black stockings under a green satin dress and her feet shod in fancy-gal boots. Petticoat ruffles peeked from beneath the skirt. It'd be a story he'd want to hear tell of later. If there was a later.

As she motioned the fuddled deputy steadily back, her eyes found Greywolf's. Her look crackled with intent. The deputy stumbled past the desk and Dark Eyes' fingers made a quick grab for the ring of keys atop its cluttered surface. Astonished, the hefty man paused. Without a word she thrust the gun at him. He resumed his clumsy backward shuffle, his eyes venomous.

It took only seconds for the lawman to realize his body was pressed against his prisoner's cage. His doughy face registered panic, but it was too late. Greywolf struck like a rattlesnake. His arm slipped between the bars and wrapped around the deputy's thick neck, forcing the man to gasp for breath.

Dark Eyes tossed the keys toward the cell, and Greywolf heard them land behind him with a clank. "Get the handcuffs," he said, his voice harsh with the effort needed to control the large, struggling deputy.

She stared at him intently.

He directed his eyes to the spur-scarred desk. "Bracelet of silver," Greywolf hissed.

Relief washed over him when understanding leapt in her eyes. She backed up several steps and perched on the desk's corner edge, petticoats flashing. Never changing the pistol's steady aim, she reached one hand behind her and rummaged through the unfiled paperwork that littered its pockmarked surface.

"I find," came her delighted yelp as her fingers connected with metal. She dangled the prize in front of her.

157

"Ya thieves 'll hang twice for this," the deputy wheezed as he lost consciousness and slumped to the planked floor.

Dark Eyes approached the small cell, holding the metal circles in her fist. "We go river now."

"Keep the gun on this hard case," Greywolf instructed as he turned to pick up the key ring and unlock the cell door. He thrust his hand out. "Quick. Give me the bracelet."

Their fingers collided as the heavy cuffs went from her grasp to his. Her touch kindled a spark. It was a good feeling. She felt it too, he knew, because she stilled, and her gleaming black eyes held his. Bad timing. He had to keep focus. "Dark Eyes!" he bit out to break the spell. "We got to hurry!"

Together they dragged the deputy's bulk into the barred room, his eyes blank and hands restrained behind him. Dark Eyes pulled the boots from his feet. "Man no can ride," she explained, deftly slipping past him, the scruffy leather foot-wear tucked under her arm. Greywolf chuckled and locked the cell door.

Surprising him again, she produced a six-gun from the lacy bodice of her dress. He watched with alarm at the casual way she waved the deadly weapon. "Careful," he said, his voice low and steady.

"I bring you." She smiled and placed the revolver in his outstretched hand.

Greywolf whistled under his breath and tossed her an appreciative grin. He slid the revolver into his waistband and grabbed two bandolier belts that hung from a nearby wooden peg. On the way out, his fingers closed on the deputy's rifle. The two fugitives slipped into a near moonless night.

Dark Eyes crept forward, leading Greywolf across the desert toward the small copse of ocotillo where Washee wait-ed. She held the little pistol in her fist. Along the way he saw her hurl the stolen boots into a patch of spiny cactus, each one a shadow that flew like a hunting hawk through the secret dark. He tossed the deputy's key ring in the opposite direction.

The pony nickered softly as they approached, ready to stretch his legs for them.

Chapter Twenty-Five

River Crossing

Washee in tow, Greywolf and Dark Eyes stole across the sandy terrain. They spoke only with the touch of fingers and meeting of eyes, alert for the posse that would follow. He was grateful, for moonset brought only a bare slip of light. Enough to take them to the river, away from the menace of Yuma.

Seeking the river's scents, like a wild thing she lifted her face into the cool air and sniffed deeply. She squeezed Greywolf's hand and pointed ahead. "Big water," she mouthed. They moved forward swiftly, Dark Eyes in the lead. In no time they were pushing through rushes high as a man's head, to the torrent's edge.

The unexpected murmur of voices carried on the night breeze.

"Ahh. My father people," she whispered.

Greywolf laid a hand on her shoulder and brought his lips close to her ear. "How do you know?" he demanded, his mouth dry with sudden anxiety.

"I know words they speak. Help us okay."

"Lord, I hope you're right," he grumbled.

In silence, they crept toward the voices. She signaled Greywolf with a raised hand—wait—then threw back her head and uttered a single, raptor-like cry. In seconds an answering shriek split the air.

"Come you," she instructed. Tugging at his shirtsleeve, she stepped sideways pulling Washee with her. Greywolf followed. They struggled hidden in thick river grasses, stopped and listened, then moved on.

Suddenly, the rushes parted. Five warriors stepped out of the tall grass, war lances in their fists. The hairs on Greywolf's neck rose like hackles on a dog's back. He gaped at the braves. Circles and stripes of yellow, black, and white covered their faces and bare arms. In the thin sliver of moonshine the paint seemed to glow, igniting splinters of terrible memories. They looked savage.

Wary, he watched Dark Eyes approach the men, regal in her bearing, even got up in that outlandish dance hall dress. Her attire with all its petticoats seemed a source of amusement to the fearsome group. He held still as stone although his heart drummed in his chest. She spoke in a tongue foreign to his ears. Curious glances told him she was explaining the situation. Although he couldn't see her hands, he imagined the graceful dance they performed as she communicated her needs.

Talking done, she wheeled around and walked toward him. Triumph sparked in her eyes, visible even in the shadows. She nodded in the direction of the five men. "Quechzen people. These friend. My family Miwuk. Same blood. We cross river now. Is good."

Her cunning amazed him. For the first time since he'd been pounced on and tossed into a jail cell, Greywolf realized real freedom might be possible. Hope filled him with new energy.

Ignoring the quiver in his gut, he dipped his chin in understanding and stepped up straightaway to acknowledge her kinsmen, arms folded protectively across his chest. The warriors looked him over in silence, then drifted back some and spoke amongst themselves with much pointing.

Greywolf turned to Dark Eyes. "What are they saying?" he whispered. Her low musical chuckle hummed on the breeze and he raised a questioning eyebrow.

She placed her hand on his. A streak of heat flared where her fingertips rested. It fanned out along his arm, warm and inviting. Her unexpected touch was at once reassuring and extremely unsettling.

"They say Father be ... mmm ... surprise," she informed him.

"That sounds mighty perilous." Although he took pleasure in her speaking his tongue so well, he frowned and pulled away. "Let's cut dirt now. I'm ready," he said. "Let's go! We best get shed of the law, quick. And I don't much want to be subjected to their bad medicine either," he added, inclining his head in the direction of the braves, who leaned on their lances a short distance away.

"I tell," she said, and marched off to relay his concerns to the men, who had followed their interaction with a mixture of suspicion and impatience.

When the tallest of the five motioned him forward, Greywolf complied. His body and mind tense, he joined Dark Eyes in the circle of Quechzen warriors. Did the men understand what he'd said? What more did they expect of him?

Leading their horses, the group slipped single file along the sandy banks of the Rio Colorado. At a wide bend in the river where water rippled over hidden rocks, the painted men lifted their lances and the party halted. Their lilting voices, pitched low, carried a set of instructions only Dark Eyes understood. After hurried discussion, she offered Washee's lead rope to a lean young warrior and climbed aboard his pony. Greywolf saw the fellow nod his approval, and his gut told him the horse had crossed many times. At least Dark Eyes would make it to the far side.

Greywolf followed hand signs made by the tall brave with intense eyes and found himself astride a muscular animal, a mustang maybe, short-legged and eager to move. Its black and white mane gleamed as though it, too, had been painted.

For several minutes, the warriors exchanged muted words with much gesturing. Then two of the war party gathered the last horse, and vanished like ghosts into the grasses.

"They wait, catch trackers. Lawman posse," Dark Eyes whispered as she and Greywolf sat on their ponies between two mounted warriors.

From beneath half-closed lids, he studied each man. Hawk feathers and bone ornaments decorated their long, wild hair—as ferocious looking as their war paint—but their body stances and behaviors bespoke no threat.

It seemed like a long time before the fifth warrior leapt onto his pony and splashed into the river, slicing the glinting currents. He turned when he reached the far bank and cupped his hands around his mouth. His throaty raptor call floated across the water, signaling come ahead. Single file ponies and riders approached the swiftly moving water. Wild shouts and whoops of their Indian guides spun them forward: first came the lean warrior astride Washee, followed by Dark Eyes, her legs cradling her horse's sides.

Greywolf set his mouth in a thin line and rode into the rippling water next. Just ahead he heard splashing as Dark Eyes moved straight into the swifter currents. Deuce! He couldn't see her clearly. Horsetail Man, as Greywolf had named him, brought up the rear.

One hand wrapped in thick mane, clinging hard to the animal with his legs, Greywolf urged his spotted mount on. Low clouds parted. He saw Dark Eyes' pony flounder in the deeper water and slip downstream. The animal struggled unsuccessfully to regain its footing. She cried out as rough waters pulled her from his back.

"Hang on," Greywolf shouted.

A flurry of white churned toward him. Keeping one hand anchored in thick mane, his other shot out and grabbed at the roiling water. His fingers connected with a handful of petticoat and he held on, cursing their damned adventure.

Sputtering and gasping, Dark Eyes surfaced seconds later, eliciting a snort from the sturdy little paint. She struggled against the tumbling waters and managed to wrap one arm around Greywolf's leg. Holding fast, she paddled furiously with the other hand until they reached the far bank, several yards away.

Just ahead of them Dark Eyes' horse splashed onto dry land, shook the water from its coat, and quietly joined Washee to nose the ground for fodder. Behind them Greywolf heard the Indian brave who brought up the rear urging his horse on.

In the near dawn, Dark Eyes and Greywolf huddled together on the sandy bank, shoulders barely touching, soaked clothes clinging to their heaving bodies. Exhausted from her struggle in the Rio Colorado's angry foam, Dark Eyes shivered in the cool air. Her hair hung wet, splayed across her back, shielding her from Greywolf's concerned glances. Nearby, the three warriors spoke softly, their melodious language a comfort to her.

Across the river, bloodcurdling screams and the sound of gunshots split the predawn quiet. Her eyes flew open and settled on Greywolf. The scent of his fear was strong. She saw it claim his features as he returned her gaze.

"You have bad spirit sit in heart," Dark Eyes said. She scooted around, and arranged herself so they faced one another. "My people stop lawman." Her eyes fixed on his and refused to release him.

"I remember something," he said at last. He pulled away from her. "It's so horrible. Terrifying." His body quaked with the memory. "Your people," he stammered. "Blood and screaming. Lots of screams. War clubs. Many warriors." He stared into the darkness. "I can't see ... I don't know ..."

Dark Eyes spoke gently, her hands quiet in her lap. "You look me, Greywolf." She waited for his eyes to meet hers. Choosing her words carefully, she rolled the sounds of his language around in her mouth before she continued. "My people, my father people, no make fight. Also have great sadness. Village afraid white man sickness. Very bad medicine. Many deaths come—mothers, babies. Cruel thing.

"Strong men use *jaw-e, mukul*, bow and arrow for hunt; sometimes *kupe-ta*, gun, for get meat. *Hopu-inu*—my mother—gather foods. No want war my village," she said, willing him to understand. Seeking to ease his trouble.

His eyes softened as she spoke, and her heart felt warm as a bearskin in the sun. She heard his breath steady. He shifted toward her and settled his weight alongside her. When his arm gathered her shoulders, Dark Eyes offered him a smile. "We make good heart one another," she said, but puzzled over what else in his remembering would bring ice to his eyes.

Chapter Twenty-Six

Riding the Storm

Sara glanced up at the tall trees. So unlike the desert scrub brush of home, they formed a lofty canopy, green and leafy, feathery limbs dancing against the sky in a constant light breeze. Sunlight scattered through a collection of clouds, piercing pines and cottonwoods, dropping spots of gold on the track. Squirrels chattered, skittering along branches. Warbles of unfamiliar birds sang in her ears. The fragrance and sounds of this forest were a welcome diversion from her constant concern about Matthew. Overhead, clouds shifted, and shifted again.

Lord, she was tired of sitting, buttocks pressed against hard leather, knees bent and legs molded along Cherry's sides. She and Marco had been riding since sun-up. Here and there the track widened, allowing them to ride side by side, although they barely spoke. Sara squirmed in her saddle, attempting to stretch her legs and her back. It was surely past midday.

Her belly made unseemly noises. Time for lunch. Thank goodness that strange old man let us take water and some hard biscuit from his larder. He was a queer old codger, and that's the truth, she mused. She guided Cherry around two large rocks and slid both feet from the prison of their stirrups, allowing them to dangle. A sigh of pleasure strummed through her as the tension in her ankles released.

Memories of Jonas' scruffy looks and raspy voice came to her. She longed for a pencil nub. I wish I'd thought to pack a writing tablet. I have tales to tell. I'll write a good bit for Pa's "gazette" about my experiences along the trail. Then, perhaps he won't be so furious if he does catch up with us. She rubbed the reins between her thumb and forefinger, feeling the comfort of well-oiled leather. When we reach Yuma, supplies ought be available. Frowning she slid her feet solidly back into her stirrups, wondering if they'd have such.

Something unseen rustled in the thickets around them. Cherry's neck stiffened, her nostrils widened and ears shot forward. Sara felt the mare's concern in her fingertips. The leather reins relayed the message as surely as telegraph wires. Tension built in the muscled body beneath her. Instantly mindful, Sara swung her head left and right, peering into the heavily wooded areas that lined both sides of the trail.

Above, a line of heavy, black clouds appeared. Probing breezes skidded around tree trunks and through branches, skimming her arms, causing them to prickle with chill. "Easy girl," she whispered. "It's just the wind."

Fallen logs thick with crawling things lay against standing trees; their trunks obscured by tangles of vines that crept up and up, in an endless search for sun. This was unfamiliar territory. Sara suddenly yearned for a patch of pure desert sunlight to warm her skin. "How much farther, Marco," she called, wanting to share her thoughts. Wanting to feel safe. Maybe it was time to seek shelter.

Wind gusts picked up in sudden fury, swallowing her question. Anxiety sat in the saddle with her now. Leaves and small branches dropped like rocks and scattered on the trail. Both horses snorted and shied, their ears at attention again, alert to danger. In seconds, the sky showed dark and ominous through gaps in the leafy canopy. Around them the forest came alive, creaking and swaying in response. The tang of decaying vegetation and moist air filled her nostrils.

She watched Marco move ahead. His rifle rested across his saddle. "Ahh, Dios," she heard him shout, his head moving from side to side. Probably watching for rattlers in their path, Javelinas crashing out of the trees, and men—the most dangerous of all.

Thunder rumbled, sounding like iron-rimmed wagon wheels rolling over wooden bridge planks.

"Marco," Sara yelled, as the first raindrops splattered her face.

Cherry jigged, feet dancing, hooves beating an uneven tattoo on the ground. Her tail swished back and forth signaling displeasure. The stiff-necked stance of Marco's bay, ears now flattened back against its head, was not good news. Sara frowned. Her lower lip caught between her teeth, she walked the mare forward. Her hands held her agitated mount easy on the bit, as they approached Valiente. If they were lucky, the horses, reassured by close proximity to one another, would simply move on with little upset. She wasn't encouraged.

She saw Marco secure his rifle. He plainly felt the tension palpable in the bay's body. He closed his legs around Valiente's sides when the first crack of lighting grazed the treetops. As the animal reared, eyes rolling white with terror, he tipped the bay's head down and urged him forward.

Sara pulled Cherry around, forcing the frightened mare away from Valiente's panic and into a tight circle so she couldn't run. Sitting deep in the saddle, she watched Marco's horse come down hard on the track and bolt forward as the next clap of thunder released a jagged streak of yellow light. It came to ground nearby, sparking a tree branch that exploded in a shower of glowing cinders. Valiente, crazed with fear, ignored Marco's attempts to calm him, and fled as though the devil himself was chasing them.

"Oh, Lord love a duck," she shouted and jammed her dripping hat down on her head. This was a wreck about to happen. She wheeled Cherry into position and kicked her into a lope, then a gallop. Pressing hard into the stirrups, she bent forward over her mare's neck. Horse and rider flew after the runaway pair. Coming alongside the racing animal, Sara and Cherry paced him stride for stride. The beast slowed to a lathering run. Sara glanced at Marco. "Yank those reins hard," she screamed, hoping he'd hear her over the ruckus of wind, rain and pounding hooves. "Now! Do it!" Her breath came in short huffs.

Still moving Cherry at a run beside the frightened horse, Sara leaned in and slid her fingers under Valiente's wet bridle. She curled them tight around the soggy leather, foamed with sweat. Sitting deep, feet pressed into the stirrups, toes up, heels down, legs in front of the cinch, she tilted her hips forward and pushed back into the cantle. Cherry obeyed without hesitation. The mare shifted her weight and brought her hindquarters beneath her. Her broad croup sank low. Legs steady, she slid ten feet along the wet, sandy road to a perfect standstill. In answer to Sara's silent prayers, stinging fingers clamped on Valiente's headstall and Cherry's sliding stop combined to bring the runaway to a jolting halt.

Marco, reins still clenched in both hands shot straight up out of his saddle and unceremoniously smacked down into it. Sara heard the thwack of seat against leather and knew he'd be sore by morning.

Her arm muscles burned from the effort of hanging on to both horses. Wet, blonde curls lay in disarray over her shoulders. Her hat hung dripping against her back. Breaths came in jagged gulps as Sara slowly urged Cherry into a walk. She kept hold of the bay's face. When they made several quiet steps together, she rewarded both horses with words of encouragement. " G' boy, G' girl. Good babies," she crooned in her sweetest, lowest tones. Her "Whoa," brought them to a easy stop.

At last, Valiente stood still, thanks be. "You've exhausted both of us," she chided and drew a deep breath. Heaving ribs, flared nostrils, and flecks of sweaty foam on the bay's face told the tale. Overhead the heavens were strangely silent, although a cold rain continued to fall.

Next to her, Marco, soaked through, mopped his face with a wet bandana, his humiliation obvious. "Mother Mary," Sara whispered, her face turned upward into the deluge. "Give me strength." Unsure of what else to say, she waited for Marco to speak.

His brown eyes turned on her. "*Este es malo*," he shouted, red-faced with exertion, embarrassment, and anger. "*Mi palabras, marcar, Sarita.* Heed my words." He lobbed the soggy bandana in her direction. "If I am unable to handle my own horse, we must return. *Immediamente!* We are no longer *niños.* This is a dangerous game."

Sara, not unused to her friend's temper, shrugged and ignored his embarrassment. "You know I will go on without you, *amigo*. Instead of hating me, you should be grateful I was able to stop that silly horse of yours. You've done the same for me once or twice. No?" Forcing a smile, she teased. "Perhaps you prefer to be tossed in the mud?" She watched his sparking eyes settle some. "We are waterlogged, *compadre*. Can we find some sort of shelter?" It was her peace offering. He'd make the decision, and reclaim his pride.

"*Si,*" he muttered. Glaring at her, he lifted his reins. "*Es possiblé no hay shelter. Pero es muy importante* to speak of this journey … and we will speak of it."

She gritted her teeth and fixed her eyes on Marco. "I need to visit the necessary," she said, deciding to heed the demand of her full bladder, rather than squabble in the drizzle.

"Do what you must," he bit out and politely looked away.

Dismounting, Sara walked Cherry toward a thicket of brush and bramble and wrapped her reins around a sturdy bush. Muddy water streamed over her boots and wet pine needles sank underfoot at every step. "Lord, this weather is ugly as a mud fence," she grumbled, and yanked at her sodden leather skirts as she searched for cover.

Her needs answered, Sara stood amidst a circle of tree trunks and fumbled with the rawhide strings of her riding leathers. "I wish I'd had Lena affix buttons," she murmured, as she threaded each opening and pulled the closures tight.

After several long moments, she emerged, wet hat thumping soggy against her back.

Droplets had turned to a new downpour carrying leaves and bits of twigs into her hair. Bending, she shook her head and attempted to pluck the assortment of vegetation from her wet curls. Her rain-slick fingers yanked at equally wet pine needles to no effect. A comb would be pleasing, she allowed. Finally, exasperated, she straightened and began her slog toward a nickering Cherry. In the distance, Sara heard iron wagon wheels rumbling in the heavens once again.

Chapter Twenty-Seven

Forced Surrender

Two men rode single file through a forest of fir and aspen. One rider lean, clean-shaven, and young; the other older, his face etched by concerns, his hair and mustache the color of ashes.

"Yuma's coming up ahead, boss." Gage Evans slung the words over his shoulder at Will Coulton. "Best we get on the main track. Heck, if we don't, we may miss 'em."

Evans pulled his well worn Stetson off and swatted it against his thigh. "Damn trail dust three days runnin' sure does wear on a man," he groused. He raked fingers through his thick hair. Repositioning his favorite hat on his sweat-damp, dark-blond mane, he pushed it low on his grimy brow.

A few yards back, Coulton reined in his mount. "Wait up, son," he ordered. Yanking a bandana from around his neck, he mopped beads of sweat off his brow and glanced upward. "Looks to me like we've got weather coming on," he growled.

Swearing, Evans turned his eyes toward a darkening sky. "Yep. Let's cut over first chance we get."

"I sure as hell hope this plan of yours works," Coulton bristled, riding in beside his lanky ranch foreman. He pulled at his mustache, jaw muscles clenched, eyes grim. "Where are those kids?"

Gage, unaccustomed to seeing his employer quite so riled up, tried to reassure him. "We'll find em' Mister Coulton. I can track anything. Folks are the easiest."

Moving forward single file again, the men turned their horses off the deer trail and aimed at a right angle through the trees. They picked their way around feathery branches of mature evergreens, fragrant with pine resin, and saplings, showing tender green in the sullen light.

Overhead, treetops shifted, bowing to the pressure of mountain wind and sudden clouds heavy with rain. Branches sifted a cloudburst, sending a spit of drizzle into the forest. Gage Evans grinned and turned his face upward to the falling droplets. "Next best thing to a bath," he told his horse, as the heavens opened and the onslaught began in earnest. "Best we keep goin' boss," he said, turning in his saddle to check on the older man. Coulton nodded.

Always alert for trail dangers, hunting opportunities, and today, the sound of riders, Evans' keen tracker's ears snatched at discordant notes in the symphony of forest sounds, chaotic and restless with the storm. Something flagged his attention— wet footfalls, not likely made by bird nor beast. Head tilted, he reined in the big grey and lifted his hand, signaling Will to do likewise. Yep, there it was again; the slap of booted feet stomping atop deep layers of rain-soaked pine needles.

Silent as a panther, Gage swung out of his saddle, and motioned at Will Coulton to come up and take hold of Thunder's reins. "Stay here," he mouthed. His eyes, arrow sharp, hunted through a tangle of trees and moisture laden vegetation, intent on seeing the one small thing that didn't fit.

"Well, I'll be," he muttered under his breath. His focus narrowed. "She looks like a drowned cat." Silent, and still as a statue, he watched her tugging at her hair, trying to dislodge the fistful of pine needles ensnared in her wet curls.

"Dagnabit!" Sara shouted into the wind, her words tossed away by the gusts.

Amusement and annoyance flashed quick as lightning across Gage's face. She's a hellion, a pretty one—but a hellion all the same, he thought. Traveling with her had to be a torment. Even soaked through and through, standing in a downpour, she was fighting with her hair. He liked watching the argument, but the rain was coming harder now, and he had a job to do. She'd not see or hear him until he was right on her.

Though her face was turned away from him, Gage knew it was rosy with exasperation. He'd bet his life on it. Cautiously, he slipped closer. A horse whinnied nearby—its cry piercing the deluge. The set of her head told him she'd heard it too.

As he expected, she gave up the battle with her tresses and spun toward the sound. She'd gained only a few steps before Gage strode from behind a tree and directly into her path. A startled shriek escaped her lips as she jumped backward and sat down hard in a puddle.

He moved deliberately. Keeping his eyes neutral, he wrapped a hand around her arm and pulled her upright.

"Let go of me," Sara snarled, drenched to the bone and shivering.

"I believe your pa wants a word with you," Gage said. He tightened his grip. Despite her struggles he turned and dragged her through the trees.

Will Coulton unclenched his jaw and raised his eyes toward Heaven. "Thanks be," he declared as he glimpsed his foreman striding through the forest, pulling a bedraggled, flailing, angry Sara along with him. Bless it, she seemed well enough—and mad as a jo-fired hornet. The girl had some perk in her! He straightened his complaining back. She'd not make this easy.

His lips tightened. He didn't look forward to confrontations with his strong-minded daughter, but the issue of Matthew's disappearance had to be addressed. Telling her his long-kept secret would be painful, but that, too, had to be done. He'd given Lena his word. It was the clean thing to do. All of a sudden, he was deep weary, as if every one of his years laid like sacks of feed grain heaped on his shoulders. Drawing a quick breath, he sat, reins loose in his hands, and watched them approach. He shook his head, thinking it best to head on to Yuma, get some good grub, dry out and clean up. Tomorrow, he'd put things to right.

Gage yanked Sara into the small clearing. There was a measure of menace in Coulton's look. He could feel the girl quiver under her father's stern scrutiny.

"Pa," she sputtered, and lifted her head to gaze up into blue eyes so like her own—now fixed upon her, narrowed and icy. She looked like she wanted to howl. Instead, she gritted her teeth and turned her wrath on her captor. "Take your hands off me," she shouted, and twisted out of Gage's grasp.

Breathing hard, Sara swung back to her father. "I'm sorry, Pa, but I did the right thing. Sorry I worried you." Her shoulders slumped in apology.

Gage, however, still saw the devil sparking in her eyes. He wondered if his boss saw it, too. Best move before this little she-cat makes any more trouble, he thought, and stepped around Sara.

"Beg pardon, Mister Coulton. This sposh and squall—it won't quit any time soon, and we are all wet to the skin. We should be heading out, sir. Marco has to be waiting nearby."

In answer, Coulton gathered his reins and handed the big grey back to his foreman. "You two ride double. And don't give me any sass, daughter," he warned, his voice hard. "Just do it. We're for Fort Yuma. My map shows it not far. We'll pick up Marco and Cherry on the way. I expect you'll be sure of where your pony waits, girl. Let's get going."

Evans legged into his saddle, leaned over and extended a hand to Sara, a determined set to his mouth. She favored him with a flinty look, but allowed him to hoist her onto Thunder's back. He turned toward her with mischief in his eyes.

"Hang on," he ordered.

"I am familiar with the finer details of riding horseback," she snapped. "I have no need of your instruction, Mister Evans."

Truth of it was, she had no choice but to throw her arms around him and do just as he said.

Chapter Twenty-Eight

Fort Yuma

Four damp, trail-dirty riders moved with purpose through the tented premises of B. Handley's Mercantile. They gathered up clothing: shirts, newfangled blue canvas pants, thick socks, unmentionables, and other wearable necessities. A coffee pot, grounds, biscuit flour, beef jerky, rifle and pistol ammunition, and a small number of personal extravagances were also required by his new customers, including a supply of pencils and three writing tablets.

Will Coulton glared at Marco and Sara, his anger with both of them still raw. He turned and stepped up to the counter, plunking an armful of provisions down. The huffing proprietor, Buck Handley, followed close on his heels and deposited a second pile of provender atop the first, then hitched his pudgy body under the wooden planking that separated customers from his shelves of potions and ointments. Checking through the items with practiced fingers, he calculated the amount owed with several quick scratches of his grease pencil. "That'll be one-hun'erd-three, mister," he decreed.

Coulton counted out the bills and handed over the requested payment. Shopping completed, he shepherded the scowling travelers back into the dusty Arizona sunshine. Arms filled with packages, the four marched single file along the Yuma sidewalk toward Estelle's Rooming House.

Sara kept her eyes downcast. The last thing she wanted to see was Gage Evans' broad back. It was the height of humiliation to have had to ride for several miserable hours with her arms flung about him. And, of course, as luck would have it, he was leading this parade and she was stuck walking right behind him. He is so arrogant, she fumed, and set her feet down hard with every step. Her plans were a mess. Everything was going to blazes.

Behind her she heard Marco dragging his feet. He'd hardly smiled all morning. She knew he'd been woefully contemplating his disgrace. He'd been a misery to behold from the moment her father had ridden up and demanded he follow them to Yuma. Sara gripped her purchases tighter. I can't worry about Marco now. I have to find Matthew.

Could it get any worse, she wondered, as she climbed the rickety staircase to the bedroom she shared with an old biddy not even of her acquaintance ... and at a rooming house. Imagine. The only hotel in Yuma had turned them away—all the accomodations being taken. Disgusted, Sara toed the door open and dropped her bounty on the one bedstead. At least Pa and Marco had one another for company. They had only to share with Gage Evans, who was no stranger to them.

It was a comfort to see that the bath she'd requested had been set just inside. Wishing no interruptions, she shoved and tugged until the sloshing tub rested almost against the door. I best get on with it if I expect to bathe in private. Brushing curls from her forehead, she wriggled from her muddy shirtwaist, stepped out of her damp leather riding skirt and yanked off her boots, underthings and stockings. "I hope they make Mister Evans sleep on the floor," she sniffed, and stepped into the oversize tin bucket that served as bathtub for Estelle's guests.

The miserly allotment of water was tepid, not comfortably warm against her skin, but it was clear of muck and floating scum. Her flesh went to goosey-bumps as she sank down, forced to pull her knees nearly to her chin. Determined to enjoy her few privileged moments of solitude and clean bathwater, Sara picked up the small chunk of lye soap provided and washed mud splatters and grime from her hair and body.

Her toilet completed, she stood up and swept water away from her person. Then stepping from the tub, patted herself dry with threadbare squares of bleached white muslin provided by Estelle. She put on her new pantaloons and camisole, glad to be girlish enough to forego a corset. She chose a soft, cream-colored shirtwaist, fastened the tiny, blue buttons, and tucked the ends into a brown skirt that skimmed the tops of her new boots.

Standing in front of the large, cheap-made, tin looking glass, Sara ran a comb through her wet curls and pulled them off her face with a buttermilk-hued ribbon she'd selected at Handley's. "I'd better hurry," she said to the distorted image that stared back. Father was waiting to speak with her. She expected a tongue lashing for her disobedience. Certainly, there'd be a fight over her search for Matthew. Most likely he will try to force my return home. Good Lord, the entire situation was so horrible it set her teeth on edge. Scowling, she turned on her heel. Defiance stirred in her heart.

As Sara made her way down the short corridor toward her father's room she heard the thud of strident footsteps. She knew her father's habits. He paced when he was particularly disturbed. It had always been so. She paused. It sounded as though he was speaking to someone. Rather than knock, she gently turned the porcelain doorknob and pushed.

"Father?" she said, slipping into the room.

Will Coulton whirled to face her looking like he'd been caught in a trap. He strode the length of the room, steps measured as a metronome on the worn piece of carpet beneath his feet.

"Afternoon, daughter," he said fixing her with a nervous glance. He grasped her by the elbow and deposited her on one of the two chairs the room provided. Surprised when he didn't pull up the other, she watched him resume his pacing, his boots beat a tattoo, filling the silence.

"Pa, what is it you wished to speak of with me?" she finally asked, confused by the wretched look on his face.

He stopped and stared at her, unease in his eyes. "I know you are upset with me, and I am none too pleased by your treacherous disobeying of my wishes," he began. "Make no mistake, I shall have that out with you. However, I have another matter of which I am bound to speak." Will sank onto the edge of the room's one bedstead.

A terrible struggle showed plain on his features. Concerned, she watched him put his face into his hands. "What is it Pa? Are you ill?"

He lifted his head. "No, not ill. I am unsettled with the need to tell you of … this other matter. My news will be a shock of a different stripe." He paused. "I know of no easy way to say my piece, daughter, yet it must be said, and I will be square with you. It's past time you knew."

With a start, Sara realized the muttering she'd heard when she first opened the door may have been a rehearsal of the conversation he planned to have with her. What could be so upsetting, she wondered, and swallowed the lump of apprehension lodged in her throat. Then she heard four words that would change the constancy of her life.

"Marco is my son," he said, eyes brimming.

Her breath came short. Her father's words seemed to ricochet inside her. It seemed she could not grab the reins and bring them to stillness. Her pulse ticked in her throat like a clock measuring the undoing of her reality, second by second. Her life had been a lie. And Marco's as well. She was glad to be seated, for she felt faint.

Her father regarded her for several anxious moments.

At last, she stood and stepped toward him, all thoughts of Matthew overridden by his astounding announcement. "Why did you never tell me?" she demanded, gripping his hands in her own. Her words tumbled out and fell like sharp rocks. "How can this be? Why did you keep it a secret? You must speak of it all. Now."

"It … it happened soon after your blessed mama's passing. I could not come to reason. My heart was tortured. I wished to follow her. It was Lena helped bring me from despair so I might raise you, for you were but a sweet infant and deserved a loving father."

"Lena?" Tears leapt unbidden into Sara's eyes. "Pa, Lena is special to me, as is Marco. They have always been as family. All these years you kept the truth from me. I needlessly longed for kin of my very own." A hollow pain tangled in her belly.

"I know, and I am heartfelt sorry, child. Lena never wished to hold it a secret. She was wiser than I, and metes no blame. I'm aiming to set things right with you young 'uns today."

Sara swiped at her eyes. "Have you told Marco?"

"No. Not yet. We were … are … not bound by marriage contract. Although Marco is your half-brother, he will not be recognized as a Coulton," Will responded, voice gruff, the pain of his admission exposed in the sag of his shoulders and despair that twisted his mouth.

Sorrow hummed in her—for her father, for Marco and Lena, for herself. She simply could not sort it out. Sara glared at her father. Anger tinged the words she flung at him.

"Pa, why did you not take Lena to wife? What were you thinking to deceive us like this? To cheat Lena of her rightful place and Marco of his standing in life!"

"I did what I thought best to protect all of us, Sara. To honor the memory of your mother ... to protect Lena. To protect you youngsters," he said, sadness and defiance in his tone.

"What you did was a betrayal." Her voice rose. "You must do the correct thing! You have surely shocked me. My life is not as I believed it to be. I am glad to find a true brother in Marco. He has always been my best, my first, my oldest friend. Pa, he is your son. He must carry your name. Lena has been mother to both of us all my life. Lord, she is the only mother I've ever known. You've wronged us. This is shameful. Perhaps you wished most to protect yourself," she spat, narrowing her eyes. "Can you not see it?"

He looked at the floor. "I am sorry, Sara. I know my deceit is causing misery. I never intended harm. Can you find the heart to forgive me?"

"Pa, in truth, I cannot until you straighten out this mess."

"I plan to speak with Marco today," Will said. "Lena and I are concerned with his knowing the truth. He has always adored you, Sara. These feelings can become complicated. He is near a grown man." His eyebrows lifted in question. "Have I made it clear? We feared a peck o' trouble brewing between you two, taking off together like you did."

Their eyes locked in unspoken understanding, spinning her thoughts to Marco's recent odd behaviors. She cringed at the thought of what might have happened.

"He has been moody, and I have been some uncomfortable in his company during our trip, but you have naught to fear. I ignored his peculiar aspects," she snapped. "Your selfishness will cause him heartbreak. He will be mortified, humiliated, though his sinning t'was only in thought. You must find a way to give him your name."

Sighing, Will nodded and pinched the bridge of his nose. "God A' Mighty, I am fagged out, purely exhausted."

Sara understood his anxiety. Their conversation, afire with emotion, took the starch out of him. She saw it in the small things: the way his eye caught the single, white curtain's every flutter, as it rippled in the sun-soaked breeze. His jaw twitched. He was jumpy as a cat, his face haggard and nearly as bleached as the curtain.

He glanced at his pocket watch. His shoulders slumped. "Noon and then some. Marco will be waiting for me in the downstairs parlour," Coulton stood, his features drawn in an unhappy frown.

"Best go then." She stepped back and gazed at her father, saddened. She'd pray that Marco move past this. The world had spun on its axis and some things would always be different. But she was strong. Why, I feel the elder here, she realized, astonished. Her next words seemed to leap from her mouth on their own, like trout from a stream.

"Well, Pa, I am still your daughter and I care for you deeply, but I am well nigh a grown woman and I know what needs to be done. You take care of your missteps. Right them!" she added, her blue eyes boring into his. "I will find Matthew."

Will Coulton returned his daughter's stubborn stare. "Sara," he said, warning in his voice.

She pressed her advantage. The matter of Matthew needed settling, and soon. She lifted her chin. There would be no turning back from this day, and both of them knew it. "No Pa. Put your own house in order. I have to tend Cherry. I'll see you at supper." Spinning on her heel, she strode to the door. She hoped Handley's Mercantile would be open for business this afternoon. There was something she needed.

Chapter Twenty-Nine

Shifting Plans

Will, Marco, Sara, and Gage gathered to share their evening meal at Yuma's only hotel, the very establishment that had refused them lodging when first they'd arrived in town. This eventide, they were seated in the large dining room, at a table of generous proportions. Cloth napkins gleamed white against its polished wood surface. Sara surveyed the area. It was empty save for a dandified fellow and his female companion.

She'd been plenty disappointed when Pa had been unable to secure rooms. "We're plumb filled t' bursting," the clerk had said, pointing to the register. "We got a couple immigrant folk makin' thar way fer Californy ta' farm the land, but most is gold diggers."

It seemed a good number of the guests had foregone the evening meal, and instead repaired early to the town's numerous establishments of drink, gambling, and the charms of soiled doves. Even now, at the supper hour, the entire street was lit up and raucous. Gunshots and drunken shouting mingled with the plink of tinny pianos. Horses screamed, and the thunder of numerous riders swelled and faded.

Perhaps it was for the best that the hotel failed to give their party purchase. She could hardly picture what sort of carrying on would beset the place when the lodgers staggered in, befuddled, tick full of blackstrap and barleycorn. Meantime, she intended to enjoy her meal if she could. This was not a slap-bang eatery. After all, it was the finest Yuma had to offer.

Sara glanced around the table at her supper companions. She'd seen Marco ride out with their father in the afternoon, and wondered what had passed between them. Tonight he seemed pale under his dusky skin, as if he'd been ill. His eyes though, told a different story. They held a mixture of pride and anger. Mostly he refused to look at her. Embarrassed, she guessed, recalling Pa's concerns about the direction of their childhood friendship.

Her father, his blue eyes flat serious, had placed himself between Marco and that Evans man. Pa certainly had no trouble returning her stare. Frowning, she snapped her attention toward the ranch foreman.

Gage sat, rocked back in his chair, broad shoulders and muscular arms encased in a clean, white broadcloth shirt. Long legs, and toes of his boots flat on the floor kept his fixture from tumbling over, she noted. Abashed at her unseemly interest in his seating arrangements, she turned her eyes to the nearest window and straightened her shoulders. *Mother Mary, he looks as if he's no care in the world!*

Sara toyed with her silverware, turning the eating irons this way and that. Then, appalled at her breach of manners, she grabbed her napkin and pulled her hands into her lap. The man gave her nervous fits. She was sure he had followed her every movement with those green eyes of his, although they appeared half closed. She stole a look. Yes. He had seen her fidgeting. She was certain of it when his gaze boldly traveled up to her face and returned her glance with a lazy smile. His hair, relieved of its trail dust, showed gold in the dining room light. Uninvited warmth pinked her cheeks. *Why am I even taking notice of this … this bushwhacker.* It was past time to return her attentions to the important matters at hand.

She breathed a sigh of relief when the waiter approached. Her father, as she knew he would, took charge of the menu selections. He requested soup, chicken pies, and sweet tea for all of them. Meals ordered, he dismissed the server and settled his eyes on those gathered around the table. Gage brought his chair upright.

Her father's silent appraisal of his dinner companions seemed to go on forever.

"I'm peckish, fair pinched with hunger," Sara said, hoping to divert him. There was no response. Tension became palpable. Frightened of what might ensue, ready to stand her ground and fight, she waited in the stillness. Hackles bristling, she vowed to run if need be. *Matthew must be found.* She could hear Marco and Evans' measured breaths. They were on alert now, seats pulled close in to the table's edge.

Finally, Will Coulton spoke, his voice cold as a nighttime blow of desert wind. "We've got some dust to settle here." He laid his hands on the polished wood slab, palms down. He looked at Sara, then Marco. "I've been sorely provoked, chasing you two up and down mountain sides and worrying for your safety this last while. And I've made some decisions that you *will* abide by."

She stared into her lap. She could feel the slats of the chair-back pressing uncomfortably against her spine.

"Mister Evans has proved himself to be a fine and trustworthy man. You will either continue on with his assistance and protection, Sara, or we will return home, and this foolishness of yours will be done with. I can surely use your help getting the paper out, and you know it."

With a guilty start, she realized that he'd left the newspaper with no one at the helm, and the ranch without a foreman. "P … Pa," she stammered, thinking to express regret. Then unable to find any words, she simply clamped her jaw shut, and tried to imagine what journeying on with that intolerable Evans person might be like. It was unthinkable.

"If you wish to persist in this infernal search, I'll require you write some words of new places and scenes you come upon, for publication. Is that understood? And I'll have you home within six months—Matthew found or not." His palm smacked the wood surface for emphasis. "Those are my terms, daughter. I'll expect your answer before we leave the supper table tonight."

He shot a glance at his foreman. "I'll be wanting a few choice words with you, son. We'll set a while after this get together winds down. I'm putting a mighty big responsibility on your back."

Sara stole a quick peek at Gage. He didn't look happy about the prospect of traveling with her either. But giving up was not an option. Not when she knew Matthew was just ahead.

"In any case," her father announced, "Marco will return home with me. His mother expects him, and I have need of his help at the ranch." His eyes were unyielding. Blue marbles. He ran a hand through his silvering hair, smoothed his mustache with long fingers. Falling silent, he busied himself with unfolding his table napkin and tucking it into his shirtfront. Sara knew he had much to consider and a fair amount to contend with at home.

She glanced across the table at Marco. Her brother fingered his eating utensils, head bowed, eyes hidden. Sara saw the stiff set of his shoulders. He must be confounded by the news just as she was. She embraced having a true brother.

She loved him. In time, she knew he'd accept her as his blood sister and forever best friend. Although the truth shocked and saddened her, it was also a blessed gift they'd been given. Returning home with their father would be a good thing for Marco; they had plenty to hash out. What plans does Pa have for him, she wondered.

By the time the waiter set steaming bowls of soup before them, she had agreed to her father's terms. The rest of the evening meal was devoted to discussing preparations. Plans were laid to purchase a pack mule and more supplies, and at Pa's insistence, have a meet-up with the sheriff.

"Meantimes, let us hear what you know of this Matthew business," her father urged.

Sara shared the discovery of Matthew's pocket watch. Marco described what they knew of the Indian, the stolen black horse, the tracks he'd seen, and his certainty of two riders, then several.

The ranch foreman spoke of trail routes that might take them into California. Sara concentrated on devouring her chicken pie and listened to the wrangling going on around her. She didn't care to invite conversation with Mister Evans.

Later that evening, Sara tiptoed to the big boardinghouse bedstead and climbed in without making a sound. She surely did not wish to disturb Mother Twombly, already asleep and snoring.

Gingerly, she pulled at the shared down comforter to free what small scrap of covering she could, and wiggled beneath its folds, careful to keep to her side of the mattress.

She closed her eyes. It had been a long day. Tomorrow, Marco and their father would be heading home before the sun was straight up. Then it would be just her and that Evans person moving ahead. Pa had fixed *her* flint. Worries about dealing with the foreman tempered the excitement she felt. Lord, she'd be forced to make parlor talk and put up with his cocky attitude. At least her afternoon trip to the Mercantile had been fruitful. She'd be wearing those odd-looking riding trousers soon enough. Knowing sunrise would make the start of a busy time, she turned onto her back and drifted into an uneasy sleep.

Chapter Thirty

Reluctant Partners

Sara could scarce believe she was out in the borderland wilds with Gage Evans her only companion and protector. But it was true, and she'd brought it on herself.

She snuck a glance at the lean silhouette that rode alongside her. He sat comfortably astride Thunder, the big grey stallion that was Matthew's pride and joy. His hat, brim angled and set low, hid his eyes. He looked mysterious, she thought. At least he was a skilled horseman. She'd give him that.

Sara deliberately ignored his long legs resting casually against Thunder's sides, his booted feet fixed solid in the stirrups. She was curious about the fancy, silver spurs he favored, though she'd not seen him put them to serious use. "Lord love a duck," she muttered into the breeze. "I wonder what will come of this journey, as I can barely imagine having a civil conversation with the man." She set her jaw. "Danged if I'll be asking him about his outfit anytime soon."

Behind him, the sturdy little pack mule, Murphy, plodded steadily on. Merely recalling the manner in which her traveling companion addressed her concerns regarding the poor mule was aggravating. He'd scoffed at her worries about the poundage the modest-sized beast carried. And he'd rolled those green eyes of his and chuckled when she settled a name on the coarse-coated creature. She had done her best to disregard the man. As for the trousers she wore, he'd simply quirked an eyebrow and offered an amused grin. Thanks be, he'd made no comment.

The entire morning had been an ordeal. The mood somber. Just thinking of her farewells to Pa and Marco had her teary-eyed and wishing she had headed home with them. Nettled, Sara dug her heels into Cherry's sides, lifted her reins and trotted out in front of the foreman. Never mind all that. No sense feeling sorry for herself. She had a job to do. She hoped her quarrelsome cohort hadn't noticed her upset.

While she rode, she reviewed everything the sheriff told them early that morning. The meeting in his squalid jailhouse had been helpful, but the man, repulsive. He was a shifty sort with a stubborn set to his jaw. The sneer in his voice had grown quite pronounced as he recounted the villainous treatment he and his deputy encountered, "bare-a-week past, at the hands of the damn savage and her horse-thievin' squawman," as he referred to the pair.

"Them creatures made it across the Rio," he'd snarled, slamming a beefy fist into the papers that cluttered his desk. "Nearly killed us. Him an' his injun friends."

"Pa? Don't you see? It's got to be Matthew," she'd said, excitation galvanizing her. "They're right ahead of us!"

"Girly, them painted-up braves that run the river ain't 'bout to let you folks cross it," the lawman said. He spat tobacco chaw onto the dirt floor, opened the door and showed them out. "We got the Army comin' in spring. They'll stop 'em," he bellowed at their backs.

She pure hated those men.

Mister Evans had shown no fear, she conceded. On the contrary, he'd raised his eyebrows and stared at the man with contempt. In fact, after they were out of earshot, he'd allowed as how he "might have given the sheriff a similar haul down, the man being a lout and all."

"Keep an eye out for the river." Gage's voice startled her from her musings. "Should be up ahead soon enough," he called. His command was irritating as sand blown into her eyes.

"Don't tell me what to do," she huffed, hurling the words out like rocks.

They rode on in ornery silence, single file, until Gage moved off to the right. He tapped his horse into a trot with the end of his reins. "Let's go north a-ways."

Indeed, Sara soon heard the rush of water, smelled it on the breeze, too. Seemed he knew what he was doing. She pushed Cherry ahead to catch up and worried about Murphy, who was gamely working his shorter legs to keep pace with Thunder. Before long they pulled to stop on a flat strip of golden sand and gazed at the clear, calm water flowing beyond it.

"This is a perfect place to cross. California is just the other side," he said, and urged Thunder forward.

She eyed the expanse. The current seemed fair mild. She didn't see any savages either. So much for the Sheriff and his ill-spoken predictions. Loosing her reins, she guided Cherry into the river. Moving deeper, wet to the knees, she stepped nearly neck and neck with Thunder, hoping the mule was a strong swimmer. The faint scent of rotten egg prickled her nose. She glanced upward. How odd. The very sky looked yellow-like all of a sudden. "Mister Evans," she shouted, and pointed toward the heavens. He looked up just as the rumbling began.

The river roiled like a kettle of muddy water at the boil. Both horses bolted, frantic, struggling to escape the commotion, their eyes white with terror. Sara leaned in, wrapped her arms around Cherry's neck, and clung like a burr in a sheepskin coat. Beside her, Gage Evans directed his attention straight ahead, his dismay and astonishment obvious.

"I don't like this," she shrieked, as bits of black rock and ash rained down on them. The smell of sulfur floated strong in the air. Her eyes smarted. She could see a wisp of steam rising from the river's surface. The water soaking her legs felt warm. *Mother Mary, what in heaven was happening?*

Gage's voice cut through the maelstrom. "Earthquake!" he yelled. "Get to land, Sara!

Move that horse. Now!"

He let go of Murphy's lead rope, and she saw the creature strike out for the far shoreline.

Reining in growing panic, she urged Cherry forward. Grateful the mare was willing to follow the little mule toward solid ground, she gave Cherry her head and hung on. Gage urged Thunder through the calamity. She could hear him whistling and yelling, "Git on! Yah! Eyah!" like he was driving cattle or turning a stampede. Staying astride their terrified mounts until the animals gained purchase on the far shore, the two slid from their saddles. Sara was petrified.

"Officially in California," Gage panted. He surveyed their surroundings. The situation remained perilous. Along the horizon, brush fires loomed like a broken line of blazing torches. Acrid smoke fueled by blood-red flames lit the skies. He looked at Sara and realized the fires were the least of it for the moment. She was wan as a ghost beneath the ash that smudged her face, her eyes round and pale as full moons. She stood too still, clinging to her reins with a frozen, white-knuckled grip. He could see the sheen of perspiration on her cheeks although she shivered in the occasional shards of late afternoon sun that poked through the smoke-dark hullabaloo above.

Beneath them, the ground continued to shake in snatches. Behind them the river had calmed. He wrinkled his nose. The air had a new peculiar odor—the tangy, smell of a lightning storm. Thank God, they'd made to shore, mule and all. "I've heard stories about this quakin' business from cowboys who've been to the gold fields, but sure as shootin' they didn't tell about steaming rivers and hellish horizons," he jawed.

Cherry and the stallion skittered and snorted, their eyes still frenzied. The mare, nostrils flared, pulled hard against the reins, and reared, trying to escape the shuddering ground. Sara screamed, ear-rending and shrill.

"Wake up girl, dad blast it!" Gage barked across the several feet that separated them. "Work that horse. Give 'er some slack. This shaking won't last but a bit more," he shouted, hoping it was true as he struggled to keep his footing, calm his horse, and stop the mule from running off with all their supplies. He hoped he was right.

"*Dang it!*" Sara's panic was *not* the most helpful in their situation. Grim, he looped Thunder's rein loosely across a bush, and hooked the mule—who finally stood calm in the midst of the uproar—to a nearby branch. Then, he spun around and stomped toward his frightened charge, covering the ground between them in a few long strides. He wrapped an arm around Sara and collected Cherry's reins. "Talk sense to your horse, by gum!"

She trembled against him, near as fiercely as the earth itself had. He wanted to linger and hold her, give comfort. Instead, he forced her behind him as a smoking shower of black rocks fell to ground inches from where they stood. Sara sank to her knees, sobbing.

He could hear her weeping as he got busy calming the mare. He moved along with Cherry's nervous back-ups, her head flung upward at every step, then asked her to come forward with a light tug on the reins, as he quietly talked a lot of nothing. He breathed a sigh of relief when the horse finally stepped into him, stopped moving her feet, and lowered her head for a moment. "Good girl," he whispered. As he reached up to scratch her forelock, she backed away.

Sara's crying fit had gone to sniffling. Reins in hand, Gage turned. He studied her face. Dash, she was a mess. She looked a guttersnipe—her mug all streaky with tears and dirt, her hair sooty and tangled. But something inside him moved off-kilter. She'd touched him, yet hadn't lifted a finger. This was a different Sara, all her sass and obstinate behavior gone. He wanted to gather her in his arms and soothe the panic that ran wild across her face and leapt in those blue eyes of hers. Instead he ran a hand through his hair, dark with dust and black ash.

"Listen," he murmured, keeping his voice low and steady. "The worst is over. I need you to get yourself under control, woman."

"I c ... can't," she began. A fresh flood of tears spilled down her cheeks, making tracks in the smudges. "It ... it seems the world has c ... come to an end," she sobbed, staring at the infernal red horizon.

"Tarnation, Sara, this horse needs you," Gage spat out. *And damned if I don't need you myself.* He pressed a hand to his forehead. *What am I thinking? Am I losing my mind?* He set his mouth in a hard line. "Listen to me! The ground seems about done shakin' and we best figure a safe way out of this mess. If we're gonna have a chance to outrun the brush fire we've got t' get to higher ground quick as we can." He reached out and grabbed her arm.

Several feet away, the big grey screamed a warning and stamped in terror, sending sand and pebbles flying. Distracted, Gage looked up. The breeze had intensified. The fire was moving fast through the chaparral. No time for comforting.

"Dry those tears and let's get outta' here," he ordered, pushing his bandana into her hands. "I've got to get to Thunder before he bolts and takes that mule and what's left of our supplies with 'em." He knew his tone didn't speak of kindness and wasn't surprised when she pulled her arm out of his grasp, indignant.

Sara clenched a fist around the cloth. She dabbed at her face and blew her nose, cursing the hiccups that had replaced her tears. "What are we going to do?" she wailed.

"Take your horse," he spat and shoved the reins at her, praying for the best.

Cherry laid her ears back and shot Sara a terrified look, the mare's brown orbs, dark as gooseberries.

"It's okay girl," she croaked, trying to calm herself. Fighting fresh tears, she pulled a deep breath and squared her shoulders. She turned toward Gage. "I've got her," she hiccupped.

"Mount up then! We have no time to spare," he said, and strode away, all business, heading for Thunder and the braying mule.

The fiery horizon seemed to race toward them. Flames crackled close, consuming nearby clumps of low brush and mesquite. At a run, Gage leapt into his saddle, slapped the grey stallion on the rear and dug in his heels, hanging on to Murphy's lead rope with an iron grip. "Let's go," he shouted and pulled the grey's nose around to the north, away from the ugly, red-hued smoke that churned like the devil's own thundercloud. Simply breathing was painful. Thunder pranced forward, frantic to be gone from the frightening sounds and smells of the place.

No longer trusting the ground beneath them, both horses stepped short and snappy. Their tails flicked in displeasure with every step. Gage hoped that Sara, busy handling Cherry, would soon feel like herself again. He was determined to keep moving at a brisk pace as he led them away from the end of the world.

The trail steepened and the ascent became more difficult. He pressed his legs into Thunder. Behind him, he knew the mule was forced to a near lope to keep up along the rising track. Sara rode at Murphy's rear. She'd agreed to urge Murphy on. He glanced back to check on them.

"Mister Evans, exactly where are you taking me?" she shouted, wiping at her dirt-covered face with the even dirtier back of her hand.

He smiled as Sara's words reached him. She sounded her unruly self. At least that part of his plan was working. "To where we can breathe," he called over his shoulder.

The first threads of freshening air, cold and clear, washed across his face. Gage drew in a grateful breath. In a short while, he pulled to stop and turned in his saddle. He saw shock in Sara's eyes and wondered if he, too, had the ghastly pallor of a corpse under gritty smears. She'd have a hissy fit if she knew how unseemly she looked, tallow-faced with only mud and dirt to hide it.

"It's best we continue on 'til nightfall. We'll make camp tonight in the mountains," he said, and turned back to the business of riding.

She sighed loudly. "Mister Evans, I am anxious to settle for the evening as soon as possible. I find myself in need of water and food, and the comfort of a warm fire. Besides, poor Murphy needs to rest."

Gage stiffened in annoyance. "Just like you to try and jab a spoke in my wheel," he threw over his shoulder. "We'll move on 'til dusk hits."

"That man can't abide taking instruction from a woman," she protested under her breath.

"Nothin' but prattle," he told himself. Jaw clenched, he knuckled down for a long ride.

Morning dawned clear and chilly. Sara sat as close to the heat as she dared, her clothing yet some moist from that horrid river crossing. At least I am shorn of my petticoats, she thought with satisfaction, or I'd be wet through and through. September was nearly half gone and the small fire scarce offered enough warmth to suit her needs. "I am damp and perishing of the cold," she announced to Gage, who was on the other side of the embers, checking their saddles for water damage.

"We'll be on our way soon enough. I want to be certain the vittles and the rest of our supplies are mostly dry," he said, without even looking her way.

She shuffled her feet and inched them closer to the fire's rim. Her boots were just short of dried. She eyed the notebook she'd purchased back in Yuma. It had been wrapped in oilcloth, along with her limited wardrobe, so it was useable. Picking it up, she flipped it like a flapjack to ensure the pages had no moisture. She planned on penning a letter to her Pa real soon.

"Will we be getting to a town of any size?" she wondered aloud.

Gage turned. "I think it's more likely we'll see some mighty peaks in the coming days. Soon after, we may start dropping into a more civilized situation."

"That's dandy," she said and jumped up. "I am ready to pack my goods and move on."

"I've heard tell there are some astonishing views along this trail." He motioned for her to take her saddle.

Pleased to be doing something other than sitting, she lifted the saddle and got busy readying Cherry for the day's ride, glad to see her mare quiet and soft-eyed.

The afternoon came a bit warmer. Even Murphy and the horses seemed fair delighted with the sunshine and ambled happily in its embrace. Mister Evans' prediction as to the scenery was correct. She had never set sight on grey, stony mountains of such magnitude. They stopped once and dismounted to view the spectacle from a ledge, both struck by a tiny slip of silver threading its way through a valley far below. Are we descending into that?" Sara asked, eyeing the sheer rock walls that held the winding river prisoner.

She practically sang with relief when her appointed guardian flashed that lopsided smile of his, and said they'd be picking their way around the formidable granite summits and save the valley for another time.

"These peaks are ripe for snow," he said lifting his face to the breeze. "We'll look for a track that skirts 'round 'em and move quick."

"Bless me, I pray to be warmer tonight," she said, and swung herself onto Cherry's back, eager to move on.

Fall
1850

Chapter Thirty-One

Into the Valley

Mountain wind blew raw through the high country in late September, a harbinger of deep snows and long, icy nights. Dark Eyes and Greywolf, swathed in bedroll blankets, sat warming by their cook fire as they had many evenings before.

"Speak me now of your people," Dark Eyes said, wanting to know everything about the man she was bringing home to her clan village. In their quiet times she'd seen him stare at nothing, struggling to capture memories, battling Coyote for his stolen past. Tonight she saw pain flash in his eyes. Maybe the Great Spirit had pushed Coyote to release some of Greywolf's first life, and return it to him.

"My father and mother ... were good people," Greywolf said, his gaze focused into the darkness beyond their fire. "I was so young. I couldn't save them from ... from those savages." His voice turned hard. "They took my little sisters. I'll never see them again, either." He bowed his head.

Dark Eyes heard his grief, bitter as gathered acorns before they were pounded down and water-soaked. Each time he spoke of such things it was the same. Coyote had been busy causing sorrow and death in Greywolf's growing up days.

Within her own family she had seen Coyote's mischief. She knew the sadness and anger his tricking could bring. Her heart shared Greywolf's sorrow. She wished to comfort him.

"I tell you story of *Wonomi*, worldmaker of The People," Dark Eyes said. "Longtimes back, *Wonomi* make all things—trees, rocks, animals, and the People—all good. He work hard, make perfect world for live in, make death a place to visit.

"Coyote, his helper, not so good. He destroy some *Wonomi's* fine work. Make mischief, break things, fool people. We call Coyote smooth-tongued. Strong spirit. Sly. He like sound of People cry, so change death to place no can leave. Now Coyote enjoy noise of weeping all times. He make danger, hurt people. He visit my family, take father's small son. No fault me. He visit your family. Bring evil. No fault you."

She watched him and wondered if her words brought his heart from the cave of despair. Would he speak again? Greywolf looked up.

"My ma and pa called me Matthew. My name is Matthew."

His mouth creased up at the corners, showing he welcomed the memories though they were foggy and bittersweet.

Dark Eyes smiled back at him. "Mah Tew," she repeated, delighted to be learning the sound of him. "Mah Tew, how call your sisters?"

His scowl returned. She saw him pull against Coyote's thick smoke that allowed no seeing. Would he win this battle?

"Elizabeth and Rachel," he said after a long pause. "They were beautiful." His voice caught as though speared. "Rachel's hair was soft as cornsilk and bright as the sun, and ... L... Lizzie was a tiny, dark-haired angel."

"Mmmm. You say me more your sisters," she entreated.

"I ... I don't remember much more than that," he said, glancing at her, his eyes sick with torment.

"I like hear your family, you care them," she said softly.

She watched with her heart as Mah Tew stood and gathered his blanket around him. He brought his sturdy frame to sit beside her. "Thank you," he whispered against her hair.

Dark Eyes sighed and leaned into him. "We come my clan village, four suns maybe. Good people happy know you." She lifted a hand and stroked the eagle feather that lay between her breasts. Their eyes met then, the dark and the grey. She felt herself still as Mah Tew gently brushed his lips against hers, leaving a trail of fire that seared her very core. His gaze sought hers again and he brought a hand to her face, his fingertips tracing heat along her jawline in the icy night. She trembled; her breath quickened. Dark Eyes pressed her face against him, helpless to resist her need to touch him and wary of her growing feelings for this man.

"We sleep now," she said, voice uneven, pulling her blanket more tightly around her shoulders. She was ready to lay tight against her companion for extra warmth, and comfort the feel of him always brought. Tonight there was something else. A new need. "I like mouth touching," she murmured, as he stretched out beside her.

"Dark Eyes," he whispered. His look sent heat.

She, in the way of her people, was free to share Mah Tew's sleeping blanket each evening. Three times they made the music of man and woman after the sun had gone to its sleep. He was always gentle and as if with magic, fanned her desire. Under the blankets, she curled toward him and welcomed his wanting with her own need.

Later, as she lay cradled in his arms in the way of *waliki*, he spoke of the future. "Dark Eyes, I wish to marry. To make a life with you. Do your people have this ceremony?" he asked. "Will your father be angry?"

"I like be wife, but father must first give blessing. He want me find husband." They whispered of children. Although she gave no promise, she listened well. His words were powerful. A new happiness tumbled through her. Attachment to the man brought to her by the Spirits was deepening. Her sleep was rich with dreams.

Morning came to the *Tuoluome* meadow, bringing chattering blue jays to ground, and woodpeckers busy in the trees. Her companion stretched and groaned. Dark Eyes studied his waking and could see he felt the ache, night-cold ground left in his bones. He climbed out of his bedroll and came to stand beside her at the edge of their camp place.

"It's mighty cold for such a clear morning," he said, and searched the heavens for a sign of the sun. The smell of snow rode the wind gusts. The golden globe he sought was not in plain sight. His arm slid around her shoulders. "Do you want a fire?"

Dark Eyes smiled. "You sleep like old bear. Sun longtime walk down high walls to make warm near river. Now, live behind *Tis-as-ack*," she said, and gestured at a single massive rock that seemed to have lost half of itself. Its rounded dome scraped the heavens.

He stared around them at several enormous stone mountains looming dark against the blue sky. "These are the biggest rocks I've ever seen."

"This place of my people, *Wonomi* make longtimes before." Pride shone in her voice. "Very strong medicine *Yosem-it-e* clans. Chief *Tenaya* village in big valley by fast water." She pointed at a thin, winding ribbon glinting far below.

He peered over the edge, amazed. "Good Lord, that's a long way down. How many days' journey to the river?" he asked, hugging himself in a useless attempt to get warm.

"*Awahne* place of my aunts and cousins. Big village. We come *Awahneechee* people, two suns. I think big snow soon. We go. Be safe. Now break camp."

Shaking her head in wonder, Dark Eyes gathered her bed-roll. She never spoke many words with any man, but Greywolf was different. *Mah Tew*, she reminded herself. She knew in her heart she would be *oha*, wife to him. He would be *opu*, husband to her. His true name was to be Mah Tew Greywolf. Much talk and thoughts of family and the future brought energy to her feet. Her clan's village was so close, the journey nearly over. She moved quickly.

"Mah Tew Greywolf, we take trail of black bear." She walked toward a stand of tall trees and pointed. Behind her the scuff of his boots came close. His arms, strong and sure, encircled her. He pressed his lips against her ear. She heard the smiling in his voice when he whispered, "It is good how you say my name. I like the sound of it."

She turned and made a circle of her own arms. "Not long you see Father, Mother, Grandmother," she said. "They go far. Leave *Olumpali*. Make long walk meet us."

Mah Tew Greywolf frowned. His eyes darkened. "How are you so certain your father will be in this valley of yours?"

"I tell river cousins when we cross big water. Ask give words to father. He come," she said with certainty. She felt his body tense and knew fear churned hot in his belly.

Dark Eyes and Washee rode out first. "Many places hard ride, must walk horses," she said, as she climbed onto her pony. Mah Tew heard every word, though her voice was barely a hum. How does she do that, he wondered?

He watched her navigate tight switchbacks as she picked her way along the rocky trace. Sometimes she dismounted and looked intently at the ground before making decisions. Other times, when a new track crossed their path, she inclined her head and lifted her face to the breezes before choosing a direction. Maneuvering this way and that, one track feeding into another, they proceeded steadily toward the valley.

The straight line of her back bespoke strength and determination. She fascinated him—a stranger in every way—yet someone he had come to trust. He had no memories of a home. She had become his home. He was learning the ways of her people. What little he knew of their customs felt comfortable. Dark Eyes twisted in her saddle from time-to-time and looked back. Her eyes found his, and they warmed him. Their ponies walked single file, eating up the hours.

"Not ride," Dark Eyes called to him in that husky hoot of hers whenever safety became an issue. He marveled at her ability to anticipate places where, forced to dismount, they led the horses along narrow hard pack, or over loose sandy stretches. It was perilous. In these mountains a misstep would mean certain death. Though his surefooted Indian pony maneuvered the trails, never stumbling, he took good care after his hard-soled boots spawned two near slips on scrub roots and loose rock.

The show of splendor made up for the danger, he decided. At one of the widest vistas he stopped abruptly, astonished to ride in the midst of such unending beauty. He drank in the glory of soaring rock mountains that touched the sky all around him, the slashes of tumbling water, and the deep, green canyon that nestled thousands of feet beneath. Great satisfaction washed over him. The majesty of their surroundings awakened an oddly familiar stirring. Something about worship—a church? *Where did that come from? Was it another small memory?* The moment slipped away. He drew his brows together in a thoughtful frown.

"Dark Eyes," he called, his tone pitched low in the same way she always hallooed him. "Let's set a while here."

They climbed off their horses and he came to stand beside her. One arm held her close, the other gestured at the awe-inspiring view of stone and forest, the silvery wet of early fall water spills. "This work of the Lord is supreme," he said. "I like seeing it with you." She favored him with that quiet grin he was coming to anticipate. He felt her body softly acquiesce, melting easily against him. They stood, tiny against the drama, and he felt a harmony, devoid of fear. A serenity of spirit he relished.

Afternoon crept into early evening. Dog-tired, the two riders found a place to settle for the night. In the cooling air, they spoke in intimate tones while they prepared their camp on an outcrop overlooking the valley.

Matt Tew pulled down the bedrolls and saddles. He let the horses loose to graze— nibble leaves and twigs more likely, he thought. There wasn't real fodder on a ledge this high up. He carried their blanket rolls to the clearing. "Tonight it's your turn, Dark Eyes. Tell me of your family." He contemplated her quiet movements as she unwrapped provisions and cooking baskets. "Tell me of your father."

He settled himself against a boulder. The subject of her father always made him nervous.

They'd be face-to-face in a matter of days. Knees drawn up, he palmed some pebbles, shaking them like a pair of dice in his loose fist.

Dark Eyes turned from the task of laying their meal. He watched her sit, then scoot back against a massive fallen tree trunk. Folding her long legs across one another, she looked out at the big sky stones, still untouched by the shadows that darkened the valley below. She was thoughtful. He knew she sought the words to make her answer.

"My father is wise man, Mah Tew. Has many horses," she began. "He leader in villages, like father before him. Make life good way. No wish warriors fight." She paused and brushed her hair back with slender fingers.

The musical sound of her speaking soothed him. Usually he enjoyed trading words with her. It was sweet. This time, however, he had a hard question to ask and planned to toss it straight out. Mah Tew studied the ground. *I best just say it.* He discarded the pebbles and pressed his fists together. "Does he hate white men?" His eyes flashed mistrust at her.

She returned his look steadily. "Standing Bear have big friends, white men in village *Olumpali*, place of my growing up. In *Ahwane* is fine leader, helps cousins. Knows heart of men not all same. Father will know heart you," she reassured him.

"I guess that means he won't kill me right off." His tone was harsh. His few searing memories snaked deep as he spoke the words.

"Mah Tew Greywolf, Father meet you well! Make best way for me. No kill!" She sounded outright annoyed. "Standing Bear have strong spirits, give many power him. He make good medicine. Coyote careful, for Father more brave. I try tell you." She thrust her hands out, palms down, a wall between them. "No talk more this," she said, her eyes boring into his, her frustration visible.

"Okay," he sighed. "Sorry." He forced aside hot tendrils of anxiety and changed the subject. "After supper will you tell me of your grandmother?"

Dark Eyes took a deep breath. "Is good. We speak Owl Woman," she agreed, and calmly returned to her meal preparations. "Need fire tonight Mah Tew." She smiled at him over her shoulder. "Tomorrow we come to valley. You speak father of marry. He make blessing."

He pulled his mouth into a semblance of a grin and went toward the trees to collect kindling. No matter how often she told him her father would give welcome, he couldn't quite believe it. "I'll find out soon enough," he muttered, wondering if he could ever rid himself of fearsome memories—so different from what he felt for this woman—and from her.

Chapter Thirty-Two

Under Granite Walls

Mah Tew Greywolf craned his neck. Around him, granite soared thousands of feet into the cloudless sky. He could hardly see where the stone peaks topped.

"I feel joy of small child," Dark Eyes murmured, as they rode side by side along the river. "Water name *Wa-Kal-la*," she told him. "This is place of my younger times. My family sometime visit, stay summer with Chief Tenaya family."

"I know nothing of your valley or how to live in it, Dark Eyes, but it is truly beautiful," he said, gazing at the bright rush of water at his feet.

"Not always like this," she confided. "I tell story of *Wa-Kal-la*. In old times, man who sleeps beneath ground move and make *yowan-owits*, earthquake. Big explosion come. Ground drop under feet of '*Olomko*'—The People. Hear great roar. Big flood, cause them run for lives. Many drown. Now is river long in valley, water still hurry past. Is tale *Yo-sem-ite* chief share to all children."

She was so at home in this magnificent place, he marveled. She had memories of a childhood here. He saw the way her eyes shone with excitement as she pointed out favorite places to bathe in the sparkling flow, to sun oneself, to prepare food.

"Mah Tew, look. This rock good. At top has fine pounding hole for make acorn flour." She pointed. "And here, find yellow stones in sand, make river shine. In time of warm sun, catch many fish."

As far as his eye could see, mighty boulders rested in the lazy currents or sat like small mountains on its pebbled banks; perfect for climbing, if you were able to scramble up their slick sides. Trees of different kinds grew everywhere. Pine needles carpeted the ground. Her valley was captivating.

"Brother Snake and squirrel make home, too. Share with birds, deer, bear," Dark Eyes explained.

In the distance, he saw two cabins and wondered who lived here besides native people. Settlers maybe? He might stop by and knock on the doors to say hello sometime.

An unexpected smattering of water droplets misted his face. Mah Tew twisted in his saddle. He stared upward, following the sweep of Dark Eyes' arm and was astounded.

She laughed at his surprise. "You touched by *Pohono, Wa-Kal-la* cousin. She make big jump greet you. Is good you see now. Soon cold make long water stiff."

"We call this 'waterfall,'" he said. "But I have never seen water fall so far. Never seen such long water," he amended.

"I show many things you not see before." Gleeful, she turned Washee toward a stand of the tallest trees he'd ever seen. The valley was a place of giants.

"Look there, in trees, *Awahneechee*. My people come, bring welcome." Dark Eyes encouraged Washee with a sudden press of her heels against his sides. She headed for the huge, red-barked grove at a rapid trot, one beat short of a gallop.

This was the moment he'd been dreading. Instinct told him to follow, but his body and mind were reluctant. He hoped the familiar fear sweeping through him like an ill wind did not show on his face. Mah Tew Greywolf shivered involuntarily in the warm sunshine. "Drat it, hold up," he called.

When his words reached her ears she spun Washee toward him and returned to his side.

Her pony and his stood neck and neck, as though they might race at any moment.

"We ride together," Dark Eyes said softly. She smiled into his eyes, and his heady rush of terror subsided, although it still quivered in his belly. He nodded. In concert, they rode slow, stopping beneath fragrant branches, where a group of young men and several women awaited them.

Mah Tew did not dare take his eyes off the scene before him. Dark Eyes climbed off Washee. A dozen men attired in deerskin leggings and loincloths surrounded her. Blankets wrapped their shoulders, covering bare chests. Women, barefoot, tiny in their apron dresses, some toting babies, pushed forward. They were so different from Dark Eyes with her long legs. Many of the women had some sort of thin, dark, dotted line running from lip to chin. He'd ask her about it when they were alone. Here and there in the crowd, he noticed an occasional bird feather, small bone, or ribbon adorning a head of long dark hair.

The braves and women chattered, waving their hands in excitement and joy at seeing Dark Eyes again. He guessed they'd all be about the same age. She clasped the shoulders of several in greeting. Some grabbed her shoulders and held her close. Mah Tew saw tears. These people had meaning in her life. He shut his eyes. For a moment he longed to know all those who dwelled in his own lost past. He remembered so little, and what he did recall left him feeling alone, unanchored, anxious.

"Mah Tew," she called, bringing him back to the moment. She gestured in his direction, and the group turned its attention on him. He set his lips in a careful smile. The faces of these people did seem open and cheerful. He saw curiosity in their eyes, although suspicion was plain on the faces of two or three young men. I'm suspicious too, he thought grimly.

"You meet sister cousins, brothers. *Olomko*—my people." She motioned for him to dismount and join them.

Swallowing his discomfort, Mah Tew Greywolf complied and found himself staring down into the eyes of brown-skinned strangers. Most stepped forward, reaching to clasp his shoulder and repeat his name. In return he repeated each of theirs. His smile began to feel real.

"Come, we go now village my cousins." Dark Eyes grabbed his hand. "Meet Father." She pointed toward another grouping of tall trees.

Through clustered red trunks he glimpsed a distant splash of green: a meadow thriving at the foot of a massive rock that towered toward the heavens. Numerous cone-shaped forms dotted the flat grassy space. Leading their horses, they meandered toward the place of her parents, flanked by—what was the word? *Olomko*. The People. He rolled the sound around in his mouth and liked the fullness of it. But, her father ... an uneasy prickle snaked up his spine.

While they walked, trailed by her friends and relatives, Dark Eyes commented on the varied shapes they passed, each unlike anything he'd seen before.

"This *chuck-ah*," she said of a tall square structure set on stilts and lined with rabbit skins. "Is storage for winter food; fill with acorns."

"What is this place?" he pointed to a large, circular thatched roof sitting low to the ground.

"Ahh, *kaul-kotca*, dance house. Dig deep in earth. Make sacred place for gathering times of Water people and Land people clans."

They walked on and soon were surrounded by the cone-like buildings he'd seen in the distance. Some of the group that strolled with them fell away, melting into various huts, each of which stood twice taller than a man. He saw smoke coming from the tops of several.

"Sleeping houses, call *u-ma-cha*. Like white man living places," she explained. "Make of tall poles, tree bark, sometimes grasses. Have good smell."

As he listened to her speak, he realized they were coming close to a special dwelling, the farthest of these houses. His heart raced. Outside, a man and woman stood, silent. The man wore his graying hair in two long braids. A woven blanket of red and blue covered his shoulders. Beneath it, Mah Tew could see the cut and fabric of a white man's shirt. Deerskin leggings wrapped his long, thin, slightly bowed legs. The man held a carved pole in one hand, its tip resting on the ground. He stood with authority, his stance proud. Plainly, Dark Eyes' height was his gift.

The small woman who waited with him had no blanket. She was clothed in a beaded deerskin apron dress and moccasins. Her black hair, divided into three braids, was not yet speckled with white. She did not move, but a mother's joy leapt in her face.

"Father, Mother," Dark Eyes said, her voice laced with excitement. "You come, Mah Tew." She motioned him forward. "Hold horses." She dropped Washee's rope reins, and her feet began to run as of their own accord. He walked toward her cautiously, leading their ponies. Feeling it best not to disturb the reuniting of family he stopped at a respectful distance, and tried to control his apprehension.

He watched as Dark Eyes threw herself at her father's outstretched arms. The old man glad to see his daughter, marked their reunion with much affectionate clasping of shoulders. Mah Tew heard emotional chattering as Dark Eyes clung to her father. After several moments she was gathered to her mother's bosom. In the way of all mothers and daughters, the two hugged, wept, and soon were deep in conversation, their heads bent close together.

While the women enjoyed their tearful homecoming, Standing Bear's attention turned to Mah Tew. The headman's eyes were piercing. Black as obsidian. Mah Tew breathed deep and returned Standing Bear's penetrating stare, trying to keep his own expression level and quiet. He was keenly aware of his lack of standing in this valley. He was an outsider. A muscle in his jaw twitched.

What can I say to this man? Like any parent, he'll want to know who I am. All he sees is that I am a white man who arrived at his home in the company of his daughter. Inwardly Mah Tew squirmed. The canyons and gullies that lined the old man's face spoke of a long life and many experiences. Of wisdom. What Dark Eyes says of her father is true; he can feel the heart of a man, Mah Tew thought, and hoped he'd not be found wanting.

The long-held terror that lived inside him ratcheted back several notches, to be replaced by a different anxiety. He had so little to tell. *I can speak only of my feelings for his daughter. To me, it is perfectly clear. We are the same, she and I, although we are different.* He knew he had a great deal to learn. He'd have to prove himself. He wondered what her family would decide. Would they give him a chance, or chase him out?

At his back, he could feel the heat of a dozen pair of curious eyes watching the drama unfold.

Dark Eyes, her arm entwined with her mother's, looked over at Mah Tew. He was straight-mouthed, standing stiff under Father's scrutiny. She must make introductions.

"Father, Mother," she said. "This Mah Tew Greywolf. In desert I come him, weak as ill child. Coyote make him mischief. Take his old times. I sing to bring healing. Give name Greywolf." She smiled. "He *hoja-pah*—very brave. Good man. We travel many moons, come to valley. His people *waliko*, high people, they give name Mah Tew." Dark Eyes moved to Greywolf's side and pulled him toward her parents.

"This my father, Standing Bear. Is *Hoipu*, headman *Olumpali*. My mother, *Wipajahk Halah*, Eagle Feather Woman," she said, smiling at the woman before her.

Mah Tew nodded in acknowledgement. "I am glad to know you, sir," he said. Unsure of proper etiquette he did not offer his hand.

Standing Bear dipped his chin in response. His black eyes glittered but showed nothing.

Their greeting had gone well. Dark Eyes was pleased. Now Mah Tew would say to Father, she was wife, his *oja*, and ask her father for blessing. She wished she could hear what would be said between them, but that was not the custom of her people. Instead, she stepped forward. "I take horses, Mah Tew. I visit more Eagle Mother." She smiled. "See you when midday meal."

His grey eyes serious, Mah Tew laid the reins in her outstretched hands. Dark Eyes turned, tugging the horses forward. She had much to tell her mother.

"You come *u-ma-cha.* We speak." Standing Bear gestured an invitation to several men.

Mah Tew watched as they came forward and were ushered into the family's sleeping house.

He motioned to Mah Tew. "Now your time enter," Dark Eyes' father said.

Mah Tew crouched, his long frame folding like a squeezebox, he ducked through the opening, followed by the old man. Outside, there was good-natured laughter from the gathered crowd. He had to admit he must have been an entertaining sight as he made himself small enough to fit through the entryway.

Standing Bear arranged himself atop a stack of rabbit and deerskin sleeping blankets. He stuck the point of his intricately carved *hoipu* stick into the ground and bade Mah Tew Greywolf to be seated. The other men settled cross-legged on bare dirt, their backs against the *u-ma-cha* wall. Mah Tew found a spot among them and sat, arranging his legs in the same way. In the center, a stone-ringed fire pit glowed with still-warm embers.

Eyes closed, the old man hummed to himself for a few moments before he spoke. "Name my daughter *Oloki Kalanah*, Raven Dancer. Must know true Spirit name," he said, sternly. Mah Tew nodded, and tried to anchor the unfamiliar words in his mind.

Standing Bear offered a sly smile to his assembled guests. "I hear you call Dark Eyes," he said. "I call '*Wate,*' blackberry, her name from youngest days. We same, eh?"

The men found this information humorous and slapped their legs in approval. Surprised, Mah Tew grinned and waited for the old man to continue, not sure of what to expect.

"My daughter pick you; I no pick." He fixed his eyes on Mah Tew. "She not want young warriors. She refuse old medicine man with many good magic. *Oloki Kalanah*, strong-headed. Has much spirit power." He shook his head to indicate how difficult it was to understand a daughter.

Mah Tew returned Standing Bear's gaze. "Yes sir," he said. "She has much spirit power and true strength of heart. I respect her ways. I pick your daughter, too."

Standing Bear continued to stare at Mah Tew. "I like know you more, Mah Tew Greywolf. My daughter tells Coyote take past times?"

Uneasy, Mah Tew nodded. "I have few memories," he admitted, unwilling to tell Standing Bear of the horror he remembered.

"I say you learn fool Coyote. I teach." Standing Bear said. "After make good dance for marry, men have sweat lodge ceremony grow your Spirit guide strong. I choose special Shaman, strong dancer, help you. Now must talk of daughter's new life."

"You be *salipah*, son-in-law." He turned his sharp eye on the other men sitting in the *u-ma-cha* and tapped his carved wooden pole on the ground twice. "What is your work, Mah Tew Greywolf?"

A small swell of interest riffled around the circle. Mah Tew saw several heads nod in support of the question. The old man waited, still as a lizard on a sun-drenched rock.

"I would like to open a general store, sir. I'll sell to the mining camps. There's all kinds of supplies needed." Mah Tew blinked. Where had that come from?

"As bride, *Oloki Kalanah* is worth many clamshell money. How feed her? Feed children?" Standing Bear leaned forward awaiting a response.

"Well, sir, someday I will have a *rancheria* with crops and livestock." He looked into Standing Bear's eyes. "I'll rely on hunting for now. I can learn many ways of living. I'll learn your ways. I will take care of her, sir. I give you my word." He paused for breath and continued. "I have few coins in my pockets. No paper money or clamshell money, no land. What other bride price will be good for you? What can I give?"

There was heated conversation among the men that sat with them. Several glanced in his direction. They must be tossing around ideas for a suitable bride price. He was certain of it, and worried. Maybe they would reject him, find him unsuitable, for he had naught to contribute.

Standing Bear said nothing, allowing the discussion to continue for several minutes.

Finally, he held up a hand and the group fell silent. Faces grave, they looked from Standing Bear to Mah Tew, awaiting their headman's decision.

"You make hunt with *Ahwahnee* braves," the old chief said. "You bring *tunaka*, bear: head, skin, plenty meat. You bring many wild turkey for wedding feast. Make big time dance. But first, you build marriage house. I teach." His eyes drilled into Mah Tew's. "These things you must do before snows fall and valley sleeps in white."

Standing Bear placed a second hand on the *hoipu* stick. "Later time you bring six good horses, give to Eagle Feather Woman. It is the way of The People."

Mah Tew Greywolf was solemn. "I will try to do all you ask, sir. When I have money or livestock I will make a good gift."

"Do you not search for yellow stones?" Standing Bear asked. His face grew suddenly harsh, his eyes fierce. "Many settlers and blue coats want come this valley for yellow rock live in river."

"No, sir. I do not. I think it better to sell what folks want to buy." *Did I once tell someone else that same thing?* An image flashed in his mind. And then it was gone, leaving no echo. He shook his head in confusion.

Standing Bear grunted in response, as though the matter were settled. One of the men produced a pipe and tobacco. It was going to be a long day, Mah Tew realized as the ritual pipe was lit, and his soon-to-be father-in-law began to instruct him in the way of building a proper marriage house. He wondered what else he'd learn about in this valley—or remember.

Chapter Thirty-Three

Finding Angels Camp

Although moved to exclaim aloud over the raw beauty of their surroundings, Sara had no interest in exploring its splendor. She was fixed upon Gage's promise of a warmer clime—and the sooner the better. The past few afternoons had provided some relief; however, each setting sun brought unwelcome drops in temperature. It would be simply devastating to pass one more night in the bitter cold, her lips blue as high-country lake ice, and her feet stiff. Why, last night the water they carried had frozen solid.

Nevertheless, come late afternoon Gage dug in his heels. "We've made good time. These animals need to rest, Miss Coulton." His voice left little room for argument.

Sara legged Cherry over and rode beside him. Sullen, she stared around at meager greenery, its growth a victim of thin sunshine and glacial nights. "What do you propose?" she challenged.

"I reckon we'll be settlin' in for the night."

She held tears of frustration at bay. "Have mercy, sir. Am I to find myself chilled to the marrow, suffering in this bleak mountain air once again? I say we continue on."

Gage raked her with those unsettling green eyes. "Buck up, woman," he spat. I don't give a feather for your whinin'.

My concern is the critters. I don't want 'em turning up lame." He stepped off his horse. "I thought I heard a trickle of water over yonder. I sure can smell it close by." Thumbs hooked in his pants pockets, lean, muscular legs planted wide, he joggled his shoulders to and fro. Trying to loosen his back, she supposed, deliberately turning her head away from him.

Fury flared quick and hot in Sara when he handed her Thunder's reins and Murphy's lead rope. Why, I'd like to up and leave him walk, she fancied. It would serve him right. She shook her head, and rued the promise she'd made to her father.

"Wait here," he instructed as though he'd plucked the thoughts from her head, then turned and stamped off through the undergrowth, rifle in tow.

In a melancholy frame of mind, she dismounted and tethered the animals to chunks of rock. Feeling like a critter caught in a snare, she pulled saddles and bedrolls down and awaited his return.

That evening, after a deplorable meal of beef jerky and hot tea, they huddled by a beggarly fire. It barely made a dent in the frigid conditions that gripped their camp. Gage gave her his sworn word, making use of picturesque language that brought blush to her cheeks, that tomorrow the trail would at last start down from these intimidating granite heights.

Further conversation did not interest her. She could barely keep her eyes open. Numb as an ice block, she watched the dazzling pinwheel of stars that carpeted the night sky. It seemed the firmament itself was made of sparkling bits of ice almost close enough to touch. Pulling her jacket snug around her torso, she mumbled a cursory goodnight, and making what nest she could, slipped beneath her horse blankets. Head resting on her saddle, she slept fitfully, sandwiched between wintry air and freezing ground.

Thank the Lord. Just as he'd pledged, next day they descended into truly warmer precincts. The sun rose toward high noon in the bluest sky as they rode through groves of mammoth trees, admiring their broad trunks. Farther down, a faint wagon track gave on to a running creek. Shaded by oak and cottonwood trees, they followed its pleasant burble, walking their horses along at a leisurely pace, hardly a word passing between them. Little Murphy brought up the rear at a near trot. Sara found herself smiling.

The creek widened. Up ahead the clank and scrape of shovels and pounding of pickaxe against rock rang out. "What might that commotion be?" Sara inquired.

"I'm not quite—"

His answer was cut short by the sound of a weapon being cocked close at hand.

The owner of the long-barreled pistol, a disheveled man of indeterminate age, stepped from behind a tree. He was soaking wet from his worn boots to the brim of his filthy hat. Even his wild, unkempt beard glittered with scattered beads of water. "Yer trespassin'," he growled. "Git offen my claim."

Gage pulled up short and tipped his hat. "How do, sir, name's Gage Evans. This here's Sara. We're up from Yuma— just passin' through and searchin' for a place to rest a bit. Our stock is bone weary, and the young lady is hankering for a camp spot to call home for a time."

The fellow narrowed penetrating eyes and studied first one then the other, seeming to ponder the explanation, shooter at the ready. "I be Seth," he grunted after his thorough looksee. He stepped up to offer Gage a handshake. "You folks come dang close to Angels Camp. This here's Angels Creek. Thar's hunnerds of blokes placer mining this loblolly. We ain't lookin' fer company," he cautioned.

Seth inclined his head toward the tangle of sun-sprinkled trees surrounding the track on its far side. "If 'n ya keer fer a purty place that be kinda quiet like, jest head off beyond them groves." He waggled his thumb. "Thar's plenny of livin' space away from the diggins." he said, and with a quick nod toward Sara, stomped off into heavy brush.

"Let's have a gander," Gage picked up his reins and headed into the trees. Sara followed. They searched the area and, just as the old fellow said, found a small golden meadow complete with a trickling streamlet.

Gage surveyed the expanse. It looked near perfect. There was plenty of grazing for Cherry, Thunder and Murphy, and not another soul in sight. Nearby, a whole mess of trees provided privacy. And to boot, the location evidently wasn't far from town.

"See there." Sara pointed at a purely flat spot in the partial shadow of a big black oak tree. "What a fine campsite that will make. Lord love a duck, I am so tired I could sleep for a week!"

He gazed at her and nodded in agreement. Weary as a hunted jackrabbit, he was ready to put his feet on solid ground for a while. Before he swung a leg down and stepped from his saddle, Sara looked at him expectantly.

"Perhaps, Mister Evans, you will see your way clear to visit the town that miner spoke of and fetch some supplies. We are plumb out of coffee, and I would pure succumb for an egg or an orange." Her lips bowed in a meager upturn.

Keeping his expression neutral, he held out Murphy's lead rope. "Tether the mule, Maybe get some unpacking done." That said, he turned Thunder and rode off.

"I need to rest, and I'll be penning that letter to my pa," Sara called toward his disappearing back. Then she pulled her notebook and pencil from her saddlebag, settled herself against a tree trunk and began to write.

September 1850

Father Dear,

I write to let you know of my safety and whereabouts. Mister Evans and I have arrived in California. We find our-selves on the western side of mountains called The Sierra Nevadas.

This is a land of extremes and great beauty. Certainly one cannot help one's self ... its glories must be admired. There are many trees. Most unfamiliar. Among the most magnificent are those called redwoods. They cluster together as families do. Their branches are adorned with lacey green needles, and their reddish trunks reach easily into the sky. From a distance, we have seen large brownish bears with humps against the neck. Grizzly bear, Pa, quite ferocious, I hear tell.

There are boulders, grey rocks that sit in the earth, but whose crowns pierce the clouds. A great roaring of water spills from them into the streams and rivers that sit deep below.

We have come through much excitement on our jour-ney. Mountain nights are bitter and presented quite a trial. Mercifully, we have dropped a bit into a warm valley today.

Along the way we rode through a grove of trees that were unnaturally large, as though made by giants. One cannot determine their topmost branches, as they simply graze the heavens. I believe they are called Sequoia. Their trunks are wide as a barn. Truly, Pa, you could drive a stagecoach clear through. One feels so tiny ... small as an insect in their presence. I felt as though I stood in church.

Gage returned to find her curled up in the tall grasses, hunched over her writing. He swung off Thunder. "I bring news, Sara."

She turned, pencil in midair. "And what might that be, Mister Evans?" Now, her words held the snippy tone she seemed to reserve just for him.

"I've seen the town," he said, hanging on to his temper. "The good news is they have a trading post, a postmaster, a bank, and church services about once a month. The bad news is the passes will be snowed over in a week or so, and impassable 'til spring. We'll be spending our winter in Angel's Camp. No question about it. Folks suggested we find accommodations to see us through. Seems shortly the rain and chill will be formidable down here, 'specially for a lady."

He saw shock register on Sara's face as he spoke. She put her pencil down. "You mean stay beyond the six months Pa allowed me? He'll be mad as wet hen," she choked.

"These mountains get twelve foot of snow or more. Trying to cross will be certain death."

Her eyes turned thoughtful. "Well, I suppose we'll have to make the best of it. We'll not be able to search for Matthew in such conditions, either."

"I heard tell of a cabin we might have use of," Gage said. "But for now, let's stay put a while and get the lay of the land." He saw that mulish look of hers pop up, even before she spoke.

"Fine. I just want to be quit of freezing at night," she bit out.

Staring at her in a fury, he raised an eyebrow. "Fine, yourself," he snapped. "I'll just save this orange for supper." He opened his hand, displayed the fruit and shoved it into his saddlebag. He thought about the saloons he'd seen along Angels Camps' main street—its only real street—and pulled a hand through his thick hair. Dealing with her persnickety attitude was darn near enough to turn him into an accursed elbow-bender. He wished he'd thrown back a glass of whisky while he'd had the chance.

Best I go in search for firewood he reckoned, before I tangle with her again. In a temper he started toward the copse of trees, wondering what it was she recorded in that infernal notebook of hers.

She glared at him and resolutely returned to the task of completing her letter.

Seems at this time of year, the days are still quite warm in the lower areas, but the nights are already icy. We are told to expect heavy rain and three or four foot of snow in the valleys during winter months, In a matter of days, snow will fall heavy in the mountains, twelve or more foot. Trails over the passes are snowed in without respite until late spring, according to those who reside here. They tell shocking tales of the Donner Party, who not three years prior perished in these circumstances. Trapped in winter snows, buffeted by storms, they starved and froze to death, Pa. Even little children. I know you will recall headlines shouting out their terrible plight.

Mister Evans has determined, and I agree, such conditions render travel unsafe. Therefore it is best we pass the winter in this place. I shall write when we are settled. I know my particular news will not please you. But, of necessity we must adjust. Rest assured I shall comport myself properly. I expect your Mister Evans will write you as well, since he passes no opportunity to exert his will and fulfill his responsibilities.

In my search for Matthew, I plan to question all whom I meet and have no further news for now.

I remain, Your Loving Daughter

Sara Durann Coulton

Chapter Thirty-Four

Homecoming

Dark Eyes sat cross-legged in the shadow of a black oak tree, mixing basket tucked between her knees. Her fingers worked acorn flour that would become bread for the evening meal. She separated tiny bits of nut shell from the coarse meal with her fingertips, and watched Mah Tew build their *u-ma-cha*. Father had quickly chosen the marriage house site, inviting Grandmother Owl Woman to make a blessing using special plants that pleased the spirits. It was a short walk from her parents' home.

Several feet away, she saw Running Deer and Laughs Like Dog squatting in a small patch of shade. The young braves eyed Mah Tew and talked among themselves, their words quiet as drifting smoke.

Mah Tew had set the long poles first, as Father taught him. Now he placed thick, wide strips of tree bark over them to form conical walls. Despite the new headband he wore, sweat glistened on his face. His shirt lay forgotten, tossed to the ground, and his shoulders held the sheen of moisture. The look of him pleased her. He was strong and handsome, muscles rippling as he worked. Her busy fingers halted their kneading as memories of his touch flooded her senses.

Dark Eyes sighed. There was much to do before the time-of-stiff-water, when the silvery flows that roared into streams and river would still, turning to ice as they dropped. *Tunaka*, big bear, would sleep, hidden until spring. There was no time to waste. Frosty air already stung the valley nights. The hunt would be next, then the dance Mah Tew must hold for their marrying.

"Soon you finish outside of house, then my turn," she called to him, feeling compelled to hurry their preparations.

"I have plenty more I need to get done to prove myself to your father, Dark Eyes." His tone was sharp. "He expects me to make a special hunt. I've been told to bring back bear—head, skin and meat. I hope I can do it."

"You sound like father say you must lift great boulders to mountain tops with one hand and, chase *tunaka* with other. Listen me, Mah Tew," she said. "When you make hunt, take two men help."

He turned toward her, all attention. "I'm listening, *Oloki Kalanah.*"

She smiled, liking his saying of her true name. "I think be good you invite Running Deer and Laughs Like Dog. They clever hunters. Have strong backs." She tilted her head to show where they sat, and was pleased when Mah Tew nodded.

"All time you search for *tunaka* is my job fix inside *u-ma-cha*. I make good sleeping place, bring all cooking tools. Mother give two big rabbit-skin blankets. She say you tall as tree. Need many rabbits." Dark Eyes threw him a teasing glance. "Hard work, you. Maybe I reward," she hinted.

Mah Tew grinned and positioned another bark slab. His tone was lighter. "Reward?" His eyes held sudden hunger. "Ahhh. Then I will complete your house before the sun goes down."

Delighted, Dark Eyes imagined the perfect marriage bed. Pine needles covered by dry grasses would make a soft place to spread the rabbit skins for warm sleeping. She had gathered the materials needed. When they lay in it together, she would tell him of the child that *Wowoni*, bringer of life, had given into their safekeeping. Silently, she rejoiced in their good luck, cherishing her secret. They would make fine sons and daughters.

Her dinner task completed, she set the basket aside and dusted acorn flour from her hands. She had much more to do before their marriage time: weave household baskets, collect herbs for healing and cooking, and sew deerskins for warm shirts and leggings. She'd find acorn and pinion for storage against the hunger of a long winter, for the cold time had many moons. As was the custom, her closest sister-cousins offered to assist, and Dark Eyes was grateful. She'd ask help from Grandmother and Mother too.

"Mah Tew," she called, "I have much work do. Must get Mother help. You come evening meal. Yes?"

"Okay," he said. "Make me your special bread."

Dark Eyes grinned. She loved to talk with him, to speak of little things. She stood and grabbed her mixing basket. "Okay," she echoed, comfortable tossing the word back at him. "I go now." It gave pleasure to know his eyes followed her as she walked toward her parents' *u-ma-cha*.

She found Mother sitting under a tree working long strips of willow into a tightly woven basket, perfect for cooking acorn bread. Eagle Feather Woman made a soft smile when Dark Eyes approached.

"How is your day?" Dark Eyes asked. She set her mixing basket on the ground, folded her legs beneath her, and joined her mother in the shade.

"I am well, daughter, but let us not speak of me. It is better you tell the story of your journey home and the white man you choose as husband." Eagle Feather Woman glanced at Dark Eyes. "How will he feed you? You must think of these things. Life with this man will be a different way for you."

"Truthfully, I knew fear when I came upon Mah Tew close to death in the desert. But I gave what healing I could and quickly was no longer afraid. It seemed what the Great Spirit wished of me," Dark Eyes said. "Soon my heart whisper of *wyny-c*, my walk around. '*We-lek*', take him in, it said. 'Bring to *wasa-ma*, *Ahwane* round house.' I listened well, for it is best not to make long travels alone." She patted her mother's shoulder.

"Though Coyote has taken his past times, each moon rise we sit and talk, I learn much about his way of being a kind man. He is my friend. He makes laughter." Dark Eyes smiled and her words were tender. "Mah Tew is not as young warriors and other white men are. Much sorrow has come to his life; in payment he is granted deep spirit and learns a grateful heart. I think Coyote maybe will give back his past times."

"I see he honors our ways and is respectful of your father's instruction. That is good," Eagle Feather Woman said. "Will he take you to live in a white man's village? That may be difficult, my daughter, even dangerous. Only two suns ago, I have heard talk of disturbing behavior in this valley. It is the way of his people."

"Mother! I am his people! Now *you* are his people. Mah Tew Greywolf lost his family to fierce Apache raiders. His heart was sick. He has learned of our ways from me. I speak many words of our *Olumpali* village, of our family, and tell stories of Old Days. Like Father, he does not wish to war."

She fingered her spirit feather and felt the tiny pouch filled with bits of the prized yellow metal. "I do not know in what place we will live, but I wish to be close to you."

"Do you have warning of others from his past times?" Eagle Feather Woman asked. "Few times I think he may have known a special woman," Dark Eyes admitted. The thought brought troublesome feelings that quivered inside her like a snake's rattle. She shook her head to dislodge her unease. "His caring belongs to me now; this I know. I must walk my path."

"Will you make grandchildren for my old age, daughter?"

Although Dark Eyes had not told her parents of the child she carried, her mother's canny, watchful look, held suspicion. *Forgive me, my mother. I will not share a secret today, for I want to tell Mah Tew first.* "Of course I hope for children," she said, speaking a truth.

Eagle Feather Woman nodded. She seemed to accept the answer and all that was unsaid between them.

"For now, I wish to speak of Mah Tew. He is good hunter. Father will see this. He knows the way of white man coins. Father teaches him of *ke-ha tiwah-pa*, our shell money. I do not fear, Mother. Do not worry so." She moved closer to Eagle Feather Woman and took her hands. "I follow my spirit guide as you taught me."

The two women sat quietly for quite a while, then Dark Eyes frowned. She recalled her mother's cautioning. Was something amiss here in the valley, where she planned to bear her child? She turned to Eagle Feather Woman. "What is the disturbing behavior you spoke of?" she asked.

"Aiyee, my daughter. There has been much talk of white settlers coming to find the yellow pebbles that make their home in the river. Many *yhy-ty* ... bad. They show no respect. Elders say men want our earth, our nest—the land of the Old

Ones. Some tell great violence will come. Villages in high rock places have troubles, I hear."

Dark Eyes felt her heart pitch in her chest. The hairs along her arms prickled. Unease knuckled her spine.

Chapter Thirty-Five

Vigilante Afternoon

Alongside the overgrown trail, Sara basked in sunshine. A downed log braced her back. She stretched out trouser-clad legs, crossed her booted ankles, and savored the fragrance of wild mint growing in profusion on both sides of the road. Nearby, Cherry grazed silent as velvet in the shade of a huge, black oak. The only sounds were the hum and chirp of grasshoppers enjoying the heat of the day. Cradled in the pleasures of California's Indian summer, she smiled, feeling decidedly lazy.

It was a perfect afternoon for woolgathering. She contemplated her decision to stay in this area until spring. Gage had insisted. It seemed strange that blizzards had already left several feet of snow over the mountain passes making travel unsafe, while hereabouts, today's warmth served to make her a bit drowsy.

She wondered if her father had received her letter explaining the necessity of changing the plan made in Yuma. Gage had written to him also, assuring him of her safety. Her thoughts turned to Matthew. He was so different from Gage Evans. Perhaps she needed to think more about that. The notion rippled—a small, cautionary voice. She chose to ignore the tiny disquiet that flitted in her head. Instead, her eyelids fluttered. A small nap was tempting indeed.

Cherry's sudden snorts and pawing swept away her musings. She glanced up, concerned, and saw her horse alert, ears forward, nostrils flared. Sara listened hard, and reached for her hat, dog-eared, but still useful enough. It sounded like hoof beats. Her eyes sought Gage. He sat on the crest of a large jagged rock, soaking in the afternoon's quiet, a shotgun cradled in his arms. His back straightened. She was certain he'd heard it, too.

"Sara, grab your horse and get behind this rock," he ordered in an undertone, confirming her concern.

She leapt to her feet and strode to Cherry's side. Swiftly, she pulled her rifle from her saddle scabbard, fisted the reins, and moved the mare.

Gage surveyed the trail from his perch. "Not likely it's soldiers," he said, voice low and tense. "I don't know what they'd be doin' up here."

He stood, feet planted on a small granite ledge, his shotgun hanging at his side now, barrel down, his finger resting on the trigger. Sara, nodded at his words, and readied her rifle, her mouth dry as a sand hill, heart thudding. The pounding grew louder.

Four sweat-covered horses galloped toward them, halting several feet away in a cloud of yellow dust. She peered from her hiding place. Their unkempt uniforms and battered hats identified the riders as militia, or worse: vigilantes. Sara had heard talk of militiamen in Angels Camp. Surely they were hooligans, more than a few rules short of soldier. Indeed, they looked more than capable of causing harm—the bottom of the bucket.

Gage's smile didn't quite reach his eyes. "Howdy," he said, voice even. "What brings you this way?"

The closest rider spat into the road, leaned an elbow on his pommel and stared up at the ledge, plainly assessing the situation. He seemed to take particular note of the shotgun.

"Looks like a Hawken's, eh? Nice piece of iron." His shifty eyes grew greedy.

No answer was forthcoming, the air surly with menace.

Sara watched. Four against one. Gage wouldn't have much chance alone. Her hands were cold in the heat. Gage waited, silent as a scorpion. She knew he was poised to strike. She had to stand with him and chose that moment to step from her hidey-hole, rifle at her shoulder.

Startled, four pair of eyes turned from Gage to Sara. The men pulled up on their reins, backed their heaving mounts just a step or two, and looked hard at the gun muzzle pointed their way.

Sara didn't like the cut of them. Crass and dirty. Her heart hammered. She summoned all the bravado she possessed. "You'd best move off!" she demanded.

"Hell, girl," said the man who looked to be the youngest of the four, his red-rimmed eyes intent. "Careful where ye pernt that gun a' yorn," he warned. His gaze boldly roamed her from head to foot. "Yer a purty little thing," he rasped and glanced at his companions. Turning back to her, he leered, His lips parted in a ghastly semblance of a grin, exposing the black of rotted teeth.

Sara saw his eyes dark with unwholesome interest. *Skinny, hard-faced, and dangerous as a pit viper. Lord, he's the devil himself.*

He stood in his stirrups.

Oh Mother Mary! I hope he's not planning to step off that horse. She trembled, thankful that Gage swung his weapon up right then, sighted along his shotgun barrel and aimed it neat at the bumptious fellow. She couldn't see Gage's face now. It was veiled by his shock of dark blond hair. *He means to protect me.* She released a breath and turned her attention back to her own weapon and the other three.

A brash voice boomed in the malevolent silence. "Shut yer big bazoo, Carney. And siddown!" The order came from a bearded giant of a man, walking out of the trees, lathered mount in tow. His jacket pulled tight over his wide girth, he sported remnants of lieutenant's stripes at his hefty shoulders.

Carney's cohorts smirked.

"Ye heard me, man." The giant scowled at the offender until Carney complied, resentment riding in his eyes, his demeanor grim.

No comments were offered.

Satisfied, the "lieutenant" turned his attention to Gage and Sara. He pulled the well-chewed stump of his cigar out of his mouth, and gave Gage a long, considering look. "We come down from Sacramento. Wild up thar wi' celebratin' statehood. Twixt that an' gold, folks is gone crazy with it. We're headed back into the valley t' join our reg'ment." His small eyes blinked lizard-like from the recesses of his round, red face. "Got no need to disturb ya t'all. Ma'am. Sir." He tipped his hat, climbed into the saddle, and lifted a beefy arm to motion his men forward.

Sara kept her attention on them until they were out of sight, her rifle positioned for business. "Lord love a duck! They were a dreadful bunch."

"Yeah, bad hombres. Ugly customers. I hope that's the last we'll see of them." Gage slid from his roost, shotgun in hand. She was sure she saw a new flicker of respect as his eyes met hers.

She leaned against the big boulder and lowered her weapon. "You'd think soldiers would be sent in to keep some order here, with all the fighting and stabbing and shooting that goes on day and night. The miners are wild men!"

Gage chuckled. "I agree. The mining camps are unsightly and highly uncivilized." He lofted an eyebrow. "Certainly an unsafe place for a young lady such as yourself. It's a good thing your father thought to send me along to protect you."

"We needn't discuss that," she bristled. "You know perfectly well we're stuck here until spring. I'm bound to write for my pa about all I see happening. Lucky for you sir, I can handle a rifle, too." She stuck out her chin. "I won't have you laughing at me."

As though he hadn't heard a word she said, he fell into thoughtful silence. Sara glared at him. He ran his hand along his shotgun's stock. "That was odd," he said softly, taking no notice of her temper. "Those riders were not soldiers nor militia. They were vigilantes. I wonder what's happening in the valley?"

Her eyes narrowed at his words and she shook her head. "I don't know, but the gang of them were on the prod, hoping to kick up a row. They scared me, the no good lappers—nothing but drunks." She sheathed her rifle and gathered Cherry's reins. "I want to get into town and see about that cabin you spoke of. I *am* tired of living in the woods."

Chapter Thirty-Six

The Hunt

Dark Eyes awakened before the sun made its long sweep over the edges of gray stone peaks and slid into their valley meadow. Mah Tew Greywolf had gone. She could feel the emptiness, the lack of his presence in the place around her. He had disappeared in darkness to climb high into the mountains and make his hunt.

Two suns ago, she'd peeked from beneath lowered lashes when he approached Running Deer and Laughs Like Dog. The young men withdrew and hunkered down beneath a tree to consider his request, taking the proper measure of time before giving their answer. She had not misjudged their generous hearts. As she expected, both agreed to accompany him.

Yesterday, at sunup, the three began their fasting and laid plans for the hunt. She heard much hooting and chatter and saw many hand gestures as they learned to speak with one another. Then, comfortable in their alliance, they packed up bows and arrows and two rifles loaned by Chief Tenaya. The Awaneechee chief strode into their midst and thrust the long guns onto their saddle blankets. "One for Mah Tew, the other you share," he decreed, and stomped off without another word.

Dark Eyes made acorn fry bread. "You take," she said, and Mah Tew stuffed it into their packs. They would not know hunger. But danger was always near during a hunt. Only the Great Spirit and luck could protect them from Coyote's mischief. Each carried a knife on his belt, and her man, she knew, always secreted another in his boot. The last thing they did before darkness was roll up heavy blankets and tie them to their small saddles, resplendent with beaded flaps.

Last night, Running Deer, Laughs Like Dog, and Mah Tew retreated to the men's sweat lodge. She knew they continued their fast until moonset, the best time to ask the Great Spirit for success. It was Mah Tew's first experience of a purification ceremony. She wondered if he found it to his liking? Before the moon rode across the black sky and bathed the valley in its silver light, she'd seen Father and an old medicine man coming from the men's sacred place.

Now, peering out into the pre-dawn mist, Dark Eyes touched her hand to her heart and wished the hunters well. She was thrilled. Her marrying time was coming closer. Perhaps today Mother and Grandmother Owl Woman would present her with the beautifully beaded ceremonial dress worn by generations of land-clan brides. She was to become a wife. And later, in the time of flowering and swift water, would be a mother. Unable to contain her elation, she did a little jig, her feet beating a rhythm on the bare ground in front of her parents' *u-ma-cha*. "My heart is full," she sang.

This morning Dark Eyes planned to finish Mah Tew's fine wedding leggings and shirt. Gathering her bone needle and sinew strands she readied them to sew the shirt pieces together. While her sharpened bone knife dug tiny precise holes in the soft leather, she thought about her domestic needs. She already had a good mixing basket, a *het-al,* for preparing acorn flour. Baskets of many other sizes were necessary for a proper household—for drinking soup, collecting water, and carrying cooking rocks. These they would receive from her clan cousins. The soft rabbit-skin blankets made by her mother were ready to spread in their marriage house. She'd do that this afternoon. In their *u-ma-cha* everything would be perfect for beginning as man and wife.

Soon she and Mah Tew would be celebrating their union with family. Land and water clans in nearby villages would come to feast and give them luck. She lifted her face and sent her words to the sky, her voice husky with emotion. "My excitement is strong, Great Spirit. I do all necessary for a good dance. I have waited long times to be shown the man meant to be mine."

After the hunting party's return, Mah Tew must make his plan for the dance. Then, Father will send runners to the villages and small tribelets. Each runner would carry knotted strings to give to invited guests—the knots told how many suns until the celebration time. A large flat outdoor space had already been chosen for the festivities.

Several days before the wedding, tradition dictated Mother lead Dark Eyes to the women's sweat hut, where six women of the village awaited. Some years older and more experienced in life than Dark Eyes, their job was to ready the bride for her marriage day. She'd be welcomed with singing and flute playing, and they'd shoo Eagle Feather Woman away. Mother's only task was to prepare the feast. Dark Eyes knew some of her sister cousins had agreed to help, for it was a big undertaking.

Friends who had already made their own unions chattered about the ritual as they ground acorn flour or wove baskets. First she would bathe with special herbs and make a fast for two suns. Afterwards, gathered around a fire built with sacred roots and leaves, she and her helpers must implore the Great Spirit to keep her heart strong in her new life. Then, she'd call upon her own spirit guide to lead her in the correct ways of being wife and mother.

Finally, she'd make a second bathing and rub her skin with sweet smelling lavender.

The women would help her dress, fix her hair and, for the last time, put in place a headband with a long fringe of finely beaded strands hanging from it. Young unmarried women wore it when they danced, to conceal their roving eyes from posturing young men. To accept his bride, tradition dictated Mah Tew remove it, showing her time of living with a husband was about to begin. A smile spread on her face, and Dark Eyes ducked her head, suddenly shy. Though she was alone today with her private thoughts, soon the entire valley would escort her to the marriage bed.

Seven suns came and went. This cool morning, Dark Eyes bathed at the river, washing her hair with soap root and chatting with the other girls. Sudden whoops of victory, and many voices crying welcome spilled into her ears. Had the hunters returned? Leaping from the water, she grabbed her bathing blanket, her breath coming in short, excited whooshes. *"Henhen,"* Mother would have scolded. "You breathe too fast."

But it was Grandmother who greeted her as she ran barefoot toward the village, water dripping from her hair, soap root and friends forgotten. The creases in Owl Woman's ancient face mapped her toothless smile. Her hunched body blocked the path. *"Oloki Kalanah*, Raven Dancer, you need not hurry. I give news. Our hunters have returned." Her gnarled fingers pointed. "It is good, my granddaughter. They bring much meat and many skins. Mah Tew Greywolf make worthy hunt for *tunaka*. His pony walks heavy with burden. Laughs Like Dog hauls deer meat, and Running Deer carries turkeys for feast. It is a good day."

Dark Eyes clasped the old woman's shoulders with delight. "Ayiee, Grandmother. Thank you. Mah Tew has done all Father required of him. It is well. Preparation for the dance can begin." Her heart jumped like a jackrabbit. "I want to hear story of their hunt," she declared, trying to step past Owl Woman.

"You must dress now against morning chill," Grandmother chided, unmoving. Her black eyes squinted as she surveyed her granddaughter, who shivered with excitement and the cold. "Be wise, child. Greet your betrothed with dignity," she counseled.

Unwilling to defy Owl Woman, Dark Eyes bent her head, clutched her wet covering close, and slipped into her parents' *u-ma-cha* to exchange her blanket for warm deer-skin coverings. She was determined to join in the greeting, to hear of Mah Tew's bravery and the dangers he'd faced. Skin still damp, feet bare, she hurried out toward the sounds of celebration.

Attempting to keep her feet from racing, Dark Eyes approached the throng. Joy rushed through her at a gallop when Mah Tew embraced her shoulder and asked that she sit near the victory fire with him.

The crowd jostled and chattered like a flock of pea hens, falling silent only when Laughs Like Dog stood and acted out how, *tunaka,* the big angry bear, roared a challenge. "Mah Tew climb tree to fool him, but Father Bear wants sit in tree, too." He flung both arms against a nearby tree trunk for emphasis, as Running Deer demonstrated how Mah Tew stayed on his perch and took aim. "His arrow fly true, one time into heart. Not need gun."

Both young warriors brought fisted hands above their heads in recognition of Mah Tew's success. Women clapped. The men dipped their heads and offered words of approval.

"Bear give up spirit quick," Running Deer added. "Maybe no like man with wolf hair on face," he chortled, drawing laughter and teasing shouts from the braves who sat close by.

Dark Eyes beamed with pride for Mah Tew's fine hunt. Tomorrow Father might send out his runners.

Chapter Thirty-Seven

Looking for Lodging

A ngels Camp, sure as a gun, was a gold town. This afternoon it bustled with miners. Excitement charged the very air. Shouts of hurrah came to her ears from all directions. Sara gawked at the sights as she and Gage rode down the main street looking for the real estate office. Dusty, ramshackle tents housed everything from bawdy establishments and saloons to farrier businesses. Behind the local laundry works, smoky fires burned beneath huge cast iron caldrons. Everywhere new construction was underway. The sounds of hammers rang out steadily, contributing to the general din.

Rivera's Trading Post seemed to be the most civilized business on the rutted byway. Sara found its clapboard façades and painted signs advertising Eggs, Butter, Washbasins, Tools and Brooms—a comfort after all those weeks on the trail. It was one of the few completed wooden structures in town.

A huge banner hung unfurled above the trading post doors, nailed in place. "CALIFORNIA ATTAINS STATEHOOD" it proclaimed in red letters. Below the banner a swad of men hoisted tankards of beer and clanked whiskey bottles in celebration. Outside the mercantile's doors a tall man stood surrounded by a crowd. "Californians!" Sara heard him shout, "My good friend Mariano Vallejo has sent word. *Estamos Americanos!* We are the newest state in the Union! Rejoice!"

"Gage Evans, did you hear that? We've come riding into history. I will write about this day in Angels Camp. Arizona may be next."

"I had no idea what all was happenin' here today. We have been plumb outta contact," Gage marveled. By criminy, I'll bet there's gonna be a passel of celebratin' comin' up. Tuck outs, dances, and maybe a parade."

Sara peered around at the commotion in the street. "These rowdies must feel they've got a fair shake. My Lord! They're tickled pink and roostered to a man."

She turned away from the interested glances of rough-cut men crowding the thoroughfare—their faces unshaven, hair long and tangled, their clothes desperate for one of those very washbasins advertised at Riveria's. It was disgraceful to let yourself go up-the-spout just because you are held separate from your family, she thought, statehood or not.

As though he had read her mind, Gage turned toward her. "These boys do look a bit like we did after our river crossing, eh?" Amusement flashed in his green eyes.

Sara shrugged her shoulders and favored him with a "humph!" She didn't much appreciate being reminded of that unpleasant experience. She'd been terrified and filthy from head to toe. Would he never let her forget it? Besides, she hated how those eyes of his made her fidget. However, she surely admitted taking comfort in riding with Mister Evans today, for there certainly wasn't another woman out on the street.

Apparently, the land agent was available. He stood, picking his teeth, in front of a poorly made sign nailed to a dismal canvas tent, which tottered toward collapse. "Real Estate - B. Lockey," it stated. Her eyebrows rose in consternation. "Mister Evans," Sara whispered. "I hope this cabin you've heard tell of is not falling to pieces."

"We'll see it soon enough," he answered, and lifted a hand in greeting.

The agent, one Benjimin Lockey, led them up a tight, rutted track to a property on the outskirts of town. "This be it," he said, as he rode in beside a dilapidated fence that ran along one side of the land. The gate hung out of fix, half off its hinges.

"A lot of room for improvement," Gage noted.

Sara's eyes followed his, taking in every detail of rotting fence post and rusted wire. Set midway into the acreage along a rutted track was a small structure. The dirt-floored cabin at least seemed sturdy built. Dismounting, they walked clear around it before they stepped inside.

"Good bones," B. Lockey intoned.

"It's got a fireplace," Gage pointed out, "and a cookstove. We'd be warm." He flashed a mischievous grin. "And maybe well fed."

Sara stared at him, speechless. She pointed to the ceiling. "I see sunlight shining down where it ought not be. Lord help us should it rain."

His eyes followed her finger. "I can fix the roof and put in a new door. We'd be cozy all winter," he assured her. "We'll not find the likes of a fine home up here, so pull in your horns, Miss Coulton."

She glanced around. There was only one other room; a small sleeping quarters. A flutter of heat flushed her cheeks. She felt her ears burn. "Surely you do not expect me to share a bedroom, Mister Evans," she questioned in strangled tones. "We will need proper sleeping arrangements."

"Don't get yourself in a pucker, woman. I'll fix a place for me to bed down. We've got a few weeks yet before winter blows in." Gage peered out a dirt-encrusted window. "Looks like there's room for a good number a' horses and space to corral them for training, and even a water pump," he said. "I'm hankering for a civilized place too, Sara."

Benjimin Lockey cleared his throat. "Ma'am, the clime remains mostly mild yearlong, fine for chickens and vegetables. And we sure do have need for some decent trained horseflesh around here," he said, attempting to encourage them. "Besides, if'n ya rent the place, you'll be true Californians," he informed them.

Unresponsive, Sara turned a circle, and looked in despair at the dust, the falling-to-pieces table and chairs, and the torn cloth at the windows. *What a mess. And Lord, how in tarnation will I cook?* Lena hadn't taught her all that much, and her fancy finishing school had mostly shown her how to pour tea and plan menus. She squared her shoulders. Well, he'll just have to eat what I know to prepare, or we'll starve, she decided. That will have to do.

Behind her she heard Gage and Lockey come to an agreement. Although she was dismayed at such meager surroundings, she was dreadful glad she'd have a roof over her head, poor as the cabin was.

Gage headed for the door. "I'm goin' into town and arrange for some wood to be carted out here. I'll be back before nightfall," he announced. "Best I get it done today. Nothing will be opened tomorrow what with the hullaballo and party planning."

"You'll do no such thing," Sara informed him, hands on her hips. "I'll be riding in with you and stopping at the trading post this afternoon to set up a housekeeping account and pick up supplies. Why, we don't even have a broom."

While Gage made arrangements for wood and a wagon, Sara paced the confines of the trading post. Trailed by the sales clerk, who had indeed clearly been enjoying a bit of celebrating, she pointed out her choices. Mister Jonley fetched her goods: a sturdy broom, several yards of muslin to cover the one bedstead, some cheery blue-and-white calico for the windows, two coarse-woven, heavy blankets, rough burlap and flour sacks to make into rugs and rags, two notebooks and several pencils, a bucket, vinegar, candles, some city-made soap, a lantern, a cast iron pot, and two skillets. *What else do I need?* Consulting her list she selected a couple of big bowls, wooden mixing spoons, striking matches, lamp oil, and several tin plates, knives, forks and spoons.

Next she moved to the baskets and barrels of foodstuffs. "I'll take six eggs, two pound of flour, a half pound of salt, bacon, tea, butter if it's available, dried black beans, and, oh, a small sack of potatoes. I'd like some vegetable seeds as well. The kind that fare best for winter planting," she said, hoping she seemed knowledgeable about such things. "And 'er … two pound of coffee beans, sir, and a grinder."

At the counter, Mister Jonley totaled her purchases, carefully noting them in a small account book under the name Mister William Coulton.

When Gage walked through the door, Sara could scarcely believe her eyes. Just beyond him she saw a wagon filled with lumber, a nail keg, saw, hammer, a couple of sturdy ropes and a shovel. *He certainly is a clever fellow,* she thought. *How did he manage to lay in his supplies so quickly and find a conveyance to boot?*

"I'll be returning the wagon to Mister Rand's lumberyard in the morning," Gage said, following her gaze. He strolled to the counter, settled cash on the bill and picked up several of Sara's purchases.

"I thank you, Mister Jonley, and assure you my father will send a draft to cover future expenditures within the month. I expect to be doing business with you regularly." She favored the clerk with a sweet smile.

Jonley's ears flushed pink. "That'd be jest fine, Miss Coulton," he stammered, and bent to the task of wrapping the last of her items and toting them out the door.

Packages loaded into the wagonbed and horses tied behind, Gage helped Sara onto the bench seat and took up the reins. The two thanked the man for his help once again and headed toward their little cabin, traveling only a wagon length ahead of deepening shadows.

Sara quivered with the early evening cold but kept primly to her end of the buckboard seat. She had never slept unchaperoned in a house with a grown man, a stranger, and one so … so … cheeky to boot—always looking at her with that cocky grin. *Why, if it wasn't on his lips it was in his eyes.* Sometimes she saw something else behind his visage. She pulled her shawl tighter around her shoulders. *I'll not think about that!*

Winter
1850–1851

California
Chapter Thirty-Eight

Marriage Bed Secrets

Gray and thick, smoke rose from the *u-ma-cha*'s fire pit and out the smoke hole, circling around itself in December's early morning fog.

Inside, Mah Tew Greywolf, propped up on one elbow, looked at his bride. "You are a fine woman, Dark Eyes," he breathed, voice husky. He brought his hand to her cheek, and gently stroked her face. His reward was a fluttering of eyelashes and a sleepy smile as she snuggled deeper into the blankets.

Mah Tew lay back, shoving his arms beneath his head. They had been married almost a month now. Life had been busy. Living among her people was enjoyable. Their humor and respect made for a good life, different from what was before.

He thought back. Thankfully, the hunt had gone well, as had most preparations for the wedding celebration. Learning of the groom's responsibilities had been worrisome. Standing Bear and several of the men had shared information about the rituals of the dust-up. At first he was sure he'd look the odd stick, trying to fit in. He grinned remembering Laughs Like Dog's attempts to teach him some of the simpler dance steps.

After their shouts of laughter died down, he was more than certain he'd embarrass himself.

During the festivities, with a few cups of Manzanita cider under his belt, he'd managed all right. Dressed in the handsome beaded shirt and leggings that Dark Eyes had made as his wedding gift, he'd felt right dashing. Folks were curious about him, and he was just as curious about them. It made for some interesting conversations.

Their marriage dance lasted four days. These people sure liked a get-together. They ate, visited and danced, rested up, and started all over again. There was always a group stampin' their feet and chantin' to the music. Children and dogs ran and played. Men from Pomo villages brought bird whistles and tail feather costumes. Dark Eyes had enjoyed herself, beautiful in her marriage dress, so graceful in her movements. She glowed with an inner light that warmed his heart.

He thought the drums, the flutes, and the rattles would never quiet down. But, late in the evening on the fourth night, the carrying on came to a halt at last. Sated guests repaired to their sleeping huts or gathered around fire rings to rest until dawn allowed safe travel. As was the custom, he and his new wife were escorted to their *u-ma-cha* by the last of the revelers.

Exhausted and happy, they'd climbed into their soft rabbit skin blankets, smiled into one another's eyes, and promptly fallen asleep. It was in the morning, after they had enjoyed one another in their marriage bed for the first time, that Dark Eyes shared her secret with him.

She'd nestled in the crook of his arm. "Mah Tew, I have special goodness to tell you." He'd looked into her eyes. They had been more intense than usual, dark and shimmering with excitement.

"Speak your mind ... wife." He liked saying the word. "Let's hear your goodness." He'd pulled her closer until they'd lain face to face.

She'd blushed, brown cheeks pinked, as she touched her belly. "Mah Tew, we have gift. *Wowoni*, bringer of life, has given us sacred seed that grows within me." Dark Eyes had watched his face carefully, her tone cautious. "We will have child in time of Spring."

His breath caught in his chest, he'd held her gently, not sure how fragile she might be. "Dark Eyes, you are everything to me, and now to have a babe ... I am a lucky man," he'd whispered against her lips. They had lain wrapped in the warmth of their blankets as the winter sun rose in the sky, man and wife talking and laughing, making their plans.

Mah Tew stretched and sat up. He, too, had a secret and would speak of it this morning. He was ready. He'd carefully considered the wisdom of sharing his news, for he did not wish to upset his bride. If he wanted only truth between them, he best tell it. He pulled a rabbit skin blanket over his shoulders and stood to bank the ashes still warm in the fire pit. It was only then he decided exactly how to say it.

His mind made up, he crawled back into their cocoon blankets. "Wake up, sweet girl." He waited as she struggled from sleep to sitting. Facing his bride, he put his hands on her bare shoulders. His eyes searched hers. "I bring something to share, Dark Eyes." His voice serious, and he saw a shadow of unease flutter across her face. "Don't fear, my wife. A "goodness," as you say it, has happened.

"You know of the sweat lodge ceremony your father made for me after our marriage. He brought a fine shaman to teach me the ways of it. The shaman chanted his powerful magic while I made the fasting so I'd be ready to meet my spirit totem and find my strong way. I hoped, if I proved worthy, maybe Coyote would give back my old times to hold in my memory. You and I have talked of that.

"When I made my quest, I was freed from fear of the past." He took her hands in his. "Coyote gave me back one memory. An important one. It is right to share this with you. In my past times, there was a woman, a girl. I cannot recall her face or the shape of her, just the feel of her presence. I was also given this knowledge: to make a life with that person is not the way of my spirit. Not the good way for me."

He felt Dark Eyes tense, although she never took her eyes from his. He drew breath knowing he had to finish his tale quickly so she would understand and suffer no grief.

"The name you made for me is true. Father Wolf is my spirit guide. He came to sit with me and told of many things. 'The person of my past times can only be a friend,' he said. We made prayers about the path I choose to walk with you. He showed me the way of happiness. And, before he took his leave, he spoke these words: 'I give to you the gift of knowing your man-heart in its deepest place.'"

Mah Tew touched her cheek and felt tears beneath his fingertips. "You are so brave, my wife. You bring me gladness. My heart belongs to you, *Oloki Kalanah*. You are my mate in life and spirit. We are the raven and the wolf." He grinned. "I feel clear and strong as a wolf. So now, it is time I give to you the words my people speak when they wed. I don't make fancy talk often, so listen well. It is you I love."

Dark Eyes' smile dazzled as Mah Tew drew her into his arms.

Chapter Thirty-Nine

Mountain Cats

Sara padded barefoot from her bedroom at sunup and rubbed sleep from her eyes. On this early December morning the cabin was warm. Most often, Gage awakened before first light and came in to bank the stove fire. She frequently found a kettle of coffee, hot and ready for sipping, set neat atop the cast iron surface.

Since November, she'd abandoned cotton stockings and snugged her feet in heavy-knit, woolen stockings, hosiery usually worn by men. Today, dressed in a sky blue shirtwaist, her favorite Yuma trousers, and swathed in a wool shawl, she breathed in the enticing aroma of Gage's cowboy coffee. Brown gargle, he called it.

Grinning, she poured herself a steaming cup and sat down at the table. She glanced around the small room. Gage had repaired the roof. She had proper swept the floor last night. Curtains she'd sewn from checked yardage hung slightly ajar on newly clean windows. It was right cozy.

Drawn to the nearest vantage point, she stood and peeked out at the corral Gage had built. Pushing the bright, blue-and-white curtain aside she saw him standing with his latest charge: a sweet golden-dappled colt, all legs, its still-short tail bobbing and dipping. The two stood nose to nose. She could see the white vapor of their mingled breath in the cold morning air.

Sara chewed her lower lip. She did like to watch Gage Evans. His brown leather jacket, scuffed at the elbows, hugged his broad shoulders and fit him close all the way down to his hips. She gulped, ignoring the uptick of her heartbeat, and turned away. It was certainly the horses; she simply enjoyed seeing Gage work his stock, she concluded. It was nothing more than that! She resumed her contemplation of the scene. The wee powerhouse started to paw and toss his head this way and t'other. She wondered what might happen next. Horse babies didn't know their own strength.

Hat pulled low on his brow, head bent, Gage kept on talking to that young un'—barely a yearling, maybe. The colt's ears flicked back and forth in response to his words. He was firm but gentle, and fair in his dealings with them. Those critters loved him though he didn't cotton to slipping them treats. Mostly he'd rub their foreheads and scratch their ears. "That's all they need," he told her now and again, flashing that lopsided, maverick grin of his.

Whenever he saw her toting carrot stubs or a pinch of sugar to share while she checked paddock water buckets, he'd shake his head, his thick hair almost to his shoulders, and look at her with unreadable eyes. She'd straighten her shoulders and pretend not to notice, but wondered what he was thinking. Despite the nervous palpitations he engendered, she found herself hankering to know him better.

Sara frowned. So much had happened since the day Sheriff Brenner gave her news of Matthew's disappearance. It seemed like years, not simply months ago, that she had anticipated marriage, then, desperate to find her missing swain, had taken off with Marco in tow.

Her thoughts had not been on Matthew lately. Winter in the mountains brought its own challenges, and they were complicated. Though the frosty season brought her searching to full stop, her footing wambled in new ways. How had things settled out at home for Marco and Lena? Pa hadn't said in his letters. Shaking her head, she opened her notebook, picked up her pencil and began to write.

December 8, 1850

Dearest Father,

I trust this letter shall find you well. Winter has finally come to our little corner of the world. We have not yet suffered much snowfall, although we get a dusting now and again, as light as sprinkled sugar. The mountains are deep with it. In the main, the season offers icy evenings and chilly mornings, along with occasional gully washers.

We have come to find a suitable house with proper and civilized living arrangements in this new state of California, in a small town called Angels Camp. It is a blessing to have the comfort of a roof over my head. This is rough country, Pa, but be confident I conduct myself properly, as I was raised. Gage Evans, for all his stubbornness, has been a gentleman. I dare say he will not veer from that path, although I am fair certain you know that.

Mister Evans sees to wood for cooking and heating. He is quite busy making needed repairs and constructing a feed barn and stalls. I am helping put up fencing. Local residents often call upon him and pay well for his assistance in breaking and training their stock. Thereby he helps to sustain the household. We hunt so as to have meat. Our neighbors are good family people.

Recently, I have heard tell of a newspaper located in a nearby town, and give thought to speaking with the editor regarding work. I shall of course write for you, as promised, of the local color. Here, I have penned a glimpse of the gold camp life:

Pa, a thousand or so miners residing along Angel's Creek persevere despite inclement weather. Their canvas tents soak through and through. All becomes mildewed. Their belongings are soggy for weeks on end. However, they care not one whit—and persist in digging their claims, shoveling mud, sand, and gravel from the creek into their homebuilt rockers, and sifting for even the tiniest gleam of yellow metal.

What they do reap from their arduous labors, they take into town to spend on whiskey, cards, and the occasional woman. There are few females here of any ilk. Mister Evans assures my safety when I am abroad purchasing supplies and the like, so you need not worry. I see many a remarkable sight and will relate what I can.

The streets are either ankle deep in mud—a hazardous situation for man and beast, and terrible for the wagons—or between storms, ruts and holes dry hard as cast iron, making for troublesome transport. Our Arizona dry washes are like fine carpet in comparison.

The town continues to grow apace with buildings springing up overnight like wildflowers. Even in winter, gold seekers arrive daily to make their fortunes. Commotion seems the norm in Angels Camp, and certainly at Angels Creek, for which the town is named.

Her thoughts drifted to the fisticuffs she'd seen on the way to town, not a week prior. Two bewhiskered men, old friends that traveled together from Kansas to make their fortunes in the goldfields, hoisted shovels and set upon each other. Cussing and stomping around in the rush of creek water, the drunken miners threatened to kill one another over some imagined slight. Cold breezes had carried rank body odor and worse to her tender nose.

Thank goodness Gage intervened and removed the shovels to a spot high up on the bank, setting them next to a pile of empty whiskey bottles. The two fellows still pounded one another in the creek bed, soaking wet and swearing, when she and Gage left to journey on toward Angels Camp. The incident might worry her father. She'd relate it at a later date.

Sara nibbled the top of her pencil. Oddly enough, she *did* like her new situation. It was raw and daring. That was something she'd not tell her father either. Instead she'd explain how everything in California seemed larger than life, louder, quicker. No matter the season the place burst forth flaunting the grandeur of its being. She was about to return pencil to paper when Gage burst through the door bringing chilled air swooping into the small room.

She looked up.

"Mornin' Sara." He knocked his hat against his thigh and stepped nearer the table. All male, his presence filled the little cabin, and brought unbidden heat to Sara's belly. "I'm taking on another pony, a filly, just coming two, from the Teddo place. I should be home in time for supper."

"Morning. I thank you for the coffee and the warm stove. It's nice against the cold." Folding her arms across her chest, she eyed him cautiously, willing her body to behave. "Gage, have you heard any more of the mewling that reached our ears last night? It really gave me pause."

"Nope. You be careful though. Could have been mountain cats. Mama and cubs, maybe. Don't start beating the bushes. I mean it, Sara. The mamas can be hellfire vicious."

She lifted an eyebrow and tried to ignore the green eyes that shot through with gold sparks whenever he got worked up about something. "I know that, Mister Evans," she informed him with as much dignity as she could muster. "It's just ... it was an odd sound—almost human—and the nights are getting so icy."

"Likely cats," he repeated.

Gage surveyed the cabin and a smile slipped, quick as a whiffle, across his face. "The place looks right comfortable with the curtains, nice and tidy, too. My ma would think it a well cared for home." He reached for his shotgun, strode to the door, and turned. "Your rifle is loaded and ready to fire, woman." His eyes held hers. "Don't be a shanny. Heed me. Don't try to skungle them cats. Take care, Miss Coulton." And he was gone.

Sara dropped her pencil, ran to the door, and flung it open just in time to see Gage and the big gray heading toward the gate. "You take care yourself, Mister Evans. Please give the Teddos my regards," she called after him. "Of course, I'd surely be grateful for any news of town goings-on that you can bring me."

He lifted a hand and she knew he'd heard her. Then hunching her shoulders against the nip in the air, she quickly retreated into the warmth of the cabin. *What on earth am I doing, running at his back shouting orders?* He *was* a distraction.

Settling again at the table she attempted to resume her writing. Unable to regain enthusiasm for the task, she added only a few sentences:

As for Matthew, we keep an eye out for a man who answers his description, and our search will contin-ue as the weather permits. I concern myself with your situation, Pa, but trust you are well and send my fondest care to Lena and Marco. You may safely send posts and your banknotes in my name to Rivera's Trading Post, Angels Camp, California.

    Your dutiful Daughter
    Sara Durann Coulton

Sara closed her notebook, her concentration all but gone. She'd post the letter on their next visit to town. Her face knotted in a scowl. *That Gage certainly does get me all stirred up.*

Eager to do something physical, she resolved to check her winter plantings. She and Gage had prepared the earth together and he'd built a sturdy fence around the garden. Sara had to admit they were a good team. He was handy, and a hard worker. Pushing away from the table, she shoved her curls up under her hat, pulled on her boots, and started for the seed plot, shovel and work basket in hand.

There was a nip in the air, but the work was strenuous enough to start her to sweating. She was on her knees, punching small holes in the red dirt of the Sierra foothills when the mewling began again. *What is that?* Sara got up and stood perfectly still, giving it her full attention. She was going to solve this mystery right now.

Recalling Gage's warning, she retraced her steps to the cabin, fetched her rifle, and headed toward the brush and trees just beyond the corral. The mewling became a thin cry. She turned toward the sound.

"Oh, Mercy," she gasped, and stared, astonished, at a young woman huddled in a mess of brambles, her face and hands scratched, her blonde hair long and tangled as her hiding place. Dirty fingers pressed a squirming bundle to her breast, trying to mute its increasingly outraged cries. Desperation and terror spun in the girl's blue-grey eyes.

The two women gaped at one another. Then, spurred to action by the insistent howls of the infant, Sara gathered her wits about her and spoke to the affrighted mother. She offered a tentative smile. "Hello, my name is Sara. Who are you? Are you hurt?" She made a show of placing her rifle on the ground and stepped a little closer. "Do you understand English?"

For what seemed a terrible long time, the girl searched Sara's face. "I am Rachel, wife of Crossing Waters," she said. Her words were halting and thready as the rustling of leaves in the cool breeze.

"We must get you free of the stickers." Sara knelt. "Rachel, kindly come out of there," she scolded. "It is not a fit place for your child." She brushed the red earth from her fingers, and held out her hands. Her voice softened. "Let me help you. Please. Hand me your babe, then you climb out. The baby will be safe. I promise." She managed a reassuring grin. "Don't be afraid. No harm will befall you. I shall surrender the child to you immediately."

Rachel grimaced and eyed Sara, hope and distrust sparring in her gaze.

I reckon I shall have to exercise that most elusive of virtues, patience. I must help her. Sighing, Sara returned the look with what she hoped the girl understood as kindness.

It seemed to take forever, but at last Rachel lifted shaking arms and handed the infant into her steady grasp. Sara cradled the wailing chickadee. She winced as she watched Rachel work her way out of the bramble patch. Moments later, the tiny thing rested loudly in the protective arms of its scraped and bleeding mother.

The girl looked to be not much older than Sara. Her deerskin dress and leggings were torn and stained. Once beautiful beaded moccasins, now shabby and frayed, protected her feet. Her hair was sun bleached nearly white, and her face quite browned as though she'd been without proper shelter for some time. She had a basket of some sort strapped against her back. Its trappings were tied together with beaded strips of leather. Tear tracks streaked her cheeks.

"Let's get back to my cabin." Sara said, and pointed toward the structure that sat beyond the garden fence. "Surely you must be starving. I'll make food, and you can tend your nursling." The girl rubbed at her mouth. Looking hard at her guest, Sara turned, picked up her rifle, and led the way home. Mountain cats, indeed!

A light snow fell, and soft flakes fluttered in the eventide as Gage rode Thunder through the gate, a chocolate yearling in tow. On his right, the windows of the cabin glowed like beacons. Sara must be using every candle we've got, he thought.

Swinging off the big gray, he led both horses to the modest barn he'd built and settled them in. Chattering softly to the critters, he pitched hay, topped water buckets and put up his tack. It was true dark when he closed the barn door and headed toward whatever dinner Sara had prepared ... for him ... for them? *Oh heck, only thing I know for sure is I'm hungry. And cold.* He shoved one hand into his jacket pocket and his legs ate up the distance to the golden windows. He pulled the door open.

The heady aroma of fried beans and brown gravy captured his nose. It swirled in the air amid infant cries. Slowly he closed the cabin door. His eyes swung toward a young woman wrapped in a bed covering. Beaded moccasins peeked from beneath the folds of cloth. She was settled comfortably in a rickety chair. The wiggling personage in her lap made cooing sounds. "Sara, what in tarnation is goin' on here?"

She arched one of her fine eyebrows. "This is the baby you were so certain I'd imagined, Mister Evans," she gloated, mischief hovering at the corners of her mouth.

He grinned, determined not to take the offered bait. "So this is our little mountain cat, ehh?"

Sara nearly fell as she leapt to her feet in response. He'd not seen her this excited about anything before now, except finding that fiancé of hers.

"Gage, meet Rachel and her baby boy, Carlos Running Horse. Rachel, may I introduce my... my..." she stared wildly at him for a moment, "a friend, Gage Evans."

Gage nodded politely in Rachel's direction. Food forgotten for the moment, he wandered over to have a look at the tyke. "Handsome child," he said and smiled down at the two.

Rachel hesitated. Fear shadowed her face. She drew back, squeezing the child hard against her body.

Her sudden terror was clear. "Don't take on so, Missus, I'm no mudsill," he said, keeping his tone soft as a filly's nicker. "I'm not wantin' to harm your chickadee. Good eve to y' both."

The dread melted from her features, although no smile was forthcoming. "I thank you," She shaped the words carefully, as if she'd not used them in a long time.

His gaze jumped to Sara. "I know a story when I see one. Who's doin' the tellin' is my only question." He sat down next to their visitors and grinned at Rachel, hoping to further give her ease, and awaited the tale.

"Well—I found them tangled up in the brambles, not a space from the garden. The babe was truly wailing," Sara said. "They were alone, cold, and you can see, grievously in need of tending, so I bid them come home with me." She stopped to catch her breath. "Perhaps you can persuade Rachel to tell us her story."

"Has she eaten?" Gage asked. He glanced round. "Have ya, Ma'am?"

"I shared my dinner with Rachel. I'll fix you a plate. I baked soda biscuits, too."

Gage placed a fist on his stomach. "I'd be much obliged. I'm real hungry, ladies."

She brought his supper to table, and Gage wondered, as he did every evening, just how long his teeth were going to last gnawing on Sara's version of baked goods. Deliberately, he set his biscuits to soak in the gravy. She watched him with hopeful eyes, and he decided not to embarrass her tonight with teasin' about her cooking. He shifted his attention away from his dinner. "I think it best we give Miz Rachel time. Can we make a pallet on the floor? Maybe let her get a full night's sleep?"

He grinned at Rachel. "I think you'll tell us your story, just not tonight. I'd say, when you're feelin' ready." Then he fell to devouring his supper, biscuits and all, without another word.

Chapter Forty

Sorrow and Celebration

Gage pulled his jacket tight before he stepped into the cold, clear dawn. The smell of snow flurries permeated the air. He held his gloves between clenched teeth, and with icy fingers fumbled buttons into their assigned slots. Then, yanking on his thick leather gloves, he hauled a stack of kindling from the pile set against the lean-to where he slept, and headed 'round the corner toward the cabin door.

He glanced at the kitchen window in passing and was surprised to see Sara standing at the iron sink so early; the sun just barely making a run at the night sky. Her pretty golden curls, tousled and gleaming, fell in long loops around her shoulders. Miss Coulton mesmerized him this morning—not that he'd tell her about it.

He stopped, ears burning in the near freezing breezes, and watched her measure out the coffee grind. When she lifted her head and stared back at him, he stamped his feet, the spell broken. Gage resumed his trek to the cabin's little front porch; it was time to rekindle the coals, anyway. The plank door swung open, surrendering to the pressure of his shoulder. He stepped inside and shoved it closed with his booted foot.

The scene before him was downright domestic. Appealing, really. Rachel sat at the table. She looked a sight better than she had that first night some weeks ago. Sara had plunked herself down in the most comfortable chair in the room, a rocker. She dandled little Carlos Running Horse on her knee, and a smile broad as a canyon shone on her face. She was full of surprises, he thought. A dangerous woman, his boss's daughter. Something about her brought out the tenderness in him. He hadn't yet decided what he might do about that unfamiliar feeling.

"Morning ladies." Gage greeted them. "I trust you slept well?" He set his armload of wood against the far wall and busied himself fortifying the stove's cook fire, and starting a blaze in the fireplace.

Out of the corner of his eye he saw Sara playing a game of peek-a-boo with the chortling tyke. He watched, transfixed for a moment as the babe nestled against Sara' bodice, his pudgy fingers grabbing at her smiling mouth. She laughed softly, and Gage felt a notable hitch in his usually steady heartbeat. He looked away. Uh uh, I am not going down that path, he vowed, and returned to stoking the fire.

When the crackle and pop of burning wood told him the cabin would be warm as toast in a few moments, he wiped his hands clean and sauntered over to join the womenfolk.

Sara rose as he approached. "Sit down, Mister Evans," she offered, snuggling the baby on her shoulder and rubbing his back. "Guess it's time to put the kettle on. I suggest you get better acquainted with Rachel's son while I tend to breakfast."

"Sure thing. That'd be just fine." He settled himself in the big rocking chair and held out his arms. "Hand down the little one. I'll set with him a bit—that is, if his mama don't mind?" He flashed a sociable grin across the table at Rachel, who favored him with a cautious smile.

Setting the babe on his lap, Gage cuddled him and enjoyed the mouthwatering aromas of sizzling bacon and fresh coffee that soon permeated the cabin. He gave Rachel an appraising stare. "You and Sara look enough alike to be cousins," he said, taking in her clean scrubbed face and scratched hands folded in her lap. She was wearing one of Sara's shirtwaists, and it seemed a close-to-perfect fit.

"How about telling us ... what in the world brought you to hiding in our brambles with your young 'un? Where do you hail from?" he asked, as Sara set the coffee kettle and three cups and spoons on the table. He watched her turn back to fetch a tray with a plate of last night's warmed up biscuits, a pitcher of milk, and some of her precious hoard of sugar, along with a platter of crisped hot bacon chunks, steaming porridge, and three hand towels. Appetite getting the best of him, Gage carried Carlos to the table and slid onto the near bench. Sara chose a seat on the opposite side, next to Rachel. She poured their coffee.

Between sips of the rich, hot liquid, sweet with sugar, and bites of bacon and biscuits, Rachel spoke, her speech halting, as though she might not choose the correct words. "My husband, Crossing Waters, was a good man. We lived with his family, be ... because mine is g ... gone." She paused and looked at her lap. "Our home was part way down the stone mountains." Her voice trembled. "All had been well since I came to be with them many years ago. Then, counting back three times of the round moon, bad things happen ... happened. Soldier men, cruel and greedy, visited our village. They made warnings to my family and our neighbors. 'You leave,' they said, 'or we will make you go.'" Rachel's hands tightened around her coffee cup and pressed it to the table.

"How old is Carlos Running Horse?" Sara asked, gently.

"He has eight moons." Rachel looked at the flames dancing at the hearth and sighed deep. Guttural almost.

Gage leaned forward in his chair. He could see the tears standing in Rachel's eyes, ready to fall. Sure enough, a sob tore from her throat as she continued. It was as though once she began to speak of it, she couldn't stop.

"After a time, the elders and young warriors, including my husband, decided to fight. They believed their spirit gods would protect them, for those men had no right to chase us from our homes. But it went badly—the men came back and stole our horses. They ran the cows off and killed our dogs, but they had not finished.

"One day," her voice sank to an anguished whisper, "they returned and murdered our neighbors. They burned the village. People were screaming. My husband was so fierce with grief and anger he forgot to be afraid. He jumped from our hiding place, and those men shot him dead." Tears spilled down her cheeks. "I held myself still as stone and nursed my son so he did not make a sound. After a while the killers thundered away on their horses. I ran and ran for many suns. Then I walked from the high rocks until the moon was round, and made a resting place in your bramble bushes." Rachel wept, her hands limp on the tabletop, her breakfast forgotten.

Gage rocked the sleeping baby in his arms, thinking on the story. He watched Sara reach over and clasp Rachel's hand, her own face wet with tears.

"You poor thing." Sara scooted closer and wrapped her arms around Rachel's heaving shoulders. "You are safe now." She smoothed the girl's cornsilk hair, much like his own mother had when he and his little brothers grieved for their Pa. "We'll be family to you," she said. "I'm so sorry for your loss; we both are." Rachel's weeping turned to sniffles and hiccups.

Gage looked across the table at Sara. Over plates of uneaten bacon and biscuits, her eyes met his in perfect understanding. They'd encountered those very men.

Despite the warmth in the cabin, he felt a cold anger and its companion, sorrow.

During his adventuring years, he'd spent time with Piutes and Apache in the Northern Arizona territory, learning to live the best and worst of tribal life among "The People," as they spoke of themselves. He'd endured a painful rite of passage, becoming a blood brother when his Indian comrades honored him. Brotherhood was his reward for having saved the life of a young brave attacked by an angry bison.

He held a certain respect for their native ways and the beliefs that sustained their tribal families in time without measure before the white settlers came. He knew firsthand the treacheries of the soldiers and the wasp nests of politicians' lies. The last thing he wanted to see were more grievous acts of slaughter—spurred by government greed for land and what lay under it—taken in the name of homesteaders and gold seekers. He had a foot in both worlds and had witnessed a passel of sorrow on both sides.

In the silence that followed the telling of the story, Gage stood. The strike of his boots against the floor made the only sound as he carried the sleeping child to Rachel. Once the baby rested secure in her arms, he turned and picked up his hat and gloves from the hearth where he'd left them. "I have chores to tend to," he said, voice gruff. Tugging the Stetson low on his brow, he pulled the door open. "I'll see you ladies later." It closed behind him with a thump.

He knew exactly what had to be done to gladden the womenfolk. Grabbing a saw and slinging a curl of rope over one shoulder, he saddled Thunder and led the stallion into the trees. For a good while they walked through the forest and Gage evaluated the greenery, peering left and right.

"It's gotta be near t' perfect," he told Thunder as they trudged along, fallen needles cracking underfoot. The forest's piney smell lifted his spirits. "It'll be the little bit's first Christmas. His Mamma can use some cheering-up, as well," he said. His eyes raked a sturdy little tree. "Looky there, Thunder. Can't be more than five foot. This'n is right pretty, nice and thick branched," he informed his horse and dropped the reins.

Thunder, watchful, nibbled on low hanging foliage as Gage sawed through the trunk and wrapped the fallen tree in coils of rope. He whistled for the stallion and climbed aboard; the rope dallied around his saddle horn, its end in his fist. Sara will be delighted, he thought. He chucked and Thunder moved forward, slow and steady, dragging their prize to the cabin.

Sara flung open the door when she saw him coming through the gate. "My heavens," she exclaimed, her eyes wide. "A Yule tree!" She grinned from ear to ear. "Rachel, Rachel come quick. Gage has brought us a gift," she called. "I think it will be just right for the cabin." With that, she flew off the porch, icy air forgotten and helped Gage haul their tree inside.

Rachel gawked. "I was a child when last I had Christmas." Her eyes filled with emotion. "I am shivering with the scent. It brings memories."

"The fragrance of Noel, of a tree, is something I could never forget either." Sara breathed in the perfume of pine resin sticky on her fingers. "Oohhh," she sighed and ran to Gage. She boldly reached up to peck him on the cheek. "Thank you."

Feeling like a hero, Gage smiled. "I guess I'm for hunting us a proper turkey. By my reckoning, the big day is coming a week from Sunday."

"We'll prepare a feast," Sara warbled. "Let's gather pine cones to make some pretty decorations. I have hair ribbon, and we can pop some corn kernels and string them. The chickens won't miss 'em."

Rachel's face lit like a candle. "I'd love that." She giggled, all shadows gone from her eyes.

"Get t' work ladies. I'll set the tree a'standing tonight."

Gage winked at Sara, and stepped outside, his own grin stretched broad on his face. We'll be celebratin' our first Christmas together. The thought warmed his heart, although sometimes bein' around her unsteadied him. He was struck when her eyes turned thoughtful and her smile soft. A'course that'd be when she wasn't sparkin' fire, he noted. Livin' beside this woman all winter was sure to be a challenge.

Chapter Forty-One

Suspicions

Sara could hardly believe it was January. A brand new year had begun. *1851.* She stared out the window at Gage's retreating back. Her eyes drawn to his long legs outlined by the new fangled canvas pants he wore. The trees and ground were white-frosted this winter morning. His boots made dark tracks as he strode toward the covered shelter he built to hold their hay. Today he'd put up the last wall. She hugged herself and rubbed her arms. There were secrets he held close. She saw it in his face sometimes—or heard it in his tone of voice. *Though it may be an intrusion, I shall ask him about his upbringing at my next opportunity. I can't help it. I am fair dying to know more about him.*

Only yesterday she'd peeked at Gage from beneath her lashes while she fixed dinner. How manly and comfortable he always looked with Rachel's tiny boy sheltered in his muscular arms, the chickadee's dark head resting against his broad chest. She squeezed her eyes shut against the image, but not before she felt the heat of a blush that went right to the roots of her hair. *What on earth has gotten into me this morning?* It seemed as if she were standing on wobbling ground, everything topsy-turvy in her thinking.

Across the room, Carlos Running Horse awakened and squirmed in his mam's cuddle, working himself into a tirade of angry wails. "Hungry again," Rachel said, as she loosened his bindings and brought him to her breast to suckle. She perched in the old straight-back chair Gage had found in a deserted shack and hauled to the cabin.

"Settle in the rocker, Rachel. It is the most comfortable seat in the house," Sara suggested.

"I believe I will. I have not enjoyed such pleasures since my sister and I nestled in our mother's." The chair creaked, its wood joints crooning as she rocked. "It sounds the same."

The two sat in companionable silence for a long while. Sara, aware of an unseemly rumbling in her belly, nibbled on a piece of biscuit.

She gave Rachel a curious glance. Then another. "There is so much more I want to know about you. How about we trade some tales? I'll tell you where I grew up and what brought me to California, and you do the same."

"Some of my memories are comforting and some are right terrifying." Rachel's voice was somber, heavy with unnamed pain. "I haven't spoken of the past in a very long time, although it creeps into my thoughts."

Outside they could hear the attack of hammer against nail as Gage bent to his task.

Sara nodded. "I was ... am ... promised to a young man I met not so long ago," she began, feeling anguish of her own as she spoke. "He worked on our ranch in Arizona." Sara's eyes clouded. "One day he simply disappeared. We ... my pa, the sheriff, and I, learned he'd fallen victim to outlaws. I defied my father and ran off to find him. Pa caught up with me bime-by. A lot has happened since, but, simply put, my fiance's trail led me here, to Angels Camp in the company of Gage, my father's foreman." She stared out the window, memories flooding in.

"While in the telling, I may as well say that Pa was not comforted by my choice of a beau, and in my present situation, I find myself fair confused about my promised troth. That is quite enough about my plight. What of you, Rachel? Tell me of your mother. Mine died when I was born. My father raised me—he and Lena, who keeps our home."

"I was born in Ohio." Rachel closed her eyes. "My Da and Ma farmed. I recollect how green it was back East in the summers. In the winters it was mostly barren 'cept for deep white snow." Rachel smoothed Carlos' hair and laid him over her knees. "When I came ten years old, Da started talking about land for the takin' out to the West. Afore I knew it, he and Ma decided to start off. Like so many others, me, my grandpa, and my sister and brother spent nigh on two years in that Conestoga wagon," she said, her birth language flooding back to her.

"That must have been exciting," Sara said, trying to imagine the journey.

Rachel looked up, eyes bright with tears of remembrance. Sara winced, angry with herself for giving voice to such a thoughtless remark. "And tough to leave all you'd known," she added in a rush. "I've been so few places until now."

The hammer beat out its irregular tune. Sara stood and carried the coffee pot to the stove. Picking up the poker she stirred the fire in its cast iron belly, until it hissed and crackled. The pot would reheat quickly atop those flames.

Rachel busied herself in the rhythms that made a background to their silence. Her hands rubbed and patted the baby's back by turns, urging a burp from his rosebud lips. After he produced a suitable bubble, she rearranged her clothing and wrapped him snugly in his blankets.

Sara brought over two cups of warmed jo and handed one to Rachel. "I spoke out of turn and did not mean to wound you. I ask your forgiveness."

Rachel smiled her thanks and took the cup. "I think we shall be fast friends," she said. "It has been a lifetime since I have had a companion who reminds me of my old life."

When the babe slumbered peacefully in her arms, Rachel resumed her story. "We saw a lot of country. We did our lessons with Ma, in the wagon mostly, but sometimes under a tree or aside a stream." Her lips turned up at the memory. "We had to share our food with the less fortunate in our train, and that was a hardship. The worst was the freezing cold and the scorching heat. I learned to be ever so grateful for any small comfort that came our way. Then, finally, Da said we were getting into the true West, closer to California."

Sara saw a shudder cross Rachel's face.

"Th ... that's when it happened. We were in the path of a raiding party, their faces streaked with fearsome paint. They attacked without mercy. People were shrieking. Our wagon was afire, I remember. Da and my brother climbed out, and Ma handed my little sister down to them. I helped my granddad. He was old and bent. He moved so slow I left him resting beneath a buckboard.

"Then everything went out and out wild. Those savages killed Ma and Da right in front of me. I grabbed my sister's hand. She was only six. We started to run and I lost hold of her. They took her, and a second later they scooped me up too." Tears burst from Rachel's eyes like buckshot from a gun—and just as suddenly stopped. "Lizzie was hardly but a baby," she whispered.

Sara, saddened with sharing the horror of such a memory, jumped up and threw her arms around Rachel as best she could.

She offered a hand towel, but words refused to come out of her mouth. *Unspeakable* was her only thought. She grieved for her new friend.

"I don't know what happened to my sister, or my brother, or Grandda. I pray for them. I believe the entire wagon train perished. To this day, it pains me to speak of my loss."

"I know someone with a like story," Sara said. Her eyes locked on the girl.

The infant in the crook of Rachel's arm squirmed, pulling his tiny fists into his mouth. Sighing, Rachel pushed her feet against the floor, setting the chair in motion and her small son back to dreaming.

"Mother of God, Rachel, surely anger would consume me if my family were harmed," Sara said at last through clenched teeth. "Were these attackers your late husband's people?"

"No, Sara. I was lucky. The murderers traded me to a different tribe, to a family for I know not what. I was for a long time brokenhearted, but the people were kind to me. I was chosen by their son for marriage; he was a good man. He loved my yellow hair. 'Hair That Is Sun,' he called me."

"You held affection for him?"

"Yes, I cared for Crossing Waters. Kindheartedness and evil live among pale skins and those of The People. I have known both." Rachel pressed her mouth into a thin line and stared at Sara, the exhaustion of reliving the atrocities etched on her face. She rocked. Her little one held tightly to her.

Outside all hammering had ceased. The frost had melted, and a soft rain was falling. It must be getting to midday, Sara realized, as she looked at the table still littered with breakfast's remains. Time had fled while they were engrossed in conversation.

"I'll pick up here and get some chores done. Why don't you rest?" she said to Rachel. "With all our talking, you must be plumb played out. It seems a perfect time to have a lay-down. The chickidee will be your comfort. Later, we can visit again and speak of happier things."

Sara's mind spun as she cleared plates, wiped the table, and stored the leftovers for supper's stew. Grabbing the broom, she brushed the floor clean of twigs and crumbs. Then she grabbed the grain bucket and headed out to feed the chickens, all the while mulling over her suspicions. She needed to think some on this before she spoke with Gage. Would he turn a deaf ear? Mock her?

Chapter Forty-Two

Driven Out

Mah Tew Greywolf stood knee deep in snow. He leaned on the gate that gave entry to Joseph Donnegan's homestead. The flat land around the small cabin had been cleared; not a tree remained. Probably every stick was used to construct the modest family cabin and barn sitting beyond the fence. Donnegan himself was bundled against the cold, gloved hands resting on his pickets. He'd lived long and hard from the look of his grizzled, old-timer's face, and the greasy gray brown hair that straggled from beneath his hat.

"Howdy," Mah Tew said. "I'm—"

"I knows who ye be. Yer the young fella livin' with the injuns. Din't 'spect ta see the likes a' you at me home place. Speak ye piece, man."

"I come for information, mister. I've seen a passel of armed men around the valley these last weeks. Can you tell me what's afoot?"

"Wal," said Donnegan, "you shur'n set yer'self a hard road, son. Thar's trouble comin' close by any time now. Them boys is vigilantes. They ain't a givin' up. Those fellers got no fear of Teneya, chief or no chief." He stroked his beard. "You and that squaw a' yourn best be movin' on afore ye come ta grief."

Mah Tew regarded the settler with a level gaze. Heat fired up behind his smoke-grey eyes. "I don't plan on puttin' my *wife*," he emphasized the word, his voice a growl, "in danger. I hate to move on in winter. It's harsh, and she's big with child. But if what you say is true, I fear staying in the valley any longer. I don't aim to have her suffer the loss of family like I did mine."

"Gold, son, that's what it's all about. It's settin' in the rivers and under the dirt." Donnegan spat into the snow. His eyes glittered. "I got some plans a' me own."

"It don't seem right," Mah Tew said. "Thugs running villagers off their family territory. These people been in the valley for thousands a' years. They tell the stories."

"Son, their time's 'bout done. S'all about progress herein. Fact is, I'm considerin' putting in a hotel and stage stop m'self. This here's a mighty fine place. Folks is likely ta want a gander at it. These savages don' make no good use a th' acres."

"Heck. It's plain sorry what side of the fence your boots come down on. Ta split it fair, The People been living off this land, feeding their families a deuce longer'n you've been alive, mister, by a thousand years or more. Seems like good using to me. I told you true. Your eyes are set on the prize to be taken and it's a damn shame," Mah Tew snapped. He turned heel and stomped toward his horse, boots digging crevices in the heavy drifts.

"I'd head fer Jackson, boy," Donnegan called after him. "Sure to be work thereabouts, got a couple general stores, carpentering, and placer mining if ye have the stomach for it."

Concerned about his own safety and that of the village, Mah Tew rode sure and steady across the valley. He shadowed little used deer tracks, slinking through the trees, dark and quiet as a mausoleum in winter's late afternoon. He had to warn Standing Bear, and pack up their *u-ma-cha*. He and Dark Eyes would leave in the new morning hours one day from today, snow or no snow. She'd not welcome his news.

The argument had gone on all day. "We are going. It is settled. Pack what you most want. I'll see to the horses," he said, tone grim. Resentment rose in his wife's eyes, coal dark and sparking. Her breath made white puffs in the night air. A scattering of snowflakes fell, a silent harbinger of looming challenges.

When her parents came to make their farewells, they talked of her safety and the expected dangers in Chief Teneya's village. "You must leave here," Standing Bear told her. "Husband's plan is sound." Still, she fretted.

"I want baby come before travel," Dark Eyes insisted.

His toes about numb from tramping around in wet snow, Mah Tew continued to lash baskets to the litter they would pull. "It's not safe I tell you! Not for you, not for our child. Pack," he ordered. *Blast. We've already quarreled on this same track more'n twice over.* "Our babe will be birthed in Jackson less'n you dawdle and we end up bringing him forth on the trail." *A woman in a family way was a caution and that's the dang truth!*

He watched as Dark Eyes reluctantly wrapped the last of their acorn bread and blankets. She glared at him. "You have cradle board? Must take. Birthing bundle inside."

Mah Tew nodded. "I promise."

Hands clasped around the swelling mound of her belly, she asked, "What of Father and Mother?" Her concern hung in the air thick as tule fog. "I do not wish to leave them."

Mah Tew wrapped his arms around her bulk, well sheltered under a cloak of rabbit skin and deer-hide. He wanted both to console and encourage her.

"Your parents will leave in five sun times and follow our track. We must be as ghosts so no notice is taken of our travel." He brushed snowflakes from her cheeks. "I have spoken with Standing Bear and Eagle Feather Woman to lay the route. There's bound to be bloodshed real soon, Dark Eyes. This is a bad time for the valley. I must protect you and the baby. We have no choice."

Dark Eyes leaned into Mah Tew's embrace with a sigh of resignation. "Then, my husband, we must ask for *tyl-y*l, strong medicine on journey." Just beneath the surface, a flicker of stubborn pluck ticked in her voice. He smiled into the darkness. He had jumped his biggest hurdle.

She brought a small pouch of sage from beneath her coverings and held it toward Mah Tew for lighting. Sweeping the pungent smoke with cupped palms, Dark Eyes made prayers to the four corners, the Wind, the Water, the Earth, the Sky. He waited quietly, for he'd come to respect the power of these rituals. Only after her chanting did she turn her eyes to his. "I like you help me sit pony," she said, and walked toward Washee with that peculiar belly-first gait she favored lately.

Mah Tew breathed a sigh of relief and did some bargaining of his own with the Lord, as he mounted his sorrel gelding in the moonless time of coming dawn. He moved his horse forward, beckoning Dark Eyes to do the same. It would be hard, and many more days' travel to reach safety beyond the granite mountains.

Shrouded in darkness, they slipped away unnoticed. He led, threading their horses through the needle-thin line of trees, sheltered from prying eyes until the track started to climb. He hunched his shoulders and yanked his jacket collar up against the cold. "Let's buckle to, and we'll be quit of the flats in no time. The higher we are the safer we be."

"Mah Tew," Dark Eyes voice drifted to him in that almost inaudible tone that flowed so easily into his hearing. "When we pass Dance House I see great crowd people."

He pulled his horse up and turned his head. "Yep. They meet to prepare for the comin' assault. I imagine many will skedaddle to the four winds." As he'd expected, there was no reply. She had to be grieving the unsettling of her life. When she did break her silence, it was to announce her need to stop and relieve herself. She spoke up in that regard several times as the crowning sun swept the sky to orange, then rose above a wintry, cloudless blue expanse.

Mah Tew, impatient with the delays, speaking little himself, helped her on and off Washee to visit the necessary. Rifle in hand, he aimed to keep the two of 'em invisible and get good quit of the valley.

Early on the second evening they made camp in a circle of fir trees. The rising wind had a vicious bite, slashing at Mah Tew's hide and fleece wrapping, searing his face. Dark Eyes lurched from Washee's back, into his waiting arms, spent. Her features were hidden. Only her eyes and the tip of her nose, red with cold peeked from a swaddle of shawls and blankets.

Mah Tew shoved snow, pushing it to shape four thick, sturdy walls to shelter them from the bitter wind. He made a small fire inside their makeshift enclosure.

Arms gathered over her belly, Dark Eyes sat by the meager warmth. She'd loosened some of her coverings. Now her attention focused inward. Finally, she looked up. "Our child wish to meet you Mah Tew. He kick and wiggle. Make me hungry."

Though layers cloaked her lower face and muffled her voice, he swore he heard her teeth chattering.

"Like ponies, we have snow eat tonight. Maybe still have pine nuts? You bring food me, please," she said, blinking away the tiny ice crystals that settled on her lashes.

He fumbled in the saddlebags with frost-numbed fingers, finding acorn cakes and sticks of deer jerky to share. When he carried the food to where she sat without complaint, he marveled at her courage—her being in so delicate a condition. Such a wife warmed his heart.

"You are a wonder, Dark Eyes." He brought icy, chafed lips to her forehead and planted a kiss. "I promise you, little mother, not long after five suns rise, we will come to a place that is not so cold. A place of *waliki*, my people."

She tilted her head, apprehension in her eyes. "I not know all ways of your people. Only little bit." She shivered.

He cradled her shoulders. "You will be just fine, wife. I will keep you safe," he whispered, and hoped he could.

Following a sparse evening meal, Mah Tew tethered the horses where they stood, haunches braced against the wind, licking the snow's icy crust, nosing for feed below the surface. Grateful that white flakes no longer fell, he spread Eagle Mother's marriage gift of rabbit skin blankets atop the frosty surface and brought Dark Eyes to lie spooned in his arms. Bundled in cloaks and covered with saddle blankets, it felt pert near warm. She snored lightly only minutes after they bedded down, leaving Mah Tew to drift into sleep, turning thoughts of their future over in his mind.

The trail led them downward on the ninth day, sun shining warm against their backs. Mah Tew strained to see across an icy expanse of glistening snow, so white, the shine was near to blindin'. *Dash it!* He squinted and hooded his eyes with his hands.

"We are here," he all but shouted, pointing down a small slope at a group of structures. In the distance, shouldered together in two dark rows, they looked like nothin' but children's building blocks.

Dark Eyes, too weary to speak, gazed at him, her black eyes clouded. She was the very picture of exhaustion, her dusky face paled. Worrisome smudges rode beneath her eyes. Travelin' near 'bout a week or more, it was plain enough, the cold had taken its toll.

"Only a little further now, sweet," he said. "We'll make camp just below the snow line—there, by those oaks. You can rest a mite. We'll get to town in the morning and see about lodging and some kind a' work for me."

Chapter Forty-Three

The Milk Cow

It was nigh on suppertime when Gage set off for home, pulling his purchase behind him. The going would be slow along the treacherous canyon road that provided the shortest route to the cabin. He had little choice, he thought ruefully. Taking the road up and around through Angels Camp would mean an even longer ride.

It had been quite the task to find precisely what he needed. Using a shortcut to get home meant he'd be in the saddle for only a couple more hours before he arrived with his prize, and a letter from Sara's pa. And wouldn't y' know it, the temperature was droppin'. His toes were numb in his boots.

"Let's go," he said, urging Thunder into a steady walk. He pulled his hat brim lower on his head and tugged his jacket collar up to meet it, as though that, and his thick hair would actually keep him warm. Never mind, he knew the drill. Just keep going. Think about the cabin and the hot meal waiting. He pulled his bandana up over his nose. Frostbite would be particularly unpleasant.

Fiddler's Stew bubbled in a cast iron pot. The heady scent of carrots, onions, bacon and beef filled the cabin while Sara fussed with the biscuit dough. Her eyebrows drew together in a frown. She looked up. "I always seem to wreck my biscuits," she said to Rachel. "Gage says they'd make fine cannon fodder, though I'm not sure how knowledgeable he is about cannons."

Across the room, little Carlos sat in Rachel's lap. His chubby fingers grabbed at a small smooth stick his mother had carved for him earlier in the day. "My ma always said not to be mixing the dough much. Just toss it lightly and roll it out," Rachel offered, smiling at Sara's determination to conquer biscuit making. "The stew smells real good already," she added.

Tightening her fingers around a wooden spoon, Sara pushed it into the floury mixture and attempted to follow Rachel's instructions, twirling the mass gently to and fro several times. Then, giving it one solid stir for good measure, she turned the mix out on the tabletop and eyed it suspiciously.

"I must confess: Lena, who raised me, tried to teach me to cook, but I was always busy with my adventures and never paid much attention. Now I am fair laughing stock in the kitchen," Sara admitted. She chewed at her lower lip as she concentrated on rolling out the dough and cutting it into squares just right for baking.

"I don't know that much about cooking either," Rachel said. "Just the wee bits I recall from my mama ... and preparing the traditional dishes of my husband's mother. We did not have fine kitchen tools in the village—mostly baskets, pounding stones, spits, and fires."

Sara slipped the biscuits into a cast iron pan and sat them atop the stove to cook up. "I see you feed Carlos bits you have chewed. Is that the way of your husband's people?" she asked, watching Rachel's mannerisms, for any likeness to Matthew's.

"My milk has thinned since we lost our home. I feed him in the only way I am able," Rachel answered. "In the village I learned from the women to chew whatever I eat to a soft mash, and feed him with my fingers." She smoothed his dark hair, thick and growing straight up, like porcupine quills. "I know it's different when you have a kitchen. I do remember my ma spoon feeding my baby sister gruel and jar fruits."

Sara looked out the window at a family of chattering jays doing a happy dance, their blue-feathered bodies plump with grub worms and seed. She grinned. "I know. We'll go into town tomorrow for supplies and get whatever you need—perhaps some fabric to make a shirtwaist for you, and gowns for the tyke. It shall be a pleasant day for us. I haven't been for awhile."

Rachel bit at her lower lip. "I have no money to repay your kindnesses." She moved Carlos to her other knee.

"I admire your skill." Sara pointed at the stove. "You can teach me all you know of cooking and help tend the place. We certainly cannot abide your child and yourself being alone and unprotected. I know the good Lord would have us love our neighbors. Besides, it's grand to have a woman friend. There's mostly men in Angels Camp."

Rachel favored Sara with a tremulous smile.

"It's settled then!" Sara beamed at Rachel.

While they laid the supper table, the women continued chatting, discussing supplies, what Rachel knew of putting up vegetables, and the challenge of rearing a child.

Before long, the mouthwatering aroma of baking dough spiraled into Sara's consciousness. She pulled the biscuits from the stove. They looked simply delicious, big and puffy as blooming roses. Just wait until Gage tastes these beauties, she thought. Lord, she wanted him to get home in the worst way.

The wintry night had fallen early, grey skies deepening into a leaden sunset. Now it was dark, icy, and still. Even the branches of the fir trees didn't flutter. Silence wrapped the little cabin, causing the sudden bellow that broke the evening quiet to be all the more frightening.

"What was that?" Sara said, feeling the blood drain from her face. She strode to the hearth, her skirts rustling around her booted feet, and pulled her rifle from its spot.

Rachel stood and stared at the darkened windows, when a second brawl echoed the first.

"Get Carlos to safety!" Sara hissed. Her tone prompted Rachel to grip the baby so tightly, he whimpered as she raced into the bedroom.

Sara heard a horse whinny. Was their livestock being threatened? That wouldn't do. Gage would never forgive her if they lost even one horse. Stealthily, she moved toward the window nearest the door. Might it be a grizzly? One of those evil-tempered brown monsters? As luck would have it, the night was nearly without a moon—black as pitch. The devil's own playground. She couldn't see a thing. Clearly, she'd have to open the door and fire scattershot.

Perhaps she'd scare away whatever it was.

Holding her breath, Sara pulled at the door's leather strap and peered through the narrow crack. She lifted her weapon, and blinked. Not ten yards away, she saw Gage encouraging a reluctant black-and-white cow, its udders heavy with milk, to cross the yard toward the nearest pasture. The poor beast bellowed again, breath white in the frosty air.

Sagging with relief, Sara pushed the door shut and sank back against it. *Thanks be I didn't shoot him!* "Rachel," she gasped, "there is naught to fear. It's Gage. He's brought us an outraged milk cow."

Rachel, her face still fright-pinched, appeared at the bedroom doorway, arms coiled around Carlos. "That was a dreadful scare," she said. "I still fear the militia men. You are brave. It is a blessing, a gift of the Great Spirit that my son and I have come to you, Sara." She lay Carlos on a square of folded blanket set on the floor, and stood. "All the fuss has me craving to eat. I'll help you get dinner to the table."

Gage came through the door, his face so reddened and raw from the cold, it burned. He moved to the hearth, pulled off his gloves, and added a log to the flames. Curiosity hung in the air. The women watched him expectantly. They'd have their questions, but he was freezin', saddle sore, and mighty hungry. Tend to first things first, his ma always said.

"Hmm. Something smells doggone fine," he announced, and turned from the fire to seat himself at the table. "I see you two have been busy."

Rachel gathered the baby and slid onto a bench while Sara ladled hot stew into three bowls. The serving done, she sat down next to Gage.

"I would like to give thanks before our meal," Sara said, staring at him with unusual intensity.

What was she thinking? Gage wondered, as they joined hands across the table and bent their heads for the evening prayer. Following a chorus of amen, the clink of spoons against plates, and "please, pass the," were the only sounds heard for several minutes. Finally, pushing away her supper bowl, Sara spoke up.

"You all but scared us to death," she said. Her voice dripped with exaggerated sweetness, though her words were peppery as she passed the biscuits to Gage for the third time. "I thought we had a grizzly out there."

He shook his head. "Nope." He reached for another golden square.

"Hmmm. These biscuits are darn good, Sara."

"I nearly shot you, sir."

"Best ya' didn't. I would have missed this fine dinner, woman," he said with a wink in Rachel's direction. Sara's cheeks grew rosy at his words. He smiled, his eyes catching hers, admiring her flour-smudged face until she looked away. Food always did put him in a better frame of mind.

"It is good you brought a cow. Where did you find it?" Rachel asked.

"Oh, I stopped in town and Mister Jonley over at the trading post sent me on up the road to Jackson. He knew some folks looking to sell a bossie. It was a long trip over, and a longer trip back dragging that old mama cow behind me. I thought your young un' would be needing the milk."

"Thank you. My son will grow strong because of your generosity. You are a good man."

"Yes. Thank you," Sara echoed, her face still flushed.

"My pleasure, ladies," Gage replied with a casual dip of his head.

Sara cleared the dinner dishes, while Rachel said her goodnights and retired to the little bedroom with sleepy Carlos.

When they were alone, Gage joined Sara at the sink. He pulled the letter from his pocket. "This here's for you."

Sara's eyes widened. Stepping forward, she snatched the paper square from his fingers and stared at her father's careful script. Then, stuffing it into her apron pocket, she murmured. "Much obliged."

"Twan't nothing," he said. Giving her a three-by-nine smile, he grabbed a flour-sack dishrag, and dried as she soaped and rinsed plates and utensils. Several times she turned and studied him as though she had something she wanted to say. He saw confusion flitting across her fine-boned features. "Let's put the kettle on," he suggested. "I could do with some hot tea before I turn in."

Suddenly, she whirled on him. Her hesitation seemed to vanish like mist before a strong breeze. "I have to talk to you, or I shall burst," she said, her tone low, intimate. "Rachel, she ... she told me quite a lot about her life. I know it sounds pure crazy, but what she said ... it is the same as Matthew told me of his family and their tragedy—even the people, the names she spoke, though she did not name her older brother." Sara's voice shook with the saying of it aloud. "I believe Rachel to be one of Matthew's two sisters, the older of the two."

His jaw clenched. Her words riled him. Truth be, he was sick of the subject of her beau. Vexed, he fought to keep his voice even. "Dash it, Sara. That is an amazing yarn. Have you told Rachel of your suspicion?"

"No. I wanted to share it with you first." She ducked her head. "Do you believe it possible?"

"I'm struck all of a heap. It's a piece a' news I want to hear with my own ears." He felt his eyes go hard. "I think we must speak with her about it, ask her brother's name. That will surely be binding." Behind him the kettle sputtered. "Let's keep it on the quiet for now. A few days will be time enough to settle the matter. I don't hanker to upset the girl. And I have yet to milk that mama cow t'night," he reminded her.

Sara turned her head. "It would be right fine to reunite them, as they are all the family either has left."

Gage stared at her, surprised by her words. This was the first time she'd not referred to her own need to find Matthew. Were her feelings shifting? If so, he craved the change. He welcomed a chance to know her better. Though what might come of it eluded him. It might be downright pleasing if she gentled herself where he was concerned. His expression softened as he claimed his cup of tea from her trembling hands.

Unable to help himself, he touched the warm silk of her cheek. Her beautiful blue eyes shimmered with unspoken yearnings as she raised them to meet his. His breath caught. Who did she yearn for? Swallowing hard, he found his voice. "Sara," he managed, hoarse. His fingers trailed along her freckled nose and over her curls in a caress that left his fingertips heated.

"I know, you have to tend that cow," she breathed, "I'll see you come morning."

She favored him with a smile, clear and sweet as summer grass. Did she feel the burn of his touch? Those eyes of hers told him, yes. Was it his imagination? He watched her pad toward the bedroom, and marveled at the ruckus goin' on in his heart. Sleep wouldn't come easy tonight.

When she heard the cabin door thunk shut, Sara slipped into the main room. Wide awake, wrapped in her shawl, she pushed the rocker close to the fire's banked coals and sat down. Eagerly, she drew Pa's letter from her pocket. Leaning close to catch the light of an oil lamp resting on the mantle, she tore open the missive. Anticipation of news from home was only one of many emotions that unsettled her tonight, she began to read.

January 10, 1851

My Dearest Daughter,

Lena and I were pleased to hear from you. I hope this letter finds you well. We do worry for your safety in your winter home. Nevertheless we are enjoying the stories you send. I am publishing these entertaining vignettes with your byline, which is as it should be—and have got good comment on them.

I have news that will warm your heart. You know I asked for Lena's hand quite a while back and have been awaiting her response for many a week.

Although she was overcome with such a bold action after all these years, she has finally agreed to make an honest man of me.

Indeed the tying of the knot is upon us. We search for a Padre willing to join us, or a preacher. I believe we will simply get hitched with only the Sheriff as witness, and have a wedding celebration when both our children are here to celebrate.

Marco's schooling will complete in the Spring. He intends to come home, and I will train him to manage the ranch and its business. These are many changes I never planned for, Sara. It is my hope that you have forgiven us and will embrace my decisions. Lena frets about how you will feel in your heart about the new arrangements as well. She adores you.

You might send some word regarding these matters.

Your loving Father,

William Coulton

Chapter Forty-Four

Ladies' Day

Sara fooled with her hair. Pulling it this way and that, she squinted into the looking glass with no satisfaction.

"Seems to me, you are mighty concerned about prettying up this morning. For Gage?' Rachel shot her a sly look.

"Hmmph. I have no interest in that ruffian," Sara insisted. "Most times I'd like to pin his ears back." She recalled his fingers caressing her cheek. How his touch brought uninvited warmth to her belly. She'd keep her secret close.

Rachel chuckled, "I see the way he looks at you."

"Oh, bosh! He's admiring of me on occasion, like when I doctored Thunder's crumbly-toe with my hoof salve."

"You two are bucking the herd. You fancy one another. It's plain as day."

"Nonsense. I don't care a whit," Sara declared, and wondered if it was true.

The cabin door opened and banged shut. On the far side of the curtain, they heard Gage toss kindling and chunks of wood into the stove.

Sara pressed her lips together in a fit of pique, snatched up her brush, and forced her curls into submission. When they were properly pinned and tied with her favorite blue ribbon, she smoothed her cream-colored, high-collared shirtwaist and glanced down at her cornflower blue skirt. Truth be, she hadn't gussied up like this since that last evening in Yuma. "I'll have to see his face sometime if we are to get to town today," she said, and stepped into the cabin's main room. Flames crackled in the stove's belly.

"Mornin'," Gage drawled. "I trust you slept well?" Taking his sweet time, he scrutinized her person.

Sara felt her face go beet red. "Good day," she replied. Her gaze flicked here and there, as she tried to escape connecting with his impudent eyes. She cribbed her fingers into fists and walked to the sink, showing him her back.

"I see you have provided morning milk for the babe," she managed to say, as she measured out coffee grind and ladled water into the kettle from a tin bucket sitting next to the stove. "Today, Rachel and I mean to ride into town for some female shopping. There is quite a bit we have need of," she informed him, hoping her color had returned to normal. "Perhaps there is an animal in the barn I can ride? That will allow Rachel to set up on Cherry."

"I expect you'll be needin' an escort," he said. "Let me think on it. I doubt Murphy will do for hauling your purchases. It's time we find a buckboard … what with you women and a baby wanting to gad about."

"That is quite a plan, Mister Evans. It's probably best we *let* you join us," Sara allowed. "However, I'd like a word with you first."

"Agreed," he said, and smiled like he'd won a prize bull-riding contest.

She eyed him warily. "I guess there's no putting off my questions any longer. I'll speak my thoughts this evening. I simply have to know. I'd appreciate keeping our queries about Rachel's family dry 'til tonight. I don't want to spoil a fine excursion."

"Fine." He strolled to the table. "Speaking of family, where is the little shaver? I'm hankerin' to dandle him on my knee whilst I pull down a cup of your nice, strong coffee."

"He lays on my back, safe in his cradleboard," Rachel said, as she joined them and picked up two plates. Sara followed with the coffee pot and a third. They ate without further conversation.

His breakfast biscuits and eggs dispatched, Gage stood. "I'll get right to saddling Cherry and Thunder. Rachel, Sara thinks it best you set Cherry, and I believe she's right. Sara can ride with me." His eyes danced with deviltry. "It's been a while since we rode double, hadn't it?" The lopsided, boyish grin he shot her set her pulses to thrumming. "I'll find us a wagon for the ride home. You ladies enjoy your coffee now."

Gage grabbed his hat and headed for the door, leaving Sara to recall being hauled unceremoniously up onto his horse in a mountain storm, forced to cling to him all the way to Yuma. It would be a different story today. His arms would encircle her.

They arrived at Angel's Camp without incident. Thank heavens no dry gulchers jumped from the trees to rob them. Although she and Gage were chock-up in the saddle, they hadn't miseried one another at all. In fact, she'd quite enjoyed the ride. She looked over at Rachel, and smiled, pleased that she'd handled Cherry well.

"Mister Evans, do let us take our leave right here," Sara instructed as they approached the trading post.

Legging in to a hitch rail, he swung down, and fighting billowing skirts, courteously assisted their dismounts. "I reckon I'll have the horses over to the Livery while I take care of some business," he said. Then with a small bow, he pulled his Stetson from his head. "Allow me to take you ladies to a midday feast at Miz Hannigan's eatery. I'll meet you here come noon."

Rachel smiled her assent and handed Cherry's reins to Gage.

"We shall see you when the clock strikes," Sara agreed. She grabbed Rachel's arm and hurried up the steps to the trading post.

The store did a brisk business, even at this early hour. Miners looked for shovels and lamp oil. A couple of soiled doves perused the French soaps, bright parasols resting casual-like against their shoulders. Plain women picked supplies for their families, staying as far from the fancy ladies as they were able, Sara guessed. Mister Jonley was up to his ears in conversations and explanations.

Rachel gaped at stacks of merchandise and full-to-brimming shelves, her eyes bright with emotion. "I am overwhelmed. I have not been in the likes of such an establishment since my twelfth birthday."

"I knew you'd take pleasure in this store. We must make the most of our time," Sara said. "As I remember, we need cotton flannel for baby gowns, flour sackin' for swaddling squares, shirtwaist fabric, needles, thread, blanket yarn, and some gentle soap for bathing the child. The two bent to their task, perusing bolts of cloth and sacking as they waited to be served.

Sara fingered calico, patterned with small brown flowers on a cream background. "Look here. Do you favor this for your shirtwaist and skirt? It's a fine compliment for your coloring."

"Why, yes. It's lovely." Rachel pressed the fabric to her cheek, grinning.

At last, a frazzled Mister Jonley greeted them, his eyeshade catawampus on his forehead. "How do, Miss Coulton," he said, and bobbed his head politely as Sara introduced her companion.

She was grateful when Hiram Jonley showed courtesy to her young blonde friend who carried a papoose on her slender back. She well knew Rachel had concerns regarding how she'd be received here in town.

The clerk, his spectacles sitting low on his nose, measured lengths of cloth and suggested a finely milled soap for the tyke.

"I think we shall need several clean bottles and two of those black rubber infant nipples I've heard tell of, if you carry them, sir," Sara said. Ignoring Rachel's surprised glance, she piled their choices on the counter willy-nilly.

"We have the bottles and a pap spoon. I'll have to order the rubber teats," Jonley told them. "Will you be wantin' the *Ladies Monthly Magazine* you spoke of earlier? It'll need orderin' too."

"Yes please, do order that as well."

"I think we best get four yards of oilcloth," Rachel suggested, shyly. "It will keep our bounty clean to home and we can toss it over the table for dining."

"Yes, ma' am," the clerk agreed, and hustled off to scissor it.

"Vittles next." Sara grabbed Rachel's hand, and tugged her toward the foodstuffs. Flour, coffee, bacon, dried beans, tea and several jarred fruits soon filled the remaining counter space.

"Mister Jonley, kindly total our purchases and pack them for transport. I wish the full amount put on account." Sara dazzled him with a smile. 'We shall collect our merchandise in short order." She turned toward the store's entrance. "First, I must post a letter to my father."

"Miss Sara, jest hold on. There be mail from your pa, here. Came in with the payment of last month's billin'. I'll fetch it." He fumbled around in his big file cabinet and produced a letter.

Accepting the thin envelope and thanking the man, she scooted out the door, nearly knocking over a stack of wooden boxes in her haste. Rachel strode after her, rushing to catch up.

Snatches of conversation concerning an upset of some sort in the *Yo-se-mite* valley flew around them as they hurried along the plank walkway. The words militia and war barely caught Sara's ear, so intent was she on assuring her letter to Pa traveled on today's eastbound stage. She scarcely noticed the disapproving stares that settled on Rachel, girlish in her borrowed frock with an unlikely burden strapped to her back. Unaware of the commotion his presence caused, Carlos cooed and chortled at his audience.

The clang of the midday bell sounded, loud as a shriek, as Sara completed her transaction with the postmaster in the new Angels Camp post office.

"It must be near on noon. We'd best not dilly dally," Rachel reminded her. "Gage will be along directly."

"I know. And we've yet to pick up our purchases."

Errands completed, they headed back to the trading post. The women waited outside the doors, seated on a quick-made bench Jonley rigged using two crates and a length of lumber. They kept a sharp eye on the purchases mounded at their feet—wrapped in brown paper and tied with ropey hemp, piled in slatted boxes, and topped with a basket chock full of food items—chatting all the while.

"I hope he gets a wiggle on," Sara sighed. "I'm nigh unto starving, aren't you?" She fingered her pa's missive, eager for news of home, hankering to read it. Then Gage pulled up in a buckboard just as he'd promised, Thunder hitched to the front and Cherry tied to the rear. Pa's letter would have to wait.

"Ladies, your carriage awaits." He jumped down. "Our new transport is in fine condition, not a nick on the wheels nor a bullet hole in the body. Take a look."

Sara and Rachel approached the acquisition, both agreeing, "It will serve us well." Its sturdy bed was full of fresh-cut lumber, the piney scent pleasing. Sara marveled again at how he always so quickly found whatever was needed. "Makin' his jack," the miners called it.

She and Rachel gathered up string-wrapped bundles and handed them into the wagon. Mister Jonley stepped out and lent a hand with the boxes, admiring the solid build of the conveyance. In short order, every package and basket sat alongside the wood lengths. Gage laid oilcloth and tied down the entire pile.

He joined them on the walkway, brushing dust from his sleeves. "Shall we dine?" Placing his hand at the small of Sara's back, Gage guided her along the dusty planking as the three started off toward Miz Hannigan's eatery. Although she tried to ignore it, she did feel kind of breathless to have him touch her so personal like.

The town was a'swarm with activity. Their progress, slowed by Angels Camp bustle of humanity, required the ladies to bring hankies to their noses. The multitudes, mostly male and unwashed, stopped to confer, argue, and peer at the tents that lined the only street. Sara slipped her arm through Rachel's as the trio worked their way forth.

They dodged boxes and burlap bags passed hand to hand, as citizens stacked wagons with supplies for the camps and homesteads. The road was no better, crowded with horses and carriages vying for space, pitching up clouds of dust and clods of dirt. Curses and shouts split the air, as drovers staved off near collisions. It seemed ever more folks were moving in since statehood was declared, taking up farming and opening businesses.

"Right here," Gage said. They pulled to a stop before a wooden door flanked by three small-paned windows.

Rachel removed Carlos from his carrying cradle. She toted him into the restaurant on her hip as he wiggled gleefully. Sara, delighted to find wood flooring under her feet and real walls around her, exclaimed, "It makes no never mind that the roof is canvas; the place feels like a fine eatery." Then inhaling the aromas of well-prepared food, she fell silent.

Widow Hannigan, plump as a ripe pumpkin, rushed to and fro seating a stream of hungry customers for the noon-day meal. Hailing Gage, she directed their party to an empty table and rushed off to ferry platters of roasted meats and root vegetables to waiting diners.

The sight of the baby's black hair and brown fingers grabbing at strands of Rachel's golden locks caused curious glances, a smile or two, and several disapproving frowns. Each of those well met with sharp-eyed defiance by Gage and Sara, as they made their way forward and seated themselves one on either side of Rachel.

Widow Hannigan delivered an armload of cornbread, gravy, and steaming roast beef platters to her guests. She smiled warmly. "I guess there be four o' you counting the sprite. Here ya are folks." She beamed as the two young women reached to help her unload the feast.

Sara closed her eyes and breathed in. "The smell of it is pure heaven, ma'am."

"Ain't ya gonna make introductions?" their hostess demanded of Gage, ignoring the fact he was chomping at the bit to feed.

Sara liked her instantly.

"Miz Hannigan, meet Miss Sara Coulton, and Miz Rachel Crossing Waters and her son, Carlos Running Horse," Gage said, eyeing the platters with lust. "Sara, Rachel, this here is Miz Hannigan, owner of this fine establishment."

"Pleased ta make yer acquaintance, ladies." The older woman's eyes twinkled. "I dare say that's one fine looking boy ya got there," she pronounced, beaming at Rachel. "You folks jest wave a hand should ya need a thing more," she added, and strode off toward the door where a crowd had gathered, waiting to be seated.

"I don't recall ever visiting an eating house. Ma always did our cooking," Rachel said. She cuddled Carlos, her smile radiant. "This feels good to me."

The four of them had scarcely tucked into their meal, when a male voice boomed over the general hubbub. "Halloo, Evans."

All eyes turned toward the tall, broad-built speaker, conspicuous in a store-bought fancy plaid shirt and fine, woolen jacket. A wide-brimmed, leather hat covered his dark, curly hair. Gage stood and offered his hand as the man reached their table.

"Afternoon, Mister Rivera. Have a seat."

"I believe I will," Rivera said, and snatched his headgear off. Glancing around the table with interest he settled his bulk in the remaining chair.

Delighted to see her esteemed guest, Miz Hannigan hurried over to set a plate and eating irons before him. "Good day, Angelo," she all but shouted.

Chatter in Widow Hannigan's eatery suddenly hushed. Whispers hid in corners, as diners took note of the town's mayor, and new owner of the trading post, making himself comfortable right there at Gage Evans' table, with those women and that baby.

"And who might these lovely creatures be?" Angelo asked.

Once introductions were made, he fixed his eyes on Sara, then Rachel, upon whom he bestowed a generous smile. "Call me Angelo," he boomed, allowing a wide-eyed Carlos to capture one of his thick fingers.

"Mister … er, Angelo, won't you please share some of our bounty?" Sara gestured at the platters.

"Gracias, Senorita, thank you. Don't mind if I do." He stretched a thickset paw toward the closest serving spoon. Between enthusiastic mouthfuls, he brought his dinner hosts news of the goings on in the area. "Changes come to the deep valley. *De verdad*. It's true. There's a regular war on. General Bunnell's militia—and that mob of self-appointed vigilantes— they run the Indians out. Chief Tenaya and his family are fighting for their land, but most are fleeing. Can't say I blame 'em. I heard Tenaya lost one of his sons to a bullet already. *Está desgracia*. A disgrace."

Rachel flinched, fisting her fingers into a ball. "I lost my husband to the vigilantes," she confided.

"Them polecats ain't comin' up hereabouts to make their messes, Miz Rachel," Angelo assured her. He reached to give comfort, and her hand disappeared easily beneath the canopy of his. "You and your *hijo*, your young 'un, are safe."

"I allow that is a relief to hear," Sara said, glancing at Rachel, who suffered a slight reddening of her cheeks.

Over coffee and juicy berry pie, the talk drifted to the challenges and rewards of breaking horses using this method, and that. Sara and Rachel listened, fascinated, as Angelo, son of a Spaniard and an English woman, told stories of his childhood in the wilds of Mexico—all the while bouncing young Carlos on his knee. "And I hope you enjoyed your visit to the trading post," he added, explaining that he'd recently purchased the place from one Henry Moore. "I have added space and merchandise to please *las familias,* the families who settle here.

When it came time to move on, their dinner companion thanked Gage for the meal and smiled broadly at Sara and Rachel. "Welcome to our town, ladies," he said. His voice carried throughout the room as though he had used a speaking trumpet. "I'm pure glad to have made your acquaintance. Like as not, I'll be seein' you soon."

He clapped Gage on the shoulder. "Let me know when you wish to pick up my colts. I'll see to it you have some help, *amigo.*" The men shook hands and Angelo walked through the restaurant, watch fob in hand, nodding to various folks as he headed for the door. Sara and Rachel sipped the last of their coffee, and the three made ready to depart.

"Mister Rivera is indeed a gentleman of the first order," Sara said to Gage as they rose to leave Widow Hannigan's. She leaned closer and spoke quietly. "I do believe he took a liking to Rachel."

"Seemed to," Gage agreed, and placed a hand at the small of Sara's back again, steering her toward the buckboard and an impatient Thunder.

"You ladies wait a moment," he said, and went to check Cherry, who was pawing dirt at the wagon's back end.

"I find Angelo quite kindly," Sara whispered to Rachel as Gage came around and helped them onto the bench seat. Rachel, fussing with Carlos, made no effort to respond, although a faint blush pinked her cheeks.

As they rattled up the track to their cabin, Sara realized her world had tilted again. It was suddenly filled with moving pieces, new people. It felt like everything was flyin' out of its rightful place. *What news did Pa's letter hold? What upheaval will this evening's talk bring?* She feared it would be a tangled skein.

Chapter Forty-Five

Ruffled Feathers

Sara darted around the cabin, skirts swooshing along the dirt floor as she piled sundries, fabric and foodstuffs onto the table. She glanced out the window. Pulled alongside the hayshed, their buckboard stood empty. Gage had unhitched Thunder and Cherry and taken them into their shelters earlier. He'd unloaded his lumber and was busy stacking it inside the shed.

The day had flown by, so full had it been. Her thoughts wandered to their ride into town. Heat again curled along her back and around her middle as she recalled the feel of his chest, muscled and lean, pressed warm against her spine. She wondered if he had felt her fervor. Her face flamed. In self-defense, she spun away from the window. *Enough of this lunk-headed thinking.* It was getting on to dark. Before long, she and Rachel would be busy fetching supper. She wanted the chores done first. They'd need time for talking after they ate.

"I'll put up our supplies, Rachel. Why don't you tend to young Carlos. Once he's fed and off to sleep, you and I can prepare the evening meal. I am coming to enjoy cooking. I purely love learning from you. You've a way with the kitchen arts."

The young mother smiled and bent to loosening her son's swaddling blanket. "I think you most like to pleasure Gage's appetite for tasty food," Rachel said, as she disappeared into their sleeping quarters, her squirming baby boy gathered in her arms.

Sara popped her head through the curtain divider. "I own impressing him is quite satisfying," she confessed. "But I've chores to tend to and can't be dwelling on that."

True to her word, she bent to the task of organizing their ample purchases. One by one, she opened boxes, bags and packages and searched for the best storage containers. She poured coffee beans into the tin beside the grinder, refilled large pottery crocks with black beans and flour, and heaped potatoes in a square wood crate that sat in a cold spot nearest the door, away from the heat of the stove.

As she tucked fabric and thread into her sewing basket, Sara's attention turned toward the question she must ask of Rachel tonight, and how best to broach it. Often, her direct approach caused vexation. She didn't wish to cause her friend pain.

Preparing supper had gone well. Thanks to Rachel's fine suggestions, it had been tasty indeed. Eating however, was simply a devilish distraction tonight. She tried not to fidget as dinner conversation moved easily from talk of Miz Hannigan's establishment to a discussion of Mister Rivera and his tales of Mexico.

Rachel seemed relaxed and enjoying herself at table this evening. She'd successfully fed Carlos hunks of bread soaked in warm milk, using the new pap spoon. Swaddled again, he slept soundly on their bedstead behind the curtain.

Gage consumed several portions of eggs and potatoes before he, at last, sighed and pushed his plate away. Sara, in a fair ferment, seized the moment. She sprang to her feet, scooped up the supper dishes and deposited them in the sink. She closed the blue gingham curtains against the night chill. It was time. There was no sense in putting this off any longer.

She carried three steaming cups of chamomile tea to the table. Answers were needed. She'd mulled a while over how best to raise the subject and thought to begin by drawing Gage out a little. "Tell us some about your family," Sara coaxed, as she placed a cup before him.

He looked up. "Well, I don't know that it's all that exciting. The crux of it is, I purt near raised both my younger brothers back in Missouri. Pa fell sick with the influenza and died when I was comin' sixteen. We took his passing hard. Ma sure needed all the help she could get growin' up those little hell-raisers. The boys loved to ride with me." He smiled with the remembering.

Sara saw softness in his eyes, a desiring almost, and wondered how long it had been since he'd seen his family. Over the months, she'd noticed him posting a letter or two in Angels Camp. Writing to his ma, she expected. Pulling her gaze away before he was discomforted by her scrutiny, she turned toward Rachel.

Nervous, folding her hands in her lap to keep them still, she murmured, "I know you had a big brother you adored, Rachel. Truth be, your tale of losing him has remained with me. You never did name him. How was he called?"

Distress and the pain of loss rose in Rachel's eyes, causing Sara a pang of guilt. Still she had to know.

The three sipped in silence for a few moments. Behind them the hearth fire crackled and popped. Her question asked,

Sara glanced at Gage and saw his jaw clamped tight, a furrow bunched between his brows as he regarded Rachel with sober eyes. He seemed uneasy, wound up as a cat about to bolt for safety. Sara's body tensed. *What was he thinking?*

Rachel set her mug in her lap. "His given name was Matthew. Matthew Jacob Davies," she said tenderly, a river of sorrow in her voice.

Tears sprang unharnessed from Sara's eyes. Stunned and confused by her inability to control her emotions, she turned toward Gage. She wanted his strength, needed to connect.

Gage stared hard at Sara for a moment. He slammed a hand against the table, knocking his cup sideways, causing tea to splatter.

Eyes sparking fury, he stood and shoved away from the table. "I'll be checking on the livestock," he muttered, voice edged rough.

Alarmed, Rachel looked from one to the other, "What on earth is goin' on?" she demanded.

Gage offered no reply. Grabbing his jacket, he threw a "g'night," over his shoulder. Boots scraping hard against the packed dirt floor he headed for the door. It thwacked closed behind him like the crack of a pistol shot.

Sara watched his retreat through the watery blur of tears, that overflowed and spilled down her cheeks.

"I fear I am the victim of shock, hearing your words. My ... my... the person for whom I've been searching, I believe him to be your brother, Matthew. But everything has become so entangled now," Sara sobbed. "Forgive me, dear Rachel. How selfish I am." She gripped her apron-skirt and swiped at her tears. "Of course, this is wonderful news for you."

A kaleidoscope of emotions—hope, joy, disbelief, and bewilderment—fluttered like quicksilver across Rachel's face.

"My brother? He lives? You have set eyes upon him? You're certain? What do you know of his wellbeing? I thought him perished."

"I know he has been seen by others. In all likelihood, we shall find him and you shall have your brother by your side once again. Your family," Sara whispered, sniffling.

Trembling, the two women clung to each other, seeking comfort in the tumble of their emotions.

"Rachel you have become as a sister to me. I pray you will understand that I must reconsider my promise of marriage to Matthew. Your brother is a good person, but my feelings are as unclear as the horizon in a dust storm. Whilst it's a misery that Matthew has not yet been found, my feelings for Gage persist and grow stronger. I believe I care some for the man."

"How can I ever thank you for saving my life and that of my son, taking us in as family, and now," Rachel's voice quavered, "giving me hope of seeing my beloved brother again. My husband would say, 'The Great Spirit brought our paths together. We have big magic.' We *are* sisters, now. Nothing can change that."

"Do you mean Crossing Waters would believe our meeting was part of a greater plan for each of us? Our destiny?"

"That is a true way to understand the beliefs of Crossing Water's people," Rachel said. Their faith is guided by the power of their Spirits. The visions they bring are strong."

Sara's thoughts slid to Gage. She wept anew until her entire body was spent and speaking almost too much an effort to make. *Blessed Virgin, what will I do when Matthew is found?* After a moment she leapt up and paced the room. "I am confounded by all I feel. Why did Gage storm from the house? He looked distraught, beset with anger, it seemed." She plopped down in the rocking chair. "I don't understand why. I wished to talk with him. Gage has turned from me, and I cannot bear it."

"You can bear it. You must wait and see what will come of this. Be brave in your heart. Take your own counsel." Rachel urged Sara out of the old rocker, toward the little sleeping room they shared. "Let us retire and give dreaming time to soothe. It will be best to make good prayers for Matthew and for you to know your true yearning."

"I guess that is so. What more can be done? I feel torn in two." Sara headed toward the alcove they shared. In truth, she was exhausted; however, sleep came slowly, and her dreaming was unsettled.

Chapter Forty-Six

Angelo's News

The muted rumble of voices aroused Sara from slumber. Still thickheaded with sleep, she heard Rachel welcoming a visitor. Male from the sound of it, she decided. She threw back the covers and gasped as a wall of icy air settled around her. For a moment her heart leapt. "Lord love a duck!" *Was Gage home? No. It was fearfully cold. He would have made a fire.*

Darting across the frost-nipped dirt floor, she bundled into her heaviest shawl and poked her head around the curtain that served as a door for their sleeping quarters. A numbing chill crept into her bare feet, stinging her toes.

Why, it's Mister Rivera. What is he doing here? She rubbed her eyes. There was a surprising amount of light coming through the window. *It must be well beyond sunrise. Heavens, I slept long.*

Thoughts of the evening Gage had stormed out chased around in her mind like a dog after its tail. He'd been gone several days. Sadness and confusion settled over her as it did each morning since he'd been gone. She shuddered as much from the memory as from the frigid swirl of cabin air. *Confound it.*

Rachel turned as though she had the ability to see right through the curtain. "Sara, do please come out here. Mister Rivera has some news to share."

"I shall in a moment. Let me dress," Sara said, and set herself to find the nearest warm clothing to properly cover her person. Then, wrapped in her wool shawl, feet encased in heavy leather boots, she joined Rachel and their unexpected guest at the table.

"Mornin', Miss Sara," Angelo Rivera said, appraising her with worried eyes. "I had an early visitor couple of days ago, *temprano,* sunrise just," he told them. "Gage stopped by and asked me to watch after you ladies and the tyke for a while. He's headed into the deep valley to have a looksee."

"He's left us completely? Isn't that journey quite dangerous? It's midwinter and there's a war going on." Sara pulled at her lower lip with her teeth and wondered if Mister Rivera saw how deep-pained her heart felt. "Well," she said, as she fought back tears, "I am overwrought thinking of the harm Mister Evans might suffer."

"He seemed a bit distressed, ma'am. Perhaps he was needin' to go off and reflect a bit. *El necesita pensar.* Sometimes a man has to settle down his hash. *Comprende?* Understand? He thumped his hand on the table. Gage means to return soon, I am sure. Meanwhile, don't fret yourself. I'll see to it you have enough wood and come checking on you from time to time. I do believe you're looking a bit peaked, Miss Sara. We can't abide that."

Rachel glanced up, smiling her agreement.

"I am feeling quite fine," Sara insisted, yanking her shawl even tighter.

"I brung one of my horses to leave with you folks. Well-broke gelding, name's Sueño. He'll be safe for Miz Rachel to ride." His eyes sought Rachel's.

Sara saw her look down in haste and stare into her lap, unwilling to meet his gaze. *Why any fool can see he's smitten. I must speak with Rachel about this situation and her future wellbeing ... and about Gage and my own.*

Angelo's voice interrupted her musing. "I'll bring in enough wood to tide you over for a couple of days and I'll set a good fire this morning before you perish with the cold. We'll get the stove goin' too. Then you women keep feeding it. It is *muy frio*, very cold this winter. And, Miss Sara, it would please me if you used *mé nombre*, my given name, as do my sisters."

"Thank you Mister Riv—ah, Angelo, for being so neighborly," she said, polite and shivering. *It surely couldn't be any colder outdoors.*

"My pleasure, Senorita. *'Perdoname. Tengo trabajo.* Excuse me, I have work." He pulled on his gloves and stepped outside to pursue his task.

After a hearth fire roared, goodbyes were said, and the cabin door closed at Angelo's back. Sara turned her attention to Rachel. "I'm concerned. Gage was upset when he took leave of us that night. It was my tears must have provoked him. Though I have anger at his leaving, most often I am saddened. And now I worry for his safety. What can be done?"

Rachel smiled. "Why don't you set for a time and cuddle Carlos. He'll keep you busy. I'll heat the kettle, and we can make a plan over hot tea. We'll have plenty to do and time to think while Gage is gone."

With the little one in her arms, Sara looked up. "And by-the-by, you surely know Mister Rivera is taken with you, Rachel. Have you no interest? I think he'd do anything for you and the babe."

No sooner had she spoken the words, than Sara heard the clatter of the kettle as it dropped from Rachel's fingers, struck the stove, and thudded to the floor. She grinned despite herself. *Well, I dare say, that was an answer of sorts.*

Chapter Forty-Seven

Death and Life

Gage sat, his back pushed against a redwood tree. "Blast that gal! She's turning me into a crazy man," he declared, his words spilling into the wind. Somehow—he wasn't sure exactly when it happened—his heart had opened, and she'd slipped right in. He'd never felt as aggravated by any female and drawn to her, all at once.

To be sure, he'd had his dalliances, friendships of a sort that lasted days, or even weeks. But he'd always moved on without a backward glance. He shut his eyes. He'd had this same conversation with himself for far more'n week. It was gettin' old.

The be-all-of-it is I can't seem to let go of her, he finally admitted. Sara was different. *Heck, I'm hostage to her spirit, her laugh, her sass, the way a blush pinks her cheeks.*

He'd about gone round the bend when he heard her teary prattlin' about that boy she'd been searching for. "Matt. Still wet behind the ears," he grumbled. *I've never been jealous before. It's a bad business. Its best I cut dirt. What I need is to stay away. Clear my thinking. Maybe it's nothin' a bottle a' tonsil varnish won't fix.*

He savaged the hard tack and a strip of jerky, part of the grub Angelo had stuffed into a saddlebag and handed to him the morning he asked his friend to look after Sara and Rachel.

"I'm headed into the deep valley. Be back after a while," Gage told him, accepting the gift. "*Muchas gracias, amigo.*"

Angelo asked no questions, but offered warning. "There's a war going on. It's not all palaver. Militia's shedding *mucho indio* blood. Take care, my friend. *Vaya con Dios.*"

Gage tipped his hat, climbed into his saddle, lifted a hand in farewell, and trotted into the brisk dawn. He'd been out on his own for near two weeks.

He figured he'd reach the trail that crested the huge stone mountains tomorrow. "Get ready for big snow," he told the grey stallion, as he packed up gear and swung into the saddle. "We've got a good climb ahead of us, and it'll be dang cold," he declared. "At least I *know* how to deal with hard weather." His heels whispered against the stallion, and Thunder moved forward.

Picking their way down a rock-strewn track, Gage stuck the reins between his teeth, pulled his hat low on his head and his jacket snug around him, fastening every button. Wind bit at his face.

It was hard seeing the ugly work the militia had done. The carnage bore the truth of Rachel's story, and it sure as shootin' didn't improve his mood any. Indian villages burnt to the ground. Bodies of women, children, and the old marked with the cruelty of their dying left him heartsick. There'd be no burying them. The earth in these mountains was frozen.

Grim, he did what he could. For weeks he wrapped the lifeless in what tattered cloth he found, placing the corpses with their heads facing the home of the Great Spirit, crossing their arms over their chests when he could. Finding caches of unburned sage, he sprinkled the sacred herb over the departed to help ease their passage into the Land of the Dead. It was bad. A soul-harrowing experience.

Wrapped in his blankets at night, he stared into the unending swirl of stars and thought of Sara. Feisty, stubborn, shiny-as-a-new-coin. Smart, too, with all her scribbling. She had pen to paper just about every day. Writing letters to her pa, and those made-up stories she was always talking of. He wondered if she wrote about him. "Humph." He tugged his blankets tighter. His emotions veered like an out-of-control buggy headed straight for a cliff. He wanted to stay, keep her close. He wanted to run. Praying for relief, he closed his eyes and slept.

Next afternoon, as he neared the valley floor, a steady stream of fleeing villagers passed him on the trail. Women carrying babies on their backs and leading children by the hand trudged upward, wrapped in furs and blankets against the cold, feet encased in deer hides and ice. Even the youngest carried baskets or pouches. The elderly struggled through snow drifts, heads down.

He heard the shouts and screams of mayhem and the pop of rifle shots echoing below. He knew the drill. All the young men stayed behind to defend their land, their villages—the places of their ancestors, of their people since time began.

He trotted Thunder forward, closer to the fighting, picking his way through heavy snowdrifts. Despite the chaos, he couldn't stop thinking of Sara. She'd be indignant about all this, furious at the injustice. She'd surely be writing about it. He scowled. 'Course she was probably taken up with talk of Rachel's brother. Just thinkin' about it made his head ache. Or it could be my heart. He reined Thunder in, and looked up, needing to take his mind in a new direction.

That's when he saw them.

The old man, wrapped in a ceremonial blanket, walked with pride, stabbing his talking stick into the snow to assist his climb. Lips pressed tight, he gazed directly at Gage, his dark eyes hard, angry, defiant. Leading a mule loaded with only a few meager possessions, his wife trudged beside him. The woman, thin and shivering, struggled and coughed, her face drawn with the effort of each step and the bitter cold.

Gage sat astride the stallion quietly, watching. This is an important man. A chief, maybe? A leader. He was sure of it.

The old woman stumbled and fell in deep snow. He heard her speak soft words to her companion. Then shaking her head, she seemed to motion him to go on without her. In that moment, Gage made his decision. Moving Thunder forward several small steps, he gestured in greeting. "I see you have troubles, and I wish to help."

The old man straightened his back and plainly assessed Gage, evaluating his horse, full saddlebags, and the rifle lying across his thighs. After several tense moments, he said, "I Standing Bear, Headman *Olumpali*." He looked toward the woman. "This Eagle Feather Woman, my wife. We travel meet daughter and new husband in place call Jackson."

"I'm Gage Evans, blood brother to the Apache."

Standing Bear nodded. "Maybe Great Spirit send you."

"I think he may have," Gage agreed. He climbed off Thunder and nodded his respect. "I can get you and your wife to Jackson, sir."

"You want make travel up mountain?" The headman regarded him thoughtfully.

"Yep. Guess I do. Jackson's not that far from my cabin. We'll ride together for safety. I'll be glad for the company." He grinned, something he hadn't done for many days.

The old man's wizened face wrinkled in a smile. "Today, travel together good. I think more before choose to make big journey with you."

Gage brought Thunder closer and helped Eagle Feather Woman onto his saddle. Leading horse and mule, the two men turned from the valley floor and sought cover for the night.

Camped partway up the granite mountains, tucked in a circle of boulders, they shared a meal of acorn bread, jerky, and melted snow water. The sky was inky black with only a sliver of moon. When Gage bid his new friends goodnight, he rolled into his blankets, rifle cradled in one arm. Although he was fair certain militia and vigilantes were busy creating sorrow in the valley, he wasn't taking any chances. Bad enough they'd made a small fire earlier.

Pillowed on packed snow, arms crossed beneath his head, his thoughts drifted to an idea he'd been considering for a while: settling down in California. He liked the weather, the scenery, most of th' folks he'd met. The place seemed fit for ranching and cowboying. Heck, there was good need for his talents right there in Angels Camp. He'd been savin' enough of his horse breaking and training pay to maybe get a piece a' land of his own.

His mind wandered to the edge of his cliff. Sara. He'd never spoken about this to anyone. *Was it time to head on home and do some talking?* His brows gathered in a frown. *"Would she even be there?* Blowing out a sigh, he closed his eyes and vowed to sleep on it. He'd shake it out in the mornin'. That decided, he fell into a light sleep.

In the thin light of dawn, under sky-high peaks, the three travelers packed in silence, preparing for a trail that rose before them like the rising sun.

"I'd be much obliged if you folks would set my horse for a spell," Gage said, breaking the early morning hush. "Until I find us another mount."

The old man's dark eyes flashed. "You *waliki* good character," he pronounced, and solemnly gave his agreement to partner up on the big journey to Jackson.

Relieved at Standing Bear's choice, Gage pulled on his gloves and helped Eagle Father Woman and Standing Bear onto Thunder's back. He walked, leading the mule, rifle slung over his shoulder.

Stepping through drifts and bare patches, he gave his future serious thought. The idea of running his own horse ranch felt right.

But, Sara? He still couldn't shake her from his head. *Hell's bells!* He hated confused thinkin'. Truth was his loneliness had teeth, and its bite stung. He gazed at the man and woman tucked together in his saddle, and in that moment, knew he'd been heart-shot. *I'm not worth a straw without her. There's only one way to quiet my hunger. Have Sara by my side for a lifetime.* Though it made him doggone nervous, fact was, he'd fight a grizzly for the privilege. He swallowed hard and set off with new resolve.

As they had for several twilights, this evening the three crouched around a meager fire. They'd tracked away from voices and hoof beats all day and been able to avoid any confrontations. So far they had not fired a single shot.

Tonight, a shared meal of acorn bread and the roasted meat of two squirrels he and Standing Bear had snared warmed their insides.

Gage hunkered down, closer to the heat. "Tell me of your daughter," he said. "Do you know whereabouts in Jackson to seek her?"

"She go with husband. Carry gift of child in belly." Standing Bear squatted. "Husband *waliki*, like you." His gnarled fingers gestured at Gage.

"A white man?"

"*Aiyee.* He Mah Tew Greywolf. He give map for go Jackson. I lose. No have. Must make search for daughter."

Poking at the fire, Gage turned the information over in his mind. They were traveling slow. It could take several more days, even two weeks to reach Jackson. And who knew how much longer to find the couple, if, in fact, they were still in those parts. Food was runnin' low. The old woman was coughing something terrible. He worried about her survival. It wouldn't do to be dragging her from place to place.

He thought about Sara, a plan forming. They'd go straight to the cabin. It was closer. The women could properly care for Eagle Feather Woman, while he and Standing Bear rode down to Jackson and searched. Then, he'd return and declare himself. Praying Sara would forgive his sudden leave-taking, he hoped she'd look favorably on him for the good deeds he was doin'.

He glanced at his traveling companions and wondered how this change in plan would sit with them?

Spring
1851

Chapter Forty-Eight

New Life

On a sunny late March morning, Dark Eyes greeted the spirits and gave thanks. She trundled her bulk around their camp. Murmuring to her unborn child, she stopped at the edge of the meadow beneath a big oak tree, then the fire ring. She could feel Mah Tew's eyes tracking her. "I show baby new home," she explained, when she completed her circle of the site.

Many sunrises, Mah Tew rode to Mister Charley's farm for work. Each afternoon he brought new foods to her. Butter, white man sourbread, cheese, black beans. She ate and grew strong. Today, he not work. Sabbath—now time to speak my God, he'd said.

Thirsty, she stepped to a mound of unmelted snow and scooped pristine palmfuls into a small, tightly woven basket, and picked up two flat stones. "You make fire, heat rocks, husband," she said, and placed the stones and basket in his outstretched hands. "Need water for drink."

"I'll take care of it. You are large with child. Shouldn't you rest?"

Contented, Dark Eyes settled herself against the wide trunk of the grandfather black oak tree at the center of their clearing. Its thick branches, graceful and rugged, reached in all directions. Closing her eyes to feel the peace of its canopy, she stretched her legs straight out and rested her arms on her belly. "Moon grows big, round as my belly. Baby come soon. Maybe time of seven suns, maybe more quick." She made marks in a nearby patch of damp soil to indicate her expectations.

Mah Tew dropped an armload of kindling next to the stone ring he'd built. "How can you know?" he asked, as he arranged a small mound of sticks in its center and topped them with the larger firewood he'd gathered.

"My baby tell me," she said.

"Don't worry. I'll be sure to seek help first thing when I ride for town tomorrow."

Dark Eyes laughed, a low musical chuckle. "No need," she gently chided him.

He stared at her, shock etched sharp on his face. "Are you funnin' me?"

She drew her legs up, setting a fence between them. and stubbornly returned his shocked glare. "No good speak this with husband. Spirits no like. Is for woman job." This was not the first time he had tried to talk of the birthing. She didn't say another word.

Tight-lipped, he busied himself, preparing the fire. "Don't seem right," he growled at last, breaking the silence.

She watched without comment as the small blaze heated her flat stones. When he placed them in the basket and came to sit beside her, his face was shadowed with concern. "I must get a midwife for you, Dark Eyes."

"*I wife*. What midwife is?" she asked, suspicious, in a bit of temper.

"It's such like the women in the village who might assist you. A woman who helps the baby come into the world. My ma had one for her lying-in times." He scowled. "Please, Dark Eyes. I don't know a darn thing about safe birthing a young un.' Pullin' a calf would be another story." He reached for her hand.

A small sigh escaped her lips. She loved his touch. It seemed her hunger for his skin against hers was always alive. Even now, she marveled. He slid his hand and hers under her cloak, and placed his fingers gently on her belly. His big hand resting with hers across the expanse of her stomach warmed her. She could feel the good magic they sent to the new life she carried.

She looked up at him. "Midwife is white man way ... a stranger." Dark Eyes sighed and drew her brows together. "Husband's mother make best help, but no can have. No need *wunenapi*, medicine woman. *Wonomi* say, 'Baby have safe journey to my arms.' I believe," she said with confidence.

Seeing his eyes darken to the color of charred wood and his mouth turn down in distress, she relented. "Midwife come later, okay." She pushed herself up, unwilling to think any more about it. "I get acorn bread. We need eat." She headed for their saddlebags.

Basking in early spring sunshine, soothed by heated drinking water and fortified by a small meal, Dark Eyes felt a surge of energy. While Mah Tew tended to the horses and laid a comfortable sleeping place for them, she wandered around their campsite, peering surreptitiously into the nearby trees, stretching her legs and musing about the life they would make in this place. Jackson, it was called.

She felt both fear and excitement. *Change more hard now I carry gift of new spirit in belly.* "Like mother bird, I need make nest," she muttered. She thought about her parents. Did they have upheaval in their lives when she was but a new spirit? Were they safe? Would she ever see them again?

Dark Eyes awakened refreshed, as a new sun reddened the sky. Her sleeping had been dreamless. Mah Tew had added wood to the coals in the fire ring. A merry little blaze spread warmth to where she lay. He was several feet away readying his horse for the ride to town. She sat up and stretched, enjoying the comfort. "Mah Tew, I greet you," she called.

"Mornin' wife. I am glad your sleep was quiet. Stay by the fire. I'll bring warm water and bread." He rummaged in the food baskets and handed her a small packet wrapped in leather. "This here is the near finish of our food stock. I must gain the start to Jackson early today so I can get my plowing work done and get paid. We need white-man money to live in this place." He bent and planted a kiss on her brow while she nibbled at her morning meal.

Swallowing a mouthful of dry acorn bread, she looked up at him. "Mah Tew, I have gift share you." She fumbled in her cloak, pulling at a circle of tiny stitches. "You need come here." She patted the ground next to her.

When he sat beside her, she smiled and took his hand, pressing a small pouch into his palm. "You look," she said.

His thick man fingers pried open the tiny bag and pinched at its contents. "Luddy Mussy! Where did you get this, woman?"

"My cousin gift for trip home. I save. No give Father. He has many horses. I keep for marriage. Is good? Yes?"

"Why, Dark Eyes, this little pile of yellow metal will keep us from hunger. We can save most all of my work pay. After a spell, might be I can open a store of my own—just like we talked about." He tumbled her back into the blankets, his face alight with hope. "This is treasure," he said, "and so are you."

"Hmmm, where my water for eat rest of acorn cakes, husband? You must be hurry. The sun grows old in sky."

He brought the water bladder to her, warmed from sitting near the embers. "1 don't like leaving you." Mah Tew frowned. "I want to gather some vittles after work and check on a place I heard of—for us to settle into. Maybe it's best I take you with me. I'll not be back 'til late evening."

"Mah Tew, Spirit guide tell me is time find water that race free. Need make birth hut where water rush." She pointed. "Maybe find in trees."

"I want to watch over you," he insisted.

His anxiety pierced her like cold wind. She shook her head, wondering how to make him understand. "Evil no come me. No bad medicine." She touched his face. "You look mad wife. Maybe I let come. Okay?"

He made a small smile. "*Mid*wife," he said, and lifted his arms in a gesture of surrender. "Okay. You have your long knife?"

"I keep," she assured him. "*Wonomi* watch over me. I know."

Throwing a backwards glance, face stark with worry, Mah Tew climbed into his saddle and rode off toward Jackson.

Dark Eyes watched him go. She rummaged among their belongings and found the deerskin-covered sack her clan women had woven for her. This she slung over her shoulder. Then fingering her spirit feather, knife in hand, and alert for the sound of running water, she walked into a copse of trees. She felt a small telling pressure beneath her big belly and rubbed. "My baby you seek entry into world. This day I welcome you," she whispered. "Father surprise."

At the side of a creeklet, its bed barely wetted with a trickling flow of cold, clear water, she rested for a short time. There she left her birthing bundle. Now she must find a proper place to welcome her child. Not far from the creek's edge, she came upon a cluster of redwoods. In their center, brush and vines had grown into a thatch almost as tall as she was. Cautiously, she investigated the tangle and found promise.

Making prayers to the four corners, Dark Eyes slashed at the undergrowth, creating a narrow opening. Panting with her exertions, she knelt and cut through dry twigs, green vines and leafy shoots, carving out a small circular space.

Attentive to the warnings of her body, she stilled more and more often, biting her lip as unfamiliar pains circled from belly to spine. The upheavals in her lower back intensified, a signal that motherhood came closer. Determined, she worked on, slowly clearing a floor space, and scraping a shallow, round depression in the earth. She filled it with soft fallen needles and grasses to receive her child.

The hut completed, Dark Eyes struggled to her feet and fetched her bundle. Crouched before the birthing place, she unpacked medicinal herbs, healing sage, a shawl to bind the child to her, a water bladder, and soft, chewed deerskins she had carried all the way from the valley. Biting back moans, she sprinkled sage over the bedded floor and laid the deerskin in a pile, as Owl Woman had instructed.

Only then did she hurry to rest beside the creek and listen to the birth song of her body. In one hand she held her knife. In the other she gripped her eagle feather for courage, and asked to be unharmed by forest hunters. She wished no visit from coyote, wolf, or man. She meant to live to see her *u-ti*, her baby.

In the warmest part of the day, the striving of her unborn babe grew ever more demanding. She knew it was time. Fisting the small stick Mother had given her, Dark Eyes crept into her birthing hut, grateful the spirits of her ancestors had allowed her to complete the proper preparations. Shedding her beaded shift, she folded it and placed it at the entry, atop the shawl. In this sacred place, *Wonomi* safeguarded mother and child. She arranged herself on the soft circle of grasses. Over and over she squeezed her eyes shut, clamped her teeth against her prayer wood, and made no sounds for the clamor in her body.

Soothing spirit visions gave her strength to shepherd new life as the baby journeyed from its sheltered place within her. Panting, she obeyed the shriek of muscle and bone, shifting from sitting, to hands and knees, and back again. Slick with sweat, mouth too dry, she whimpered. Her small mewlings grew until anguished groans escaped her clenched jaws when finally, no placement of her torso provided respite.

"*Wonomi*," she thundered, bawling as a surge of pain forced her to a crouch. Her child was coming now, twisting and turning in his fight to greet her. She grunted and squatted, pressed her head into the roof of the makeshift hut, feeling the pressure of his head and shoulders splicing her, she yowled like an injured bear and—with a mighty push—brought forth her baby onto his welcoming forest bed. A son, as had been foreseen.

Dark Eyes wept with the joy of him and the sound of his thin wailing. She cradled his slippery little body atop her own. Sitting up, she fingered her spirit stick and twisted it around the cord that still tethered her son to the spirit realm. She used thin strips of deerskin to carefully tie off the birth cord close to his belly in two places. Then, making a prayer for sure hands, she sliced through it with the obsidian knife of her clan, bringing their *u-ti*, their baby, fully into the world. His cries of greeting grew robust. Relief washed over her. She touched each perfect, tiny finger and toe as he suckled at her breast. Gratitude filled her, and she offered thanks to the Great Spirit as she lay back to await the afterbirth, which came quickly.

If she were in the bosom of clan and village, she'd stay in her birth hut for seven days, enjoying the crown of motherhood, under the care of her own mother and sister-cousins. Her husband would guard his wife and new child. They'd speak in whispers through the hut wall.

Alone in this thicket, she had no choice. She must move to safety—away from wild, forest animals. She wished for Mah Tew, as she lay curled with their boy, cleaning him and herself with small pieces of deerskin. Her first tasks of motherhood completed, she gathered her strength and rose with effort from her bed of grasses. She struggled into her shift, bound the child to her with the shawl, and carried her son to the creek's edge. The afterbirth and bloodied trappings she buried near the water. She left no trace of his birth. It was the proper way to assure the health and wellbeing of their child.

Then, according to custom, she stepped into the rill and made the prayer Mother taught her. She dipped her son in the running wet of the creek to ensure strength. His howls of protest were indignant. For a moment she wondered if she'd properly carried out the ritual. To ease his distress, she bundled him into the larger deerskin she'd brought and placed him against her nipple to suckle. His instant silence bespoke forgiveness. No harm had been done. She longed for Mother, Father, Grandmother, and her clan cousins, wanting their guidance on this new road.

The sun was almost gone to its rest when Dark Eyes arose, and cuddling the baby, now swathed tightly in the shawl, made her way back to camp.

It was there Mah Tew found them lying beneath a canopy of glittering stars that looked as though they had nearly dropped to earth, almost close enough to touch. Overseen by a crescent moon, wrapped in blankets, his child lay swaddled against his wife. The babe's tiny, fuzzed head peeked from amidst the folds. Astonished, he yanked his hat from his head and fell to his knees. "Thanks be to God," he said softly.

His heart thudded, as he reached out a hand to tenderly caress the mother of his infant. "Dark Eyes," he whispered, voice cracking with emotion.

She smiled sleepily, "*Wonomi* bring you son, Mah Tew."

He hoped the digs he'd found for them close to town would be good enough.

Several days later, Mah Tew loaded the horses with all they owned. Dark Eyes sat Washee, her face a stoic mask. No stranger could guess the discomfort of her tender, unhealed birth wound. His son, swaddled in the cradleboard, rode comfortably against her back in contented sleep.

"I go at walk," Dark Eyes stated, flat out.

"We'll move slowly," he promised, understanding her demand.

True to his word, they traveled at the walk for more than two hours. He saw concern grip his wife's face as they passed near town. She'd been wary of moving close to the white man houses. She'd heard too many stories, seen too much. Skirting Jackson's main streets, he led them up a dirt track that gave onto a rutted ditch of a road, then pulled to a stop beneath a large tree.

Dark Eyes stared with distaste and curiosity at a dirty canvas structure. Its roof set at a slope like a small hill was held in place by ropes attached to oak tree branches.

"This our home? *No um-a-cha*?" she asked, disappointment plain in her voice.

"Yes. It will do for now. Don't fret, wife. We will be warm and dry through winter. It is far from strangers. We must think of safety while we wait for your parents. Drawing attention is unwise." Anyway, it was the best he could do without using their nest egg. He climbed out of his saddle and looped the reins around a lower branch. "There's grazing for the horses and hunting will be good. We even have a little corral."

Mah Tew walked to Washee and helped his family down. "I've purchased cooking supplies and got you a good broom." He grabbed her hand. "Come have a look," he pleaded, urging her toward the rickety wood porch. "Let's get inside, and you can see for yourself. It will be okay."

California
Chapter Forty-Nine

Serendipity

Sara sipped her morning cuppa joe, a scowl on her face. In the six weeks since Gage had stormed out the door, it seemed like she awakened out of sorts and beset with guilt every day. Her romantic affections for Matthew were fading. She seemed unable to keep her heart from pulling in a new direction. Many a sunrise, she struggled from sleep, her mind slapping at nightmare visions that plagued her dreaming. Gage mortally wounded. Slipping from a cliff face. Freezing. Starving. His blood, a bright stain in the snow, leaving a trail for fearsome wolves. "Perhaps I'm cursed to lose the fellows I care for," she lamented. "Perhaps I bring the devil's own luck."

Rachel tried to soothe her friend. "No such thing! You simply need to clear your thinking. This misery of yours is trying, and I fear for your health. Ride into Angels Camp," she beseeched. "See who is new come and who's struck it rich. Explore a bit. Visit the shops. It will do you good."

"Your reasoning is sound. I must find a diversion or I shall start raving. I'll take Sueño and jog into town. Perhaps I can find a story of interest to relate for my father's paper. He likes the tales I've sent him thus far." She set her cup down hard, spilling coffee on the table. "Maybe I'll ask around about Matthew. I need to do something besides sit in this cabin waiting to hear from Gage, or I'll simply go crazy with it!"

"Carlos and I will be fine here," Rachel assured her. "Mister Rivera is due for a visit. He's left me a trustworthy pistol, so you take your rifle. Just promise you'll be careful, Sara. Gage wouldn't want you roaming afar by yourself."

"Then he was foolish to take off. I don't know if he'll ever come back. He has broken my heart." She shuddered. "Thing is, I find it dreadful hard to accept. I long to see him." Holding back tears, she went to saddle the gelding.

Giving her promise to return before supper, Sara climbed on Sueño and rode for town. She left Cherry to enjoy the shade of the corral that sat behind the cabin, knowing Rachel would need a fast horse if she had a dire emergency.

Despite her despair over Gage's absence, she was grateful for the sun warm at her back. The old red gelding's gentle gait and the light breeze tickling her neck chased away tensions. She savored the expanse of rolling, oak-studded hills. Feathered grasses, still winter-green, made a lush carpet stretching in all directions. I surely suffered a case of cabin fever, she mused. I guess 'twas the cold and grey brought me low.

It was hard not to feel a bit hopeful today. The very landscape enchanted, and the sky showed a magical cornflower blue. She sang a chorus of "Oh, Susanna" for the joy of it, smiling when the gelding's ears waggled back as her voice rose and fell.

Memories of Indian summer rides she and Gage took while they still camped in the woods dogged her. When was it that their bickering had taken a turn and become something different? Lately she had come to respect his fairness, his capable mind, and acts of kindness. I like him, she mused, even if he is ornery.

As the road passed within earshot of a nearby creeklet, the familiar sound of men's rough voices and the clank of pick and shovel disrupted the sleepy clip-clop of Sueño's hooves, disrupting Sara's thoughts.

"Mother Mary," she snapped, suddenly alert. Shifting the reins into one hand, she rested the other on her rifle stock. Tendrils of tension crept back into her shoulders. She urged her horse into a lope, hoping to get past the commotion and into town without delay.

Sueño moved ahead at a measured pace, his hooves kicking up dust as the road passed close to the rain-swollen, turbulent waters of Angels Creek, muddied with the efforts of a thousand men obsessed with the search for gold.

Dashing her hopes of an uneventful ride, a big-bellied, bearded man, his clothing fit for burning, jumped up at the sight of Sara and the big horse pounding along the trail.

"Hiya voman! Coom here," he shouted. Turning, he poked his bare-chested companion with a gnarled finger and gestured toward her.

Not yet noon and the pair were befouled with drink. Disgusted, she put her nose in the air in response to the whoops and hollers of the miners. When they flung their shovels aside and started for the bank, gazing at her with heated eyes—quick as a cat—she spurred her mount into a full gallop, leaving the men knee deep in the cold creek water.

"I will never get used to this sort of ignorant behavior. It scarifies me every time," Sara confided to Sueño as they ran. "Do you suppose they behave in this manner around *their* womenfolk?" When the track finally turned away from the water's edge, she allowed her mount to slow and her own muscles to loosen. As horse and rider returned to a leisurely walk, her thoughts reverted to planning her day.

Rachel is clever. I must bestir myself to some purpose. Find something to inspire me. In his last letter, Pa had asked for another of her stories. It's time I provide one, she decided, although she'd leave this episode out. She'd heard talk of Jackson. Exploring the nearby gold town would be an adventure.

Sara stared down at her saddle horn, her thoughts drifting. Gage would never have permitted such a gallivant. Perhaps there'd be some danger, it *was* farther afield than she'd been before. But writing about it might be just what she needed to help her quit grieving for the man who'd stomped out of the cabin, and on her heart.

Sensual notions, traitorous and unbidden, swung round in her head, evoking memories of the evening his strong, calloused fingers heated her face like a struck match at every spot they touched. And those astounding green eyes of his, roaming her person, causing fire to curl in her belly and unfamiliar muscles to quiver deep inside. Such stirrings were new. She found them both alluring and entirely unsettling.

She wondered again if he'd known the reactions set loose in her body and perhaps within his own. Face flushed, she squirmed in the saddle. The moment certainly had been a great deal more than simply pleasant. Sara chewed her lower lip, miserable with his absence. She'd not felt this same fullness with Matthew. Now, that attraction seemed like a schoolgirl's crush, something from another life.

Fears for Gage's safety plagued her. Try as she might, she could not stop imagining bullets and arrows flying. A war, and Gage in the midst of it. *I best face up to my sentiments.* Struggling with the truth, her heart thudded. *I hunger for him. Oh my. Have I fallen in love? Rachel seems to think so. Surely not love ... he is so exasperating.* Emotions bucked and kicked until there was no way to avoid the flood of feelings. Overcome, tears burned behind her eyes. *I have fallen in love.* It came clear as a sunny day. *My future will always belong to Gage.* Quivers of joy and sorrow shook her.

"Dear Lord," she hastened to petition, "do forgive my begging, but I must! Will I never have the chance to tell him of my feelings? *Please* bring him home to me." Excitement, hope, and despair somersaulted in her heart. She was upon a new beginning that might never have a chance to betide.

All this thinking and lamenting made her want to flee something fierce. Taking a breath, she straightened her back and lifted the reins. Jackson it'd be. "Come on, rattle your hocks," she hissed and pressed her legs into the gelding, anxious to be on her way.

The sun had got straight up in the cloudless blue, when small wood-built houses came into sight on either side of the road, their tiny, gated front yards resplendent with budded pink and red climbing roses. Reining Sueño in, Sara slowed him to a walk. Her eyes took in a busy scene. Just ahead she saw sleek one-horse buggies, single riders, and larger wagons, moving with purpose down what seemed to be a still muddy main street. There were quite a few buildings. The town was some bit larger than her digs. She'd ask after Matthew. This was a perfect distraction.

Sara knew a general store could be delightful or quite disappointing, depending on the happenstance of deliveries. Today, she was in luck. In front of a large shop, its doorway stacked with goods, she dismounted, tied up Sueño, and strode to the entrance. Happily, she found writing books in good supply, a generous selection of pencils, and a length of handsome light flannel. Carlos was growing like a young colt and in need of new gowns again. Women bustled through the store alongside her, some wearing fine outfits and even proper hats, picking and choosing their necessities. Before taking her choices to the counter, Sara pulled her composition notebook from her satchel and scribbled quick descriptions of their finery.

"You've quite a village here," she ventured. Encouraged by his interested glance, she continued. "North a ways in Angels Camp, gold-seekers over-run the rivers and creeks. I find their rowdy, vulgar behavior tries my temper. Have you the experience of unruly folks here in town? I've heard no gunshots or swearing."

The man nodded, his fingers twisting twine into knots. "Indeed. Gold or no gold, one never can predict what sort of rudeness and brutality one might come upon here in Jackson," he confided, glancing at the busy road outside his door. "There's outlaws come through and plenty of shootin'." His voice sank to a whisper. "We are in need of an honest lawman, to be sure."

Making mental notes of their conversation for the article she'd send her father, her thoughts turned to Rachel's brother. "I wonder, do you know of a Matthew Davies hereabouts? He'd be a newcomer. Brown hair, grey eyes, not quite six-foot."

"I cain't be right sure, Ma'am, we get so many. Mebbe. Why doncha ask down at the jail. That bunch usually know who comes and goes. Head to the right. It's some eight doors up."

Sara thanked the fellow, gathered her treasures, and stepped out onto the planked sidewalk to survey the busy main thoroughfare. Outlaws. Vigilance was called for.

She checked on Sueño, then started toward the sheriff's office. She hadn't gone but twenty steps when a slender Indian woman, sitting atop wooden steps that gave to the rutted street below, caught her attention. Her arms cradled a squirming bundle. She looks no older than I, she thought, and stopped mid-step to stare at the tiny cooing baby. A boy, she guessed, some months younger than Carlos Running Horse. She could not tear her eyes from the child. His skin was so much lighter than the rosy brown of the regal woman who held him. Why, wee as he was, he looked almost familiar.

Head tilted, forehead drawn into a dark crease of frown, Sara tried to give name to the vague suspicions tiptoeing in her head. She ran her fingers through her tangle of curls. What absurd thoughts. *I should move along. Best I get back before sunset.* But her boots seemed rooted in the plank walkway. *Didn't that awful Yuma lawman say Matt traveled with an Indian woman?* Possibilities swept through her like bats stirring at dusk.

After a few moments, she was compelled to lift her head and stare directly at the comely young woman, who reached into her deerskin pouch and removed what looked to be crumpled paper … or cloth.

She watched intently as the woman unfolded a lacy white square and tucked it beneath the infant's chin. *Can it be? No. No.* Sara gasped. On the lace-rimmed hankie were the very initials she had embroidered in azure blue: SDC. Her feet suddenly came unglued. She stepped closer. *Yes. I am certain. It is! The handkerchief I made and gave to Matt when he left for Tucson is a bib for this lambkin.* "Oh my God," she whispered, her heart pounding in her throat. People strolled by, intent on afternoon errands, but Sara neither saw nor heard them.

All thoughts of the sheriff gone, her emotions churned, bouncing in every direction. Is Matthew alive? Had she found him? It will mean joy for Rachel. *Who is this woman? I simply must speak with her.* Despite her sorrow at losing Gage, Sara tingled with anticipation. She could not allow this moment to pass.

Her heart pulsed hard, thudding in her ears,. Tongue thick in her mouth, throat cracked-dry with anxiety, she pressed clenched hands against her chest. So excited that she could barely breathe, Sara opened her mouth to gulp in the Sierra air, fragrant with pine and sage. Then, not entirely sure she could actually speak, she tried clearing her throat. Her words seemed to come from far away, but they were distinct enough, "Ahem. Pardon me," she began.

Chapter Fifty

A Mystery Solved

Dark Eyes lifted her head. Taken aback, she considered the stranger. Who is this *ohant*, a *waliki* woman who speaks to me? She has crown of sun-hair like many whites, but she does not make tame. It wild, like nest of curling yellow snakes. She glared, her black eyes probing Sara's blue ones. Uneasiness quivered in her belly.

"What you are want?" she demanded, mindful of Sara's gaze fixed on the baby. Dark Eyes enfolded the infant tightly in her arms. "No can have." She looked at Sara sternly. "Little Hawk my son."

"Nuh, no," Sara managed to say. "No, I ... I want to know where you got that handkerchief," she blurted, pointing.

Dark Eyes glanced down at the small white square Mah Tew had given her. Then, scooping the cloth from beneath the baby's chin, she proudly displayed it for the pale haired woman, holding it up with one hand. "Present," she said, dipping her head a tad. "You like? My husband give. Very fine."

The *ohant's* knees seemed to wobble. Legs unsteady as a wounded deer's she sank down until the women sat side by side. Dark Eyes clutched her infant even more protectively to her breast. She studied the white woman whose eyes feasted on the lacy square.

"You have sun hair," she said. "You pretty." Watching the *ohant* out of the corner of her eye, Dark Eyes put the lace-trimmed square back into her pouch with deft fingers. "You come for catch shining stones?" she asked, looking at the girl.

"Gold? No, I do not seek it. I live near here, in Angels Camp, and I am searching for an old friend, Matthew. My name is Sara," she choked out. "I think your husband may be my old friend. Your infant has some of his look."

Dark Eyes was not sure what she felt about this white woman who looked directly at her, worry and excitement in her eyes when she spoke. Perhaps the woman was sick with bad thinking. Like Greywolf had been when his face was not good and his eyes were dark as caves. She must be careful. To be rude and refuse Mah Tew Greywolf friend a wish to visit was not the gracious way of her people. She felt a flutter of threat in her chest; it was soft, like a moth against skin. Was this the person of his past times? She often wondered about that woman.

"And the handkerchief, it is familiar to me," Sara whispered.

Dark Eyes looked Sara up and down, her gaze sharp as the knife she carried at her waist. She saw that the woman's packages had fallen from her lap and lay forgotten in the damp of the road.

"You are woman of my man past times." Dark Eyes set it out between them, voicing her worst fear. "I am Dark Eyes, wife to Mah Tew Greywolf," she warned the yellow-curl woman. "I no give him for you." Her eyes flashed. Something grim and wild burned in her heart. "You make fancy cloth present," she challenged, patting her carrying pouch. "I see is true."

"It is true," Sara admitted. "Once, a long time ago, wife of Mah Tew, I thought we would wed. But so much has changed."

She looked from the knife into the Indian woman's obsidian eyes. "I no longer set my affections upon him. Friendship is all I offer. I am truly pleased he has married; you may be sure! Yes, I made the handkerchief, the present, but your man has made it his gift for you. It is as it should be, for I have given my affections to another."

"What you want to say Mah Tew?" Dark Eyes asked. Suspicion laced her words.

"I want to say, Matthew, your wife is lovely. That I am pleased she has such a handsome son. I surely want to know if my friend is well. And most of all, I want to tell him I have found his sister Rachel."

Dark Eyes lifted an eyebrow. "He speak of sisters some days."

Above them an eagle soared and shrieked its high-pitched whistle. Dark Eyes looked up, welcoming her Mother's spirit guide with joy. The *ohant's* news would not cause harm. She felt a settling, an easing. Mah Tew and her son, Little Hawk, would not be torn by this woman. She had a fair heart. Maybe *isak ol ok*, she is friend.

"It is good." Dark Eyes laid her fingers over the feather always tucked at her breast, gathered in a strengthening breath, and made her decision. "You want come home with me?" she asked.

Sara bobbed her head three times in quick succession, curls bouncing around her face, lips pressed together, her hands clutching one another as though strong ropes bound them.

"You must think I am a crazy person, and maybe I am," Sara muttered. "Yes, I want to come home with you," she said. "Please take me to see him. I have fine news."

Dark Eyes wondered what Mah Tew would say when she brought this 'hut tut,' this hummingbird, to him. Standing, she grasped Little Hawk's swaddling cradle, laid him in it, and tightened the laces that would hold him snug. Setting the cradle on her back, she stepped into the street to gather the *ohant's* fallen packages and stowed them in the wagon bed next to her own, while the white girl fetched her horse. She kept an eye on Sara who checked Sueño's saddle and pulled a rifle from its scabbard before she led him to the wagon and handed over his fine made leather reins.

Accepting the animal, Dark Eyes tethered the horse to the wagon's rear. She could see that age and disposition would make it easy to pony the dark gelding with the long mane and tail. He would walk behind giving no trouble. Little Hawk rested comfortable and safe against her back, making a welcome, warm place between her shoulders.

The *hut tut* pulled herself onto the small buckboard and placed the long gun at her feet. Dark Eyes glanced at the wagon bed one last time, then climbed in. She spoke softly to Mah Tew's horse standing in harness, lifted up the driving reins and made a tsut tsut sound with her tongue. The buckboard lurched forward.

The *ohant* studied her, watching her handle the cart as they trundled along. She could feel it. She knew the woman had seen her knife. Did she have fear? Perhaps she was brave, a good person to know. She scowled. Was Mah Tew to be friend to this *ohant*? This pretty woman?

Not ready to speak, Dark Eyes instead looked inward, recalling how the Great Spirit had led her to the meeting of a husband. And how Mah Tew had looked on that day: confused, near death, his past times taken from him. She thought about the way he'd pulled the little square of white from his pocket and turned it over and over, staring at it as though it held a secret he could not know.

Finally, he'd given the pretty square to her. And Dark Eyes remembered wondering, who made this gift to him?

As they traveled, she spoke of these things. She knew her halting words were heard well by the woman of Mah Tew's past times, for the sun-haired *ohant* did not speak until the story was told. The sun moved across the sky, and Sara shared some of her tale, describing Matthew's disappearance. "I, too, made a long journey, following your trace," she said. She told of getting caught in the shaking earth and spreading fires, and of Gage, and how he helped her through the ordeal.

Dark Eyes listened closely to the words. She frowned and shook her head when Sara spoke of the sheriff at Fort Yuma and saw that Sara also made a bad face.

Plumb talked out at last, both women sat silent. The day was more than half gone now.

There was only the creak of the wagon and caw of jaybirds as they moved slowly along a narrowing track. Black oak trees peppered the hillsides. At the foot of a huge boulder that stood like a sentry, Dark Eyes gestured to the right. Slapping the reins she turned up a rocky rise that was no road at all. They were jounced and bumped on the hard bench that served as seating until Dark Eyes brought the buckboard to a jolting halt next to a small corral.

"I bring Mah Tew Greywolf see you," she said, and climbed from the driver's perch. "You wait."

Chapter Fifty-One

The Invitation

Sara watched Dark Eyes make her way toward a seedy canvas shelter, it's roof held aloft by thin branches. The young woman slipped inside. Sara waited, scarcely able to sit still. "I have found him," she gulped, thinking of all her hostess had shared of her life with him. Matthew has taken this Indian woman—quite lovely and obviously smart—to wife. What of the injuries he suffered? Was his mind well? The moments stretched long; it was hard believe that her search had come to an end.

Then, as though she'd seen him yesterday, Matthew appeared and slowly walked in her direction.

In a moment of grave disquiet, Sara glanced at her rifle and considered picking it up. Instead, she stood and climbed from the buckboard, hands empty. She couldn't take her eyes off him. Something that had been coiled tight inside her loosened, and she felt a broad smile roll across her face. He was alive. *Thanks be!* His hair was longer. He looked leaner, too. His features had a different cast. He wore leather trousers and a beaded shirt. Surely his life has changed him, she realized with a start. Most likely, she'd changed some. He was friend and stranger, both. Perhaps he'd not know her. She shivered in anticipation, suddenly curious as a young filly.

"Hello, Matthew," she said. Thinking of what Dark Eyes had told her, she chose her words carefully, fearing to unsettle him. "I am Sara. Do you remember me? I know you."

Mah Tew Greywolf stopped and stared. He shook his head as if to clear cobwebs from his thinking. He peered at her as though he had need of a hand lens. "You are the one, the person of my past time," he finally said, voice cautious. A look of amazement wavered between them.

"Yes," she grinned. "I am that friend. Once we considered marriage. But much has happened since then. It seems so long ago, Matthew." Sara saw effort working in his face and reached out to touch his arm. "Do you recall Arizona? The ranch? Durann Canyon?" she asked.

"No, but I ... I've seen you before." He blinked. "Just flashes, quick pictures," he said, and searched her face.

"I am so glad to see you! We've been seeking your where-abouts for near a year. Oh Matthew, I've much to tell you. The most important news I bring is that I have found your sister Rachel. Your wife told me you recall Rachel. She lives in Angels Camp with me."

"Rachel?" he repeated. His eyes widened in disbelief. His face contorted as though the grief he stored deep in his bones was dissolving beneath his skin. Tears burst from his grey eyes, and he held his hands against the sides of his head, as though he might explode. "Dark Eyes," he called hoarsely.

His wife waited in front of their meager shelter. Sara could see uneasiness in her stance, her features carefully set to give nothing away. At his cry she stepped from the thin strip of porch and started toward them. Her strides were strong and her face held questions. Dark Eyes slid quietly to his side and embraced her husband, leaning close and saying words of comfort, Sara was sure, although they spoke in a tongue unfamiliar to her.

"I am married to a fine woman. We have a son," Matthew told Sara when he was able to speak again. He put his arm around his wife's shoulders and made a formal introduction.

Sara smiled at Dark Eyes. "We are well met, Matthew, and have spoken quite a lot during our ride here, mostly about how you came to be together. I am happy. You have a splendid family. Your son is darling."

"And Rachel, my sister, is she well? Is she all grown up now?" he asked. "The last time I saw her ..." Horror swelled in his eyes as he remembered. He blinked it away. "I am addled to find Rachel is alive. I thought she must be—"

"She is well, Matthew, and also has a son. Carlos Running Horse is not much older than your own boy. You are an uncle. Rachel is a strong and winsome girl. We have become as sisters. She is teaching me to prepare tasty vittles. I know she never thought to see you again in this life. She'll be blissful."

"I would like nothing better than to see her. I must see her."

Relieved that no complicated explanations were required and pleased to be a good friend to Matthew and his wife, Sara glanced around the clearing—sparse and isolated. "I want to take you to her," she said. "Please come to Angels Camp with me. There is room to stay. You are welcome and will be comfortable. We have a sturdy cabin, a milk cow, a mule, and several horses. We have managed a sizeable vegetable garden, too. The hunting is good, and Rachel is there thinking about fixing supper right about now. We would love to have you," she finished breathless, looking from one to the other. "I fear, perhaps, it is not easy for your family, living here in Jackson all alone."

Mah Tew turned to his wife. "There's been precious little work, Dark Eyes. We've not found a safe place to live. I think we best accept Sara's invitation. I must see my sister, and I want you to know her. We can take our belongings and have a long visit. If it is good, we can make our home thereabouts."

"What Father and Mother do if come?" Dark Eyes said, voice edged with challenge, worry painted on her lovely face. "They not find me."

Mah Tew gripped her hands. "I know you are afeared' over their dangerous trek. They will come," he said, smoothing her black hair.

"We expected Standing Bear and Eagle Feather Woman weeks ago," Matthew explained to Sara. "They may be caught in the fighting down in the valley."

"Why don't I make a map," Sara suggested. "I'll nail it to your shelter. My cabin is not far from here, some less than a half-day's ride. They shall find us, or us them."

Dark Eyes fixed her gaze on Mah Tew. "You believe the *ohant* speaks the truth?"

"I do. It feels right, wife."

Dark Eyes fingered her eagle feather and dipped her head in agreement.

Sara heard eagerness in his voice as he turned and relayed their decision to accompany her.

"There is work at Angels Camp," she told Matthew as she searched through her saddlebags for paper and pencil. "The town's general store has a brisk trade. It's fair to bursting with supplies," she said, thinking of Angelo Rivera's talk of expanding. "Are you still interested in selling foodstuffs, tools and such?"

He nodded in answer, but said nothing, though his eyes were full of questions. Surely he was beset with impatience at the thought of his lost sister, gone forever, never to be seen again, now only a short while away. Sara wondered if he would come to recall all the missing pieces of his life and if holding his grandfather's watch might shake loose his memories. They'd have precious time to share their stories.

She fervently hoped Dark Eyes and Rachel would fall in with one another, be sisterly. She could imagine Carlos Running Horse and Little Hawk romping together as they grew up. Her California family was bourgeoning—missing but one. Gage, she prayed silently, come home to me.

Straddling the horizon, smudging blue heavens with its splendiferous display of pinks and orange-edged greys, the sun would soon sink. They best make haste. Sara placed the map under cover of canvas, a rock holding it fast. She and Matthew gathered the family's few belongings and packed them in the buckboard, speaking little, while Dark Eyes put the babe to her breast. A full belly would ensure his slumber on the journey.

Mounted on Sueño, Sara was anxious to be off. She'd lead the way. Dark Eyes sat, reins in hand ready to shepherd the wagon, Little Hawk snug against her spine. Mah Tew astride Washee would ride shotgun.

"Time to get!" Sara called, and put her spurs to Sueño's sides.

Sara expected they'd reach the cabin maybe an hour past supper. She knew Rachel would worry herself to a lather for that entire hour, but she'd be almighty thunderstruck when they rode in.

Chapter Fifty-Two

A Full House

Rachel's shrieks of relief at Sara's safe arrival soon turned to breathless silence, then full on hysterics that swung from tears to laughter, and back to tears when she saw her brother Matthew ride into view, a small buckboard rattling close behind him.

"Dear God," she shouted, rushing at him. "We've been apart since you were a boy, but I knew you soon as I set eyes on you," she sobbed, and near tore him off his horse. They'd gripped one another so tightly, and for so long, that Sara feared the two would swoon from lack of air.

His wife, seated in the buckboard, remained stiff and regal as a woodcarving, reins in hand. She watched the scene unfold. Her face a mask, as her husband clutched the weeping woman who ran at him like a wild thing. At last, Matthew, face red with emotion, turned and fetched Dark Eyes and their babe. She stepped down and stood, stock still. Her back straight as the handle of a horsewhip, she smiled warily at Rachel, who, beside herself with with gladness, fair leapt upon her and wrapped her in a sisterly bear hug.

It was just as warm and exciting a reunion as Sara had hoped. Long after all should have been abed, Rachel and Matthew chattering like magpies, made small forays across the borders of life changes and losses each had experienced. As they explored these avenues of sadness and joy more fully in the coming weeks, she expected they'd find solace and comfort. That night, each time she glanced up from her writing, brother and sister were touching each other's hands or faces to make sure they weren't dreaming. Rachel still looked as though she wanted to laugh and sob all at once, and Sara saw tears in his eyes.

"You look so grown up, but yet the same. I've missed so much," he choked. They gripped hands and held fast when words were not enough.

Dark Eyes sat close to Matthew, clasping their sleeping son to her breast and saying little. Sara wondered ... does she know the whole of Matthew's childhood story? Had he shared what he did remember? Does she feel threatened by this upheaval? Knowing her questions were for another evening, she held her tongue and instead layered quilts to make a cozy sleeping place for Matthew and his family when, finally, they bid their goodnights.

A few days later, Sara drew Matthew aside and quietly placed the silver watch fob that had been his grandfather's, into his hand. "I stumbled across this in the Arizona sand. You must have dropped it," she said, and related how she had reached Angels Camp in her search to find him.

Matthew listened, his face a study in concentration. "Thank you," he said at last. "I ... I may have dropped it. I was confused." He put a hand to his head. "I didn't know it was mine. A lot of my remembering is missin'." He looked at her. "You seem familiar. I feel I know you, but I have no recall of anything about that time. My apologies."

Emotions spun. For a moment Sara was piqued to be as a ghost to her friend. She felt an unexpected twinge of loss, followed by a guilty, bloom of relief. "You have done nothing to apologize for. All is as it should be," she assured him, smiling, even as she thought sadly of losing Gage.

Once in a while, she'd see Matthew take the watch from his pocket and trace his fingers over the inscription. She wondered again if any more of his memories would return. He never spoke of it with her, but he shared his worries with Dark Eyes. Sara often saw them deep in conversation. When they wished to speak privately, they repaired to the porch and huddled close. She often heard laughter, too. Dark Eyes was good for him. He was different now. A man devoted to his family. It felt so right.

A few weeks later, Sara gazed around the cabin's main room. It looks cozy and comfortable, she thought with satisfaction. On the table, a lantern glowed bright. The fireplace hosted a roaring, toe-warming blaze. Her feet rested on sturdy plank flooring. It was a miracle; Angelo and Matthew had installed the pine boards in a mere two days of nonstop hammering and sawing. Although the women were forced to spend much of both days outside with the little ones, the effort had been well worth it. Just this afternoon, the men raised the hearth with flat rocks and a mud mix, lifting it to the height of the new wood footing. Now the fireside was perfect, too. "The results are extravagantly fine," Sara exclaimed as she swept up the debris—bits of rock and dried mud.

Dark Eyes and Rachel made a platter of fry bread in celebration. Angelo and Matthew devoured their reward with gusto. Sara bit into the hot pillow, its crust browned and glistening. Her eyes widened in pleasure. "Ooooh, delicious," she decreed. Sinking into the rocker, she closed her eyes, relishing the taste, when like an ambush, Gage popped into her head, uninvited. She knew he'd love this savory.

"No more muddy feet and wet shirtwaist hems," Sara murmured from her perch on the rocker, forcing herself to a new topic. She simply had to stop thinking about Gage.

"A good safe place for Carlos Running Horse and Little Hawk to crawl about and romp," Rachel sang out. She turned to her sister-in-law. "What do you think *Oloki Kalanah*? Do you like the new floor for the babies?"

"I like. Make warm and dry." Dark Eyes held her wiggling infant son in the cradle of her lap, her legs crossed.

Sara smiled, life had gladdened. They were blessed. From the start, Rachel took pains to include her new sister. They cooked together. Dark Eyes conquered the iron stove in an afternoon. In soft murmurs of a shared tongue, she often reassured her brother's wife that she belonged, for Rachel knew the grief of living as an outsider. Little Hawk had never enjoyed so much attention, as his auntie refused to release him from her embrace until her Carlos awakened for feeding. Only then did she relinquish him into his mother's keeping.

Down to her bones, Sara recognized Rachel's sense of completeness. Open-hearted family affections pulsed in every corner of the log house, she thought, even in the dust motes. Around her, the voices and laughter of people that mattered hung in the air. It was such a comfort to have them here. Only Gage was missing. It would be lovely to see him jigging Carlos on his knee. Of course he'd missed the reunion—the whole reason for the adventure the two of them had undertaken. *Where are you?* She rolled her eyes heavenward, feeling more than a touch of sorrow.

But there was a heap to be grateful for. Dark Eyes and Rachel had bonded quickly, sharing their motherhood, the native culture, two languages, and their love of Matthew, or Mah Tew, as Rachel sometimes called him now. Rachel certainly loved Dark Eyes' given name. It often rolled off her tongue. "*Oloki Kalanah* has the sound of a song, so pretty," she explained, causing her sister-in-law to smile.

"I have other name, too," Dark Eyes said. "Mah Tew, you tell story of Father name for me." They'd all chuckled when Matthew explained how he and Standing Bear found something in common when the headman heard Matthew's name for his daughter, saying he himself called her '*Wa-te*, for her eyes dark as blackberries.'"

During these early spring days, Rachel and Dark Eyes weeded the garden on hands and knees and had begun the planting. Sara often minded the young un's, keeping Carlos from tasting grub worms and such while her friends worked the soil. If the wind tossed up a storm, she bundled the babies indoors and found them to be an entertainment.

"I do like caring for the little ones," she confided to Rachel one afternoon. "I'm surprised it pleases me so."

"You see to the children right well," Rachel agreed, wiping muddy hands on a burlap rag. "They're safe and happy with you."

"They make me chuckle," Sara admitted with a smile.

Early each evening Angelo came to sup. He always spoiled the household with his gifts of sweets—bringing a box of chocolates or Miz Hannigan's cookies—setting them in Rachel's hands, along with his heart. Stories were told with the passing of supper plates, bringing to mind more recollections shared, and questions to be answered over coffee, tea, and dessert. Matthew mostly listened, his eyes thoughtful. Sara was enthralled. She soaked in the words and, in the evenings, made notes in her lined books.

There was so much for the siblings to catch up on. It was, Sara thought, as though they were starving folks sucking in details like warm gruel, they couldn't get enough to pad their bones and give them peace. Her telling of how she came to know Matthew and descriptions of life on the Coulton's Arizona Territory ranch avidly interested all.

She spoke little of Gage but yearned for him to come home, to know he was well. How he might receive her admission of love was another matter. Sara looked over at Dark Eyes and knew she had worries, too—about the safety of her parents—although she did not speak of her concerns often.

The group had settled into an easy rhythm. This evening, Rachel and Dark Eyes relaxed atop a quilt they'd spread on the new floor. Angelo brought a checkerboard and pieces from the trading post shelves, and the men sat at table engrossed in a game.

Sara, ensconced in the rocking chair, watching the babies with a bemused smile, announced, "Little Hawk's waving arms and kicking feet have Carlos curious as a cat." She listened as Rachel, speaking Miwuk, explained the saying. Sara craved to understand her words. She turned to Dark Eyes with an idea in mind. "I wish to speak your language. Will you teach me?"

"I teach. We make time each day. You learn well, yes?"

"I promise to put my wits to work in hopes that I shall be a good student."

Gage might fancy me wise in my undertaking a new language, she reflected. I trust he'll be suitably impressed. Thinking about him scared up a fit of nerves. Her fingers twisted in her skirts. She had no wish to dwell upon her troubles, especially with the men in close proximity. She'd certainly not pursue the issue of Gage aloud. She clamped her mouth shut. *Why, such an outburst would be all-fired embarrassing.*

Their game concluded, Angelo and Matthew turned to a deep discussion of plans for expanding Rivera's trading post. Matthew was to manage the project and oversee the retail operation once he was familiar with the stock.

"*Mi trabajo*, my work will be to build a fine little hotel once Matthew's handling the trading post," Angelo informed the ladies. After a hail of questions from Sara, the women sat in companionable silence, watching Carlos Running Horse push onto his knees and rock in an attempt to crawl to his cousin.

Today as she did most days, Sara spent her chore time haying the horses, watering them, and mucking run-ins. She'd even taken to haltering and hand-walking several of the yearlings and two-year-olds. Stubbornly she figured it wouldn't do for Gage to arrive home and find them gone to wild, not after all the work he'd put on them. Doing for the critters usually lifted her spirits. Tonight, however she tread a dark path, fretful as the evening grew old, wondering if she'd ever see him again.

Chapter Fifty-Three

Unexpected Visitors

One evening, Angelo looked over at Sara, coffee cup in hand. "Tomorrow is the first of May. This tempest will be the last rain until November. Mark my words, Senorita."

Sara smiled. It was pouring big drops. Sluicing down in buckets. She bedded and fed the livestock early and came in soaked to the skin. Now it was dark, black as the devil. Nary a star to be seen. She was glad that the little cabin crackled with warmth and was full to brimming with friends and hopeful talk of the future.

On their quilt, Dark Eyes and Rachel chattered, heads bent together, voices too low to be heard. Both the cherubs had fallen into slumber.

Sara rocked herself in gentle rhythm, pushing her feet against the floor, enjoying the creak of wood on wood. She'd near lulled herself into an after-supper nap.

Suddenly, Matthew turned his head and stared toward the kitchen window. "There's somethin' out there." Alarm carried harsh in his tone.

Angelo scraped back the bench as he stood. "You women get into the back room with the babes," he ordered, and hastened

Dark Eyes and Rachel toward the sleeping quarters before the men clattered out the door.

Alert now, Sara shook her head, jumped up from the rocker and ran to the kitchen window. The moonless night gave up no secrets. She listened to the sounds around her. The horses whinnied, calling their brethren. The milk cow lowed. The creatures were feverish. However she heard no fear in their outcry. Shivers ran up her spine, down her arms and right into her knees. Hands a'flutter, she grabbed a lantern and raced to the door, flinging it wide. Hitching up her skirts, she ran 'round to the small corral in time to see three horses and riders pull to a halt, looking for all the world like a string of clay figures in the ancestor stories Dark Eyes told. Through the downpour, she glimpsed Angelo and Matthew helping two of the three dismount.

Her attention returned to the lead rider and remained focused on the cowboy, leaning on his pommel, hat dripping. This was no clay figure! "Oh my Lord," she exclaimed into the torrent. "Bless you Santa Madre, for bringing him home."

Sara's excitement grew as the he stepped from the saddle of his big horse. She'd have known him anywhere, mud covered or not. "Gage," she cried, and stumbled toward him. Her prayers had been answered.

The tall cowboy turned toward the sound of his name. "I'll be," he muttered. There she was, lookin' half wraith and half wild woman, splattering through the muck, lantern wavin' and sputtering like some sort a' specter in the night. And danged, I'm glad to see her. *I figured wrong when I figured Sara Coulton to have run for her pa and safety.*

"Sara," he breathed as she stopped in front of him, gulping for air. Hanging on to his horse with one hand, Gage pulled her to him with the other and wrapped himself around her dripping hair and sodden skirts, oblivious to the pelting rain. He felt her quaking right through his poncho and leaned down to whisper in her ear, "You get on into the house now and let me bed Thunder." She wasn't the only one taken with the trembling, he realized, as waves of joy hurtled through him.

Sara lifted a wet face to his and smiled. "I simply cannot let go of you," she said, her happy tears blending with the raindrops. "I'll light your way to the hay shed first."

He grabbed her hand. "I'm not going anywhere. Soon's we wick a lantern out there, you get to the hearth and dry out. I'll be up directly. Promise?"

"I promise."

The hay shed was dark as blood pudding. Even the attached stalls were near invisible until you stood but a boot length from them. Sara held her all-but-soaked oil lamp high, and felt along the wall until she found the kerosene lantern. With shaking fingers she pulled it from its hook and handed it to Gage. He took the last of his dry flints from beneath his poncho, lit the wick, returned it to its hook, and led Thunder into an empty stall. Its gate latched, he turned to Sara.

Holding her at arm's length in the dim light, he stared at her hungrily.

"I'm h ... happy," she sniffled. Her choked breaths huffed in and out. She looked up at him and burst into tears. "But look at Thunder." Grabbing a rag she slipped into the stall and started to rub the stallion's face and neck. "Let me help," she cried as he followed her in and took her into his arms.

Gage laughed and reluctantly released her. He pulled a second rag from its hook and rubbed at the animal's withers and flank. Together they unfolded a heavy blanket and laid it over Thunder's back.

Then gathering her into his arms, he pressed his mouth against her lips. "That's enough," he said. Concerned that both of them trembled with the chill, he plucked the rag from her hand, eyed her sternly, and muttered, "Git…"

Gathering her skirts, Sara turned and scooted out the barn door, racing through the downpour toward the cabin, keeping her pledge.

Feeling her Spirit guide calling to her, Dark Eyes gripped Rachel's hand and pulled her from the sleeping area. "I must see," she whispered. Holding their infants on their hips, they crept to the kitchen window and watched the two men head round the cabin toward the corral. Hanging on to one another for courage, the women raced to the window nearest the table, swept the gingham curtains aside and peered into the wet fog.

"There is not but a tea cup of light," Rachel complained, squinting. "It seems as though Angelo is got ahold a' two horses, their heads hanging like they been ridden hard. I can make out Mah Tew helping the riders dismount." She turned and gazed around the room. "Where might Sara be?"

Dark Eyes' breath caught in her throat. She, too, had been staring into the dark. Her eyes burned with excitement. "Aiyee, Rachel. My parents, maybe my parents come." She gasped, hardly able to believe it true. Little Hawk, tucked against her waist, whimpered in protest as her hand clenched around him. "Ssh, ssh. It is good my son," she soothed, running toward the open cabin door, Rachel in tow. They arrived just in time to see Standing Bear and Eagle Feather Woman step onto the covered porch. Angelo and Mah Tew stood with them.

"Mother, Father." Dark Eyes wept now. Dropping Rachel's hand, she turned a pleading eye toward her friend. Without words, Rachel swept Little Hawk up in her free arm, and stood back, watching as her sister-in-law rushed out to greet her dripping, mud caked, blanket-wrapped kinfolk.

Mah Tew and Dark Eyes ushered the family into the cabin and over to the warmth of the hearth, voicing their welcomes. Angelo followed. He hefted a thick log from the stack he had built up against the wall and laid it atop the blaze for more heat.

She embraced her parents' shoulders, gripping them hard. She touched their arms and hands, making sure they were really there with her, not ghost people.

Though her mother shuddered with chill, her damp skin felt hot against Dark Eyes' fingers, her eyes too bright. "You must warm yourself. You are not well." she said, peeling Eagle Feather Woman's traveling cloak from her back. "Father, give blanket now. I bring new." She smiled as he placed his covering in her hands. Dark Eyes laid the blankets, heavy with rainwater, across the table so they might dry, and disappeared into the sleeping quarters to fetch fresh wraps.

Mah Tew settled the couple closer to the fire's crackling heat. He snatched the quilts Dark Eyes brought and wrapped their quivering shoulders to combat the cold.

"Rachel, Angelo." Mah Tew motioned them over. "Meet my in-laws. This is Standing Bear, *memoyi,* my father-in-law, and Eagle Feather Woman, *mempotci,* my mother-in-law," he explained, using the formal terms. "Father, Mother, this is Angelo Rivera, my sister Rachel and her son, Carlos Running

Horse. And this," he said proudly, taking the infant from Rachel's arm, "is Little Hawk, your *tca tcai,* your grandson."

"You must be hungry, I'll fix us some vittles and hot tea with honey," Rachel offered, shyly smiling her welcome to Standing Bear and Eagle Feather Woman. "We have no *nypati,* no acorn mush," she said, "but I will make *pe-kin* and *hatatah,* good bacon and biscuits.

Standing Bear nodded, obviously pleased to hear the language of his people spoken by the yellow-haired sister of his new son-in-law.

Lifting her arms in joyous welcome of the child, Eagle Feather Woman motioned, asking Mah Tew to sit close beside her. Addressing Angelo she wheezed, "You, big like tree, come circle." She made a swaddling blanket of sorts with the quilt's corner edge and accepted her grandson from his father's keeping. In the way of grandmothers, she cozied Little Hawk tenderly against her heart. "Aah, fine boy," she said, and turned to present the child to his grandfather. "Husband, you have grandson. He is brave. No cry," she rasped.

"My son gurgles and coos as though his grandmama is an old friend," Mah Tew said with pride.

The old chief turned curious eyes on the baby, inspecting him from head to toe. Angelo, Mah Tew, Eagle Feather Woman, and Dark Eyes, holding two additional coverlets, waited silently as Standing Bear ran his gnarled fingers over the baby's head, arms, and legs. His wizened face creased in a broad smile. He banged his hoipi stick against the hearth, and looked up at them.

"Fine boy you give me. Great Spirit make blessing. I teach hunt." He pulled three ornately carved pieces of wood from his traveling pouch and pushed them together until they formed a ceremonial pipe. "*Wila.* Come, Mah Tew Greywolf, We thank."

Mah Tew nodded his understanding and went to sit at his father-in-law's side. Eyes serious above his pleated face, Standing Bear lifted the ceremonial pipe and handed the sacred tobacco pouch to Mah Tew, who carefully filled the bowl and tamped the leaves to make a good smoke, as he'd seen it done several times before.

"Bless new life journey," Standing Bear said. "Bring grandson," he bid his wife and daughter. "Baby here." He gestured to the small space between himself and his son-in-law, then, turned back to Mah Tew.

Dark Eyes placed an extra blanket on the spot indicated and helped her mother lay the little one, fallen fast asleep, between the two men. Standing Bear lit the pipe, using a length of kindling as match. He made two puffs and scattered the smoke over the child then passed the pipe to Mah Tew. "You father. You say son baby name," he instructed.

"Little Hawk. My son starts life named for his grandmother's family." He drew upon the pipe twice as he'd seen the old man do and handed it back.

"I make prayer of thanks and welcome," Standing Bear said to the gathered assembly. He sang words that Mah Tew did not know. Drawing on the pipe several more times, he lifted his right hand and pushed the smoke to the Four Corners. "It is good *Oloki Kalanah*. Raven Dancer, I am honor to be grandfather," he proclaimed to the group gathered at the hearth, his black eyes twinkling with pleasure.

Lifting her grandson from his place of blessing, Eagle Feather Woman cuddled him. She stroked his tiny fingers and plump baby feet for many minutes before she was willing to place him into Dark Eyes' arms and accept a cup of hot tea laced with honey from Rachel.

She had barely put the cup to her lips when Sara burst through the door.

Chapter Fifty-Four

Gage

Sara shook her skirts and wiped at her dripping face with wet fingers. As droplets scattered in the warm room, chattering voices went silent. Six pair of curious eyes fixed upon her.

"You have missed the blessing ceremony," Rachel said, as she rushed over, rag in hand, to sop up the small flood pooling at Sara's feet. "I think you best tarry at the fire to pay your respects and dry out some." She led her shivering friend to the crowd huddled around the hearth, and scooped up the last dry bed covering. "Put this about you," she said, and looped it over her shoulders. Sara mumbled thank-you," and sank down next to two blanket-wrapped strangers.

"You look like a mudhen. What happened out there?" Rachel asked, peering at her flushed face.

"Glory has happened," she sighed, contented. "Gage has come home. I am joyous with his return."

Rachel's eyebrows lifted. "Aha," she said, falling silent.

Sara looked around, questioning. "But who are these folks that traveled with him?"

"Mother and Father," Dark Eyes said, her face aglow. "They not see note we leave in old place. Say good man guide them to me."

Sara smiled. "How did Gage know to bring them here?"

Rachel took up the story. "He found her parents on the trail, having no idea who they were. He felt it safest to bring the old woman here. The snow, the cold, and the treacheries of war were a danger, for she is fragile. Once they brought her to safety, he and Standing Bear planned to ride for Jackson, in search of their daughter and her husband."

Stunned by their tale, Sara looked from face to face. "Why, Gage has yet no idea of all that has happened," she gulped, her breath taken once again from her chest.

"And we cannot thank you enough!" Mah Tew grabbed her hands and introduced his in-laws.

Standing Bear spoke again of their journey from the valley. He told of Old Grandmother's decision to stay behind. "Owl Woman say her place with Chief Tenaya in troubled time." His eyes met each of theirs. "He need Owl Woman make strong medicine."

Sara saw Dark Eyes bow her head and knew she sorrowed at this news her father brought. In the silence, Sara heard the older woman's labored breath. She looked at Dark Eyes. "Perhaps your mother, is ill?"

Settled between Sara and Eagle Feather Woman, nursing her son, into slumber, Dark Eyes agreed. "Yes. Mother need rest. I give herbs and strong prayers. Make well. I must ask for Gage sleep place."

Sara clasped Dark Eyes arm. "There is only a small stove in the lean-to. We must keep her warm," she said anxiously. "Will you allow Angelo to get a fire going? And *promise* you will ask for help should you have need?"

"Mother, Father, I think you like stay in Gage lean-to," Dark Eyes said, in answer.

Standing Bear sitting close to Mah Tew, his *hoipa* stick in hand made his statement. "Wife suffers breathing-in-cold illness. You heal, Oloki Kalanah. You have Old Grandmother's magic," he said, and thumped his stick against the new wood planking.

It was settled. He speaks prudently and keeps his own council, Sara thought. His creviced face emanated happiness and peace.

She, on the other hand, was having a hard time sitting still. "I am fidgeting something fierce. I can set no longer," she said to Dark Eyes. Getting to her feet she smoothed back damp hair. "Please be kind enough to excuse me. I must help Rachel with the meal." She walked across the room to the stove. Forcing her eyes from the cabin door, she slipped her apron off its hook.

Sara stood near the big iron stove, enjoying its heat. "For all their joy, they look gaunt." She glanced at her friend. "They've been through a boggling time and must be tired unto death and pinched with hunger. I feel it important that Eagle Feather Woman take sustenance. Perhaps it's best I help get food on the table."

"That's a fine idea," Rachel agreed. "It will give you something to do with all the excitation bubbling in you." She passed Carlos into Sara's willing arms, and set to work on the biscuits. The aroma of salt pork threaded the air as it sizzled atop the griddle plate.

Sara jiggled Carlos on her hip. It did seem Gage was taking forever. Would he never get the animals bedded down? Her heart was so full it was nigh on impossible to wait. She leaned over the sink and peered out the window. If he didn't come through that door soon, she might have to fetch him. How long will it take to put this meal to table, she wondered? Too long. He'd be astounded when she told him who his traveling companions had been.

Meantime, with her free hand, she pulled the still-damp blankets from the table's surface and draped them along the benches so they would continue to dry. "Have we enough tableware for this gathering?" she asked, and wiped the top clean of sand and bits of twigs, letting them tumble to the floor. Best sweep this up, she reckoned, and reached for the broom.

"I have a better idea," Rachel said, sliding two skillets of johnnycake batter onto the hot stove. "Why don't you hightail it to the hayshed? Angelo will help me if need be." A sly smile played across her lips. "I know you want to. It looks like the rain has let up some." She glanced out the kitchen window. "Besides you can explain to Gage what has happened to his sleeping quarters."

Sara fair danced with impatience. "Oh, bother. You know I have been trying to keep my feet from running out to the barn. Since you will be well assisted, I will do just that. Truth be, this waiting rends my heart." She handed Carlos back to his mother.

Her own smile as wide as Standing Bear's, and as grateful, Sara slipped out the door and stepped into her boots. The moon peeped from behind silvery clouds. Rachel was right, there was but a fine mist against her face and tendrils of fog that had settled to ground. Lifting her skirts, she hurried forward. No lantern was required. It would be easy enough to find the way.

She reached the hayshed and heard Gage just beyond, pitching the dry stuff into the run in's. He hummed some sorta' tune as he worked. Shy of a sudden, Sara tiptoed toward the sound and stood several feet away drinking in the sight of him. The scent of Gage, rain-damp and sweaty, drew her. She longed to touch his skin, breathe him in. I best make myself known, she thought, just as he whirled around, pitchfork in hand.

Gage stared at her for a moment, stabbed the metal fork hard into a hay bale and chuckled. "Woman, are you part Indian, sneaking up on me like that?"

Unable to be even a foot or two from her, he stepped around the hay pile he'd been working and enfolded her in his arms. "Sara." He nuzzled her damp curls. "I feared you gone from me—from Angels Camp. It near tore my heart out when I understood I was in love with you. I missed you every day."

She smelled of rain and lavender water and wood smoke. His entire body was warming to fever. No campfire had heated him as did the feel of Sara melting into his embrace.

"I have so longed for you," she said softly. "I despaired of your safe return." She clung to him in the fervor that shimmered between them.

He looked down at her. She has feelings for me; I didn't imagine it. The realization brought a rush of gladness. Certain she was blushing all the way to her toes, he saw a new and intense gleam in her eyes. A place never fully explored sprang wide inside him. Gage brought his hand to the back of her neck. He stroked the bare skin beneath her hairline and Sara quivered in his arms. He felt her yearning and knew she, too, was set afire. Her willing response stirred his heart, honed his desire keen as a razor's edge. He wanted more, wanted to taste of her. Wanted to feel the tender fullness of her mouth against his.

Bending before the storm of his needs, he wound his fingers in her hair and gently tilted her head until her face was but a space from his own. "Sara," he breathed and brought his mouth to hers, bewitched by the soft yielding of her lips. His body aflame at the touch, he caught his breath and stepped back a pace, just as she placed her hands against his chest and wrenched herself from his embrace.

"I fear to lose myself in this blaze of sensation," she choked. She gazed up at him, her face rosy as a summer berry, and as luscious.

"Let me get this fodder pitched, and we'll head to the cabin," he said huskily. "Or I may find myself unable to treat you like a lady."

Her uneven breathing stole his resolve, made him step close again and draw her to him once more. "I want you for mine," he said. Voice wishful and ravening, he nibbled easy along her winsome cheek. Her hand caressed his face and her fingers tangled in his hair, pulling ever so gently, ignited him, searing his blood.

Sara wordless, peered into him. Body atremble, her eyes flashed with fire and emotion.

Gage clenched his jaw in an effort to quiet his rampaging desire. Sensing she was near to swooning against him, he lifted her easily, cradled her in his arms, and set her on a nearby hay bale. Gripping her hands in his, he decided to have his say, right there in the hayshed, and fell to one knee. "I have set my hat for you, Sara, if you'll have me. My feelings for you are deep held." He kissed her fingers. "I know we have a lot to reason on, some big plannin' to do, as I'm properly courtin' you, my darling girl. Though I've not yet spoken with your Pa, will you agree to be my wife?"

She regarded him with adoration and delight, still coming to ground. At first she seemed almost bashful, her tone sweet and breathy. "You have taken my heart, sir. I cannot resist." Then, unable to suppress her glee, she cried, "Yes. I give my hand. I shall marry you."

Bedazzled beyond speech by the love glistening in her eyes, he jumped up and stomped his feet to celebrate his good fortune, happy as a king.

"I've never seen you in such a froth. I rather like it." Sara patted her bodice and brushed forcefully at her skirts. "Still, we must attempt to conduct ourselves properly, Mister Evans," she declared. "Although it seems quite difficult given the spirited tenor of … of our affections." She grinned at him, her hair all mussed and curling, just the way he liked it best. His eyes met hers and found perfect understanding.

Lord! Even her voice stirred his blood. Only work or standin' in a blizzard would cool his ardor. Desperate, he grabbed the pitchfork like a wild man and turned to the business of haying the critters.

Perched on the straw bale she sat silent for several minutes, then bid him to lend an ear. "I've a story to tell," she said. "Some weeks ago, by sheer happenstance, I came to locate Matthew. I met an Indian woman who cradled an infant son. As it turned out, she is Matthew's wife, and the child, theirs. She took me to him. I brought Matthew and his wife and their chickadee here so Rachel might have family. They have been staying with us. The two people you found along the trail—they are not strangers. They are mother and father to Dark Eyes, the girl who is wife to Matthew. Or as she calls him, Mah Tew."

Gage listened, his hands slowing as her words tumbled out.

"It seems you, too, have brought a family together and they rejoice," Sara finished, pride ringing in her voice.

"I had no idea," he said, bemused. "I did what I had to do."

At his words, curiosity perked in Sara's eyes.

His brow furrowed. He wanted no ugly memories stirred this evening. "No questions, missy newspaper lady. It was a disturbing journey. Let's not talk of it just now. The fine thing is, I'll not have to leave Angels Camp. There's no searchin' to be done."

"There is more," Sara said. "Eagle Feather Woman is ill." Her voice ratcheted up a notch, "Dark Eyes requested they stay in your lean-to, and I agreed. You will bed down on the cabin floor. My father would not condone such a arrangement, so it's best not to speak of it again."

He mucked a final fork of horse apples from Thunder's stall. Life was starting anew all around him. A weight lifted from his soul. Glad to stay at her side, Gage stretched out on a nearby bale, and glanced at his betrothed. He'd planned to share all he'd figured on doing to make a good start in life for Sara and him. Real soon. Maybe right now. He turned toward her.

Chapter Fifty-Five

The Telling of It

Sara was at her wit's end today. Here she was living out in the wilderness, and she couldn't seem to find a moment's quiet. There was rough voiced shouting, sawing of logs and endless pounding of nails that came with adding two bedrooms to the cabin. For now, the new spaces would serve as sleeping places—one for Matthew, Dark Eyes and Little Hawk, the other for Rachel and Carlos. Sara chose to keep the sleeping area nearest the kitchen for her own until she became Missus Evans.

Angelo Rivera, bless his soul, invited several townsmen to lend a hand with the building. Mister Teddo, their closest neighbor had arrived of his own choosing with his Missus, children, and his young hunting dog in tow. The pup, adorable as it was, detested being tethered to the porch and periodically made a dreadful racket. All in all, it was quite chaotic.

Close to the hearth, the Teddo brood, Carlos, and Little Hawk screeched and chortled under the fond gazes of their mothers. Rebecca Teddo was telling of an amusing May Day picnic she and her mister had attended. Sara caught a word here and there, although most of the chatter escaped her notice, as she bestowed her attention upon a letter she was trying to compose.

Eagle Feather Woman, almost recovered from her ordeal, sat in a patch of sunlight with a handful of reeds, and with nimble fingers, wove a small ball for the boys to play with. Rachel had kindly set a steaming cup of lemon tea, too hot to sip, beside her a while ago. It wafted a soothing bouquet as it steeped. A devotee of Rachel's cooking, she'd already gobbled up the fresh baked raspberry tart that had accompanied it. She was healing well.

Sara didn't hear the ring of ax against wood at the moment, but Matthew and Angelo had been chopping at the base of a tree earlier, while Mister Teddo stripped leaves from larger branches. Then, under Standing Bear's watchful eyes they harvested tree bark strips and used the bare branches to construct a sleeping place for the old couple, who prepared to summer here, before returning farther north to their home in *Olumpali*. The *umacha* will be finished today, Dark Eyes and Rachel had explained during the morning meal. A relief, since the cabin was full to bursting, and Gage wanted his lean-to back.

Thoroughly distracted, Sara shook her head to clear it. Lord, love a duck! How on earth was she to compose a proper letter when she could barely think. What was it her father had written when last she'd heard from him? Sighing she picked up her pencil once again.

May 19, 1851

Dearest Father,

I trust my letter finds you thriving. I send my grand-est congratulations on your recent wedding. Please convey affectionate greetings to Lena and Marco. I am overjoyed to hear of your plans for the ranch. Marco will make a fine rancher. I expect he is pleased.

I fear I have been tardy in replying to your last missive. I have been quite bound up in life here. It did gratify me to know you found my attempts to describe a California winter in the goldfields worthy of publication.

Life has conveyed more blessings than I could have imagined. So much has happened that I am fair challenged to relate it all. I shall begin by telling you that Matthew has been found. He has flourished, although he has lost memory of his time at our ranch, and of the very incident that laid him low. We have happily reunited him with his oldest sister, Rachel, who is nearly of an age with me. She and her son, Carlos, of whom I spoke in an earlier letter, reside with us still.

He is well married, Pa, to a lovely Miwuk woman, a native of this region, and they have an infant son.. I shall fill in the details of how I came to stumble upon him at a later date. It gives my heart ease to know he is content. I enjoy Dark Eyes' company. She is a fine mother and quite clever. I daresay my thinking has changed in many aspects.

Do you recall Matthew's desire to be a purveyor of tools, foodstuffs, and such? He is to have his wish right here as he imagined. Mister Rivera, the fine man who founded our town, owns the trading post. He and Matthew will be working together to expand it.

Our little cabin hosts Matthew and his family. His mother and father-in-law, complete construction of their sleeping hut today and will spend the summer months here. Militia and vigilantes, greedy for acreage and gold, chased them from the lands of their ancestors. As I write, rooms are being added to the cabin, so you shall have a place to stay when you visit. Mister Rivera and a neighbor are assisting Matthew and Gage in the endeavor.

My biggest news concerns Gage and myself. We shall return to Durann Canyon this summer. Indeed, I know this will delight you, as your last post impressed your own and Lena's wish to have me home. But I must prepare you; we are courting, Pa. Though I cannot say when precisely it was, our bickering turned to something else entirely. Mister Evans has declared himself and I have accepted. I have stolen his heart, and he, mine.

I cherish hope that you will honor us with your blessing. Gage insists upon asking you in person; therefore, we shall leave our California family in two-weeks' time. We travel by overland stage and expect to arrive in late June.

Gage and I wish to be wed at the ranch during our visit. I assume Lena will be in a positive foment when you share my news. I'll wager she'll be aflutter with pots and pans and endless preparations of my favorite dishes the moment she hears.

I would be grateful to have you both arrange the wedding, Pa. I wish you to give me away and Lena to stand as my Matron of Honor. I think one of Gage's brothers, or both, will be asked to stand up for him. Gage has written to his mother and brothers in Missouri. I am anxious to make their acquaintance. We shall meet in Tubac and plan to have them travel to California with us for a long visit after the wedding.

Your letters are uncertain to reach me except at station houses along our route. I know not the locations as yet, but will send a note with the best suggested before we embark.

With his horse earnings, Gage has purchased our cabin and several acres of surrounding land. He plans to start a horse ranch. Gage is a fine horseman through and through, but you already know that, Pa.

I, of course, look to the pen. I have quite a few story ideas. Perhaps you and I can publish Penny Dreadfuls. I have also been asked by a neighbor to school their young children through the winter, and I've agreed. I do wonder what you will do with the Star Dispatch, Pa, now that we both know it is the writing and not the business end that draws me. Besides, at some future point, I expect we'll be welcoming our own young un's. We shall make you a granddaddy. Fancy that!

Sara put down her pencil and stretched her fingers, lacing them together and pressing them outward. *Well the hardest telling is done.* She was relieved. Although some tiny anxiety rippled in her heart, she was fair certain Pa would make peace with their union. Possibly, he'd considered such an outcome might come to pass. She pondered the thought, sipped from her own cooling cup of tea, and refreshed, picked up her pencil again.

Matthew has purchased two acres adjacent to Gage's holdings. He made the acquisition with a sack of gold dust Dark Eyes had hidden away. In the next week, work will begin on their cabin.

Mister Rivera has set his hat for Matthew's sister. I daresay in time, she and her son shall be living in Mister Rivera's splendid house. He has kindly smoothed the entry of our growing and varied frontier family into the community. We have been welcomed by most.

I simply yearn to see home.

I am your loving daughter,

Sara Durann Coulton

Finally completed! Sara dropped her pen and shook her hands, cramped with putting a river of words to paper. She heard boots scuff across the porch and turned to find Gage strolling through the door.

"How do, ma'am," he chuckled, and pulled off his dusty hat, making a sweeping bow. Wood chips and sawdust flew through the air. "Whoops," he said as he straightened and flashed his lopsided, "kiss me," grin at her.

"Gage Evans," Sara began, and screwed her face into a fierce scowl that refused to stay in place. His green eyes registered delight. Laughing, she jumped up and ran into his arms.

Acknowledgements

As I began to tell this story, I never imagined the journey I would take—from discovering the world Dark Eyes and Sara lived in, to meeting the men, women, and children that peopled that world. Nor did I understand fully the process of writing a novel and how many expert writers, interested friends, and willing family members it would take to support me along the way. Among them:

Bob McLeod, my San Francisco Examiner friend. He asked me for a two-paragraph story about an Indian woman. That 250-word piece gave birth to Dark Eyes. She refused to stop talking to me and inspired this novel.

My daughter **Paula Muscarella**, who encouraged me and gave of her time to read a first draft, then my second and third rewrites. Her perceptive developmental remarks were essential in moving the story forward to its proper ending. I'll never forget the phone call she made to tell me "You've got a book!"

My daughter **Olivia McClellan**, for sharing her knowledge and instincts concerning internet marketing and her unrelenting belief that I could do it.

Granddaughter **Sara**, the horse-loving young woman for whom Sara Durann-Coulton is named.

My grandson **John**, a computer animation wizard. In an evening, he ended a long tedious search for a particular Native American artist during my pursuit of cover images.

Beta readers: **Ellen Rix**, my sister, who pushed past her discomfort with commenting and came through for me; my old friend **Lisa Robinson** for her detailed first-draft notes; my horse mentor and friend **Sue Ferguson** who read for the horses; and fellow rider **Claire Passanisi**, who checked the galley for typos.

Deepest gratitude to my Big Rig critique group, talented writers all: **Skye Blaine**, **Laura McHale Holland**, **Marie Judson Rosier**, and **Beth Ann Mathews** for their rewrite patience, support, and expertise over a four-year period. With special thanks to **Boudewijn Boom** for his delicious cookies and an eye for detail.

My editors, **Robbi Sommers Bryant** and **Laura McHale Holland**, for sharp eyes and even sharper red pens. Their insightful comments, creative suggestions, and timely strikethroughs, brought this tale into focus.

Western artist **Don Weller**, and wife **Cha Cha**, whose talent and kindness were invaluable.

Last, but certainly not least, my fellow writers at **Women Writing the West** and **Redwood Writers**, who generously shared a mountain of information in response to my many queries.

Heartfelt thanks to each of you who helped bring this book to publication. So many helped me along the way.

Thank you!

PH Garrett's passions are writing, horses, dogs and ballet. Fascinated by the history of the American West, she lives in California's wine country and has a penchant for the cowboy way of life. This is her first novel. A sequel is well underway.

Author of numerous fiction and non-fiction pieces, her work has appeared in several anthologies: *Call of the Wild, Water, Untold Stories,* and award-winning *Sisters Born-Sisters Found,* and in the *Marin Independent Journal, Sonoma Horse Journal, Family News, Up Beat Times, Petaluma Post, San Francisco Chronicle,* and many other publications.

As an editor, she has helped others polish their written words. Find her website, stories, blog, and contact information at: www.wordwranglingwoman.com. And at: word wrangling woman/facebook/author or PH GarrettAuthor/facebook

Colophon

This book is set in Minion Pro 11.5 point and Lucida Handwriting 8.5 point.

"Minion is a serif typeface designed by Robert Slimbach in 1990 for Adobe Systems and inspired by late Renaissance-era type.

…

As the name suggests, it is particularly intended as a font for body text in a classical style, neutral and practical while also slightly condensed to save space. Slimbach described the design as having 'a simplified structure and moderate proportions.'" (source: Wikipedia)

"In 1990–91, Bigelow & Holmes created Lucida Handwriting, an informal joining script. The font became widely used after its release by Microsoft in 1992. … They evoke a distant echo of Renaissance humanist handwriting but were made in the modern age with modern tools." (source: Bigelow & Holmes)

74874148R00245

Made in the USA
Columbia, SC
14 September 2019